Promises to Keep

Promises to Keep

To my granddaughter Poppy.

Promises to Keep

Amanda MacAndrew

ANDARO BOOKS

First published in 2018 by Andaro Books
Adstockfields Farm, Adstock, Buckingham, MK18 2JE

Distributed by Lightning Source worldwide

British Library Cataloguing in Publication Data
A catalogue record for this book is available from the British Library.

ISBN 978-1-9999253-0-7

Typeset by Amolibros, Milverton, Somerset
www.amolibros.co.uk
This book production has been managed by Amolibros
Printed and bound by Lightning Source

About the Author

Born and brought up in Scotland Amanda MacAndrew trained
as a social worker in Dublin, travelled widely and subsequently
read English at Oxford while being the sole proprietor of a mixed
farm in Buckinghamshire. After the publication of her first three
novels she taught creative writing and undertook several public
and charity appointments. She has been married for forty-eight
years and continues to farm in partnership with her son. She
has three adult children and recently acquired a granddaughter.
Cherished memories of a post war childhood on the Ayrshire
coast inspired the writing of *Promises to Keep*.

Previous books by Amanda MacAndrew are *Passing Places, Party Pieces* and *Bits of String*.

Introduction to Part One

As sisters, Elvira and Maud Troubadour had been similarly reared and appropriately educated to make good wives for gentlemen. As young women, they were as unalike as the figures on a weather-house. Elvira would have gladly passed her days indoors while Maud revelled in the open air and all that went with it. Neither of them had been attracted to any gentleman that paid them any attention and both were kept well under control by their severe, ambitious mother.

Their father's sole purpose was to make money, write cheques and keep quiet, after he had fulfilled his reproductive functions satisfactorily.

Little Herbert Troubadour had preceded Little Elvira and Little Maud so, on the whole, Mr Troubadour Senior's fathering duties were done. Had Mrs Troubadour been a mantis or one of the nastier spiders she'd have gobbled him up, provided he'd managed to accrue adequate wealth for her maintenance and the gentle rearing of her brood.

Maud and Elvira only knew that their father was something in the City. What this something was, they didn't know, till after both their parents were long dead, when they discovered that they were descended from Albert Trubshaw, whose colossal glue fortune had been rendered from hoof and horn. By changing their name, the upward Troubadours could distance themselves from any Trubshaws, stuck below in the knacker's yard.

Elvira and Maud could speak French, recite some poetry (mostly heroic), thump the piano and foxtrot. Maud was plumper and prettier than Elvira and far more practical, though Elvira did become an accurate and speedy typist, which was something to fall back on, if the suitors persisted in steering clear.

Life in Surrey was stultifying; life in London was worse. In the country one could do things without having a man in tow. In London everybody else went around in pairs or boisterous crowds; only spinsters were solitary and being one of those was tantamount to failure.

Hitler's megalomaniac ambitions did the Troubadour sisters a favour.

Mrs Troubadour was mortified; not one of her children joined the Senior Service, so she retreated indignantly to Newquay for the duration, where her husband faded away like the morning moon. Not many noticed his passing. Herbert Troubadour enlisted with a regiment of foot, Elvira enlisted with the ATS and, horror of all horrors, Maud joined the Land Army.

When peace returned Mrs Troubadour had joined her husband in death, Herbert had lost both legs and Maud had married William Pollock, a farmer whose heart she had lifted together with his turnips and with whom she'd fallen in love, along with his Ayrshire cows, his Clydesdales and the gentle climate of the coastal farm overlooking Arran and Ailsa Craig.

Elvira attended the wedding in Dalmuirie Kirk when war was at its darkest. She'd been posted to Cairnryan and seen the Mulberry dockyards towed away. D-Day was imminent but the sun shone and the bride looked passably radiant in a frock devised from remnants. The groom smiled, despite his suit. Elvira was in uniform, which suited her angular figure though khaki did little for her sallow complexion.

Later that summer, Elvira's heart was broken by a handsome Territorial officer who had been too young for active service in the First World War and too old by the outbreak of the second. He busied himself with dealing with claims of indignant landowners after military manoeuvres had desecrated their acres. Major Gilbert Gilmerton was very rich but somewhat pathetic. His requisitioned mansion possessed a large garden, from where he salvaged the pompom dahlias he presented to Elvira in July. Unfortunately by September, he had given his heart, his substantial wealth and eventually, when circumstances intervened, his hand and name to a Gaiety Theatre ingénue. Firstborn Matilda arrived remarkably promptly, to be followed three years later by Grizelda, who completed the Gilmerton brood.

After demob Elvira returned to ruined London, bought a house quite close to Pont Street and let out rooms, resigning herself to spinsterhood, vaguely cultured pursuits and writing bucolic verse from within her urban shell.

Crippled Herbert Troubadour married a pretty Portuguese widow with two young children, Dorabella and Binjamin, who turned into Dora and Ben, both clever but different. Eventually Ben became an acclaimed astrophysicist, Dora a free-living, free-loving, free-thinking wreck.

In 1948, Maud presented Willie with their only child, Cecile.

Willie Pollock never admitted that he was disappointed with a daughter, but he wouldn't hear of his wife Maud adorning his wee girl's name with an acute accent. He didn't hold with foreign goings-on and took nothing to do with the Auld Alliance and such.

When Cecile reached twenty she announced that she wanted to leave home, go South, North, anywhere and see the world.

'What has got into her? What would a lass with all this want with that travelling-about caper?' Willie stretched out his grime-embedded hand to sweep the view from Dalmuirie Mains where cattle munched in fields sloping westward down to the sea with Arran and Ailsa Craig across the Firth. To the north one could see the distant houses of Dundoon and to the south, Firthside Holiday Camp's helter-skelter shielded the view of ruined Dalmuirie Keep. What else was there to want?

'What have foreign parts got that folk canna' find in Dundoon? What's the point of fancy cruises if you can go to Arran? We've bright lights enough right here at Firthside camp, for goodness sake. Where else is there to be?'

Behind the Pollock steading to the east, two obelisks defied each other from forested hilltops commemorating ancient unpleasantness of territorial religious rivalry. To Cecile they represented sentinels posted to prevent any overland escape.

'It's all here, is it not Maudie? Am I not right?'

'Yes, Willie, indeed you are,' said Maud, 'but Cecile is young. She has her way to make.'

'No child of mine needs to make its way out yonder. Is she not having a high old time at hame? There's ways enough to keep her cheery here what with Young Farmers and all that carry-on. She's got this place to mind till she finds herself some fine upstanding farmer and makes him as happy as you've made me.'

'Oh Willie, sometimes you do say the nicest things.'

'Steady, Maudie, don't go getting carried away.'

Maud was happy being rooted. Contentment sprung from being capable and enjoying the security of circumscription within a small horizon. She became big in body and the Women's Rural Institute and could number poor Lady Charity and pretty Irene Gilmerton amongst those with whom she was on first name terms, though she was closest to her sister-in-law, Avis, who had returned to Scotland after the war as the wife of Commander Rodney Wishart. She, too, had lived a secret life in Bucks during the war where she'd met her Rodney. They never spoke to anybody about what they knew, not even to each other.

The Commander left the services in 1948 and took command of the Firthside Holiday Camp which provided the Pollock and the Wishart families with more than enough excitement, a swimming pool bedecked with plastic palms and parrots and a Mount Vesuvius that erupted at prescribed moments in the ballroom. Though the Commander was nominally top dog, it was the Commander's wife who kept things humming at Firthside. Avis fielded complaints and quelled unruliness. She dealt with squabbles and disruptive children. She also appeared to revel in the organised fun. The Commander wandered the site wearing a mirthless grin and long shorts with knee socks and was puzzled by the campers' ideas of jollity. He played chess by post and did crosswords at speed, spoke several languages and read Russian novels. His seagoing career had been forcibly cut short when his brain had been required to serve his country at the most inland spot in all of wartime Great Britain. The best thing about the Firthside job for Commander Wishart was that it was indeed beside the Firth of Clyde. In winter he liked to contemplate the sea in silence.

Maud Pollock never ventured south to see her sister even before she and Elvira had their falling-out and Elvira never came north to torture herself with the sight of Major Gilmerton, her only love, now the husband of a loud, trite, vulgar, gold-digging chorus girl who sang in variety shows, 'en matelot', of seeing the sea and tap-danced in fishnet tights. Elvira regarded Maud's acquaintance with Irene Gilmerton as an abominable insult, a gross manifestation of betrayal and disloyalty. On hearing that Irene had been widowed, Elvira announced that she was not surprised. This was even before the Major's suicide was common knowledge, though once his fate was known, Elvira was vitriolic. 'That termagant, harridan, hex, gorgon, nasty cheap tart drove him to it!' she told all her lodgers and placed the silver-framed newspaper photograph of the late Major Gilmerton next to her ebony-framed parents in court dress upon the whatnot in her narrow hallway.

The rift between sisters widened when Elvira sent a bleak Christmas card of the Albert Hall comparing the wit, intelligence and promise of her adopted niece and nephew, dear Ben and darling Dora, to the obvious ineptitude of stout Cecile. This shortcoming she had detected from the single polyphoto enclosed with Maud's hand-painted attempt at a bit of holly the previous year.

Maud discovered that her sister-in-law, Avis Wishart, had an impregnable carapace of self-respect. Grandeur did not impress, nor did squalor disgust her. She laughed at small calamities, got over large ones and organised the faint-hearted into pulling themselves together. She coped with sickness and death with the same cheerful spirit that she mustered for sunken cakes and disobedient cisterns. The two Wishart sons knew from birth that they'd have to make their own way in life; unlike their older cousin Cecile, there was no farm waiting for them to inherit.

Nothing much happened that was not known to Avis. She was discreet and entrusted with secrets. She knew which couples would be disappointed when they scanned each other for intimations of mortality and found nothing wrong; she also knew who lusted after whom and who succumbed to temptation. She neither fell in, nor fell out, and was welcomed everywhere. Even her complaints were delivered with such tact that those who'd served her with faulty goods, stale groceries, bad service or late deliveries were unable to resent her sympathetic rebukes. Her strength was integral, just as her husband's intellect was never flaunted, nor did they dwell upon their ropey financial circumstances, but set themselves to supplement Rodney's meagre salary.

The Commander coached children in classics and history, but never grasped the importance of sticking to a curriculum which meant that his pupils developed a love for the subjects he taught them, but still failed their school exams. Like her sister-in-law Elvira Troubadour, Avis Wishart could take dictation and type at speed, skills she used to edit the random thoughts of elderly Charles Henrysson, who was trying to write a history of his sub-heroic family.

Henryssons habitually arrived too late at battles and lost their way to important gatherings. They were perfectly at ease oscillating between faiths and monarchs, so long as they retained their family seat overlooking their useless rock in the Firth of Clyde.

Avis would sit shivering in Dalmuirie Castle's filthy study while old Charles Henrysson rambled on between tales of unsatisfactory wills and domestic calamities. His grasp of dates was sound, but the chronology of the Henryssons was convoluted and confused by too many of them having the same name and few of them doing anything memorable except making advantageous marriages, which went wrong.

Occasionally Avis would sneak off to the opposite end of Dalmuirie Castle to give a spot of cheer to Lady Charity Henrysson, who no longer spoke to her husband. The best way to reach her quarters was along the outside of the building down a weedy walk. There was a way through the Great Hall all hung about with ancestors like the set of Ruddigore, but the hall's roof was treacherous and the electrics far from safe. Much of the ceiling's ornate plasterwork lay in heaps upon the wormy boards below.

It was Avis who suggested that some of these portraits could be sold to those who craved haughty ancestors to outstare awestruck dinner guests. Most of these fancifully dressed Henryssons were nonchalantly pointing at their family rock. Charles wouldn't hear of selling any of them till Avis suggested that copies could be made of the portraits by an acquaintance called Ian Parker who had recently completed a portrait of the Gilmertons as a family group, including the late Major Gilmerton splendid in his uniform.

Ian was sent for and a deal struck. Copies were made and the portraits sold. Ian Parker bought a flashy car and moved into Dalmuirie Lodge at the spot where the avenues to the Henrysson's castle and Gilmerton's house met. Ian Parker became a fixture.

The copied ancestors were parodies of the originals, crude and badly executed. Cross-eyed and grimacing previous Henryssons pointed with banana hands at what appeared to be a dung-heap in a puddle, but Charles affected to be pleased.

A few debts were paid and in 1968 indolent Hughie was dispatched to Cirencester to learn estate management. Lady Charity continued to manage her own dwindling wealth and Avis received a modest cheque to cover all the back pay she was owed, without interest.

Hughie came home from Cirencester no better educated but considerably elated. Like everybody else, he felt compelled to confide in Avis.

'Mrs W, you won't believe the corker I've met. God almighty, there's not a woman like her in this bloody country. She's a stunner.'

'Lucky you.'

'Too true. Phew! Now, Mrs W. Don't look so disapproving, I'm a changed man.'

'I'm delighted to hear that too, Hughie.'

'You aren't still going on about that accident I had with bloody Mount Vesuvius?'

'Relieving yourself into an automatic volcano was not an accident, Hughie.'

'No…you are right. It was damn stupid, it might have been live and given my tackle an awful jolt like when you pee on electric fences.'

'I wouldn't know about that, Hughie.'

'No, of course you wouldn't and I really am awfully sorry. It's not broken is it?'

'Mount Vesuvius? The smell lingers if I don't squirt it with air freshener, but it still works.'

'Then no harm done, what? Anyway I'll never do that again now I've discovered Dora.'

'Is that her name?'

'Yes, Dora Troubadour…what a name, what a woman, a real goer. God, she knackers me.'

'I don't believe you!'

'She does, she's wild in the sack.'

'I daresay, but Hughie, I don't think I need to know any more just now. Besides, I believe it is quite possible that your girlfriend is my brother's niece. There can't be many Dora Troubadours.'

'Christ! How odd! Your niece?'

'My brother Willie Pollock's adopted niece by marriage.'

'Blimey! Not Willie Pollock, the tenant of Dalmuirie Mains?'

'The same.'

'Christ! The Willie Pollock with that spotty dog of a daughter?'

'Poor wee Cecile…she'll get rid of the puppy fat in time. She's only just out of her teens. Dora, on the other hand, must be at least twenty-eight.'

'Surely not? She's bloody experienced, though, up to all the tricks. I didn't realise…'

'Hughie, please, I don't want to hear. Didn't Dora tell you she had relatives living close by?'

'We don't talk about that sort of thing.'

'Are you going to invite her to come and stay?'

'Christ no. I couldn't.'

'Why ever not?'

'Well, it would be kind of awkward. You see, I think she's expecting something a bit more…'

'Oh Hughie, have you been spinning stories?'

'No, Mrs W, not exactly, just a bit of bullshitting. After all, I do live in a castle, don't I?'

'Indeed you do.'

'But there are castles and castles, don't you know, like vast ducal estates aren't the same thing as vast council estates.'

'How ever did you meet? I thought Dora was at Oxford.'

'She was once but not anymore. I met her at a gig, in a swamp. We shared a sleeping bag.'

'Spare me the details, Hughie. I take it you want me to keep this to myself.'

'You are a good egg, a bloody good egg, Mrs W. I say, you couldn't lend me a fiver?'

'No, Hughie, not unless your father pays me again, and even then, no.'

'No?'

'Yes, emphatically no. You should get yourself a job.'

'Could your old man fix me up at Firthside? I could jolly along the campers and make myself jolly useful being jolly.'

'I don't think so, Hughie.'

'I wouldn't bugger about with Mount Vesuvius, I promise. You have my word.'

'And you have mine, Hughie. There is no job available for you at Firthside Holiday Camp and that is final.'

'Well, what am I to do?'

'Manage your estate. Isn't that what you have been learning to do this past year?'

'Oh God, Mrs W, all we've got left are sheep and trees. Tell me what's exciting about sheep and trees? Sheep and trees only want to die. That sort of thing rubs off, you know. If it wasn't for the thought of gorgeous Dora I'd want to die, too.'

★

Six months later, Hughie's career was no further advanced, but there had been developments down south. Dora Troubadour was seven months pregnant.

Maud Pollock snorted and said she was not in the least surprised to learn that her adopted niece was a fallen woman seeing as she had been spoilt and indulged all her life by her foolish Aunt Elvira. But then she learnt the name of the father and was mortified. The disgrace! The shame! The good name of Pollock would be dragged through the mire and be forever despised by poor Lady Charity who had commended Maud's fruit loaf at the Rural and even consented to become the Patron of Dalmuirie Memorial Hall Appeal Committee.

Willie Pollock was more concerned about his hay.

His sister Avis treated the news in much the same way as she quelled feuding campers, with dispassionate, capable confidence.

In fact, it was Avis who was delegated to tell Hughie that he was going to be a father.

'Christ all bloody mighty, Mrs W. Are you sure?'

'No, Hughie, I'm not sure. However, Dora is and I imagine she should know best of all.'

'Well fuck me slowly!'

'Hughie!'

'Sorry, Mrs W. God in heaven! Bugger me...oh Christ.' He looked at Avis like a dog caught worrying sheep. 'What the hell am I meant to do now? I haven't seen her for yonks because she went travelling, out East, I think. I don't even know where she is living.'

'Well, when I was your age men who got girls into trouble were expected to marry them.'

'God, that's a tall order. I'd never thought of that sort of thing.'

'Perhaps you should.'

He did, for a full minute and then said that he rather liked the idea. ' I wouldn't mind it if I could be like you and the Commander, but I'd rather be boiled in oil than end up like my mum and dad, living close enough to hate each other and too far apart for anything else. You know, they haven't spoken to each other since I failed my Scripture O level and Dad said there wasn't any point in learning about God because God is unknowable, which I thought was bloody deep but Mother thought was blasphemy. She's like that, you know; she can't be doing with heretics.'

'I think I know how to find Dora, if you don't.'

'Really? I've tried everything, but she seems to have scarpered. Disappeared. It's almost as if she didn't want anything more to do with me. Do you think that's possible?'

'She's fairly unusual, Hughie, in that she has always been very independent. To be truthful I don't think she's the marrying sort. But though I'm not sure where her mother lives, I do know her brother has got a job at Imperial College. You could try and get to her through him…he is called Benjamin Troubadour, Dr Benjamin Troubadour. He's probably a professor by now. My husband plays chess with his head of department, astrophysics or some such.'

'That's a hell of a long way to go to play chess. '

'They do it by post.'

'Blimey! Don't the bits get muddled up?'

Avis shook her head. 'Hughie, would you like me to put you in contact with Ben?'

'Rather, Mrs W. I'd really appreciate that. I have no idea what a pickle we would all be in without you to fix things.'

'I'll find out where you can contact her in London. Only, Hughie, don't expect her to fall into your arms and be led up the aisle. Dora is very much her own woman, I believe.'

'She's bloody magnificent. I'll never fall for any other bird so badly. She's like that witch that got to that knight and left him palely loitering.'

'*La Belle Dame Sans Merci* by Keats?'

'Could be... . They made you learn poems at school if you got caught smoking. The rhyming stuff about remembering inns was OK, but six of the best would have been better than that Hopkins junk. As for T S bloody Eliot, now that was a cruel and unusual punishment.'

★

Hughie did meet Dora again, in Ben's flat near King's Cross, but she told him to get lost. Ben walked Hughie back to Euston and tried to console him. Hughie confided all, his passion, his infatuation, his desire and his overwhelming urge to make Dora an honest woman and for the coming child to join his ignominious dynasty. Ben gave up two hours of his precious time to explain that his sister's ways were unfathomable and unlikely ever to be either dynastic or domestic. They ate cheesy Wimpys till it was time for the Glasgow train, each paying for themselves. Hughie wished Ben could be his friend; Ben was glad he was not.

Dora gave birth to a daughter and named her Miracle. Nobody dared stop her. The baby's middle names were Judith, after the feisty woman who beheaded Holofernes, and Valdite, after Dora's Portuguese mother. Hugh was on the shortened birth certificate as the father, but he was not informed of the birth.

Three weeks later Dora took off for Nepal and left baby Miracle with her mother in Wandsworth.

Part One

*T*ilda Gilmerton gazed at the stars above her bed and wondered how she could get rid of them. Her mother had put them there with the best intentions, meaning well. Real stars did not march in maddening patterns that made your head spin when you had the 'flu. When God made the heavens He didn't make a hash of aligning the wallpaper. Real stars moved in magical patterns and never played at being massed pipes and drums at the Tattoo.

Tilda had learnt at school about Venus, which wasn't a star but a planet, and how you could pick out the North Star at the tail end of the Great Bear which was also the Plough, and Cassiopeia, the beautiful lady who looked like a W. But Tilda didn't go out in the dark of winter evenings to see for herself, not even now that Daddy was dead.

Mummy always meant well. She had meant well when she asked horrible Mr Parker to add Daddy to that horrible picture downstairs with Mummy looking like a home perm advertisement and she and Grizel sulking in stiff frocks like ninnies in a Sunday School hymn book.

Now Mr Parker wanted her to call him Uncle Ian. Tilda was never going to call him anything…except slug behind his back.

Grizel felt differently. Grizel could be a sweet little girl. She was also pretty, delicate and silly. Grizel said she had nightmares and slept with a night light.

Tilda had nightmares she could never talk about and no night light could eliminate.

Had she told what she knew and what she'd seen, she would have been accused of lying, and unable to distinguish between dreams and reality. Had she persisted, she would have been labelled evil. The last witch in Scotland had been burnt alive at the Citadel because she was perceived as evil.

At home, the nights were silent except for spooky owls, whispering trees and hissing sea. Tilda preferred it when mist hid the rocks and smothered the lighthouse beams because then the fog-horns boomed and everybody was permitted to be scared. Grizel always screamed and Tilda was expected to comfort her. Grizel would cry for the daddy she had been too young to remember. Tilda didn't.

Tilda was glad that her room at home faced north-east across the Muirie burn which trickled at the foot of steep banks to the beach so she couldn't overlook either the sea or the Gilmertons' immaculate garden. Looking up to the summit of the bank she could just discern a rustic summerhouse, through the inland slanting trees. Previous generations of Henryssons probably used to pause in their games of putting and croquet to watch the sun setting over their rock across the sound. Now the place was as dilapidated as the rest of Dalmuirie Castle.

The great gale of 1956 had ripped some larger oaks and beeches from the ground. The fallen trunks lay there still, their naked earthy roots exposed. That had been a fearful night: the power failed, the fog-horns bellowed and trees cracked like guns as they broke. Mummy took strong sleeping pills during storms, to stop her thinking about poor sailors.

That was when Tilda had refused to listen to Daddy and saw him crying. That was the night that he said he was sorry. The sycamore in the garden, where the swing hung, did not blow down in that gale. Mummy had it felled several days later and the stump ground to dust.

Not till many years afterwards did Tilda understand what she had remembered seeing. At the time she was told that Daddy's heart had attacked him and he'd gone to heaven.

Only Miss Philomela Stuart MA may have understood.

Miss Stuart was the headmistress of St Quivox, the day school to which the sisters had been sent to acquire a minimal education, which was all that Mummy thought necessary for her little girls who would never get anywhere by being clever. Mummy had got where she was by being knowing and able to play the ingénue.

When she was getting to the age when she should have moved to the senior department, Miss Stuart decided to have a word with Irene Gilmerton, which was horribly embarrassing for Tilda, worse than having Cess Pollock following her everywhere and giving her useless presents.

Tilda hated listening to the two women talk about her as if she wasn't there.

'Matilda is remarkably intelligent, Mrs Gilmerton. She deserves to go far. She will be a credit to Scottish education.'

'Oh my!' said Irene Gilmerton, dabbing her cherry red lips. 'Whatever next will I have to cope with?'

Miss Stuart disliked sentences that ended with prepositions, and disapproved of chorus girls accompanied by lap dogs, but kept her counsel. After all, the Gilmerton girls' fees were always paid promptly through a most reliable and well-established firm of Glasgow lawyers. The prospect of these Clydesdale Bank cheques ceasing jarred, but it was her duty, as a dedicated educationalist, to ensure that her pupils received the very best, something beyond the capacity of St Quivox to provide.

'Have you thought yet where Matilda should continue her education?'

'I was thinking she could go to Switzerland.'

'Switzerland, Mrs Gilmerton? Matilda is not in need of rare air, she is not consumptive, her physical health is exemplary. Switzerland can give her nothing that she cannot obtain in Scotland of superior calibre.'

'She'd learn French, I daresay, and elocution and meet ever such a refined class of person.'

'That may be appropriate for wee Grizelda, Mrs Gilmerton, but it would a criminal waste, lamentable neglect and a reprehensible misuse of Matilda's not inconsiderable gifts. It would be counter beneficial to subject her to the company of over-privileged philistines.'

Irene thought Philistines were probably akin to Pharisees and reassured Miss Stuart that she had nothing against the Jews.

Miss Stuart replied that she had everything against the squandering of talents, as indeed did the Lord.

'Which lord is that, Miss Stuart?'

'Our Lord, Mrs Gilmerton, in Matthew as I recall in an unequivocal parable involving a steward.'

The stewards Irene knew served drinks, often on boats.

'Furthermore, Mrs Gilmerton I feel, and so do my staff, that Matilda is not entirely happy. This could be because she is not being stretched academically.'

'She certainly has nothing to be unhappy about at home. She has everything she could possibly want, except a father, of course.'

'Indeed, Mrs Gilmerton, you have my condolences, but that being said, I suggest you make enquiries about boarding schools in Edinburgh or St Andrews.'

'Oh no, not up here, Miss Stuart. What about her accent?'

'Matilda has a charming speaking voice.'

'Her father would not have wanted his girls to talk like they're out the Cowcaddens or off of the Broomielaw. Indeed, my late husband would have been mortified to have a brainy daughter at all, especially one who couldn't speak the Queen's English.'

Miss Stuart snorted as one grappling to suppress remarks about throwing stones within glass houses and pots calling kettles black.

Tilda cringed.

'Mrs Gilmerton, one must not dwell upon the past or speculate upon the wishes of the deceased. I imagine that there are funds enough to finance the very best for your daughters.'

Did she realise what she had said? True, there were plentiful funds in trust for the children and also for Irene, provided she did not remarry.

In the end a compromise was struck. Tilda was to be sent to boarding school in the extreme south of England and Grizel was to continue at St Quivox until she was old enough to be sent abroad.

Each summer term ended with a play and prize-giving. As ever, the play was produced, adapted and cast by Mrs Smellie. Miss Carter had turned into Mrs Smellie the previous summer, about which the whole school was forbidden to snigger. 'Smellie is a most distinguished name. Many eminent Scots have been called Smellie,' Miss Stuart announced at Assembly. 'Only very stupid people find Miss Carter's married name amusing. Oh, I see. Am I to take it from this outbreak of hilarity that all pupils at St Quivox are very stupid?'

'I'm not laughing, Miss Stuart.'

'Yes, Cecile, so I see.'

A shout came from the back of the hall, 'She who smelt it dealt it! She who denied it supplied it!'

'Who said that? Come forward, please!'

Nobody answered, but everybody knew. Then Cecile put up her hand. 'Please, Miss Stuart, it was Grizel Gilmerton.'

'And a very silly little girl she is, too. Assembly dismissed.'

Cess, as Cecile was always known, was shunned, not because of the cloying ointment applied to the peeling skin on her hands, but because of her pathetic, craven desire to be liked. She failed with everyone and fitted nowhere. However, she could sing.

The play was mercilessly cut and moulded to suit cast and capabilities. Tall Matilda Gilmerton was the hero, a prince disguised as an artist and Cecile was one of several peasants vying for his favour. She was to sing a song about having a father with 'corn-lands so wide, oxen for ploughing and horses to ride' and reputedly, 'pockets with silver as full as can be.' The song concluded with Cess looking coyly at Tilda and singing, 'you he would pay, sir, so pray, sir, paint me!' Luckily Tilda was required neither to choose nor kiss Cess and the future princess was Tilda's sister Grizel, who had nothing to do but smirk.

A ten shilling note had disappeared from Grizelda Gilmerton's blazer pocket the last Friday of term while Cecile had been fulfilling her zealous duty as Cloakroom Monitor during which she'd been known to search pockets for forbidden bubble gum and other contraband. The Monday following, the day before the play, she presented Matilda Gilmerton with a leather-bound five-year diary. Conclusions were jumped upon, the Pollocks were summoned and told that their daughter was a thief. They defended their only child furiously, proclaiming her innocence, of which they were convinced. But it was too late. Cecile Pollock's song was cut and her name removed from the programme, coat hooks and register. The miserable child was driven from St Quivox Preparatory School immediately and for ever, in a Landrover reeking of cattle dung.

It was too late to reinstate Cecile when the ten shilling note mysteriously reappeared from under the boot rack, because the concert was over. It was too late to credit her for having earned the money to buy the diary by cleaning her mother's chicken shed and hosing down her father's milking parlour, even though fur and feathers made her eyes and nose stream.

After she'd gone, nobody missed her. Few were even sorry when Miss Stuart announced that she had been wrongly accused and Mrs Smellie gave a talk on Magna Carta, habeas corpus and the principle of innocence until proved guilty to which nobody listened because it cut a huge hunk out of break.

St Quivox was better off without the girl known from then onwards as Cess Bollocks.

When Tilda left St Quivox Miss Stuart asked her if she was looking forward to boarding away from home.

'Very much, Miss Stuart.'

'And tell me, Matilda, do you miss your father?'

'No, I don't.'

'Would you care to elaborate?'

'No, thank you.'

No more was said.

It took ages to sort the things she could take to boarding school. The rules were strict concerning clutter: one photograph frame, one ornament and as a concession to childish things, one stuffed toy. Suitable books were available to borrow from the library and girls were encouraged to write diaries. Irene had got Ian Parker to arrange a framed photograph of the family portrait as a lovely surprise. Tilda arranged for it to be smashed and chewed up by Toto, who had his uses despite being the world's most dense dog. Tilda wrote a sporadic diary in an ordinary exercise book with a shiny red cover and never even unlocked the leather-bound five-year diary that Cess had given her, nor did she read the fawning message inside.

Being packed off to boarding school would be the best thing that had happened to Tilda. There, she slept on a thin, dipping mattress, on an iron bedstead with creaky springs, in a carpetless, curtainless dormitory where the long nights were disturbed by a clock that struck every quarter hour. She shared a dormitory with seven other snoring, snivelling, tooth-grinding, sleep-talking girls aged twelve to seventeen, and loved it.

London 1973

Miss Elvira Troubadour saw the saltire on the stamp and feared the worst. For some time she had been expecting her niece Cecile to be in need of somewhere to lodge in London and she spent much of most nights trying to think of a plausible reason to refuse, without being outright rude. Cecile was her sister's child after all, also Elvira's closest niece by blood if not by affection. One can't help having unsatisfactory relatives any more than Cecile could help being a cumbersome lump; it was not her fault that her father was uncouth and that her mother had gone native.

The truce between Elvira and her sister Maud only held if a considerable distance was kept between them. Elvira's Christmas card of the snowbound Albert Hall annually went north passing Maud's snowbound sheep, somewhere near Crewe.

A cut-price autobiography by some grim worthy was sent to Maud each birthday and was generally reciprocated by something dire that Maud had created, acceptable if edible, undesirable if ornate. Elvira particularly took against decorated waste bins and crinoline dollies designed to conceal telephones or lavatory paper beneath their knitted skirts.

This letter was not in Maud's hand and Elvira judged the writing to be too mature and sophisticated to be from Cecile who she suspected wrote in copybook italic or primitive script.

The sixties had stopped swinging and after just one year of the Heath government, the seventies were declining into discontent.

Elvira was baffled. The letter began, 'Dear Elvira (if I may)' and ended 'Yours aye, Avis (Wishart) and came from Ailsa Lodge, Dundoon.

After Avis had explained herself legibly in blue ink on cream Basildon Bond, Elvira remembered her to be Maud's surprisingly cultivated sister-in-law, the object of elegance in Wren uniform at Maud's wedding to lumpen Willie Pollock in 1944. Elvira had warmed to her then, especially as Avis was engaged to a lanky commander with a delightful smile and therefore was no threat to Elvira's own marital campaigning.

Yes, she was pleased to get a letter from Avis Wishart; she sat in her basement kitchen to read it with a cup of tea and a chocolate digestive to enhance the pleasure.

The pleasure was short-lived and replaced with doubt and anguish.

Avis Wishart was writing on behalf of a young friend, Matilda Gilmerton, a most intelligent young woman in her early twenties intending to study medicine who had obtained a place at the Royal Free. Matilda's mother was apprehensive about her daughter in a hostel or unknown digs and was prepared to pay a generous rent for her to have a decent place to lodge. Could Elvira help?

Elvira scrunched the letter and threw it at the pedal bin. Ten minutes of raging against the idea of housing the progeny of cheap chorus girls and she had second thoughts. She flattened the ball of paper and read it again, calmly.

Recent events made the idea of a generous rent most beguiling.

Elvira Troubadour's life changed radically with the availability of the contraceptive pill, though she alas, had no call for it herself. Neither her house, nor her upbringing could cope with promiscuity.

Her top room tenant gave her sleepless nights as the pendant light danced a jig above Elvira's single bed, while the rhythmic thrusts increased until the bedstead's brass knobs rattled and her mother's silver brushes jumped upon her Maples dressing table in time to the ecstatic coupling taking place upstairs. The terraced house had withstood the Blitz, but couldn't take the onslaught of sexually liberated London and no more could the respectable single gentleman of esoteric inclinations, resident on the ground floor, whose Third Programme concerts were incessantly interrupted by the strident telephone in the hall and whose access to the bathroom was blocked by the stream of boisterous visitors. His reaction against intrusion was either to play Wagner at top volume on what he called his gramophone, or storm off to his club to be a bore. When the meek civil servant in the basement retired and took up weaving, Elvira knew she could stand it no longer. What with lust above, Valkyries below and the whole cacophony underpinned by the loom's intermittent thuds, she even considered opting for rural calm.

She took the bus to Richmond but soon came home. Birds and grass and open spaces wouldn't do. She required drains, pavements and street lights. Something had to go and she decided the only way to survive was to sell up and maybe look for somewhere smaller.

Even the most midget place in SW 1 or 3 cost a ransom and the pleasant young man from the estate agent was dubious about the price that her dilapidated and quaking house would command upon the open market.

Her greatest friend was her brother's widow, who lived quite comfortably in Wandsworth, but Elvira couldn't countenance a move across the river. The other option was to increase the rent by way of granting herself compensation.

When she mooted this rise, all three tenants gave notice. The top floor took herself to live in sin and the World's End, then the cultured gentleman decided that hotel life would be altogether more congenial and finally the basement weaver became terminally weird and was removed by an embarrassed relative to a place of safety for her own good. The weaving had bent her wits till she developed an obsession with the Lady of Shallot and was apt to cry out that the curse had come upon her when she eyed the postman's legs on the pavement above her basement window.

It took days to clear her den of junk, mostly bottles and sacks of festering food, which had to join other uncollected trash heaped upon the street corners.

The loom remained, giving the basement the look of a torture chamber.

The house was empty of tenants, dingy but quiet. Elvira liked the space, the freedom to brew up at all hours and call the place her own, except for the increasingly empty state of her bank account. She'd have to get another job as the money she received for two days' work as Lady Westcroft's social secretary barely covered the rates.

She had once won ten bob in a poetry competition, which was a start, but scarcely a reliable source of income.

Lady Westcroft spent more in one hour at the hairdresser's than Elvira took home after two days of bill paying, flower ordering, invitation answering and compiling lists of likely people to ask to dinner. Most of the time Lady Westcroft was utterly exhausted. Her husband was long gone to his reward, likewise his widow's doe-eyes and slender figure as photographed by Lenare and displayed in several silver frames upon the redundant baby grand. Occasionally Elvira was asked to read Jenifer's Diary aloud while her ladyship reclined upon a chaise longue, cucumber slices upon her weary eyes. Lady Westcroft's age was a mystery, but she did let it slip that she remembered the relief of Mafeking. Elvira disliked her thoroughly, but put up with the foolish round of self-indulgence because the work was regular and not too taxing, though the pointless frivolity of an ancient widow, who had done nothing in her life, except be beautiful enough to catch a wealthy baronet, ran counter to all her principles, especially as Lady Westcroft reminded her of her own late mother.

At some point, forty-five years earlier, Lady Westcroft had produced an heir who was now successful in conglomerates and had also managed to marry well and select a brittle Texan beauty and succeed in breeding an heir of his own. Lady Westcroft caused Elvira to send out the stiffest of engraved invitations to the christening of this wunderkind. Piety wasn't rife amongst the Westcrofts but any objection to baptising the child were quelled by Lady W's cheque to church funds which Elvira was sent to deliver to the vicar personally. Despite her own agnosticism, Elvira warmed to the Reverend. They both thought the child's chosen name most ill-advised. Elvira didn't confide that she had a niece named Miracle.

Elvira reread Avis Wishart's letter.

A generous rent? How generous? Generous meaning enough to pay all the bills? Or generous meaning exploiting someone with more money than sense? Or generous as an opportunity to extract revenge, a dish that Elvira would be eating very cold indeed? It was eons since that harridan had stolen Gilbert Gilmerton from her, but revenge would be awfully sweet. Besides, a child ought not to be blamed for its father's choice of mother.

Irene Gilmerton didn't inspect her daughter's lodgings and agreed without a murmur. The money came from the Glasgow office of a Writer to the Signet, first a hefty deposit and then a monthly Clydesdale cheque. The rent Elvira demanded for accommodating Matilda was more than she had received for three tenants.

Avis Wishart was right. Tilda (as Matilda liked to be called) was charming. Studious and beautiful, she had started her medical training quite late, having fought her mother hard to do so. She seemed only to spend her money on accepting her sister Grizel's, almost nightly, lengthy reverse-charge calls from France. Tilda rang her mother in Scotland once a week for half a monosyllabic minute and took her holidays with fellow students instead of going home. Tilda was blessed with long legs, long hair and a slender figure. Her face was also quite long, but not in a horsey way. She wore neither make-up nor much obvious fashion and laughed infectiously, exuding a calm confidence that told nobody her secrets. Her heart was a mystery not worn upon her sleeve. Like everybody who knew her, Elvira liked Tilda a lot, despite her having everything that Elvira had failed to attain, including the prospect of a fulfilling future.

Elvira hid the photograph of Tilda's father in a drawer. She tried unsuccessfully once or twice to weave him into conversation. Was it deep grief that prevented Tilda from wanting to talk about him, or the insensitivity of youth? In quiet moments Elvira would gaze at Gilbert's picture and try to find a resemblance to his daughter.

★

It was already the autumn term when Elvira answered the door to a man with the smile of a salesman but without an accompanying case of wares. Was he canvassing? No, he was far too raffish for serious politics and surely too urbane to be spreading the Word or bringing tidings of salvation in the hereafter. Elvira was transfixed; he was clutching a bunch of dahlias.

But for his straining, window-pane checked, mustard flares he was her fantasy of nostalgia. Though dearest Gilbert would never have considered a tie clip, nor brown suede shoes in town...but those flowers. Yes, oh yes, the way to her heart was paved with pompom dahlias, red ones like these in this stranger's strangely string-gloved hand.

'Yes?'

'You must pardon this unannounced intrusion, my dear lady, but I am looking for Miss Gilmerton. I understand she has rooms in your house.'

He made it sound as if he was calling on Sherlock Holmes. 'I am a close friend of the family and Miss Gilmerton's mother asked me to drop by and see how her wee girl is getting along in the big city.'

A Scot. The fruity voice betrayed one whose accent was probably naturally more pronounced. 'My name is Ian Parker. I have a card.'

Elvira ran her finger over the card and noted that it was not embossed, but at least it was white, without pictures or embellishments. It described Ian Parker as an interior consultant, whatever that was.

27

'You may come in, if you like, and wait for Matilda's return. I am expecting her shortly.'

'Thank you, dear lady. Oh my! What an enchanting establishment, how tastefully appointed.' Ian Parker gazed in ecstasy at the whatnot beside the hat stand from which dangled deceiving male headgear concealing the inaccurate join of the faded wallpaper, before following Elvira up the threadbare stairs to her first-floor sitting room. 'How delightful!' he exclaimed. 'Can one ever have too much majolica?'

He sat on the horsehair sofa and continued to cascade compliments till Elvira fled to make tea and offered to put the flowers in water. She sniffed them, hoping for the mix of Capstan and damp khaki intermingled with bitter earthy cloves, but these dahlias clung to the sweeter smell of Ian Parker's liberal aftershave. Their velvet softness recalled the touch of hopeless love as she rattled about her kitchen shelves seeking the requested Lapsang and lemon.

The stairs creaked as she climbed back with the tray and found Ian pretending to be absorbed in the complete works of Elizabeth Barrett Browning which Elvira had won at school for recitation. The drawer where she kept her photograph of Gilbert Gilmerton was slightly open. She was sure it had been closed before, but maybe she was wrong. One should not assume the worst. After all, this Mr Parker had exemplary manners and he was an interior consultant after all. She was absolutely sure that the figurine on the mantlepiece had been moved. Ian followed her gaze. 'You must forgive me, I could not resist looking at your Preis. An excellent example, I would say. Have you had her long?'

'She belonged to my mother.' Elvira longed to ask whether the lithe lady in hideous bathing dress was worth much. That, however, would be vulgar.

There were footsteps in the street, a turning key and then the front door banged. 'Tilda, dear, you have a visitor.'

'Who is it, Miss Troubadour?'

Ian put his hand to his lips and shook his head.

'It's a surprise.'

'Oh good! I'll just dump my books and come.'

Tilda entered. 'Oh, it's you.'

'Is that all you are going to say? I've come all this way, after all.'

'Why? Has something happened?'

'No. Nobody's dead.'

'That's good. So why are you here?'

'We are having the drawing room done up.'

'We?'

'Your mother and I, we feel the call for chintz, hessian, too, and some decorative touches from Casa Pupo.'

'How horrible.'

Elvira was watching this exchange with increasing agitation. She disliked scenes. 'Casa Pupo has some lovely things, Tilda, pretty rugs and umbrella stands. It's down the Pimlico Road… not far. Wait, let me fetch another cup.'

'No, please don't, Miss Troubadour. Mr Parker is leaving.'

'I am? But I've come to take you to dinner.'

'I'm sorry. I have things to do.'

'What things?'

'Nothing I can do with you. Please go.'

'I brought you flowers from the Dalmuirie garden.'

Tilda faced Elvira. 'I am sorry, Miss Troubadour, I'm going to my room. I need to work.'

Elvira followed Tilda downstairs. 'Really! That was intolerably rude.'

'I'm sorry to embarrass you, Miss Troubadour. It's not your fault. Just don't let him in again, please.'

'I don't imagine Mr Parker will want to be let in again after the way you treated him.'

'Good.'

Tilda shut her door and slid the snib.

Now what? Elvira returned upstairs and this time she found Ian inspecting the bottom of a Coalport chocolate cup. 'What a shame it is cracked,' he remarked as if nothing had happened and he was one of Elvira's oldest friends.

'I am afraid, Mr Parker, I must ask you to leave. Matilda is not feeling well.'

'Wrong time of the month, eh, Miss Troubadour? What a lot you females have to contend with, and what a lot you inflict upon us mere males. I'm right, am I not?'

'Mr Parker! I have no idea what you are trying to imply. However, I have an imminent appointment, with a chiropodist (what, in the name of God, made her say that?) and must ask you to go… immediately. I am sorry.'

'Very well, I have many engagements of my own to attend to. I trust Matilda recovers soon. May I suggest gin. It is quite the thing for women's troubles, I am told.'

He was already walking down the street when Elvira called after him. 'Mr Parker, you have forgotten your flowers!'

'For you, dear lady, with my deepest respect.' He blew her a kiss. Every net curtain in the street seemed to twitch and Elvira blushed as red as the dahlias themselves, something she'd not done for several decades.

★

Cecile Pollock had been consigned to a hostel across the river where her life was even worse than it had been at home. Like Tilda, she'd fought hard to leave Ayrshire and now, unlike Tilda, she longed to go back. She prayed for an excuse to quit. She wanted to make an honourable escape from the lonely horrors of hostel life and to give up working as a trainee kindergarten teacher for which she somehow knew, but dare not admit, she'd never be suited. Children didn't seem to warm to her. The harder she tried, the more she failed. Even the prospect of the stultifying restrictions of rural life and returning to the horrors of Miss Short's Commercial Academy or, worse still, enrolling as a mature student at Agricultural College together with the humiliation of living with her parents, were attractive compared to her narrow cell, distant bathroom, clanking plumbing and, worst of all, the sound of other girls shrieking with laughter and having fun. She'd never needed to buy her food or share a fridge before and even though she'd had no close friends in Ayrshire, at least her parents doted on her. She didn't know about going out in the evening with boys or how to have a good time, what to say, how to laugh.

All she had ever wanted was to be needed, and the only things she ever really needed were babies. Her own babies would not only need but love her and she would make the most wonderful mother. Other people's children were blind to her virtues and capabilities, not so her own. They would dote and there would be plenty of them, all living happily ever after. To achieve her ambition Cess needed to find a father for her brood and that was the biggest of stumbling-blocks. Suitors did not flock to court her; she was the insignificant hen to whom males never displayed their enticing feathers or alluring courtship dances.

Her weekly postcards home said she was having a wonderful time. She could have confided her misery to her mother. Maud, after all, knew all about being lonely in a crowd, but Cess could not admit defeat, not after the epic battle to get away. Now that she'd emerged from her doting family shell, she had her pride, but no self-esteem.

Maud and Willie had managed to keep her home till she was twenty-one, but now she was gone, they wondered why it had taken them so long to yield. Life at Dalmuirie Mains was far more cheerful without her. Willie even talked of taking Maud through to Edinburgh for the Highland Show.

It had been Grizelda Gilmerton who had first called her Cess while she was still at St Quivox and the name followed her to her next school, too. Dundoon was not a large place. It wasn't kind, but the name, like muck, stuck.

'Nicknames are a sign of affection,' said Maud. 'After all, wee Grizelda doesn't fuss about being called Grizel and that's a horrid thing to be.'

'Not as horrid as Cess. Everybody said I stank of it.'

'They were only jealous.'

'What of?'

'Your lovely voice, for a start. Didn't Miss Stuart herself say you were the best singer in the whole school?'

'They laughed at me when I sang. They said I looked like a baby bird.'

'And what is wrong with that? Nothing! Baby birds are charming. You should be proud.'

Grizel's sniggering gang had been cool. Cool girls did not sing songs about Bonny Doon or Sweet Afton, they belted out ditties about putting on the style and boys, especially boys who crashed their bikes. Cess had stopped singing after she'd left St Quivox and gone to Dundoon High when she was twelve. That was nine years ago and still she hadn't grown out of puppy fat, acne or greasy hair, or bearing childhood grudges long after her tormentors had forgotten all about the butt of their schoolday jibes.

'You'll enjoy your cousin Malcolm's wedding when you get there,' Maud told Cess while she was at Dalmuirie Mains for Christmas, ' and you can carry our wedding present south with you on the train, which will save a deal of trouble at the post office. Not that a lampshade weighs much, but I'd not want it crushed.'

Cess knew her mother's lampshades; they weren't discreet. This prize number had been fashioned from Lady Charity's cast-off crepe de chine nightgown and lined with peach silk jersey (once a vest) then trimmed with all the bobbles and braid Maud could salvage from McCulloch of Dundoon's clearance sale. Wrapped in ironed tissue paper and tied with used cake ribbon, it was a most embarrassing object, unlikely to thrill any bride. Obscure Cousin Malcolm, a steady accountant, was marrying Maureen, a toothy young social worker, at St Columba's, Pont Street.

★

'Do you know Malcolm or Maureen well?' The young man asked when Cess was ushered into the back pew beside him.

'No, do you?'

'Not at all.'

'My mother said I had to come because he's a sort of cousin,'

Cess whispered with the lampshade wedged between them. The bride was late and the organist was encouraging sheep to graze safely for the third time.

'Same here. Mothers do that, don't they? They have different ambitions. Mine always wants me to meet new people.'

'You're related to Maureen?'

'No, I'm sort of related to Malcolm, like you.' He smiled, she was bewitched. 'That makes us cousins, too, sort of. I'm Ben Troubadour'. For Cess Heaven's gate opened, as did her mouth and she rose with the congregation at the entrance of the bride to sing The Old Hundredth like an angel in bliss.

Later, after too much pretend champagne, Cess walked home in ecstasy. Filthy puddles ruined her pink high heels and crept up her laddered tights, her straining dress became dish-rag soggy beneath her saturated poncho, while her enthusiastically floral hat turned to compost in January's most vigorous downpour. She floated back to Battersea wafted by delight in the clutches of infatuation. A stiletto lodged in a grating, a glove drowned in a drain, but she kept the address he'd given her, safe in her bra, next to her thumping heart. It was not Ben's address, but that of his mother, who lived in Wandsworth and would appreciate some help with looking after her granddaughter, little Mira.

What luck that she had met Ben, what luck that she was training as an infant teacher, what a chance to make herself indispensable, to make sure of seeing Ben again and earn his undying adoration. She imagined the consternation in Ayrshire when it was known that she was minding Hughie's bastard. What a one in the eye for her father's erstwhile landlord, what tales she'd have, what gossip, what status amongst those who'd once despised her as irredeemably dull.

He'd kissed her, albeit briefly, a peck of distant kinship, but the shocking thrill had whizzed through, leaving her spotty cheeks aglow and the roots of her lank, back-combed hair all tingly. A fluttering ache gripped her as her heart juddered, recalling the scorching touch of his lips. The memory of beautiful Ben who'd called her Cecile and told her to look after herself when they parted at the reception, eclipsed all her troubles. His looks stunned her. He had untidy dark hair already flecked with grey which he probably cut himself (when it troubled him), a generously hooked nose and lopsided smile that revealed delightfully crooked teeth. Being shortish, he was an ideal height for their eyes to meet on the level. Hers were watery blue and fringed in smudged and clogged mascara, his were as brown as Bovril behind thick-rimmed specs.

The next day was Sunday and Cess rang the Wandsworth number immediately after breakfast despite the Anvil Chorus in her head. It wasn't till noon that she got a reply. 'We have been to the children's church. The sisters make bible games and sing holy songs with much hand-clapping.' Despite nearly thirty years in England, Valdite Troubadour still spoke hesitantly with a distinct accent that Cess took for Spanish.

'I met Ben at Malcolm and Maureen's wedding yesterday and he said you are looking after his niece and as I am a kindergarten teacher I wondered if I could help.' Cess had rehearsed this spiel. It tumbled out in a garbled rush.

'Sorry, could you repeat, please.'

This time she spoke her lines, loud and slow with pauses, as if to an idiot. 'Did Ben tell you about me? My name is Cecile Pollock.'

'No, my dear.'

'Oh.' Cess sounded crestfallen.

'But that is no matter. Binjamin is always thinking of rocks or stars or things inanimate and forgetting to tell me what is important You are most kind to offer your services, but I do not need any help thank you, though Mira and I always like to make new friends. Please come to see us.'

Cess was invited to tea and promised scones.

Later, when she stood on the tiled step of a terrace-end cottage and pressed the bell she saw that the shape behind the stained glass panel was short and round. The bolts were slid and the handle turned to present a greying, smiley woman holding hands with a tiny, dark-haired girl.

'Oh my, Mrs Troubadour, hasn't wee Mira got her father's eyes!'

Wee Mira buried her head in her grandmother's apron; she was not for showing Cess her father's eyes again, not ever.

'So you are a friend of this Hugh?'

'I know him.'

'But not a friend?'

'Not exactly.'

Cess was in awe of Hughie. His stupidity was legendary, yet he exuded the ruthless, spoilt superiority of an only child who regarded lineage as more of an asset than common sense, and indolence as an inherited virtue. His jokes were the only practical bits of him and made Cess want to cry, which would make him laugh even louder. He had a long face like a dopey mule, and a loose-lipped mouth. His large blue eyes were his only good feature unless lanky height could be considered an asset, too, but Hughie's eyes were nothing like as beautiful as Ben's short-sighted brown ones. No, Hughie wasn't her friend. Cess had no friends, not until yesterday. 'But I am a friend of Ben.'

'I'm glad. Binjamin has many friends, but I seldom see them, though he is a good boy and comes often to see me and Mira, doesn't he, little one? You like your Uncle Ben, don't you, sweetheart?'

Mira removed her head from the grandmother's apron. 'I like Uncle Ben lots and lots.'

'So do I,' said Cess, bending down to Mira's level, in the way she had been taught to deal empathetically with small children.

'But I don't like you!' Mira turned her face away and clung to Valdite.

'Mira! You must not be rude to our guest…come along, let us go and find those lovely scones you helped make. I'm sorry, Miss…er…'

'Cecile, call me Cecile.'

'She smells of sick.'

'Mira! Cecile has a lovely fragrance.'

Cess stayed to tea and talked brightly of meaningful play. Mira said nothing and Valdite rattled on about how much there was to Wandsworth life. Darkness fell and it was time for Cess to leave, before the country shut down early in the government's desperate bid for economy in time of industrial unrest. Ben had not appeared in person or conversation, nor had Cess been invited to return.

'I should be going,' she said.

'Let me find your coat,' said Valdite.

Mira appeared to brighten. 'Are you clever?' she asked.

'Not very.'

'My Mum is clever, very very clever. Look!'

Mira fetched a graduation photograph of Dora in an academic gown rimmed with white fur and Cess saw that Dora was not only clever, but confidently striking, too, as she gazed, almost menacingly, at the camera with large dark and steady eyes. Even worse, Cess noticed that she was slender with long thick and wavy hair without a vestige of acne on her high cheek-boned face.

'And that is my Daddy!' Mira pointed at a packet of porridge on which a joyous, muscled Scotsman was putting the shot in a field of ripened oats.

As Cess left she told Valdite and Mira that she'd be back. Neither of them answered encouragingly.

'Till next week then!' Cess stepped out on to the lamplit pavement.

'Wave bye-bye, Mira, sweetheart.'

But Mira had gone and Valdite had to wave alone from her scrubbed front step.

★

Monday was Valentine's Day and the hostel was alive with shrieks of joy, exclamations of delight and embarrassed horror. Roses came for some, delivered by Interflora. Boys appeared clutching bouquets and chocolates; many girls were going to parties, others to dine by candlelight. Cess sat on her bed and looked at an unsigned home-made confection of doilies and crepe paper hearts, from her mother.

A mile to the north, on the other side of the river, Elvira Troubadour was alone in her sitting room gazing at a most ostentatious bouquet while fulminating silently about Mr Heath. How dare that ingratiating organist, murderer of Purcell, ridiculous sailor and inept Prime Minister condemn the country to cold and darkness? Let him try being a coal miner; the smirking, smooth-cheeked nincompoop wouldn't last a day. Let any blue-nosed Tory solicit her support and she'd soon wipe the grin from deadly Ted's puffy face. See if she wouldn't.

She imagined that she felt the same about horrible Mr Heath as Matilda Gilmerton, in bed with a mild case of 'flu in the room below, felt about Ian Parker.

Just after nine, Elvira had knocked on Tilda's door. 'Good morning, Matilda! These will make you feel better. Look what such a sweet young man from Harrods has delivered!'

Tilda's head appeared from under the eiderdown. 'You have them, Miss Troubadour, please. They'll be from smarmy Ian Parker. He'll have put them on Mum's account.'

'Are you sure about that?'

'Absolutely. Please have them. They can be an early birthday present from me.'

Elvira arranged the flowers her best majolica vase, where they looked superb. Oh, supposing someone had sent them to her? Just imagine!

The bell rang twice more that morning. Both these modest bouquets did make Tilda feel better, not that she knew or cared a jot for those who'd sent them, nor did she give a fig for the five admirers who'd sent the Valentine cards jostling each other on her crammed mantlepiece.

Tomorrow she'd get up and return to work. Today she wanted to be left in peace.

Elvira fielded six phone calls. 'Please try again another day.' All six males sounded very disappointed. Supposing just one of them had been for her? Ah well, what a silly dream, at least she'd got an adopted nephew visiting her next Friday to keep her cheerful.

Benjamin always called on Elvira's birthday and always brought a sticky Portuguese cake, a Bolo Do Gengibre, baked by his mother, which Elvira always gave to the ducks in Kensington Gardens. Had she known that Valdite always fed her birthday present of a Dundee cake, from Fortnum and Mason, to the ducks on Wandsworth Common, considerable economies would have been made by both households. But this exchange of cakes was a tradition that could not be broken. The ducks expected it.

Nine-hour electricity blackouts started two days later and two days after that Tilda decided to take an early evening bath while the water was hot and there was still light to be had in the basement bathroom.

Upstairs Elvira and her nephew were having an evening of stilted conversation huddled over the two bars of her electric fire, warming up before the inevitable power-cut.

How was his sister? Had anything been heard of Dora since she went to Nepal?

Not for a while, not since a parcel of loose beads had arrived addressed to Mira, with a note saying that she was well.

Any news of her return?

No, not a word.

And his mother, how was dear Valdite? How was little Mira? It was such a long time since they had come to see old Auntie El.

It was the buses, Ben explained. Three changes are never easy with a small child in tow, but he knew his mother would love to see Elvira at any time, Mira asked for her frequently or at least he was sure she did.

'Come the spring,' Elvira replied as if visiting Wandsworth involved scaling snowy peaks.

'I met a girl who wants to help.'

'Oh?' Elvira sounded interested. 'How?'

'Like taking Mira to the park, playing games and things.'

'No, no, Ben. I mean how did you meet this girl. What is she called?'

'Cecile, I think.'

'Don't you know? You ought to pay more attention, Ben. Cecile eh, not a very common name. I have a niece called Cecile.'

'That's her. We met at our mutual distant cousin's wedding, just down the road in Pont Street.'

Elvira sat up. Any cousin mutual to Ben and Cecile must perforce be mutual to her, too. She had a hat that needed exercise which someone (not male, alas) had once said became her.

'Was it a big wedding, Ben? Did your mother get an invitation?'

'I'm not sure,' he lied, 'but if she had, I am sure she would not have wanted to go.'

'Me neither' Elvira stated, then added, 'the postal service is reprehensible, of course, under Mr Heath, like everything else. And what did you think of Cecile?'

'She was eager to help.'

'I'm sure she was. What does she look like?'

'OK, I suppose, I can't really remember. How is she your niece?'

'She is my sister's child, your adopted Aunt Maud, I suppose, only we aren't close. We've had a falling-out since she took to being bucolic. She has married a man who knows much of cows and heaps of muck, a stranger to intellectual stimulation and urban sophistication.'

The doorbell rang and instead of going down to answer it Elvira lifted the sash and poked her head out into the chilly evening air. 'Yes? If you are from the Mormons or come to tell me what Jehovah said you are too late. What?'

Ben could hear someone shouting up from the street. 'How dare you! What effrontery, you can tell your organ-grinding Mr Heath to take himself and his silly boating cap for a short walk off a long pier.' She slammed the window shut; the majolica shuddered and the Preiss dancer teetered on her bronze tiptoes.

'Shouldn't that be the other way round, Aunt El?'

'Possibly, don't quibble. You scientists are all far too precise. Imagine coming at this hour to canvass my opinion on that grinning charlatan, it's monstrous.'

Sudden darkness and then the lights came on again in a final gasp before total extinction during which Elvira lit a couple of candles, merry red relics of Christmases long past. The fire bars turned from sunny orange to red, then faded to black and Ben announced that he ought to go if he was to get to home to take advantage of the clear sky. It was going to be a great night for stargazing. He had rigged up a telescope on the roof above his top-floor flat near St Pancras.

Then they heard a thump followed by a shriek from below.

'Great Heavens, Ben! Whatever was that?'

'Shall I go and find out, Aunt El?'

'Better not, dear. It was probably some domestic unpleasantness in the street into which one is discouraged from probing.'

But the unpleasantness came to them in the form of a nearly naked Tilda stumbling up the unlit stairs, wrapped in a dressing gown and several towels. She stood shaking on Elvira's hearthrug. Even by candlelight, it was obvious that she was caked in fragments of dusty plaster. The amusing footprints on the novelty bathmat around her shoulders were barely discernible through the layers of filth.

'Matilda! Explain!'

'Miss Troubadour, I am very sorry, but the ceiling fell into the downstairs bath. I was just about to get out when suddenly the lights went off and the tub was full of plaster.'

'How extraordinary, it has never done that before. Whatever is to be done? In the Blitz one was at least prepared for falling masonry. You are a man, Ben dear, what do you advise?'

Ben said nothing. He was transfixed.

'Dear me,' said Elvira. 'How rude of me. Tilda, my dear, this my nephew Benjamin, Dr Benjamin Troubadour. He's a professor you know, sound on the stratosphere and so forth. Ben, this is my tenant Matilda Gilmerton, who is intending to be a doctor.'

'How do you do.' Ben shook Tilda's hand which she extricated from her inadequate wrappings. 'How do you do. Actually I'm rather cold.'

Ben kept hold of her hand.

'How romantic, just like *La Boheme*!' exclaimed Elvira, sacrificially ripping a tartan rug from her threadbare sofa and adding it to the layers around Tilda's shoulders.

Ben held on to the icy, gritty hand and smiled. Tilda warmed considerably and smiled back.

★

Twenty minutes and a phone call later they were flying across the river towards Wandsworth. The nearest Tilda had got to biking before had been sitting astride a friend's Lambretta which had petrified her. This was different; this was like being borne aloft on angel wings, wafted by fumes, accompanied by a fanfare of engineering. She clung to Ben's back as they roared up North Side and past the prison to the tidy terrace where Valdite was waiting with soup and a gas-fired geyser.

'My poor child, what a calamity has happened to you! Come in at once…you will perish out of doors after such a shock. You can have Dora's room, but we must keep quiet as mice or Mira will wake up and I have only just got her to bed.'

Later, when she was clean, the three of them sat in Valdite's kitchen eating all the best things in her larder and drinking Mateus Rose which was the nearest she could find to the Portuguese wine of her youth thereabouts. Tilda normally hated it, but tonight it was ambrosia. The kitchen was cramped and she and Ben sat beside each other on the bench behind the tiny table. Their legs and arms touched each other and their hearts were knitted together. Valdite had never been so happy.

★

The bell rang at eight forty-five the following morning. Valdite answered the door in fluffy slippers. It was Cess, all brightly ready to help. Valdite looked at her through bleary eyes and told her, very nicely, to go away and come back later. No, she didn't need any help with the housework, no, she wasn't ill and yes, she was sure a trip to the duck-pond later would be fun for Mira, much later.

'When?'

The winter sun was unnecessarily bright, the traffic unusually raucous for a week-end. Valdite craved tea and aspirins. She gave Cess a pound note and sent her off to a far distant shop to buy superfluous milk and newspapers that she would not read, saying she hoped Mira would be in spurs and boots and ready to visit many ducks by ten, but not before. Valdite shut the door and slid the chain across to make sure, before returning to the kitchen to clear up last night's mess and toast some soldiers for Mira's egg.

Tilda woke from a divine deep sleep to find two large blue eyes less than an inch from her nose. 'Are you my mum?' the owner of the eyes wanted to know.

'No, I'm nobody's mum. I'm Tilda and I think you must be Mira. How do you do.'

'What are you doing in my mum's bed then?'

Tilda explained.

'But that's silly. Why did Aunt El's ceiling fall down?'

'I expect it was old and tired.'

'Like Granny?'

'Your granny isn't old and tired.'

'She is sometimes. She said so.'

Mira wanted to show Tilda everything and chatted to her incessantly while she got up, washed and dressed. She had to put on the clothes she'd grabbed in the dark before Ben had biked her from Chelsea to Wandsworth. Even her socks didn't match, but Tilda had an artless way of looking good in whatever old rag she wore. Mira insisted Tilda used her favourite plastic ladybird slide, to hold back her long, straight hair. Tilda never wore make-up, she couldn't be bothered, nor did she ever go shopping for fun. Her sister Grizel did enough of all that for both of them and was always broke. Tilda saved enough money to bail Grizel out most of the time and recently, when Grizel had needed a huge sum urgently, Tilda had been able to get hold of it for her at once and send the bankers draft to her in France. Grizel did not say what she was going to do with it. Tilda didn't ask. She really didn't want to know.

The doorbell rang at five to ten. 'Drat,' said Valdite, and Mira, still half dressed, ran to open it, but couldn't manage the chain. 'Who is it?' she shouted through the letter-box.

The flap opened towards her and she saw some teeth between chapped lips and smelt a waft of custard and old cabbage.

'It is me, Cecile. I've come to take you to feed the ducks'.

Mira knew how Valdite got rid of riff-raff. 'Not today thank you!' she yelled at the teeth, pushed back the flap and held it shut.

After a minute of pleading at the sealed letterbox, Cess straightened up and tried the bell again. Meanwhile the man parking his motorbike in the street came through Valdite's front garden gate right up to the doorstep. He was still in helmet and goggles because his arms were full of red roses.

'Hi, Cecile. It's me, Ben. Remember, we met at that awful wedding? Here, hold these while I take off my skid lid.'

'Oh Ben!' Her cold-bitten face beamed like the sun, birds sang and all the wintery shrubs burst into blossom.

The chain rattled and the door was opened, not by Valdite but by Tilda Gilmerton.

'Good morning! Look I've brought you these…I'm afraid they're past their best. I was given the lot by the man outside the station.' Ben took the bunch of blown roses from Cess and handed it to Tilda, who laughed and gave him a big kiss.

A shaft of ice silenced the birds and blighted all blossom.

'Good heavens!' said Tilda. 'Cess! Fancy meeting you here, too. I haven't seen you for ages.'

Valdite bustled out of the kitchen. 'Ben, my delight, how wonderful, another visit, perfection! So soon and look – to think that at last my son can do something romantic. Quick, let me find an aspirin, aspirin can revive everything, even roses. Come in come in, all of you, into the warm and I will put the kettle on, losing no time at all.'

But Cess couldn't stay. She had things to do, she did not say what. Nobody questioned her or noticed, till much later, that she had gone.

Summer 1974

Unlike Elvira's previous tenants, Tilda and Ben did not indulge their passion beneath her fragile roof. Tilda moved out. She went to live with Ben in his top-floor bedsitter in Sickert House near St Pancras where the buses and trains vied with each other to make the greatest din and the evil-smelling lift was permanently broken down.

Ben's single bed was all they needed. They hardly ever bothered to fold it back against the wall except when his mother called, bringing Mira with her. When this happened, the lovers got plenty of warning because Valdite and Mira could be heard puffing and protesting for at least ten minutes, while they made their ascent. Mira was now far too heavy for Valdite to carry, even at her strongest. 'Come, my chicken, let us get you some sturdy legs, Twenty-two, twenty-three, count with me, Mira. We will reach ninety-five swiftly if we count.

When they left they counted downwards like a rocket launch and let out a great cry of 'Zero!' as they reached the ground, by which time the bed was often horizontal again and occupied.

Had Elvira sub-let Tilda's room she might have been troubled about continuing to be paid her rent, but she kept her room in readiness, with the conscientiousness of a Victorian widow. Without a vestige of guilt, she banked the rent with glee, even though Tilda hadn't returned to Pont Terrace except to collect her mail since the lovers had met and fallen for each other in February.

45

Tilda also used Elvira's phone to make occasional reverse charge calls to her mother in Scotland.

Irene Gilmerton couldn't think of much to say to her daughter, apart from asking after her health and the weather. Irene never suggested she visit south of the border herself.

Irene's realm was her home from which Ian Parker, her amanuensis, sycophant-cum-major domo, companion and advisor was despatched in pursuit of soft furnishings and tasteful embellishments. He advised upon her hair, and couture clothes, planned her parties, presided at her table, hired her staff and drove her everywhere in the smartest cars. Irene did not drive. The vehicles in her triple garage were all presents from her to Ian, as was his nifty motor launch which he tactfully christened *Fair Irene*.

Though Ian spent most of every day with her, they slept apart. She in the bay-windowed double bedroom overlooking Henrysson's Rock and he in the lodge flanked by the gates to Dalmuirie Castle and Dalmuirie House, between the finest linen sheets upon the Biedermeier gem he'd extracted from Irene for his fortieth birthday.

Irene had inherited the lodge from her late husband, Gilbert Gilmerton, the exceptionally wealthy heir to the Gilmerton foghorn and siren empire, who had prudently bought it from the exceptionally impoverished Henryssons when their castle was de-requisitioned. Irene had succeeded in selling the Lodge to Ian Parker for a pittance, despite the strictures of Gilbert's convoluted will.

Nothing that her mother did bothered Tilda, provided she kept Ian to herself.

Tilda and Ben kept each other to themselves like twin stars, radiating happiness. Their love was delightfully obvious, yet Tilda never told anybody, not even Grizel, who could have guessed that something about her sister had altered, including her address and telephone number, had she not been thoroughly preoccupied with herself. Grizel, as ever, was the centre of her exclusive universe.

Tilda never told Ben about her possessions which, as Elvira reckoned, were considerable. As Ben's devoted aunt, this made her very happy indeed, but she kept that, like Tilda's rent, to herself. She no longer needed to sell her majolica to pay for repairs and after all, had not that nice Mr Parker said one can never have too much of it?

Ben throve and Tilda throve and, though her studies suffered badly, his work did not. The love-making that was his fuel, fuelled her blissful indolence. On fine nights they would climb to the flat roof of Sickert House and there, among the tanks and aerials, they would gaze at the stars and he would try and explain the movements of the universe. Tilda listened, absorbing little but marvelling that anybody could be as happy as she was then, while constellations trooped westward in stately procession, across the never quite black sky, above the city.

The distances with which Ben related were infinite, measured in billions of light years. Their time together, Tilda sensed, was finite and measured by the second.

Apart from Tilda's putative career, the other sufferer was Cess. Every week she visited Valdite hoping to have some contact with Ben and every week she took Mira to feed the spiteful ducks where Mira bellowed so loudly that they paddled off and the ugly looks of passers-by forced Cess to give in and take Mira back to Valdite. Cess didn't notice Valdite's shrinking body. She was far more concerned with her own increasing bulk, which made her more miserable than ever and her appetite more voracious.

It wasn't difficult to discover Ben's address. Cess watched Sickert House from a grubby cafe almost opposite where she drank too many weak coffees in transparent cups, Sometimes she walked by on the pretext of visiting railway stations to get timetables; sometimes she wandered towards Coram's fields or looked at bleak statues commemorating departed philanthropists and studied the graves of the distinguished dead in Old St Pancras churchyard. She gazed at the caryatids outside the St Pancras Parish Church which reminded her of Glasgow and wept quietly in her hostel cubicle at night, praying for a miracle that she knew no god would grant. Doughnuts and chocolate bars were not answers, but they were the only ones she got.

Tilda knew Cess was stalking Ben. He did not. Anyway, neither she nor Ben would have cared. At least three weeks passed before Tilda realised Cess was no longer there. After a while Valdite assumed that Cess had lost interest in child-minding. Mira was delighted and told her grandmother that the ducks were happy too.

Cess had gone home, where she was welcomed by her parents – somewhat less than ecstatically. The fatted calf lived on.

★

All through the months till the university summer vacation, life for Tilda and Ben was utterly wonderful.

War raged, bombs exploded, there were massacres and strikes, deaths, disasters and a General Election; all horrors went on happening elsewhere; lovers were invulnerable, or so they had come to believe.

One day when spring was well under way and the parks were full of nesting birds, Tilda returned to the flat early to find Ben waiting for her. She knew that she'd failed her exam, her concentration was in tatters and she was beginning to doubt her ability to even follow her vocation. At this rate it would be years before she qualified; perhaps the early aptitude she'd shown was just an illusion. Was she another bright child who'd peaked too early, who destructive gods had first made promising? She neither knew nor cared. It had been easy to be the cleverest child at St Quivox and fairly simple to study hard at boarding school, where the distractions were few and academic diligence was a refuge. It had even been easy to work when she had lodged with Elvira Troubadour. Now it was different, she had a lover to live for now, not a career in some unformed future. She knew she had failed and did not mind a bit. Remorse was for later; now was for being in love.

Ben kissed her and told her that he had news.

'News? What about? What has happened? Tell me!'

'I have been offered a job.'

'But you've got a job. You are the youngest professor in the place. What kind of job?'

'A research fellowship. A chance to work with the very best for a fantastic salary. A real dream of a job.'

'But how wonderful, Ben. Congratulations! Let's celebrate.'

His arms gripped her shoulders. 'There's a problem.'

'Oh?'

'It's at NASA, in the States, for two years.'

'Ah.' Tilda sat down on the bed. 'That is a bit of a downer, but not insuperable surely?'

'I'm not going.'

'Why ever not?'

'Why do you think? You, of course. I can't leave you behind.'

'Can't I come, too?'

'But what about your studies?'

'What about them? Surely they train doctors in the States. I can study there, if anyone will have me after my recent performance, which I doubt.'

'You won't be allowed to work or anything. They may not even give you a visa.'

Tilda looked at him. 'Do you mean to say that you are prepared to throw up this wonderful opportunity just because of me? You are mad, Ben. I'm coming with you, nobody can stop me if...'

'If what?'

'Oh Ben, don't be dense, if I am your wife of course.'

'You'd marry me?'

'Of course, if you asked.'

'I am asking.'

★

Valdite Troubadour liked hummable tunes with melancholy words. They reminded her, in a muddled way, of her youth, with their hints of gypsy passion, rhythmic Hebrew bouncy nostalgia mixed with the yearning of Portuguese Fado. When she sang in English to Mira, it was not of gathering nuts in May or rock a-bye babies tumbling from the tree tops, Valdite's bed and bathtime songs were about those having been the days that they thought would never end, and how those being young should have had their way. Mira liked the bit about singing and dancing for ever and a day; it was reassuring, like 'happy ever after' and 'world without end, Amen.'

Elvira Troubadour's taste was also for melancholy songs about what might have been, the joys of love that last an instant and 'chagrin d'amour' which would 'dure toute la vie.' She found comfort in that thought and also in being able to sing, albeit tunelessly, in French. She liked to be thought cultured. She was also good at secrets and took great pleasure in keeping the forthcoming wedding to herself, though she liked to imagine the gratifying scandal it would cause if she imparted it to her sister Maud in Scotland. That pleasure had to wait. Only she and Valdite knew. Mira knew, too, of course; she was going to be the solitary bridesmaid at Marylebone Register Office on Thursday 17th of July.

Ben Troubadour and his Tilda were impervious to pitfalls. They saw no obstacles; those were their days, and they, being young, should have had their way. They thought those days would never end and that they were free to lead the life they'd chosen.

★

Home in Ayrshire and disconsolate, Cess sang miserable valedictory ballads, all sounding much the same, to her father's unmoved cows, which made her eyes red and watery. Mostly she sang about leaving on jet planes, moving on because good times were all gone and hearing whistles blow a hundred miles. Meanwhile her mother, Maud Pollock, warbled cheery ditties about happiness, saving kisses for me and going all for Mahri's wedding, in tune with her Singer sewing machine. Willie Pollock had no time for musical carry-on.

It was another disappointing June for Scotland and Miss Philomela Stuart MA was on her way to Rothesay for a mouth-music convention while Avis Wishart listened to the Dambusters March as she drove to Dalmuirie Castle where Charles had summoned her to take dictation.

Alone in her bedroom at Nether Dalmuirie, Irene Gilmerton tap-danced in her underwear in front of a cheval mirror, for an audience of scavenging gulls wheeling above the beach, beyond her vast bay window. To dance unapplauded was the price she'd paid to marry into enough wealth to release her from having to make herself available to men. Sex had become as tedious a chore as scrubbing a floor to her, as it had been to Cora, her mother, who formed the other part of their 'sister' act, the Sweet Corenes. Irene missed the admiration but nothing else. She was an immortelle, a blossom preserved; she was no longer required to function sexually, for which she thanked God.

Cora had been a pragmatist who had no qualms as to how far pretty legs and disingenuous laughter could get a girl. Her legs had taken her from against the wall behind the shipyards to front stage at the Alhambra and into the beds of millionaires. Irene had learnt how to fake ecstasy and tolerate weird masculine demands by watching Cora. Gilbert Gilmerton's demands were easy for a childlike woman to fulfil. His pleasure had eventually provided Irene with life-long security, just in time.

Cora had died like Gilbert. Cora had done it with pills, Gilbert with a rope. Motherless Irene and her daughters had flourished without their father and never questioned their lack of grandparents.

What was always referred to as Gilbert's tragic death had released them all from danger and enabled Irene to become a celibate widow, a role she enjoyed to the full provided she retained Ian Parker to indulge her in every way, except that from which she was delighted to abstain.

Ian liked money and boys, Irene liked money and admiration. She looked at herself in the mirror and admired her legs. She was alone but not lonely.

She sang of sisters, devoted sisters who share everything except, heaven forfend, their misters. Her shoes couldn't clatter on the thick carpet as she danced the routine that had enchanted the Gaiety, but the woman she saw in the mirror was still a spell-binding ingénue. Just the knowledge that her younger daughter was approaching her mid-twenties disturbed her. Irene and her world were frozen in the nineteen fifties. She was forever young, never to be fifty, queen of her territory and terrified of change, but change was on its way because Grizel might be back from France before autumn, possibly without plans to leave again. At least Tilda seemed to be settled down south, odd child that she was. Would people think that she and Grizel were sisters like her and her mother, the Sweet Corenes?

Irene concluded her performance with a rendering of *Baby Face*, dead Gilbert's favourite.

Avis Wishart pulled the Dalmuirie Castle bell handle and found that the mechanism was rusted beyond repair so she pushed at the front door. It yielded grudgingly and she entered the vestibule, a graveyard for boots, waterproofs and sporting relics. A defunct forest of umbrellas and shooting sticks stuck out of an elephant's foot, a hare's head glared above a speckled mirror, framed with antlers. Avis reckoned the mousetrap was long overdue to be emptied as she recognised the stench of festering rodent while passing through murky glass doors into the oak-lined hall, taking care not to trip over a bald rug that once had been a bear. Meagre light filtered through the stained glass window on which draped maidens languished in a stylised rose garden, having no fun at all with a weedy bloke in a balaclava.

'Is anybody there?'

Avis felt like the traveller at the moonlit door. Nobody answered, but she did hear the distant sounds of seagulls mewing to the sugary notes of *Desert Island Discs* by Eric Coates. His music was having quite an airing this morning, she thought, as she climbed the uncarpeted stairs avoiding the wobbly finial, carved into an unlikely dragon, sporting an abandoned flat cap.

She followed the music and the smell of burnt milk till she arrived at the door behind which Lady Charity had retreated to be in a decline.

'Good morning, Nurse Coole.'

'Mrs Wishart! Is that yourself?'

'How is Lady Charity?'

'We are not at all ourselves. We have not taken solid food for several days.'

'I am sorry to hear that, Nurse Coole. Would she like to see me?'

'We've just had our tablet and we are now taking our nap.'

'Ah well, another time maybe. Actually I am looking for Mr Henrysson. He wishes me to take dictation.'

'Which Mr Henrysson would that be? Mr Henrysson Senior or Mr Hugh? We seldom see either of them though I doubt whether Mr Hugh is out his bed yet. If it is the elder Mr Henrysson you are after I fancy he may be taking a wee walk over to the sitooterie. I believe I saw him heading in that direction when Yum Yum was spending a penny.'

Avis thanked the nurse who, unlike her charge, showed no sign of being off her food, and went out along the castle front towards the south until she came to the tumbledown pavilion, behind which she found Charles Henrysson with his binoculars focussed on Nether Dalmuirie below, from which the distinct sound of a gramophone playing *Baby Face* was rising.

Avis coughed.

'Great Scot! You gave me a fright, Mrs Wishart…I was that preoccupied…birdwatching…it's one of my things. Bloody good spot this for kittiwakes and so forth. Shame about the puffins, rats got them don't you know? Bloody rats, they are everywhere. What can I do for you, Mrs Wishart? No trouble with young Hugh down the camp again, I trust.'

'You asked me to call by, Mr Henrysson, to take dictation.'

'Bless my soul, so I did. Clean forgot, sorry. Now I've even forgotten what I wanted to dictate. Oh well, there's time. Another day perhaps.'

Avis sighed. Another morning wasted on not earning a welcome pound.

'Lovely day what? Business brisk, is it, at the camp?'

Just then the xylophone call for first lunch sitting at Firthside Holiday Camp wafted across the bay, as it did when the wind was in the north-west. That didn't augur well.

'Business is fine when the weather is fine, Mr Henrysson. Campers tend to get tetchy in the wet.'

'It's a bad sign when you can see the fields on Arran. Always rains when the place is too clear.'

Avis looked over to the island and saw a small craft racing across the water from the direction of Ailsa Craig.

'That'll be that Parker fellow. I've asked him to poison the rats on me rock. I used to let the place to Gilbert Gilmerton, you know, but I haven't the heart to ask for the rent since he did away with himself. Nasty business that. Runs in the family, you know.'

Avis wanted to ask which family Charles was talking about, his or the Gilmertons, but thought it best to keep quiet.'

'At least my lot aren't batty. Those Gilmertons have bad blood, Mrs Wishart. Mad as snakes, most of them. They die raving if they don't do away with themselves earlier.'

'Every one of them?'

'Bloody nearly. You should have met Gilbert's sister. Talk about lunatic…she threw herself off the Duchess of Argyll.'

'She did what?'

'She jumped into the sea during a pleasure trip to Ailsa Craig. Nobody saw her do it, but it quite wrecked the Dundoon Unionist outing. She was washed up on the sands during the Glasgow Fair, damned unpleasant for the trippers. Her mother was worse, barking mad when she crashed her motor on the Electric Bray.'

'How sad.'

'Very. Families aren't easy, Mrs Wishart. Have you got one?'

'A family? Yes, we've a couple of sons.'

'Satisfactory, are they?'

'So far. One is hoping to read law and the other is a bit young yet to know what he wants to do, apart from cricket. He's good at drawing, though, and sums.'

'You wait.'

'Is Hughie in trouble again, Mr Henrysson?'

'You know, Mrs Wishart, I think I'd prefer it if he was. He does nothing, damn all, all day. A man should have an interest, a career, a hobby, something. All my good-for-nothing son has are vices: booze, women and sleep.'

'Sleep isn't a vice.'

'No, it's the nearest thing he has to a virtue. At least he isn't drinking or begetting bastards when he's asleep.'

Avis tried to think of something comforting. 'It must be nice to know he can beget children, Mr Henrysson. He's what my brother would call a proven bull. Anyway I like Hughie, even if he can be a bit wild.'

'A man of his age should be married. I was.'

During the awkward silence Avis cast about for something positive to say concerning the Henrysson marriage, avoiding the obvious asset of Lady Charity's reputed wealth.

'Your brother, the one who knows about bulls, where does he come from?' Charles asked.

'Our family came through from Fife between the wars. You know, the Pollocks. They were your tenants at Dalmuirie Mains till you sold them the lease.'

'Of course. Sorry, I forgot you were sister to that lucky devil. Selling that lease was the worst day's work I ever did. That land will be worth a fortune one day soon. The Pollocks will be on the pig's back. How many sons does Pollock have?'

'None, Mr Henrysson. Willie and Maud just have the one child, a daughter in her early twenties.'

'Do they, by George! Do they really? Well well. Is she...er married at all?'

'No, Mr Henrysson, not in the least.'

★

Avis dropped in on her brother on her way home.

'What did he mean about you being on the pig's back?'

Willie was at his dinner, in his cap. Maud had produced a prodigious stew; it smelt delicious. It was unfortunate that this stew's origin had spread her aitch bone in the yard during the frost last back-end as she might have lifted the champion heifer's trophy at the forthcoming Dundoon Show.

It was not exactly legal to shoot and butcher casualties oneself, but what else was there to do? The new chest freezer was a boon to those with large dead beasts to house, in parts. It took a while to eat a whole cow. Even Maud was running out of cooking variations and Cess was seriously considering becoming a vegetarian after a couple of months of eating Dalmuirie Thistledown the 4th. Willie Pollock ate on regardless with the *Scottish Farmer* propped up against the HP Sauce.

'Is that what himself said?'

'Yes, Willie. He said that he never ought to have sold you the lease.'

'Aye, well he kens that now.'

'Come on, Willie, I'm your sister. I need to know.'

'Well, don't let your boys get any fancy ideas about inheriting.'

'Of course not, Willie. Dalmuirie Mains is yours. We all know that.'

'Aye, well, there are folks that might have funny ideas.'

'Avis is not like that Willie,' said Maud. She was as welded to her floral overall as Willie was to his cap. Cess sat watching this exchange and wondered whether bathing in her jeans was worth the agony. She had no interest in farming, but somehow this conversation seemed to imply something quite intriguing. She listened carefully while pretending to be absorbed in *Nova*.

'I'm no saying anything,' said Willie, pushing back his chair. 'I've the lambs to sort for the abattoir. Will you give me a hand, hen? After all, it's you that will be the lucky one when I'm gone.'

Cess looked up. 'I'm busy applying for college, Dad.'

'Another college? What are you going to learn the now?'

'Advanced Hospitality.'

'Advanced Hospitality! What in the name o goodness is yon? Your mother can teach you all the advancement you need in that line. "Come away in and have a cup of tea"…that's hospitality, "and how about a wee bit cake, too"– that's advanced. It would be hospitable to offer your auntie a plate of stew. Och, she's away… always flitting about, that one. Now listen to me, woman, you don't need to get a fancy certificate for hospitality. Next thing will be a degree in making jam. Come on, get off your rump and show yourself worthy of your good fortune. Is that no the telephone? Away and answer it. I bet it's Useless Jock blethering about sheep dip or pulpy kidney…tell him I'm away down the steading and I'll no be back till my tea.'

Cess lifted the bakelite receiver. 'Dalmuirie Mains.'

'Good afternoon, may I speak to Miss Pollock.'

Cess didn't recognise the elderly man's voice and assumed he meant Mrs Pollock. 'Hold the line, please, I'll fetch her.'

Maud dried her hands on her overall and took the receiver. 'Hello, Maud Pollock speaking…why Mr Henrysson, what a pleasure to hear your voice. Lady Charity is not taken poorly, I hope… . Oh good…yes…oh, yes, quite grown-up…yes, doesn't time fly?…yes…oh certainly…she'd be delighted…I'll tell her…thank you so much, Mr Henrysson, most generous of you…goodbye.'

'Well now Cecile, sweetheart, who'd have thought. It appears you have an admirer. Guess what, that was Mr Henrysson himself asking whether you would go to the Unionist Ball at the Marine Hotel with his Hughie. There now, what a treat.'

'I won't go.'

'Quite right, hen. Don't even think about it,' said Willie, grappling with an obstinate boot. 'They Henryssons are up to something.'

'It's too late. I've accepted for you and furthermore, Mr Henrysson is paying for your ticket. What excitement. I can't wait to get started on your frock.'

'I'm not going!'

But she was, and did, in July 1974.

★

If Cess was honest about how she lost her virginity she would have said, by mistake, in a Landrover, on the Dundoon seafront, because she couldn't think of anything to talk about. She was also goaded by curiosity and haunted by the joke about the spinster's epitaph – 'Returned unopened.' Hughie had nothing to say either, so making euphemistic love was the only alternative to another hour of blinding boredom in the ballroom of the Marine Hotel.

From the moment they'd arrived and seen that they were younger, by at least twenty years, than anyone else in the room, even the waitresses, Hughie decided he'd either have to fake sick or get drunk. The former was unconvincing and the latter impossible as he'd brought hardly any money with him and by the time he'd bought Cess a Babycham he couldn't afford the amount of alcohol he'd need as anaesthetic against the ghastly ordeal that was the Conservative and Unionist Gala Ball. The Gala atmosphere was understandably somewhat blunted by the fact that Harold Wilson had been back in Number 10 since March.

'Can I tempt you to a raffle ticket?'

Miss Philomela Stuart supported the Tories in the absence of a Scottish Nationalist candidate; besides the Member himself had a second cousin who'd been a pupil (though not a very distinguished one) at St Quivox. For the ball she was got up to look like a veteran of the White Heather Club and was in charge of the raffle.

'Hi, Miss Stuart, remember me?'

'Of course, Hugh, I remember all my pupils. Will you be purchasing a raffle ticket?'

'What will I win?'

'We have a begonia, talcum powder, sherry-wine, a perm or tea with our Member.'

'God, woman, I'd rather die.'

Cess felt embarrassment wrap her in damp confusion as lakes spread from under her armpits and a ladder crept up her leg.

Her shoes were agonising. Maud had made her scratchy artificial moiré dress much too tight in a shade of tinned tuna. Her belly was still bloated despite her period having ended. The kirby grips with which she'd attached her not quite matching hairpiece dug into her scalp.

They didn't dance; the music was prehistoric. The Jock MacRonald Five favoured the Military Two-Step and even thought the passé Twist to be hazardously modern. The food was largely pink and, like the dress into which Cess had squeezed, equally unappetising. She and Hughie sat beneath a mural of modest mermaids wearing scallop shell bras and wondered how it was that time could creep so slowly without stopping altogether.

She didn't know when to tell him that she knew his daughter. She couldn't believe that he was Mira's father anyway, had it not been for his vivid blue eyes which looked so lovely on his little girl and somewhat loopy on him, possibly because they were usually half closed beneath droopy lids above quite pronounced bags for one of his age. Another drink and she might have broached the subject, but another drink was not offered and she hadn't the nerve to buy one for herself even though she had a couple of pound notes in her beaded bag. Just as she was about to be bold, her resolve was interrupted.

'Tell me, Cecile, are you still singing?' Miss Stuart had appeared from behind a plaster herm of Neptune.

'No, not really.'

'That is a great shame. Do you realise, Hugh, that Cecile here has a voice to rival Moira Anderson herself?'

Hughie stared and shrugged. 'Come on, let's go outside. This place is giving me the creeps. I've got some proper booze in the car.'

Miss Stuart watched as Hughie and Cess went out to the car park and remarked to Sheriff Substitute Affleck that the flower of Scotland was not what it was.

Hughie's scheme for rearing game birds had yet to bear fruit. In fact, the kit bought to enable this venture to start had not got itself out of the back of his Landrover since the farm dispersal sale at which he'd bought the dented troughs and feeders along with several rolls of rusted wire netting, a rotted tarpaulin and a dozen cockpit covers, under which he was planning to plant asparagus, one of these days.

The front seats would have to do for lust, notwithstanding the steering wheel, gearstick and muddy wellington boots.

Hughie got on with his job while Cess tried her very best to summon up the ecstasy she'd read about, which was impossible with her head sandwiched between the sliding offside window and Hughie's made-up bow tie squashing her nose. Hughie made no attempt at passionate kissing but let his chin stick into her left shoulder as he grunted and thrusted. Cess shut her eyes and summoned Ben Troubadour, but all she could feel was a battering ram between her splayed legs. Just as the pain became unbearable Hughie shouted 'Dora!' and then everything was over in a messy tangle of torn knickers and tights. The coupling had been mechanically successful, despite the gear stick and the racket of clattering junk in the back.

'Christ! You should have said. I never thought you'd be a bloody virgin. Nobody is now.'

Cess tried to wipe her tears with her skirt and left as much mascara on the front as blood on the back. Hughie was right, nobody was a virgin now.

He did have the courtesy to offer her a cigarette, which she took. She had never smoked before but she did now; it was part of the rite of passage. 'Always have a fag afterwards,' Hughie said. 'It's one of life's great pleasures.'

That was about the most profound thing he'd said the whole night. Cess breathed in, coughed, spluttered and sneezed.

The Landrover rocked and squally rain lashed the windscreen as she tried to muffle her body's explosions. There'd be no returning to the ball in that state now, even though Jock MacRonald was at least an hour from the National Anthem and Auld Lang Syne.

Her head spun and she took another puff. Hughie was right,

a cigarette after sex was wonderful. In future though she might dodge the preliminaries. They gazed out across the concrete esplanade towards where the sea must be hitting the shore. Two tiny lights flashed in the far distance on Holy Isle and Ailsa Craig, like censoring spies who'd seen it all.

'Hughie?'

'Yes? I say I am awfully sorry. That wasn't really on. You should have told me to stop.'

'No, that's fine. It was really nice.'

'No it wasn't, it was crap.'

'Hughie?'

'Yes… . Oh Christ, you're not going to get pregnant?'

'I know Mira.'

'Mira? Oh I see, good girl. You mean I don't need to worry because Mira can cope with any unwanted visitors, is that what you are saying?'

'I mean I've met Mira. You know, Miracle, your little girl.'

'Christ! The Bastard! Why didn't you tell me before? What is she like? You know I've never seen her and I don't even know where she lives.'

'Don't you have to pay?'

'I can't, I've not got a bean and anyway her mother told me to get lost.'

'Mira lives with her grandmother, in Wandsworth. I don't know where her mother is. I don't think anybody does.'

'What is she like, the child, I mean? Her mother is bloody gorgeous.'

'She is very small, very dark and has got your eyes. She is awfully fond of her grandmother and really hates to be away from her.'

'That's good, so we know she is happy. Does she know who I am?'

'She thinks you are the man putting the shot on the porridge packet.'

'Bloody Hell!' Hughie took another swig from the bottle he'd smuggled from his father's stash in the tumbledown sitooterie. Cess could see that the level had dropped from halfway down to below the label in less than twenty minutes. 'Come on, let's get you home.'

★

Willie was genuinely asleep when Cess crept up the farmhouse stairs. Maud was not.

'Are you all right?' She realised at once what had happened. 'Oh Cecile, I am so sorry. It's all my fault, I should never have encouraged you.'

'I'm fine, Mummy, just fine.'

'Oh my darling, if your father saw you like this he'd away and murder whoever did this to you. Was it Hughie?'

'Yes, but I told you it's fine. He adores me, he said so.'

'Yes, but, all the same, you shouldn't have let him do this to you. Here, give me your clothes. I'll bag them all up and burn them. Now go and have a hot bath. I'll sort the water for you.'

Cess looked at her mother with a mixture of loathing and gratitude.

★

Without a morsel of reproach or mention of fine work wasted, Maud burnt the blood-stained gown upon the farm bonfire and watched as it shrivelled and melted among the smashed crates and rotted fence posts. She also swore never to tell Willie about his daughter's dalliance with the greatest waster in Ayrshire since the notorious Herbert Henrysson who'd lost ten thousand acres of coastline playing poker in 1896. This tract of expendable land later turned into the prime plot that became Doonbury aerodrome, hotel and golf course.

'How is it, my little one, that you are so gullible?' Maud asked while kneading some comforting scones the following afternoon.

'Nobody ever offered to have me before. I've never been what men want.'

'More fool them!' Maud looked at her daughter and understood. The poor child had wanted something that Hughie couldn't give her. Her Cecile wanted lovers, real lovers, men who loved her, not just men who dispensed with their frustrations between her legs.

But her Cecile was prepared to banish that dream. Life could be a lot worse than with Hughie, very much worse. She would relegate Ben to an archive and call on him as a vicarious substitute when she needed something more charismatic than the lanky heir of an impecunious nincompoop with neither money nor sense.

She liked the idea of pushing a pram along Henrysson's Brow above Dalmuirie House, looking down upon the Gilmertons from the heights. She conjectured that she would occasionally be prepared to welcome her husband's bastard daughter to Dalmuirie Castle, when she would delight in behaving with the self-assured condescension of one who had ancient lineage and also opened fetes. She prayed to her neglected god for pregnancy, still a passport to matrimony in 1970s' Scotland.

★

Later July is not as popular as June for weddings which is probably why Ben and Tilda had been able to book the registrar for 4 pm on the 17th.

They spent the week before at the coast. There were rocks, Ben told his mother, that needed to be looked at and she being full of apprehension about the dangers of brides being seen by grooms on the eves of wedding days, implored him to reconsider.

'It is always rocks with you. Rocks are everywhere doing nothing, they will wait. They are not running away or losing nerves. Rocks do not panic; they do not even get anxious.'

'Nor does Tilda. Neither Tilda nor I are superstitious, Mother. We'll see you and Mira on the steps of Marylebone Council House, between the lions at 3.45 on Thursday. Don't be late!'

Tilda and Ben were impervious to bad omens and the dangers of getting to Lyme Regis and back upon Ben's ancient Harley Davidson. Not that either of them looked at Dorset's rocks when they got there. They rattled back to London just before midnight on Wednesday and fell into bed exhausted.

Tilda did not hear the telephone ring just before dawn. It was midday for the caller.

The sun was already high while she lay and dozed, dreaming of nothing except the vague future, safe with Ben, beside her always, loving each other for ever. She looked at the flimsy dress she'd bought at C & A for her wedding and was well pleased. Yes, she thought, this is going to be my lovely day, then she wished she hadn't. It reminded her of her mother and her sloppy songs and the fact that she hadn't even been told that she was about to lose a daughter and gain a son. The idea of Irene as mother of the bride was a cue for pandemonium. C&A would have been replaced by Hartnell, Marylebone registrar by somebody lofty and liturgical, there would have been guests, bidden from all over and unknown to either bride or groom, tents, champagne, a Pearl and Dean-type cake, speeches, tantrums, ghastly presents, huge bills, mountainous flowers: Hell.

'Ben? What's wrong? Darling, tell me!'

He was dressed in his old jeans and carrying a rucksack.

'It's Dora. She's in serious trouble, terribly ill. I've been sent for. I couldn't say that I couldn't go.'

'Couldn't go where?'

'Kathmandu.'

'What today? Now?'

'She's my sister. I'm all she's got, except Mother.'

'And me?'

'Yes, you, of course. You are my everything.'

Tilda sat up. Ben gazed at her. 'I don't want to go, Tilda.'

'Ben, darling, you must. We'll get married when you get back. Don't worry. I know just how you feel. I'd die for Grizel.'

'Would you really?'

'I hope I would.'

'I hope it will never come to that.'

'Luckily all Grizel's troubles seem to be dealt with by money.'

Ben had spent the time since the call getting his things together. He'd been surprisingly efficient and was now quite ready to go. The flights had been booked through Mr Obi on the ground floor whose cousin was a travel agent. Mr Obi also had a friend who arranged loans and was by way of being a pawnbroker. All Sickert House relied on Mr Obi and his clan.

Tilda wrapped herself in Ben's dressing gown (tatty and tartan, inherited from his stepfather) and looked around the oddly tidy room. 'Where's your telescope?'

'A friend is looking after it, along with the bike.'

'You've sold them!'

'Not exactly.'

'Why? You idiot, I could have given you the money, easily. Why didn't you ask?'

'I will never ask you for money. Do you understand? Never! Look, Tilda, I'm sorry, I've got to go now. Mr Obi's brother is driving me to the airport. He'll be here any minute.'

Tilda stood on the pavement, still in the dressing gown, as Mr Obi's brother's bi-coloured Consul pulled out into the Euston Road. Ben swivelled round upon the plastic-covered seat and waved until Tilda was out of sight.

She had never looked more beautiful, but the flat looked as if something had died in it. The unworn dress hung from the window frame and the dust prints on the shelves marked where once Ben's books had stood. The stupid man must have pawned them, too; they couldn't have raised much. Tilda could have paid for his ticket to Nepal and back without a qualm. They had never talked about money, in fact, it was quite possible that Ben was completely ignorant about his future wife's more than comfortable situation. Tilda, who wanted it that way, had originally been frightened that her great wealth would repel him, but grew to realise that he was probably completely impervious and unaffected by anything other than how right they were for each other. She missed him so much. The beanbag still bore the imprint of his body, the towel smelled of his shaving soap, the cup from which he'd drunk was dirty and once she'd rinsed away the remnants of his coffee she regretted it. 'I am being a fool,' she told the cracked mirror in the bathroom and then cried when she saw his hairs in the plughole.

His mother had cried, too, when she learnt what had happened, but for her the anxiety was doubled as it was her daughter that Ben gone to help. Dora may have been feckless, hopeless and selfish, but nothing could detract from Valdite's love for the child she had born in the middle of hostilities to a father murdered by the worst wartime brutes.

The only other guest at the cancelled wedding was to have been Elvira, but she was far too outraged by a terrorist having had the audacity to bomb Westminster Hall to be particularly distressed. After all, the marriage wasn't called off, merely postponed and her hat, which wasn't entirely suitable for summertime wear, would keep.

Tilda packed up all her things, but left the wedding dress dangling on a wire hanger like a flayed skin, to fade in the sunlight and dance in the draught.

She bought a first class sleeper ticket from Euston to Glasgow; she hadn't been home for six months.

★

Avis Wishart contrived a temporary job for her niece at Firthside Camp. She was also the one to tell Cess that Hugh's father had told her that his son had gone away. She didn't tell Cess where he'd gone, or for how long, but she implied that it was a journey of both length and importance.

Charles Henrysson's reaction was best kept quiet. 'My bloody son has slunk off to Cornwall with a disreputable shower of wasters!' he bellowed. 'Great nancy boy of his age should have got over all that bucket and spade lark and got settled down with that fine niece of yours to give me a steady daughter-in-law and a proper grandson and heir, not misbegotten females out of foreign tarts.'

Cess brooded and researched pregnancy in the Carnegie Library, taking note of her daily increase of symptoms, nausea, cravings, tender breasts, frequent pees and swelling belly, which all manifested themselves in the four weeks following the ball at the Marine. She scared herself witless reading a book by a doctor with a double-barrelled name who claimed that there was nothing to fear in childbirth. Occasional slight bleeding, she convinced herself, was not uncommon.

Hugh didn't go to Cornwall, but dossed down on a friend's floor in London till he was kicked out. Troubadour wasn't difficult to find in the telephone directory. There were only two, E and V, apart from a launderette, a barber and a theatrical costumier. E was north of the river, so it was V that must be his quarry. He set out on the hunt armed with an A to Z.

Wandsworth smelled either of brewery or rendered tallow, he wasn't sure which; it was all so damn confusing. He began his search at a statue of a naked man moving the earth with a lever and wandered up a hill through a market, into a web of streets lined with late Victorian houses, some with neater front gardens than others. The grander houses overlooking the Common were mostly offices. Hugh couldn't decide which was more forbidding, the gothic edifice of a school for the bright, or the weighty gateway of the prison for the bad, on whose door death notices used to be displayed after hangings. The gallows, Hugh knew, were still within those walls and still in working order.

Eventually he stood outside Valdite's house and wondered what to do.

'Was there something?'

A woman's head appeared from behind a neighbouring privet hedge.

'No, it's nothing, thanks.'

The woman watched as he strolled on trying to show that he often walked these streets for fun. She was probably the sort who rang the police the moment she saw anything suspicious.

Well, at least he knew where his daughter lived. It didn't look bad, he supposed, better than his friend's flat in Earl's Court. A bit cramped, perhaps. He couldn't imagine what it would be like to be a child without lots of space in which to play.

It was too early for a drink, so he wandered on to the edge of the Common and sat upon a bench to gather inspiration. Some schoolboys were shrieking and mucking about on the municipal swings and whirling each other on a roundabout, sectioned like cheese, intended for much younger children. He sat a while and brooded and did not notice a pair of young mothers looking at him with deep suspicion and removing their children from the park.

Then, after twenty minutes or so, Hugh saw her, a little girl in a pink party dress, all alone, climbing repeatedly up the steps of quite a high slide and solemnly launching herself down, sometimes headfirst, sometimes on her bottom. The dress ripped with every descent till it hung about her in tatters like a fairy doll mauled by puppies. He walked over towards the slide, but just as he got near he noticed a small woman huddled in a coat despite the July warmth, wiping her eyes. The child saw Hugh; she looked straight at him with his eyes.

Then she ran to the sorrowful old woman, who put her arm around her and didn't seem at all fazed by what had happened to the party dress. The pair walked off holding hands.

Hugh had an awful feeling that he, too, might become tearful so he walked until the pubs opened and stayed within the smoky mahogany and frosted glass sanctuary till he was broke and maudlin. That night he slept rough; the following morning he started thumbing it back home.

★

Tilda should have stayed in London. Better still, she should have gone to Nepal with Ben. She might have been useful, she might have been needed and she would have been loved. Here, at her home, she was none of these and, worst of all, it felt as if nothing had changed, nothing had happened. The place and the people were preserved like everlasting flowers, dry attempts at blossoming, aping living beauty, free to go nowhere.

Had she the energy, she would have painted over the mocking stylised stars above her single bed, but the lassitude of the west coast encouraged her apathy during the dragging days of idle anxiety.

Every day she rang Mr Obi, in case he'd received any message from Ben. Mr Obi had agreed to visit the Sickert House flat and pick up the post, but weeks passed without anything to forward to her.

Irene was plainly less than thrilled to have her daughter home, but put on a show of maternal delight and twittered about planning parties while Tilda resolutely refused to participate in anything that involved Ian Parker; Ian was involved in everything.

Eventually Mr Obi had news: an airmail letter had arrived from Nepal. Waiting for this to arrive at Dalmuirie was agony. To distract herself and to avoid the anticlimax of yet another fruitless post, Tilda decided to go for a long walk up the coast towards Firthside Holiday Camp.

The windless coastline was numbed by low cloud concealing the sun and distant islands, amplifying local sounds, while excluding all evidence of a world beyond. It was a day to induce claustrophobia in open spaces.

Two hopeful lovers had seen enough films about seaside romance to give it a try and had come down from Paisley for a day of passion amid the dunes, between Firthside Camp and Dalmuirie. They found a reasonably clean spot among the whins and bents and settled down to make the best of it.

Tilda tramped along the soft sand beneath the headland. Further out, where the sand was damp, she would have been able to see Dalmuirie Castle itself, but from where she was, only the back of the tumbledown sitooterie was visible through gaps in the late summer greenery. She looked across the water at Henrysson's Rock and then northwards to the barely perceptible and sinister outline of Ailsa Craig. Then she became aware of a moving figure walking towards her, far out, almost at the water's edge, perhaps some poor soul seeking solitude away from the frenetic jollity of the camp.

The barrier that marked the tidal limit buzzed with flies teeming in the slimier bladderwrack, beneath the brittle sea-weed crust, interspersed with fragments of salt-blunted glass, unidentifiable scraps, a dismembered doll and orphan shoes cohabiting with empty shells. She wondered whether the inhabitants of razor shells lie about on the seabed opening and shutting like piano lids or hop around vertically like underwater pogo sticks. Had she the energy she could have found out, but anxiety and apathy prevented her from enquiring about the ways of clams. Gulls were wheeling above intent on carrion and old picnics amongst the knives of sea grass.

The incoming tide was calm so, apart from the crying gulls, the only sound came from the camp's Tannoy, too loud to ignore, but too distant to understand the cheerful news it was disseminating. Walking nearer the sea was easier once she had negotiated the worm-casts and the hard corrugations that had been such a trial when she and Grizel went paddling as children.

The figure was lumbering nearer, in earphones with goggle eyes, looking to Tilda, like a magnified fly in a mini-skirt. Eventually she could distinguish that that this was no monstrosity, but a woman carrying a shoe in both hands, while looking through binoculars up at Dalmuirie Castle. Suddenly there was a shriek as the woman tripped and fell, dropping everything into the creeping shallows

Reluctantly Tilda ran to help. She had to. She was no eager angel of mercy, nor was she Hard-Hearted Hannah, but she did resent the size of the casualty. Why do the smelliest people have the nastiest afflictions and why is it always the bulky ones that have accidents?

Tilda's medical training was, so far, theoretical or related to the already dead.

If this woman was really hurt it would be quite a job to carry her clear of the incoming tide, though by the time she had got close enough to see clearly, she recognised that it was Cecile Pollock, who was already scrambling to her feet, weeping and frantically brushing herself down.

It was too late to turn away. They would have to meet.

'Hello, Cess, are you OK?'

'Tilda! What are you doing here?'

'I live here, remember? Anyway how about you? Are you hurt? That was quite a tumble. And what are you doing anyway, wandering along the shore so trendily dressed? Anyone would think you were still in London.'

'Nothing, just having a stroll.'

'I see.'

'And looking at birds and things.'

'And not where you were going. Look what you fell over.'

'Oh, how horrible! It's disgusting! Is it dead?'

'Hard to tell.' Tilda looked at the insulted giant blob diffused with sinister swirls. 'Poor lonely unbeloved thing.'

'I am not unbeloved. Not a bit and not lonely either!'

'I meant the jellyfish.'

At that point Cess started crying and Tilda looked on, discouraged and feeling even less inclined to offer a comforting hug than she did to embrace the dejected jellyfish. She was better at corpses than psychological support.

'My shoes!' Cess wailed, 'Oh heavens, my best shoes! Look, they are wrecked!'

'They might be OK when they dry out and get attacked with steel wool. Oh look! There are your binoculars. Wait there. I'll fetch them.'

Tilda waded through some yellow froth at the sea's edge and retrieved the binoculars from where they were lying amongst the ripples.

'Oh no! Those belong to Uncle Rodney. I borrowed them this morning. He'll kill me.'

'No, he won't. Commander Wishart would never do that to anybody, not even the enemy. Besides, I am sure they can't be damaged. Think what they've had to go through in the Navy. They'll have known worse troubles at sea.'

Cess glared. 'And I feel sick.'

'Poor you. Is it something you've eaten or a bug?'

'No!'

'Well, heave away, the gulls will be delighted. Oh sorry, it's no time for flippancy if you are feeling rotten. Let me walk with you back to the camp before the tide comes in too far. You have come from there?'

'Yes. I'm a receptionist. I meet people and show them around, only I felt sick so Aunt Avis told me to get some fresh air. I have to dress smartly to be a receptionist and now I can't.' The sobbing restarted.

Tilda looked at the straining, salt-stained mini skirt and the sodden suede shoes.

'Quite. Come on, let's get back. You can tidy yourself up at the camp and nobody will ever know.'

'Nobody will notice the difference, you mean.'

'No I don't. Was something interesting going on at the castle?'

'Why do you ask?'

'You didn't seem to be birdwatching when you fell over.'

'That's none of your business and never will be.'

Tilda apologised without knowing why; it seemed simpler that way. She'd done with trying to be sympathetic.

'Right you are. Well, if you are OK, I think I'll head off home. I'll be going back to London soon, but Grizel is coming here in a week or so, you two should get together. Bye, Cess, it was nice bumping into you.'

'Tilda!'

'Yes, Cess?'

'Don't call me Cess. My name is Cecile.'

'Of course. Bye now!'

'Tilda, wait please, I want to ask you something.'

Now what? Tilda sighed and then felt guilty. Poor girl, such a loser and so eager to be a winner. Such a lump. 'OK, what is it?'

'It doesn't matter.'

'Yes it does. Come on, tell me.'

'I've got this friend.'

'Yes, and?'

'Yes, really. You aren't the only one to have friends, you know.'

'Of course not. You must have hundreds.'

'Yes I do, but this one feels sick.'

'Like you?'

'No…yes, well perhaps.'

'What else does she feel?'

'Her breasts hurt and her stomach is swollen and she wants to eat coal.'

'Has she missed the curse?'

'Sort of.'

'When?'

'About two weeks ago.'

'What do you mean by sort of? Was there blood?'

'A bit, only for five days.'

'Well then, what is she worried about? She's probably got a bug or an allergy. She's highly unlikely to be pregnant.'

'Why shouldn't she be pregnant? She's as good as anybody else.'

'Cess, sorry Cecile, are we talking about you?'

'No, of course not!'

'Sorry. Well then I think you should tell your friend to go and see a qualified doctor and have tests done. Or if she doesn't want anyone to know there's an organisation that can help her anonymously. There's bound to be a branch in Glasgow, I could find out the name of the place for her, if you like.'

'Why would she need to go there?'

'They can arrange for her to have an abortion. A proper one, not a dangerous, backstreet affair like they used to be.'

'Never! I'd never do that. All human life is sacred. Surely you agree?'

'No, I don't actually, and your friend might not think like you. How pregnant do you think she is?'

'Six weeks and two days.'

'And she bled for five days a fortnight ago? I'd say she is well off the hook, especially if she gets the curse again in another couple of weeks.'

'I'll tell her, but don't you go thinking that I am talking about me, because I'm not.'

'I'm sorry it crossed my mind, Cecile.'

'Thank you and don't go thinking I haven't got a boyfriend, because I have and he adores me.'

'I'm not surprised. Now I really must be getting back. I still think your friend ought to have a test. They do it with pee and mice. It's quite easy, you know. It's positive if the mice grow breasts.'

'I'll tell her. Now I must go.'

'Enjoy the rest of your walk. Just remember if you'd like a loan to see your friend through a sticky patch you only need to ask.'

'You seem to forget, Tilda, I'm paid a salary that reflects the importance of my job at the camp. Money can't buy everything.'

'It helps, though.'

'Not with love. Goodbye.'

Tilda avoided the unappetising risk of a hug by hurrying back to the De'il's Dyke where she turned to watch the now distant figure approaching the arch at the holiday camp's gate. Even from there and without her glasses, Tilda could see that Cess was walking in a most peculiar way, stiff backed with her stomach thrust forward as if carrying something.

★

The De'il's Dyke was a rocky ridge that marked the boundary of Dalmuirie Bay and formed a fortress against prying walkers, protecting the sandy stretch where little Tilda and Grizel had paddled and swum, when they were brave enough to face both the cold and the jellyfish. It wasn't a private beach, just secluded and theoretically open to all. Sometimes Hughie would sit upon the rocks and throw things at them, seaweed and pebbles mostly, not entirely out of malice but possibly because he was a lonely lad with nobody of his own age to befriend and get up to mischief. But the Gilmerton girls had been much younger than him and didn't understand. They hated the way he sat brooding like some malign troll. They always fled home when he appeared.

Tilda negotiated the rocks and there he was, sitting outside the little cave beneath the castle bank, still staring at her as if more than a decade hadn't happened. Hughie did not daunt her now. He had the dejected air of one quite passed over by life, disengaged and entirely without direction. She could never like him, but she could feel sorry for him. 'Hello, Hughie! How are you? It's me, Tilda…I haven't seen you for ages. How are things?'

'Hi, Tilda, I hoped it was you and not, oh never mind. It is nice to see you.'

'You, too, Hughie. How are your parents?'

'You've heard?'

'Heard what?'

'Mother is on the way out. Dad has even sent for Forbes Farquerson.'

'The Minister?'

'Yes, but Nurse Coole says Mother wishes to die a Catholic.'

'Did she live a Catholic?'

'No, I don't think so. I tell you, Tilda, life is bloody grim. I wish it was me on the way out.'

She sat on a rock beside him and teased an anemone with a pebble, then felt mean as it opened up to receive a treat. 'I'm sorry about your mother. She presented me with a prize when I was at St Quivox, *Tales of the Covenanters*.'

'Did you read it?'

'No, but I looked at the pictures. They were thrillingly grim.'

'Mother has been batty for years. It's living here, it does that to you.'

'Didn't she have an accident? Something with a cello about ten years ago?'

'Yes, I was having a great time in Germany on National Service and I had to come home on compassionate leave, I can't think why. She didn't want to see me then any more than she wants to see me now. She fell from the top there.'

'But surely not on purpose?'

'I wouldn't be surprised. People do round here. Whoops, sorry I forgot about your dad.'

Tilda looked out to Henrysson's Rock and gave an involuntary shudder; a sudden breeze from the North was chilly. 'Why stay here, Hughie, if you hate it so much? Why don't you go away?'

'Where to? I've got no money, no brain, just a barracks of a house, falling trees and dying sheep.'

'At least your sheep are happy. I'm told dying is their aim in life.'

'Tilda, have you got a man?'

'Yes, Hughie, why do you ask?'

He sighed. 'My father wants me to marry well and carry on this bloody ineffective dynasty.'

'If that is a proposal, Hughie, it is the worst I've ever had! I'll tell you a secret, though: my man is your daughter's uncle. There now. That's something to cheer you up. You ought to go and see Mira, she's lovely. Very small and very pretty and, do you know, she's got big eyes exactly the colour of yours, when yours aren't bloodshot.'

'I know. I think…' He paused and wiped his nose with the back of his hand. For a second or so, Tilda thought that he looked as if was about to cry. She thought desperately of something deflecting to say and then Hughie sniffed and spoke again. ' Are you telling me that your man is Dora's brother? I met him once. He's nice.'

'That's him. Ben Troubadour, and he is very nice indeed. He's in Nepal with Dora at the moment. He was sent for.'

'Sent for? Why? Is Dora in trouble? Oh Tilda, I do hope she is OK. You know she is the only woman I've ever fallen for and yet she treats me like a turd.'

'Is that, perhaps, her charm? She's an odd person, Hughie. Neither her mother nor her brother hear from her for ages, then suddenly Ben gets a message demanding he goes to Nepal to rescue her. So he does, dropping everything, just like that.'

'Poor Dora!'

'Poor Dora, my arse. She's wrecks everything. I have no sympathy for her, only for Ben and for his mother. They both dote on her.'

'And my…er…daughter, does she dote on her, too?'

'I don't think Mira can remember her mother ever being there at all. She knows what she looks like from the graduation photograph that her grandmother keeps by her bed and every so often a grubby parcel of tatty ethnic beads and other unsuitable things arrives from places like Kathmandu, but little else. I know she forgot Mira's last birthday, so Ben and I took her to the zoo. She loved the llamas best. Why don't you go and see her some time?'

'I did try, a few weeks ago.'

'And did you see her?'

'I think so. She was playing on some swings. An old woman was with her.'

'Didn't you introduce yourself?'

'No, it was kind of awkward. The old woman seemed a bit put out.'

'Oh, Hughie, what a shame. I wouldn't let that stop me if I were you.'

'You're not, though. Lucky you. Anyway, Dora would murder me if I ever went near the child. Not that I'd mind. '

'Look, Hughie. I know this is the wrong thing to say to anybody suffering from depression, but for God's sake pull yourself together.'

'I'm not suffering. I'm just bloody miserable.'

'About your mother?'

'No, not about her.'

They both stared in silence at the blank sea. Distant Arran was concealed completely yet still the outline of Ailsa Craig loomed faintly through the dense mist

Hughie spoke. 'Everybody seems to know my daughter except me.'

'Everybody?'

'Well, that Pollock girl does.'

'You've seen Cess lately?'

'Do you really call her Cess? I like that, a bit cruel I suppose, though. Yes, I have seen her in a manner of speaking. I called her Cecile.'

'She much prefers that. Cess is what she was known as at school. What a coincidence, I've just met her myself, down there on the beach.'

Hughie started to heave himself to his feet. 'I'd better disappear if she's coming this way.'

'Relax, Hughie. She isn't, she's gone back to Firthside; she's working there. She fell over and I went to help her. She's OK now, just a bit wet and sandy.'

'What was she doing on the beach?'

'She said she was birdwatching.'

'I thought once you were inside that place you couldn't get out.'

'It's not a concentration camp, Hughie. Anyway, apparently Mrs Wishart sent her out to get some fresh air because she wasn't feeling well.'

Ding dong! The holiday camp Tannoy was in action again, though it was impossible to make out what the female voice was announcing. 'If that's Cess now, she must be feeling better. Do you have to put up with that noise all the time, Hughie?'

'Not when the wind is coming from Ireland and not in the winter. Don't you hear it, too?'

'No, we don't at the house. It's sheltered by the brow there.'

'I quite like the noise,' said Hughie. 'It's nice to know someone's alive nearby, even if Mrs Wishart has gated me from going there. This place is dead.'

'Talking of which, Hughie, don't you think you ought to go back to see your mother?'

'Before it's too late? Yes I suppose you are right, of course I should. Tilda, you've done me good. Are you sure you won't marry me?'

'Positive, Hughie.'

'Oh well, that's life.' He got to his feet and smiled. The voice from the camp became more insistent, perhaps someone's child was lost or bawling for its mum. 'I say, you don't think that is the Cess girl really, do you? She bloody haunts me, always coming to the castle on some trumped-up errand. I'm running out of places to hide. What did you say was wrong with her?'

'She said she felt sick.'

'Oh Christ!' He clutched his head.

'Hughie, you haven't been having a fling with Cess, have you?'

'Me a fling, with her? God woman, credit me with some taste. I wouldn't touch that spotty tank with a bargepole in a boxing glove.'

'Oh, that's all right then. She told me she was worried about a friend who thought she might be pregnant and I thought perhaps she was referring to herself. My mistake, she must have been talking about her friend after all. '

'At least she's got friends.'

'Hundreds apparently, boyfriends, too.'

'My mates have all gone off, got serious and grown-up and the girls have turned into wives with kids and jobs and all that stuff '

Just then they heard Charles's voice from the castle's terrace above them. 'Jesus!' Hughie gasped. 'The old fool has found his megaphone. I'd better go.'

The camp's public address system, now cranked up to overwhelm the shrieks of ghost train and waltzer riders, was in a ferment about the first sitting for lunch and competing with a disembodied voice coming from the south. 'Hughie, you bastard, hurry up for God's sake or you'll be a bloody orphan.'

Despite all this, the day-tripping lovers were still at it in the dunes but their passion was not what it was in the movies.

The tide was well in and the only way left across the Dalmurie burn was for Tilda to climb up through the woods and over the bridge. The post must have come by now; she'd need to hurry before anybody else got their prying hands on Ben's letter.

The path was almost completely smothered by bracken as she picked her way up to where the wooden bridge crossed the gully above the burn trickling toward the sea between dank rocks, far below. Once over the bridge she'd be only a couple of minutes from home.

'Hello, hello! What have we here? Little Miss Secretive scurrying through the woods!'

Ian Parker was blocking her way off the bridge. 'I saw you coming and thought I'd save you some trouble. Look what Postie brought! A wee billet doux I surmise, from a gentleman called Ben Troubadour in foreign parts, which I also observe was originally sent to you at somewhere quite a distance from SW3!'

Tilda could see the blue air letter in his pink and podgy hands as she stepped on to the bridge. 'Can I have it please.' The thought of his podgy fingerprints on Ben's precious writing was nauseating.

'Don't I get a wee kiss for acting the messenger?'

'Give me my letter, Ian!'

'Not unless you come and fetch it!' He held the letter high above his head and stood his ground, grinning. 'So you've taken up with a relative of your landlady have you? Would young Benjamin be uncle to Hughie's wee mistake, I wonder?'

'It's none of your business!'

'Au contraire, as your mother's protector, everything is my business. Especially when she gets to know that she has been paying a hefty rent for a room you no longer occupy.'

Tilda lunged forward and seized the letter. Ian grabbed her wrist and tugged her towards him but she managed to shake him off before stepping backwards onto the bridge again. The planks were slimed and her foot slipped. She clutched at the single rail which had become fragile with rot. It gave way.

Ian anchored himself by holding on to a sapling and tried to grip her arm and pull her onto his side of the bank, but he was too late. She slid away, then fell, tumbling over and over all the way down to where the burn met the shore.

Tilda lay silent, crumpled among the rocks, while Ben's letter floated off to be lost at sea.

★

The clamouring ambulance decided it for the lovers, even before the fire brigade joined in the din. They'd had enough of outdoor sports; industrial Paisley was a far more peaceful bower for those seeking romantic rapture.

Late Summer 1974

Tilda was lying on the roof of Sickert Buildings watching the white vapour trails of aircraft passing over at dawn. Soon these would broaden, break apart and disperse. Feeling for Ben, she only found a metal bar where she had expected his sleeping body to be. She closed her eyes and did not wake again till she heard a woman with a Scottish accent asking for someone called Matilda. She could not mean her, nobody had called her that for years, not since she was little. Could this person be Miss Stewart? No, not here. She opened her eyes and the vapour trails were still there, crossing each other like kisses, solid as strings.

'Wake up, Matilda. There's the girl. You are doing great. Stay with us.'

There were more people now, all in white.

'Hello.' It wasn't so easy to say that; everything was very difficult today. Had she been drunk last night? When was last night?

'Don't distress yourself, Matilda, just take your time.'

Take my time doing what? She tried to focus her eyes on these strangers in white coats. A man with carroty hair was standing looking down at her and feeling her pulse. He had a stethoscope around his neck. He was about her age, but she had never got as far in her training to carry this badge of office.

She tried to ask him who he was, but didn't know if she'd made the right noise

The Scotswoman spoke again. 'You are in hospital, Matilda.

You had a shocking accident, but you're doing great. We are all here to make you better.'

'Accident.'

'You fell off a bridge.'

'In London?'

'No, here in Scotland, hen, four days ago. You are in Glasgow now.'

'Oh.'

The effort of trying to talk and the effect of drugs had exhausted her. The next time she woke another Scots voice was saying that she had a visitor to see her.

'Ben?'

'Hello, Tilda!' said Ian Parker.

What was he doing here? She must hurry, she would be late for, late for what? There was something she was meant to be doing, something important, a secret thing and she was late. She couldn't move, her legs didn't work, nobody would help. Her mind didn't work. If only she could remember where she was trying to go and why.

'Tilda, do you know me?'

She looked at Ian's pink unwrinkled face, his piggy eyes and his too short fleshy nose. His breast pocket handkerchief matched his spotty bow tie and his lips were those of a kitsch cherub. He smelt of custard mixed with mouthwash.

Yes, she shut her eyes, she knew exactly who Ian was.

Later, maybe hours or maybe minutes, she opened her eyes again and saw that Ian was still there. This time she knew she was not in London and she was not late for her own wedding and that this lump of so-called male flesh was not and never would be Ben.

'Do you remember what happened, Tilda?'

She tried to shake her head. She could remember nothing. Then things began creeping back like scavengers to a bomb site. She remembered taking a train to Scotland and seeing her mother again and noticing that instead of fading with age, her hair had become yet more golden than before with intermittent stripes of burnished copper where none had ever been. She remembered that pretend stars still marched across her old bedroom ceiling.

'I remember walking on the shore,' she said. There had been a broken doll abandoned amongst the seaweed. Rejected toys and lost dogs made her cry, as did party hats on sad old heads and children howling for a bit of love.

'Did you meet anybody on the shore?'

She thought a while. No, there was nothing else she could find in her mind after the rejected doll.

The next day, she felt much better and they told her how Ian Parker had discovered her, quite by chance, lying in shallow water where she had fallen. 'You owe your life to him, Matilda.'

Tilda gazed up at the pulleys attached to her plastered legs and wondered whether her life was worth owing to Ian Parker. He was the only visitor she had; he was the person she least wanted to see. She didn't mind that her mother did not come and never questioned Grizel's choice of staying away. Grizel had a phobia about all things medical and institutionalised, which Tilda respected. It was odd, though, for her mother not to visit her own daughter in hospital. But she was too weary for visitors, other than Ben, who she needed and wanted more than anything else in the world. So she was pleased to be left alone and told Ian Parker as much, but his zealous observation of visiting hours persisted.

The police made a report and hoped that their cursory investigations would not be needed by the Fiscal at any inquest. When they went to look at the place from which the poor young woman had fallen, work was already well in hand to replace the rotten bridge and all evidence that might have proved useful in determining how, or why she had fallen, was obliterated.

★

'Where would we be without you, Ian dear? In an almighty mess, I have no doubt. Even poor Charles up the castle agrees with me. Without you this last week would have been chaos. It has all been so unpleasant.' Irene Gilmerton and Ian Parker were drinking dry martinis on the terrace of Nether Dalmuirie House while the sun set beyond the silhouettes of Goatfell on Arran, Ailsa Craig and the lesser Lumpie. Ian had his back to the view and leant towards Irene, patting her hand reassuringly, and expressed admiration for her nail polish.

'Grizel gave it me. It's called Sangdiange. It's French.'

'One can tell.'

'Oh, Ian, I am so worried.'

'Don't you trouble yourself about Tilda. She's doing fine. Just a few more weeks and she'll be back to her old self. Did you inform Miss Troubadour that she will not be returning to London for a while yet?'

'No, I've had that much on my plate, Ian, I couldn't get round to it.'

'Now don't you fret about that, let me sort it. I'll inform the Clydesdale, too.'

'Actually, Ian, I'm not that concerned for Tilda, all because you are so good about going to see her. It's wee Grizel that bothers me. She's so nervy, if you know what I mean, and then turning up here just like Tilda, without even a day's warning and then saying she's not minded to leave again…ever. What has happened, Ian?'

'I daresay it's an unfortunate 'affaire de coeur' that's gone awry. She'll get over it. Why don't I drive you both to Glasgow tomorrow? You could do some shopping. Were you not saying you needed a suitable hat for Lady Charity's funeral? You could visit Tilda, too. That would be nice.'

Irene looked doubtful. 'We'll see. I'll have a word with Grizel. She has a thing about hospitals, prisons, too. It's a phobia, she says. Ah, is that not her away home now?'

Irene couldn't drive but she had three cars, one for the house-keeper (when she could keep one) one for Ian to take her to the shops, and the other for him to drive her ostentatiously to prestigious events. It was the last that raced down the drive and crunched to a stop outside the front door, making ridges in the deep gravel.

'Grizel, sweetie, is that you?'

The front door was thrown open and footsteps pounded up the stairs. Doors slammed.

'My!' said Ian, 'That's a young woman in a hurry! Irene, my dear, even if Grizel doesn't want to come, do you not think that you'd like to visit Tilda?'

' I really don't like to leave Grizel alone. I feel I should be here for her. Has Tilda been asking for me?'

Ian got up to refresh their drinks and fetch a bonbonniere containing the cheese footballs he'd found at Crawfords, the wine merchant in Dundoon.

The only person Tilda had ever asked for was Ben, which was a detail he chose to forget.

'To tell the truth, Ian, I'm a wee bit like Grizel about hospitals. I'd prefer to wait till Tilda comes home, then heaven knows what a palaver that will be. Meanwhile I think I am doing more good by being here with Grizel. She's that distressed at times, it worries me dreadfully and you say that Tilda is being well looked after. Besides, I believe you mentioned that she is best kept quiet and given as much rest as possible. I wouldn't want to go and upset her. Could you be an angel, Ian dear, and organise some more flowers to be sent? Tilda would appreciate that I'm sure much more than being troubled by a visit from me, knowing how concerned I am about leaving Grizel just now.'

'Ah there we are, it takes a wonderful mother like you, my dear Irene, to know where her duty lies.' Ian took their glasses to be refilled again and Irene stared at the sea while Grizel vented her angst by slamming doors upstairs.

'Oh Ian , how am I to cope?'

Ian handed Irene her glass in which he'd placed a green olive on a stick. 'Helping you cope is what I'm here for, my dear.'

After the extraordinary chance of finding Tilda lying uncon-scious amongst the rocks in the rising tide, his speedy action in removing her from the danger of drowning and rushing back to the house to call 999, his calm efficiency in a crisis, his resourcefulness in causing the broken bridge to be replaced within a day and his indispensable helpfulness in appointing himself coordinator of Lady Charity's forthcoming funeral, most of Dalmuirie district were forced to agree that Ian Parker was indeed the hero of the hour, without whom everything would fall apart.

It was Ian who had put death notices in the papers, summoned McCreath and Sons Funeral Upholders, selected a tasteful coffin (The Peebles), arranged car parking and asked Maud Pollock to cater for the funeral tea.

Maud had been delighted to oblige. Willie Pollock, meanwhile, was in two minds. No wife of his was a hired hand, but there again, there was the alluring matter of payment. The Pollocks were no longer tenants, the farm was theirs outright, good money had been paid to the Estate and though he would join with other surround-ing landowners in attending the funeral there was no need for his women folk to demean themselves as tenant servants. Maud insisted that she wanted to do the job, Cess practically burst, so eager was she to prove herself invaluable, so a compromise was struck. Maud would be paid for all the ingredients and though she and Cess would be in charge of the mountains of ham sand-wiches and sausage rolls, they would act more as hostesses than as skivvies and would be wearing normal funereal clothes without aprons. Willie was happy, Cess was delighted and Maud kept quiet about the inevitable washing-up and clearing away, not to mention the hours of poking around the castle's toxic kitchens and sculleries scavenging for crockery. Ian organised adequate cash for supplies and reassured Willie that there would be equally adequate whisky; Crawfords of Dundoon, where he'd opened an account for Irene, would deliver on a sale or return basis and provide glasses.

Hughie and his father were, individually and secretly, quite surprised at their sense of loss and were also glad to be bulldozed by Ian Parker, as they contemplated the gargantuan task of tidy-ing up the affairs of the deceased, the disposal of Lady Charity's bits and pieces. Clearing the wardrobes of mothy tweeds and

balding furs, the cabinets of used cosmetics, stale scent and anony-
mous remedies, the drawers full of mysterious peach underwear,
stretched and frayed bits of perished elastic, rusty suspenders
and unrelated stockings were Herculean tasks. In the end Charles
appealed to Avis and offered her the entire contents of his late
wife's cupboards in lieu of the money he owed her for secretarial
services. He chose not to notice that she was less than ecstatic
about this arrangement.

★

'Any news on Aurea's replacement, Ian dear?' Irene asked.

Aurea had lasted three months, which was almost a record ,but
now she'd done what all Irene's housekeepers did, given in her
notice. Aurea was but one of a stream of Filipinas that Ian procured
through an agency that seemed to have an endless supply, though
few were prepared for the experience of living so remotely with
no other people from the Philippines nearby.

Being Irene's housekeeper was not a demanding job, the pay
was good, but despite a bus service of sorts, Dalmuirie was horribly isolated and the prospect of a bleak winter overseen by Ian
Parker, plus an invalid and a neurotic, in addition to Irene, clut-
tering the house, Aurea had had enough. She was off to Glasgow
to keep house for a quiet bachelor where she'd get a basement
to herself and the promise of a colour telly, quite near a hospital
where several of her friends were working.

'Alas, Irene, the advertisement in *The Lady*, has not borne fruit,
but never fear. If you'd permit me to consult the Philippine agency
again, I fancy you'll not be bereft. Another wee martini?'

'Very well, Ian, I've little choice.'

Had Irene ever seen anything weightier than *Bless The Bride*,
mad Ophelia might have crossed her mind as Grizel came onto
the terrace, barefooted, clothed in raggedy cheesecloth, with
bird's nest hair.

'Hello, sweetheart, would you like a drink?'

Grizel didn't answer, but sank onto the grass and started to make a daisy chain. She was astoundingly pretty in a dark and waifish way, too thin, as delicate as a wraith.

'Ian here was suggesting that we might all go to Glasgow to-morrow and see poor Tilda.'

Grizel looked up. Her eyes really were enormous, almost too big for her high cheek-boned face. 'We could go shopping, too,' Irene added. 'I'm wanting a hat for the funeral anyway and I'm sure you'd like a wee jaunt. Have you got something black yourself to wear? We could go to Dalys or maybe Pettigrew and Stephens, after the hospital.'

'I hate hospitals,' Grizel said.

'I don't think any of us like them, Grizel dear.'

'Tilda must, she wants to work in one.'

'Working is not the same as being a patient. Tilda would love a visit, I'm sure.'

'I won't go, Mum. I don't ever want to go to a hospital. Hospitals are like prisons.'

'No they aren't, Grizel.'

'Yes they are, they are exactly like prisons. They kill you in prisons.'

'Not in this country, Grizel dear, not any more.'

'They do in America. They kill you in all sorts of horrible ways, just like they kill you in hospitals here, with machinery.'

'But Tilda is being very well looked after in Glasgow, isn't she, Ian?'

'Impeccably,' Ian replied, 'but I am sure she would like to see her wee sister.'

'I am not going to that torture chamber, not ever.'

Ian continued as Tilda's only visitor until the day of Lady Charity's funeral when he was far too busy arranging everything to contemplate a visit to Glasgow.

★

No matter how calm it was, the wind always seemed to whirl around the hill-top kirkyard, as if the restless dead of Dalmuirie were resisting further intrusion, ruffling wreaths and stripping bouquets of their petals. There was quite a turnout to see Lady Charity sink into the penultimate vacant grave in the family lair. The hole was lined with white porcelain tiles like a public lavatory, and there was room inside it for two coffins.

Henrysson father and son looked suitably doleful as they released their cords to lower Lady Charity to her eternal rest.

It was a chilling thought that Charles would be expected to spend eternity beside a wife whose bed he may not have visited since his only son's conception when wartime privation and lack of heating, rather than desire, had driven them to intimacy.

Hughie wore a greenish frock coat he'd found in the attic, probably belonging to the prosperous grandfather who had decided to splash out on a vault rather than keep on burying his relatives at random spots in the kirkyard as earlier Henryssons had done, their dates and virtues now quite illegible upon their weather-battered tombstones.

The cloth of the coat had been spared by moths, but the stitching at the seams had rotted, so Hughie's every move was accompanied by a gentle ripping noise. Gaping holes appeared in the sleeves and seat, which was mercifully covered by the coat, denying the congregation a glimpse of Hughie's underpants which backed Britain in red, white and blue.

Irene Gilmerton, blonde and becoming in black and professionally managed tears, sat next to Mrs Whigham, the doctor's ample wife who'd invested in an eclipsing hat. Mrs Farquerson, the Minister's wife, was in charge of service sheets and a hopeful collection plate.

'What a most distinguished gathering,' Miss Stuart announced acidly, when Major 'Whiffy' Smellie ushered her to a seat in a side aisle. As the headmistress of St Quivox School where Lady Charity had so graciously presented the prizes, despite the expulsion of her son, she surely merited a better place in the body of the kirk, close to the Procurator Fiscal and his insignificant wife.

Tavish the Fiscal was to give the address, not necessarily as a friend of the deceased, but because he was good at that sort of thing.

Representing the Queen, Her Majesty's Lord Lieutenant, who had served under Whiffy Smellie in Korea, took obvious pleasure in commandeering the front pew for his exclusive use, causing the rest of the congregation, including, Charles and Hughie, to squash in behind him.

Olive Smellie, at the organ, observed the altercation and took it out on the obstinate stops.

Hughie read ineptly of how in his father's house there were many mansions.

The *Dundoon Advertiser*'s junior compositor, entrusted with printing the service sheet, was troubled by homonyms. 'Very piscatorial' Commander Wishart commented as the congregation rose to sing Praise my Sole the King of Heaven. Avis muffled her giggles with a coughing fit.

Even more people turned up to pay their respects and eat Maud's tea. Maud, despite every effort to appear to be a guest, found herself manning the urn while most of the guests tucked into the remnants of Charles Henrysson's cellar. She watched as Cess wove between the mourners with an ashet of ham bridge rolls and wondered where all this would end.

Avis had tactfully decided not to attend the funeral clothed in a black Hardy Amies suit that had been one of the few salvageable garments in Lady Charity's wardrobe, even though it became her mightily. She'd offered Maud a nasty tippet devised from most of a mink including legs, head and tail, suggesting it might make a fetching sporran for Willie. It didn't.

'I am so sorry about your dear mother, Hughie.'

'Thanks, Mrs Wishart,' said Hughie. 'I thought I'd feel different from this, though. Bloody horrible suddenly finding yourself part of the senior generation with all those wretched responsibilities. Loads of people seem to have loved Mother, even though she was a bit odd. Have you heard, Lena is leaving, too? She's off to live with a sister in Dalmahoy.'

'That's a good thing, Hughie. Lena has done nothing for years and you say your dear mother was odd, well she was nothing like as odd as Lena. She's quite useless today, too, no help at all to my sister-in-law, who has had to make all the preparations, including trying to get this place into a semblance of cleanliness. Thank goodness Maud has had her Cecile to help. I'm surprised you weren't all poisoned by Lena's perpetual stew. Nurse Coole told me the state of the kitchen was positively dangerous. You'll have to get the professionals in to give the place a good scrub and clear the rubbish, then find a new housekeeper, someone who needs a home and is capable of plain cooking and basic hygiene.'

'That sounds awfully expensive.'

'Come on, Hughie, you are a fine young man, you can solve these problems in all sorts of ways. Just brace up and get to grips with being a grown-up.'

Avis and Hughie were standing at the edge of the crowd. Cess was at the other side of the room, beneath one of the worst copy portraits ever seen. Ian Parker seldom had a good painting day, but bulbous Lady Clarinda was a masterpiece of ineptitude. 'She's no beauty, is she, Hughie?' said Avis, changing the subject.

Hughie gazed across at Cess, in a straining black skirt and jacket. Delphinium eye-shadow and meandering mascara did nothing for her as she attempted a sympathetic smirk. She held the ashet where she should have had a waist. 'No, Mrs Wishart, she's not.'

'She's pregnant, of course.'

'Christ! Are you sure? How can you tell?'

'She's such a quaint shape. Hey, watch out, Hughie, you are spilling your port.'

'Careful, Hughie, you shouldn't waste that stuff,' said Charles who'd come over to see whether the bucket was still in place beneath the latest leak. 'You can't afford to throw your inheritance around.'

'Hughie and I were talking about Lady Clarinda,' said Avis, 'Didn't the original sell rather well?'

'Yes that rogue in Glasgow made a mint from the old boot.

She's gone to Kentucky, lucky bitch. Not that any of the fortune she brought into this family is still about and all the money raised by her portrait has gone into fixing the drains and not a day too soon. Damn tomato seedlings were sprouting all over the shop.'

'I was telling Hughie that she was probably pregnant.'

'Undoubtedly. She had eight children in eight years, all useless, then she died. What's up with you, Hughie?'

'Phew!' said Hughie.

'Yes, the stench from those drains was fiendish,' Charles agreed.' I say, Hughie, isn't that the Pollock girl over there? Why don't you go and make yourself pleasant?'

Cess had moved to stand in front of a mullioned window. Hughie looked towards her and as she caught his eye a wave of hot red embarrassment surged across her face.

So it was true. Cess knew that everybody must now see that Hughie seemed to be transfixed by her. Maybe things would work out right, now that Ben was quite beyond her reach, her second best dream was coming true and would have to do. Maybe Hughie wasn't that bad after all, maybe she did like him a little bit, maybe it would all work out, maybe there was still hope, her situation could still be as she hoped, just. Perhaps if only she could hold on for a little longer, long enough to get him to commit to her. Enough.

Cess smiled back at Hughie, but then, just like when she'd made a fool of herself with Ben and Tilda, she realised that he was actually gazing at something behind her. Cess turned and saw a ghostly face staring through the window. Despite the distortion of the diamond panes, she knew whose face it was.

The Procurator Fiscal's faded little wife, emboldened by several sherries, approached Hughie. 'Pardon me, Hugh, I do not think we've met. I am Jonquil. I am married to Tavish.' She held out her hand.

'Excuse me, I can't talk now.' Hughie left Jonquil's hand dangling in mid-air.

When Cess looked back into the room, Hughie had gone. Looking outside again, she could see the wraith walking towards the headland and Hughie hurrying across the grass to join her. All silly little hopes that Cess had been nursing died, evaporating into the cloudy coastal afternoon, save one that still hung on by a make-believe cord.

Hughie's vision was of Dora. Who else could it be with such a delicate face fringed by so much dark and tangled hair? She had come back for him, the only woman ever to light his feeble fire, the mother of the proof of his manhood. She had come back for him.

'Dora!'

The figure turned. 'Hello, Hughie. Remember me? I'm Grizel, from next door.'

Charles Henrysson, having had far too much of his own cellar, was leaning on Avis while Maud and Cess were endeavouring to clear up.

'Let me tell you, Mrs W, that fine niece of yours would be perfect for my Hughie, a capable, solid, plain girl. That's what you want, a good cook and bottle-washer, none of your flighty beauties who want fancy clothes and flashy holidays. Her father, your brother, is a sound bastard. He'll collect a packet when he sells the land he bought off me for a song, a bloody song, Mrs W and what with his daughter being an only child...'

'Hush, Mr Henrysson, please, or Cecile and her mother will hear you.'

Rather too late, Charles lowered his voice while scowling at the view outside the deserted castle hall. 'What the hell is that son of mine doing with that imbecilic Gilmerton girl?'

Avis looked out to where Hughie and Grizel were standing in the fading light.

'They are throwing stones at the sea.'

★

Eight or so weeks had passed and Cess was still hopeful. Despite several credible indications to the contrary, she couldn't admit that this tenuous hope was as dead as the rest of her dreams. More than thirty-eight days had passed since the night of the Unionist Ball. Cess told her mother she was going to Glasgow; she did not actually suggest that she was going to see Tilda.

Maud said that was very nice of her to visit her poor friend in hospital. 'Mind you don't exhaust her. But I'm sure she'd like a good gossip. You can tell her all about the funeral and what a good do she's missed, poor soul. Give her our love.'

Cess had found an address of an efficient sounding organisation and called from Dalmuirie's only phone box to make an appointment for a consultation. The bored woman answering told her how much it would cost. Cess had more than enough saved to pay for this stage in proceedings. After all, she only wanted confirmation of her condition; nothing on God's earth was going to make her put an end to it. She never thought about how Hughie would feel, she only knew that his father would be delighted. For that alone she was prepared to make his son, herself and their just possible offspring, profoundly unhappy till death did them part, as she and Hugh would have to testify at their wedding.

At Central Station she went to the Ladies.

After that she had to admit that there was no future in going anywhere other than a chemist. Then, instead of cancelling the appointment or going to see Tilda, she bought a packet of Benson and Hedges, a Cricket lighter and sat a while in a café on West Nile Street, spluttering her way through her second ever cigarette. She had nothing inside to stunt or harm, she'd only herself to please. It was hard to accept.

If anybody started to spread rumours about her pregnancy, though, she would do nothing to suppress them. She would bear her sorrow, not her evaporated child, like a martyr. She put the rest of her saved money in a charity box fashioned from shell cases in Central Station, which philanthropic ladies had placed there to collect money for gifts to hospital patients.

★

'Poor child,' said Maud to Willie. 'Tilda Gilmerton must be in a terrible state. Fancy the hospital not letting Cecile see her, after she'd gone all that way. No wonder she's mortified.'

'They Gilmertons never make old bones and that's the truth of it.'

'Oh Willie, don't say that. Please spare us all such a tragedy.'

'Aye, well. There's no telling what might happen. I'd not be surprised if Foot and Mouth was away back the now, too.'

*E*lvira was adamant; her foot was down. Children do not go to funerals. It was a terrible time for all of them and exposing a child to the misery of formalised grief was totally unnecessary. She would be the one to explain to Mira why Granny was no longer there, and she would look after her while Ben and Dora dealt with the disposal of their mother's remains.

Valdite had clung on till Ben returned from Nepal with Dora. She had struggled to meet her children at the door, but was bent and shrunk with pain. Once they were inside, she had collapsed in uncontrollable sobs of relief. 'Thank God,' was all she could say.

Mira saw it all, understanding none of it. She certainly did not understand the stranger that was her mother. This washed up sea-witch trailing scarves and beads was nothing like the pretty, smiling young woman in the graduation photograph that Mira had taken to be her mum.

Even Aunt El was more like the sort of person other children called Mum. Granny was her mum and now Granny was being taken away on a stretcher. She was going to hospital to get better. But she didn't.

On the day of the funeral Ben brought Mira over from Wandsworth. Unpractised as she was, Elvira could see that the child was in a bad way. Not only was Mira miserable, she was filthy and unkempt.

Wasn't Miss Betsey Trotwood faced with the same problem

when her nephew David Copperfield turned up in Dover and didn't she take Mr Dick's advice on the matter? The child must be washed. But how? Betsey Trotwood had a Janet to heat the bath and do the deed. Elvira had never bathed anyone, except herself.

She and Mira went to the chemist for advice and got it. They bought bubble bath, cat-shaped soap, a plastic duck, a Mickey Mouse tooth brush, stripy toothpaste and some round-ended nail scissors. The assistant looked with grave suspicion at the smelly little girl and suggested medicated shampoo and maybe the use of a fine-tooth comb.

'Whatever for?' Elvira demanded.

'Nits.'

'No niece of mine has nits, in fact, I pride myself in never having seen a nit, not even in wartime. I'll take some ordinary shampoo for children, something that doesn't sting the eyes.'

'But quite the nicest children get nits. Half the kindergarten in Sloane Gardens had nits last year. You should also look out for athlete's foot and scabies.'

'Not in my family, you don't.'

'And don't mistake ringworm for impetigo.'

'I wouldn't dream of it.'

'Furthermore, you must not dismiss worms.'

'I daresay!' Elvira sniffed.

The holidays were ending and Peter Jones was awash with exasperated women in velvet hairbands, Hermes squares and obvious diamonds on their third fingers left, trying to get their sulky children clothed for the imminent new term.

Everybody had had more than enough of holidays, but it was the adults who had difficulty in suppressing their delight at the prospect of restoring their highlights and having at least some mornings, free from being asked why everything was unfair, furthermore why couldn't it all happen NOW.

Some mothers and children were accompanied by bewildered au pairs, whose job it was to stop younger siblings from hurling themselves off shelves, vandalising displays and tripping up the assistants. One extremely small boy was meekly submitting to being kitted out in long corduroy shorts and an overcoat two sizes too large by a uniformed and grey-haired nanny, who gave no quarter to nonsense.

Elvira, as conscious of her lack of significant ring as if 'Reject' was stamped on her forehead, looked aghast at the chaos.

Where to start? If Mira was to be bathed she would need clean clothes to put on afterwards and even if the twin tub had done its stuff efficiently there was no way to get everything dry, apart from baking it all in the oven. She remembered that pneumonia pounced on those with damp socks, so heaven knew what fatal horrors were triggered by a damp vest. An assistant told her curtly to get a number and await her turn.

'Come along, Mira, you can hold the ticket.'

But Mira had gone.

The floor was heaving with small children, but none were as tiny, dark or filthy as Mira. Oh God, the child had been kidnapped, spirited away to a ghastly fate by some evil monster or she'd broken her neck by climbing over the barrier and was lying dead in the basement amongst Electrical Goods.

'My great niece! Have you seen her? Please help me, I've lost her!'

The nanny was deftly knotting a tie around her charge's twig of a neck and had not seen what happened, but an older child, more bored than the rest, said she'd seen a little girl disappear up the escalator towards Furniture.

As Elvira strode up the escalator she saw the tangled top of Mira's head coming down. She shouted at her to wait. Mira turned and tried to tread against the persistent descent. 'I can't, Aunt El.'

Elvira rushed to the down escalator but Mira passed her on the way up again.

'Wait at the top, Mira, don't move!'

In her haste Elvira stumbled and fell at the bottom, scattering the bag of bath impedimenta all over the floor.

'Stay there, Tam!' the nanny commanded, 'while I help this

lady. 'Now then, up you get. You are Miss Troubadour, are you not?' She had a briskness born of decades of dealing with minor tumbles. 'What is the lost child called?'

'Everybody calls her Mira. How do you know who I am?'

'I am Nanny Westcroft. I recognise you from when you worked for Tam's granny. Now sit there beside him and when that young saleswoman returns, tell her we need pyjamas. I will find little Mira, she won't be far. Now where did you last see her?'

'Going back up to the top.'

Within a minute they were back. Mira's tears left tracks upon her unwashed face which Elvira mopped away after wiping her own with her clean white hanky, no longer clean nor white, when she stuffed it back in her pocket

'How can I thank you, Nanny? I don't know what I would have done without you. And this young man, I presume, is young Tamburlane. I remember having to send out the invitations to his christening.'

'Indeed he is, and a very fine christening it was, too, though somewhat showy for my taste. Now then, Tam, shake hands with Miss Troubadour. She is one of Granny's friends. Tiny Tamburlane held out a delicate hand, but wouldn't lift his gaze from the floor.

'Please excuse him, Miss Troubadour, Tam's granny had words with him this morning about his future. Now, why don't I help you get this young lady some decent clothes?'

'Oh would you? I haven't the first idea what children wear these days. I was brought up in liberty bodices and gaiters.'

Nanny Westcroft had total command of the situation. Disregarding the queue waiting to be served, she efficiently equipped Mira to face the fiercest of winters. She topped off the pile of clothes with a Harris tweed coat that would have done a child twice Mira's age and some sturdy replacements for the worn-out sandals that had pinched and rubbed her little feet to blisters. All Elvira's theatre ticket money evaporated in a welter of woolly garments, as did any chance of visiting her friend in Torquay before next year.

Nanny Westcroft didn't need to be invited. She seemed to take it as given that she should be the one to get Mira as clean as a whistle, neat as a pin, all shipshape and Bristol fashion.

Elvira was awe-struck by Nanny's speedy eradication of tide-lines by 'scrub-a-dub-dub, three men in a tub' and her 'one two three four five, once I caught a fish alive' way of dealing with fingernails and five little piggy toes. Mira's hair, frothy with shampoo, was made to stand on end while Nanny excavated her ears for fields of potatoes. When Mira stood up in the bath Tam broke his long silence. 'Where is her winky?'

'Little girls don't have winkies, Tam.'

'Why?'

'So we can tell little girls and little boys apart when they are babies.'

'Why?'

'Because variety is the spice of life. Now be a good boy and give me that towel.'

'Why do boys have winkies, Nanny?'

'Because they are very useful to have on picnics.'

Mira had been listening intently. 'What is a winky?'

'What boys use for spending pennies.'

'Can I see?' Mira asked.

'Go and spend a penny, Tam, and remember to lift the lid. Can you manage, or would you like Miss Troubadour to find you something to stand on?'

Tam could manage, just. Mira looked on, impressed.

'What do little girls do on picnics?'

'They go behind bushes. Now come along, let's wrap you up and get you dry, all snug as a bug in a rug.' Nanny turned to Elvira. 'And that's another job out of the way. The sooner they know, the better, I say. It will save an awful lot of embarrassment later on.'

Nanny towelled Mira's hair vigorously, then brushed out the tangles while telling her she was a brave little soldier. 'Is your name Moira or Myra? I must get it right.'

'I'm called Mira, like what you look in.'

'But it isn't spelt the same way,' said Elvira. 'Actually Mira is short for Miracle.'

Nanny sniffed. 'After Tamburlane nothing surprises me. I don't expect many children get called Myra now and we can be thankful that we've been spared another Lara.'

Tam and Mira played tiddlywinks after Nanny and Elvira had fed them hot buttered toast and made themselves a proper pot of tea while waiting for Mira to be collected and taken back to the chaos that was now Valdite's house in Wandsworth.

Elvira confided her fears and Nanny agreed that very often mummies were not the best people to look after children. In Tam's case Mummy was busy or away nearly all the time, as was Daddy, who travelled a lot or played golf, and as for Granny, well, the least said about Granny the better. Day school would be a good thing for Tam even if he was so very little and he would still come home to Nanny every day, at least till his eighth birthday. After that he was to go away to boarding school.

'And you, Nanny? What about you?'

'Shh, Miss Troubadour, little pitchers have big ears. Isn't that the telephone?'

Elvira lifted the receiver in the hall. 'Hello,' she said in a deceiving gruff voice.

She heard the clunk of Button A being pressed.

'Miss Troubadour?'

'Yes, who is speaking?'

'It is me, Tilda Gilmerton. Please I've got hardly any time. Where is Ben? I must find him.'

'So you have changed your mind?'

'What do you mean?'

'I was told very firmly that you were never coming back and that you wished for no further contact with any of your former London connections again, ever.'

'What? It's a lie. I am desperate to see Ben. I had an accident. I am still in hospital. This is the first time I have been able to use the phone. Please help me.'

'Where are you?'

Elvira made a note. 'I'll tell Ben, but Tilda, he is about to fly to the States. Please give me your telephone number.'

'I can't, this is a payphone. I am being sent back to my home tomorrow afternoon. Just tell him, please, that I love him and always will.' The pips interrupted and then the line died into a staccato buzz.

The doorbell rang. It was Ben in his only suit, the one he should have worn to his wedding. Today his tie was plain black.

★

It was just a few minutes, that was all the time they had together, there in the hospital with Tilda ready for the ambulance to transport her home to Dalmuirie. Those few minutes would have to be enough because Ben's hastily rearranged flight was going to take off for the States that evening. He had managed to get an overnight sleeper up to Glasgow after his mother's funeral, with barely a minute to spare to say goodbye to Dora and Mira, or to Elvira to whom he would always owe so much. All he could think of was Tilda. What monster had lied about her feelings for him? Who could do that? Why?

They had no time to waste discussing trivialities, no time to do anything except swear their undying love for each other, then just as the porters came for Tilda, Ben remembered his mother's ring.

'Wear it for me, Tilda, please, until we meet again. We'll get a wedding ring then.'

'What happened to the other one, the one you bought before?

'I sold it when I was told…'

'Told what?'

'That it was over between us.'

She was already being wheeled down the corridor when she said, 'For me, Ben, I swear, it will never be over.'

'Nor me, my darling, not till beyond the end of time.'

He managed to kiss her one last time as the wheelchair was

winched into the ambulance. Then the doors were shut, leaving him standing alone, watching as the love of his life was driven away.

That evening Tilda asked Grizel to push her chair out to look at the setting sun over the Firth of Clyde, when Ben's plane was due to pass over, but Grizel had other, more important, things to do.

Tilda sat in the conservatory watching a winking light in the sky retreating westward, unaware that Ian Parker saw she was weeping.

★

1974 declined while the world was rocked by Nixon's resignation. Then there was another Labour victory in another general election followed by the Lucan scandal, with murder happening unsettlingly close to Elvira in Pont Terrace.

In Scotland Tilda's mobility improved very slowly, while Grizel and Hughie Henrysson launched their relationship towards catastrophe. Cess grew larger, but only the most imaginative ever thought that her bulk was due to anything other than compensatory chocolate.

Tilda still couldn't be sure that she'd get to the post first before the ever helpful and insinuating Ian intervened. 'Another billet doux from your beau, I surmise...' he would say as he handed her the blue airletter. Tilda wrote back to Ben almost daily but it was equally difficult to get to the post without being interrogated until, by chance, she confided in Avis Wishart, who volunteered to act as post restante.

Avis understood Tilda's anguish, she understood her niece Cecile's anguish and she looked on with horror as Grizel and Hughie announced their intention to marry at Christmas. Nobody understood that, though the couple seemed compelled to go through with it, despite the ceremony following so soon after Hughie's mother's funeral and there being no physical urgency to make Grizel an honest woman.

Miss Stuart made a reference to the goings-on at Dalmuirie

being reminiscent of Elsinore, which only Commander Wishart understood and old Charles Henrysson muttered about the bad blood coursing through the Gilmerton veins, even if their bank account was healthy. Irene Gilmerton looked forward to a lavish wedding (organised of course by Ian Parker) though she would have preferred her younger and most difficult daughter to settle down further away than next door.

When Tilda asked Grizel why she was going to marry Hughie, Grizel replied,' Because I can.'

'But why? Do you really love him?'

Grizel shrugged. 'Of course.'

'Are you sure you aren't marrying him just to spite Cess Pollock?'

Grizel didn't reply, but flung her cup of coffee in Tilda's face and flounced out, slamming the door.

★

Once tupping was underway in November Willie Pollock had more time to think about his daughter's future.' Whatever is up with our wee girl, Maudie? She's that downhearted it's like having a death in the house.'

'She's unhappy, Willie.'

'What has a fine girl like her to be unhappy about? What's stopping her getting out and getting a job? She's got all those fancy certificates.'

'She can't find anything suitable.'

'You're right enough there, Maudie. Nothing suits our Cecile. She should take up something useful like book-keeping or plain cooking, not hanging round waiting to inflict some poor creature with her psychological claptrap. If she canna' get a steady job, she should get married.'

'Who to, Willie? She'd love to get married. That is her problem, I hate to tell you.'

'Nonsense, there's plenty of strapping lads down the Young Farmers who'd jump at the chance of courting her.'

'Are you sure, Willie?'

'No...but she could try.'

'She tries too hard,' Maud replied.

★

Meanwhile, in London, Mira found life with her mother terrifying and confusing. To begin with, Dora wasn't like a fairytale stepmother, wicked and cruel, though she was wrong for her three-year-old daughter, very different from that to which Mira was accustomed and totally unconventional.

There was nothing of Dora's own late mother about her. Of course she never washed or cooked or cleaned; those demeaning actions were well below her. She despised the mothers gossiping outside school gates or yelling. Wandsworth mothers did a lot of yelling then. They yelled at their kids on busses and in shops, threatening them with their homecoming dads if they didn't shut it, for Gawd's sake. The ultimate penalty was absolutely no telly. As Mira had no dad and her granny's telly was now dumped in the garden amongst the other breakages there was nothing normal to threaten her with.

She made her daughter call her Dora, and though she didn't go in for threats, she did make rash promises, never to be fulfilled. In fact Dora ignored Mira for most of the time and smothered her with exuberant, drug-fuelled affection for the rest, all for no reason. Mira could do what she liked, though occasionally and unpredictably Dora would explode with rage and frequently lashed out, but that was generally when she was high or drunk and Mira learnt quite quickly to dodge the blows.

The mums that filled the streets in Wandsworth with their shrill voices and collapsible push chairs did not associate with them. What friends Mira had had stayed away, scared off by Dora's ferocity. Actually calling her mother Dora was better in a way, easier than acknowledging this tornado as the woman who had given her birth. Dora called her Mira Millstone.

When Dora smoked it was not like the others with their Cadets and Silk Cuts on the play park seats, but something that smelled unlike any cigarette from a pack. She drank straight from bottles and didn't believe in soap, regular meals or manners. All property, she declared, was theft and it was fine and noble to liberate and redistribute the nation's wealth by helping oneself to whatever one wanted, if the requisite cash was not to hand.

Mira had a precocious perception of what was wrong and must have dreaded the days Dora wore her huge army surplus greatcoat, under which she could hide her booty. Granny had said that thieves were baddies and went to prison and Mira hated walking by Wandsworth prison gates, dreading the day that they would swing open and she and Dora and would be drawn inside for ever and ever, like the children of Hamelin in that poem Aunt El knew by heart, in which the rats bit the babies in their cradles. The Wandswoth rats didn't do that, but they did gnaw their way into the house. A man in blue overalls came and poisoned them, which meant they died searching for water under the floorboards. That stench stifled all others for a while.

Mrs Jenkins lived next door with her housebound husband and had been on friendly terms with Mira and her granny. Now, being elderly and childless, this old couple weren't at all taken with Dora's music or the garbage dump that had once been Valdite's ordered garden. Maybe they were the ones who called in the ratcatchers and eventually alerted the social workers, but that happened later.

Mira's salvation during those months must have been the times she spent with her Aunt El. Elvira Troubadour must have been in her late fifties and well past the age at which most women take to child care. Once a week, without fail, Elvira bravely took the three buses to and from Wandsworth in the morning and made the same difficult journey back at night after the rush hour. Often Nanny Westcroft would visit to help and they would all go together to collect Tam from school, after which they would toast bread on forks in front of Aunt El's electric fire with its canvas logs that glowed and flickered, redder than Santa Claus himself.

Tam was young for his age and found school life as confusing as Mira found her life at home. They became best buddies and played spilikins and Happy Families and bagatelle with marbles that shot around a board.

As Christmas approached, Dora promised Mira everything she wanted, even a real monkey of her own…and Granny again. Like all excited children, Mira woke early on Christmas Day, but Father Christmas hadn't been. The sock at the end of her bed hung limp and empty, no monkey, no Granny, not even a tangerine. Maybe the old boy was running late, which meant she should at least pretend to be asleep until he came so she screwed up her eyes and hid beneath the blankets. Nothing happened. Eventually she got up. It was very cold. Downstairs she found Dora on the floor snoring as loud as a bus and impossible to wake.

As ever, the house was filthy, stacked with heaps of empty bottles, unwashed dishes of festering food exuding the acrid, sweetish stench of decay. The fridge was smelly, too, its inside walls covered in blue mould. The several half full bottles of milk stank of cheese. The electricity meter was empty and certainly the telephone was cut off.

Mira managed to slide the catch on the front door. It wasn't a white Christmas, but it was dead chilly and damp; the concrete turned her bare feet to ice blocks. Father Christmas hadn't left anything outside for her either, so there was nothing for it but to go back indoors and wait till Dora woke up. But the door had shut and Mira had no key.

Luckily Mr and Mrs Jenkins had not gone away for Christmas and were able to rescue the shivering little girl, wrap her in a blanket and send for Elvira, who came to fetch her in a taxi. The taxi was just the first expense of the most extravagant and magical Christmas of Mira's entire life, a day of enchantment, but like Cinderella's moment of glory and Elvira's savings, it evaporated in the end.

Mira's life continued to deteriorate into neglect and squalor for the first few wintry months of 1975. Her weekly visits to Elvira were lifelines; just the one day of sanity and security served to counteract the six others crammed with chaos.

A couple of Elvira's majolica pots sold moderately well at Phillips Son and Neale.

Grizel's wedding had been everything that Tilda's was not. For a start it had actually happened. For Tilda, however, it felt more like some pagan sacrifice than a joyful joining of two young people wanting to spend their lives together. Of course Grizel was a beautiful bride, but all that fuss doesn't last and even before the champagne had numbed the bleakness of the December afternoon, the disillusionment of wifehood was threatening. The speeches were long and embarrassingly unfunny, made by people chosen for their social cachet rather than their love of the couple they toasted.

Tilda managed to get up the aisle without a stick, but was still in obvious pain as she limped behind the procession marshalling mortified and kilted Tom Wishart and sulky Isa Smellie in velvet bonnet and shawl, both too old to be sweet. Grizel, clad in Belinda Belville, was given away by Ian Parker, which caused no end of whispering amongst those members of the congregation who had known her late father.

Irene Gilmerton behaved like the movie star she had failed to become and wore a sensational hat that Commander Wishart said took at least twenty years off her age. He could not understand why this compliment offended her.

When Grizel was called 'Mrs Henrysson' by the photographer she burst into tears and hurled her bouquet at Maud Pollock, who immediately passed it on to her daughter. Everybody heard Grizel say, 'It wasn't meant for you, Cess, give it back to me at once.'

Cess meekly obeyed and watched as Grizel tore the flowers apart and threw the wrecked scraps at anybody within reach. By this time old Charles Henrysson, who was becoming maudlin, remarked rather too loudly that all Gilmertons were mad as snakes.

Hughie and Grizel left for a protracted honeymoon, arranged, like every other aspect of the wedding, by Ian Parker and paid for by Irene. The guests dispersed into the wintry night leaving a legacy of pointless waste and deep ruts on the lawns of Dalmuirie House .

After all that, Christmas had been more than usually anticlimactic. Ian had insisted on taking Irene, Tilda and old Charles Henrysson to Doonbury Hotel for lunch where Irene's cheque paid for turkey slices in glutinous gravy, soggy sprouts and rubber parsnips washed down with Chateauneuf du Pape pursued by frugally fruited Christmas pudding and insufficient Ruby Port to alleviate the embarrassment of adults pulling crackers in party hats.

Despite the awkwardness of contrived festivity, Tilda and Charles got on rather well and over his second glass of port he announced in a very loud voice that in his opinion, his imbecile son had married the wrong sister and furthermore it was a wise child who knew its own father.

'Oh my! Whatever can you mean?' Irene trilled.

Charles winked and tapped his nose, ' I apologise, dear lady,' then winked again. Somehow his party hat made this much more sinister.

Tilda, who hadn't been paying attention, smiled sweetly and thought longingly of the difference a year would make when all this would be far away and she and Ben would be together for ever more.

On Christmas morning Grizel had rung to say that the Ritz was very nice. That was all.

*

Nothing had been done to the principal bedroom at the castle since Hughie's parents had decided to sever their marital arrangements and move to opposite ends of the building. The big Maples bed was in good condition, having spent most of its life in idleness, though it retained a musty scent of mould. The pillows were large, the ticking stained; the original owners of the feathers had probably been eaten by bright young things who danced the Charleston. The linen was virgin and had formed part of Lady Charity's trousseau. Avis Wishart had found boxes of the stuff stored in a press that nobody had thought to open for decades. She made the bed and ran her hands over the icy smoothness of the monogrammed linen and wondered how on earth Grizel was going to cope. Love – she told herself, as she scrubbed at the greenish chipped enamel on the cast iron bath, into which hot water trickled at snail's pace and cold water gushed in air-locked spurts – love conquers all. Two lusty young people would not be daunted by jammed windows or knifing draughts.

She and Rodney had been impervious to post-war privations and had thrived on dried egg and margarine, so long as they both had each other to make love on sheets turned sides to middle. Avis put some late snowdrops in a vase on the dressing table beside Lady Charity's silver-backed mirror and buffed up the mahogany in the adjoining dressing room having washed the yellowing ivory brushes and extracted hairs that Charles had shed while it was still brown and plentiful. Avis had not been asked to do all this; she just knew that it had to be done and that there was nobody else to get it done. She did not expect to be thanked.

Since the wedding Charles had immersed himself in his family history and required Avis to type and edit almost every day. It was winter, Firthside Camp was closed and she had time to spare, though it would have been nice to have been paid. Charles did not notice what else she did. He did not come from a generation that troubled itself with domesticity, even though forty years had elapsed since the castle had an indoor staff of eight. While Avis coped with basic hygiene, her sister-in-law, Maud Pollock, kept Charles in pies and stews and invariably got her unemployed daughter to deliver them. Whilst on these errands Cess watched the erection of the new summerhouse with great interest and wished she could rid herself of the ear-worm that taunted her with 'this nearly was mine.'

'What are your plans, Mr Henrysson, for when Hughie and Grizel return?'

'What plans, Mrs Wishart? I have no plans.'

'I meant for moving to a smaller place, a manageable cottage perhaps or even a convenient flat in Dundoon.'

'Mrs Wishart! No Henrysson would contemplate leaving their castle, ever!'

'But you said yourself that you and Lady Charity quite enjoyed living down the bothy during the war.'

'One is not at war now, Mrs Wishart. Besides I've now got a daughter-in-law whose duty it will be to look after me and to manage this magnificent place that she has been so fortunate to acquire, even if all this does come attached to my idiot son.'

Avis said no more, but reflected on the diversity of personal perception as she emptied the mousetraps and put more buckets beneath the leaks in the gallery.

She looked out at the grey sea. All the islands were hiding in the mist and Henrysson's Rock was concealed behind the rebuilt summerhouse which also blocked the sight of Dalmuirie House. Avis thought that this was just as well. She knew where old Charles liked to point his binoculars and suspected that it might be agony for Grizel to see her old home from her new bedroom, should she and Hughie ever have a falling-out.

The bright new sitooterie looked most incongruous, more suited to a gaudy garden of regimented bedding plants in suburbia , or as a stately home's visitor centre selling souvenirs and ices, than the neglected grounds of an architectural monstrosity overlooking a bank of slanted trees leaning inland, battered by several centuries of prevailing wind.

★

Grizel was all gaiety when she and Hughie arrived home. They'd flown up from London with almost more excess baggage than could be crammed into the taxi. Without waiting for her husband, she stumbled over the step into her new home, her own castle and sprawled giggling on the ragged doormat.

Hughie, too, was drunk, though steadier on his feet. The celebration dinner that Irene had planned at Nether Dalmuirie was put in the larder for another day and further reheating, because it was obvious that the only thing the newlywed Henryssons could do was to go straight up to bed.

'Ah, what it is to be young and in love,' said Ian Parker, wistfully resigning himself to an evening of colour telly and an egg.

Tilda drove herself to the Odeon in Dundoon and saw *The Sting*, yet again.

Irene went to bed early, with a sleeping pill, while up at the castle, Charles coughed loudly on the landing outside the bridal bedroom hoping that his daughter-in-law would emerge to cook his dinner.

He wouldn't have minded, he told himself, if there had been evidence of joyous coupling and bedsprings twanging to mark the conception of an heir, but the place was absolutely silent, except for the gurgling of long disused pipes and the intermittent clanking of obstinate plumbing. All the cases and boxes were left in the hall under the blank scrutiny of the very dead stags.

Grizel's frenetic ecstasy was as fragile as a glass bubble. Her declarations of undying love and claims of mutual adoration had no substance. She looked like a wraith encircled by smoke, laughing at everything, while everything meant nothing. Only when she was alone with Tilda did she hint at her bottomless misery.

'You can always walk away, Grizel. There is no need to stick with a man you can't stand these days; in fact, I think that is morally wrong anyway. It is living a lie. Why do that when you don't need to? Look, the world is yours, your life is there to start again. What do a few empty words sworn to something you don't and can't believe in matter, compared to your sanity and happiness? I'll help you. You must go now before anything happens.'

'What sort of thing?'

'Well, babies for a start. Oh God Grizel, you aren't saying you are pregnant?'

'Christ no. I'm not having babies.'

Tilda asked her whether she meant now, or never, but got no reply.

'Then, if you aren't pregnant, what is there to stop you getting out? Nobody could ever understand why you married Hughie in the first place. I'm sure Mother would have given you a party if that was what you wanted, a socking great party without all that committing and death you do part stuff.'

'I wanted to marry him.'

'Why?'

'Because I could and nobody else could and I told you I wanted to be safe.'

'Safe from what?'

'Everything.'

'And do you feel safe now?'

'I don't know. Anyway I'm not leaving Hughie. He worships me.'

'Are you sure?'

'Of course I'm sure, Tilda! How could you say that? You are just a jealous bitch, just because you've never had anyone adore you. Anyway, I couldn't desert him. It would be too cruel.'

'Marriage isn't about being sorry for people. Besides, he is bound to meet someone else eventually.'

'Who? Oh I know, that ghastly Cess Pollock creature. She really wanted him you know, probably still does. Well, she's not having him, not while I've got a breath of life in me. I'd kill her or anybody else who tried to nick him from me, for that matter.'

'Don't be silly, Grizel.'

'And don't you dare call me silly. Just because you are clever it doesn't give you the right to call me silly.'

'OK, if that is your attitude, it looks to me as if you are stuck.'

'I just want to come home and for Hughie and me to live with you and Mum.'

'But Grizel, I'm going away as soon as I can, once the doctors have signed me off.'

'Where are you going?'

'America.'

'America! You can't go there. They electrocute murderers there.'

'I'm not a murderer, Grizel. What are you talking about?'

'Why have you got to go to America?'

'Why do you think?'

'I know, just to get away from here, to abandon me. That's why. You are a rotten sister. There is nothing in America that you can't have here.'

'But there is, Grizel. There is everything there for me, everything I've ever wanted.'

'I see. You are abandoning me, don't bloody deny it. You don't give a damn for me, just so long as you have your own way.'

'Oh please don't start crying again. Whatever is the matter with you? Are you sure you aren't pregnant?'

'I've already told you I'm not. Can't you understand? It's him. He's revolting.'

'He is? Then, like I said, you must leave him even if, as you say, he loves you. You owe it to yourself. No woman should ever submit to anything that she finds repulsive.'

'It's not Hughie, Tilda, he's just pathetic. It's his father.'

'Oh God, Grizel are you saying that the old man has molested you?'

'No, he just looks. He looks and lurks. Everywhere I go he is watching me. Every time Hughie and I are together he makes snide comments or suggests we ought to make him a grandfather. He even expects to eat with us and he listens outside our bedroom door. He's terrible. I want to kill him, really I do.'

'Then it's a good job you are not in America. What with him and Cess Pollock in dismembered heaps you'd be ripe for frying and no mistake!'

'That is not funny, Tilda. You aren't taking me seriously. Nobody ever takes me seriously. I hate that horrible old man and he hates me.'

'I'm sure he doesn't.'

'Oh yes he does. He told Hughie I was mad. He said all Gilmerton women were mad.'

'Then it looks as if you and I will be mad together, Grizel. What nonsense. Of course we aren't mad. He's just a bumbling old man who is losing his marbles. Come on, tell me, how was your honeymoon? You've told me nothing about Morocco. It sounds heavenly to me.'

'It's hot and full of snake charmers and holy men bellowing from minarets and old people worried about earthquakes.'

'But surely the scenery and the buildings and all those souks were exciting? Anyway you were alone with Hughie, that must have been lovely.'

'I suppose so.... . No, Tilda, you are wrong. It was really boring'

'So there is something wrong between you?'

'There is nothing wrong, nothing at all, do you understand? It's just not the same.'

'The same as what?'

'The same as before.'

'The same as it was with Hughie before the wedding?'

'No, not with Hughie.'

'With other men then?'

'Yes.'

'Lots of other men or one in particular?'

Grizel stopped picking at the fringe on one of her mother's chintzy cushions and lit another cigarette.

'Grizel, you never did tell me why you needed me to send you that money when you were in France.'

'That's none of your business.'

'Well, I think it is. You never paid me back. Not that I mind, but I would like to know what it was for. Had you been gambling?'

'I've told you, it's none of your business.'

'Did you need to pay for an abortion?'

Grizel hurled the cushion at her sister and missed, toppling a fake Dresden shepherdess on to the parquet floor where she shattered. 'Now look what you've done! I hate you, Tilda. You have no sympathy. Yes, I had a bloody abortion, so you see I am a murderer. Why don't you report me so I can be locked away, you'd like that wouldn't you?'

Tilda started to collect the fragments. The decapitated shepherdess lay among the rags of her china net frock. 'Of course not, Grizel. Anyway abortions are legal now, you know that. I'm just sorry that you had to go through with it. Were you in love with the father?'

Grizel shrugged and then the tears erupted again. 'Who?'

'The father of the baby.'

'He wasn't a father and it wasn't a baby. It was nothing, a messy lump of rubbish, that's all, something that had to be chucked in the bin.'

'Don't shout, Grizel, someone might hear.'

'Who? Hasn't Mum gone to Dundoon with Ian? There's only Juanita and she can't speak English.'

'Yes, but she's got a brain. She'll understand raised voices and tears.'

'So? Foreigners don't count. They are always making scenes.'

Tilda sat and waited. She looked at the portrait Ian had painted of them as children and wondered why her mother gave it house room. If ever something needed to be chucked in a bin it was that parody of a happy family. Mercifully the figure that was meant to be her father looked nothing like the man she remembered, which helped to make the picture slightly more tolerable.

Grizel followed her sister's gaze. 'You are lucky, Tilda. At least you can remember what it was like to have a proper daddy.'

Tilda had decided, years ago, never to discuss the day she discovered that Gilbert was dead and that she was happy. She had always assumed that Grizel was happy, too, Tilda had been much older when she realised that they would both be looking at the same event from different perspectives.

'No fathers are the same, nor are mothers and sisters. None of us are machines that obey instructions.'

Grizel lit another cigarette from the stub of her old one. 'I'm sorry, Tilda, I just wanted someone to talk to. Somebody who'd stand by me.'

'There's nothing to be sorry about. I may not understand you, but I'll stand by you, Grizel, isn't that what sisters are for? Is your new life really all bad?'

'It's OK, I suppose, if Hughie and I are left alone, which we never are in that bloody castle. If it isn't his father creaking and groaning, it's the pipes, or the windows rattling, or mice, or bats. That deadly hole is alive with pests.'

'Why don't you go and shut yourselves in the new sitooterie? It's big enough, for goodness sake. You could lock the door and close the shutters.'

'It's freezing in there.'

'Well, get a paraffin stove and some rugs. You could even make that huge, squashy sofa that Mum gave you into a bed. It would be lovely.'

'It wouldn't. It would be worse. Imagine Charles prowling round and round like the big bad wolf, huffing and puffing and wanting his supper.'

'Well, at least you were taught to cook at the school in Switzerland. I can only manage omelettes and things in tins.'

'Have you seen the castle kitchen? I can't cook in that. It's like a dungeon or a torture chamber. Anyway, we only learnt petit fours and napkin folding and what wine to serve with foie gras. I can't do bloody stews and pies and things made with that awful suet stuff that comes from around cows' kidneys and tastes of piss.'

'So what do you do for food?'

'That fat bitch Cess Pollock delivers stuff that she and her mother have brewed up in their cauldron. Hughie's father thinks she is wonderful. I can't stand her, or her food. It stinks of cow muck and probably contains toads' balls and newts' toenails.'

'Those women are saints. Is anybody paying them?'

'Search me. I expect so. Perhaps they are nicking stuff, I don't care.'

'Listen, Grizel, I've had an idea. Why don't you have a word with Mrs Wishart? She's been doing a lot of stuff up at the castle and I think old Charles might listen to her.'

'He won't. She told me she had suggested that he might like to move to somewhere smaller and the next day he sacked her, again. He does that quite often, especially when he owes her money. Tilda, I need a friend, a close friend, someone like you I can talk to and who won't let me down or tell me I ought to go and see a doctor and ask for something to make it all bearable.'

'Happiness isn't in a bottle of pills. But Grizel, whatever happens, wherever I am, I will still be your friend, I promise. No matter what, even if I am far away in America you can always ring me, send a telegram or a telex. The Atlantic is getting narrower all the time. And whatever you do I'll always stand by you, right or wrong. There now, cheer up, life could be so much worse.'

'Do you swear? Do you promise?'

'Of course. I promise, right or wrong.'

Grizel continued to confide in Tilda, daily and at length. Nothing got better. She became near to hysterics when pleading with Tilda to stay in Scotland, even threatening to kill herself if, as she put it, her sister abandoned her. Grizel may have been truthful, maybe not. Often she said too much. Tilda knew virtually everything about her younger sister's life, bar what had happened in France and the actual details of her intimacy with Hughie.

Eventually the long winter began to turn into reluctant spring.

Grizel still knew nothing about Tilda's hopes or her blinding and binding love for Ben whose copious letters she went to collect from Avis Wishart. Grizel knew none of these things because she never asked. She just said, in increasingly shrill protestations, that if anything went wrong it would be all Tilda's fault.

★

Arguably, Tilda was to blame. After all, she was the one who suggested the paraffin stove. She also suggested Ian Parker took both her mother and Hughie's father for a day at the races that dry, chilly Saturday.

Grizel's sick headache was not part of Tilda's scheme, but the fact that Hughie's car was in bits at MacNab's Garage was no bad thing.

With Grizel determined to be ill in bed, Tilda was free to spend her day preparing to fly away. She would be leaving home in a month, the moment her visa came through. Ben would be there, waiting. Of that she was certain.

They had only managed to speak on the phone once and then the precious minutes had been wasted in banalities about weather and head colds. Letters were better. Nearly every day Tilda collected those addressed to Miss Gilmerton from the Wisharts and just as frequently took air letters, addressed to Professor Troubadour, into Dundoon Post Office. Nothing was to frustrate her glorious future with the man for whom her love increased as the time approached for her to escape from the privileged cage of home. Nothing Tilda said could convince Grizel that for her, too, at least for now, the cage door was still open and that her incarceration was self-inflicted.

Each morning Tilda rose with the sun which would rise for Ben at her midday and would set at his midday, promising as the months crept by to reunite them across the sea where they would watch the sunrise and sunset together, for evermore.

Gin, Tilda was relieved to diagnose, not pregnancy, was probably to blame for Grizel's sickness when she was summoned to see her that late fatal morning. Grizel was lying among the rumpled bedclothes groaning. Even the most unpractised diagnostician could guess that she was not as ill as she professed. She might have been suffering from the after-effects of scalding her left hand while ineptly making coffee, or suspect potted shrimps, or lack of attention or hopeless boredom, nothing, Tilda thought, that couldn't be helped by a couple of aspirin, more black coffee and fresh air, though she did suggest Grizel remove her wedding ring, just in case the alleged agonising scald suddenly transformed her delicate finger into a puffy sausage.

'Isn't it unlucky?'

'Not as unlucky as having it cut off in hospital.'

'Anything is better than going to hospital,' Grizel replied, clutching her head and looking wan.

'Where's Hughie?' Tilda asked.

'I don't know and I don't care. He said something about going for a walk to look at sheep or trees or something like that. Then he might try and get Ian to drive him to the races, too. He loves racing. I don't, I hate it and anyway I'm much too ill. I told him not to bother me. I am going to spend the whole day in bed. I want to be left alone.'

'Well then, you are in the best place. Take the pills, stay in bed, sleep it off and I'll come and see you again this evening.'

'You promise?'

'I promise. Bye Grizel, see you later.'

'No Tilda, don't go, not yet.'

'I must, I've got things to do.'

'I'm feeling sick, Tilda, horribly sick.'

'In that case, you'd better not take the aspirin. I think it makes it worse.'

'What does it make worse?'

'Sickness. Listen Grizel, are you sure you aren't pregnant?'

'Pregnant, me? Don't make me laugh. The only people my pathetic husband could impregnate are cheap tarts. He can barely get it up with me, let alone perform. Even on honeymoon we were often both faking it and now with his ghastly father on the prowl there is no chance that I could ever get pregnant by Hughie, not unless I pretend.'

'Pretend what?'

'Pretend to be a cheap tart.'

'Well, why don't you? If that what it takes to turn him on. You might have to indulge him. Give it a try, it might be fun.'

'Fun? What do you know about it anyway? Oh I know, you've read it in a book like all priggish virgins. You don't know what it is like to have to pretend to be someone else in bed, to listen to a sweaty desperate man pumping away and shouting another bitch's name.'

'That's enough, I don't want to listen to any more. I'll be back later. Try and get some sleep and then I think you should get up, go for a walk and ask yourself again why you are throwing your life away here, and what's to stop you leaving. '

As Tilda walked away she could hear Grizel shouting for her, but she didn't turn back.

★

Everything was very peaceful as Tilda gazed out of her bedroom window, dreaming about her future with Ben. What should she take? What would she miss? The answer to both these questions was, very little. Of course she would come back to Dalmuirie from time to time, maybe, but not often. The sea, yes she would miss being by the sea, but sea wraps the whole world; it just depends how far you have to go to find it. Perhaps she and Ben could settle at another seaside eventually, but not this one.

Her bedroom window faced Henrysson's Brow and from it she could only see the strip of shore that was under water twice a day, between the land and Henrysson's Rock, which was out of her sightline. Of that she was glad. She hated the place; it haunted her with unwelcome, possibly distorted, memories. Apart from that parody of a portrait, the only picture she'd kept of her father was in her mind.

Smoke rose gently from behind the rebuilt sitooterie on Henrysson's Brow. It reminded Tilda of stories about wreckers, or beacons lit as warnings in stormy weather. But this afternoon was very still and the smoke was going straight up, like that of an acceptable sacrifice. It was a strange spot and time to choose for a bonfire though, but that was none of her business. She turned away to fetch a book. She was rereading *Ballet Shoes* well aware that it was more than time for her to put away childish things.

When she looked up again the smoke was belching black. This was no garden bonfire. This was a catastrophic blaze.

★

In her original statement, which she elaborated upon when required to testify in court, Tilda told the police that she had been in her bedroom sorting through her stuff for the States when she looked through the window and saw the belching column of black smoke rising. Flickering at first, then blazing, flames had enveloped the wooden building.

She then rang 999, thankful that she knew her sister to be sick in bed up at the castle with her husband and father-in-law safely away enjoying a day at the races.

Though Tilda still had not fully recovered, it was quicker for her to struggle up to the castle on foot rather than extract her car from the garage. At the bridge, she met Cess coming towards her in a state of panic. 'Tilda! Do something! Get help! I can't find anybody! Look!'

'It's OK, Cess, I've rung the fire brigade and everyone except Grizel is at the races. Don't worry.'

Then there was an almighty eruption as the flames found the spare supply of paraffin. The girls clung to each other watching as the whole bank shuddered and fire spread through last autumn's shrivelled leaves and the brittle twigs and fallen timber, legacy of the January storms.

'Christ, that was awful. Quick, let's go and find Grizel. She's not well and will be bloody terrified on her own.'

Tilda set off to the castle at the run with Cess puffing in pursuit. Her leg no longer pained her as Tilda clambered in desperation up to the level land and rushed on and into the castle with Cess behind, in tears.

'Grizel!' she shouted. 'Grizel! Wake up, Grizel!'

When Tilda opened the bedroom door the big bed was empty. 'Quick, Cess, search through all the rooms downstairs while I look up here. Grizel must be somewhere. Keep shouting.'

Please God Grizel might have changed her mind. She might have decided that she didn't hate racing after all. Let her have gone to the races with the others. There would have been room in the car, just. Yes, of course, that was the answer! Thank God!

Above the sound of Cess banging doors of distant rooms and shouting Grizel's name Tilda heard the approaching clamour of bells and sirens. Help was on its way. Another hour and the racing party would be back. Another hour and it would all be over.

When the Fire Brigade arrived the building was gone. The rhododendrons and leafless trees surrounding it had been burnt to the ground leaving charred scars trailing half way down towards the sea. The air stank and black flakes floated above the smouldering, unrecognisable remains of the sitooterie.

Though the fire was out, smoke was still rising when Ian negotiated Irene's new Mercedes between the potholes on the castle avenue and around the corner to where his wedding present to the young Henryssons had stood.

The moment she saw it Irene began to scream. She was the first person to grasp what really had happened. Tilda heard her mother's screams. The nightmare was true. Grizel had not gone racing. Tilda looked across the wreckage at the three figures, Hughie's father, her mother and Ian Parker. Hughie had not gone racing either.

A police officer, known to Ian, approached him to tell him that the unrecognisable remains of two bodies had been discovered. There was no doubt whatsoever as to whose bodies these were.

Tilda was told to look after Irene, who was now quiet and numbed with shock, and Cess was asked to take Charles, who was too confused to grasp the horror of what had happened, into the castle and contact her aunt Avis Wishart, who was the most likely person, after Ian Parker himself, to know what to do.

Ian Parker, magnificent in the face of tragedy, coped admirably with catastrophe and demonstrated the detached competence of a real professional, one who had been hardened by years of dealing with people in the grip of unimaginable horror and grief. It was an unexpected side to him, a man more used to advising on pelmets than taking charge in a disaster. He appeared to know exactly how to handle hysterical would-be helpers and those too shocked to be of any use. He could also cope with the press and make sure that the bereaved remained protected from probing ghouls.

Ian stayed at the scene until the fire was out and the site cordoned off. He waited and watched while an ambulance arrived and left with the silent, loaded stretcher.

There is no frantic rush when the destination is the mortuary.

He listened to an indifferent bird singing as the sun sank and watched a lonely seal swim to Henrysson's Rock. Later, at low tide, the island would be accessible, but it would be dark. Only he had noticed a bundle lying by the burn at the foot of the gully.

★

The media was bursting with excitement as Margaret Thatcher, aged 49, trounced her male rivals to become the first woman to lead a British political party.

The press, as a result, was fully focussed on Maggie and not much exercised about the tragedy in Ayrshire. It did not make the front pages of the nationals.

Locally, the area was rocked to its foundations, so much so that Maud Pollock felt compelled to ring her sister in London, regardless of the expense.

'Whatever is the matter, Maud? You sound most distressed.'

Elvira, who had just finished reading, for the sixth time, how the tigers chased each other round and round until they turned to butter, was glad of the break but not overwhelmed with delight on hearing her sister's voice. Guilt lingered concerning her lack of generosity to Cess while she'd been in London. 'If it is about accommodation for your Cecile, I am afraid I can't help you, Maud. Once more my rooms are fully occupied.'

'No, Elvira, I am ringing about the terrible news.'

'Well, she seems a capable sort of woman to me. At least she's given that snake Heath his come-uppance.'

'Who?'

'Margaret Thatcher, of course.'

'I am not talking about Margaret Thatcher, Elvira. Haven't you seen the papers? Don't you listen to the News?'

'No, I haven't, not today, why?'

'They've been killed, burnt to death, that beautiful young couple. Oh and Elvira, that poor old man left all bereft, it is quite terrible.'

'Who has been burnt to death, which beautiful young couple?'

'Hugh and his wife, Grizel Gilmerton as was. Not four months since their honeymoon, locked in each other's arms in a summerhouse.'

'Oh dear,' said Elvira lamely.

'Is that all you can say?'

'Just a moment, Maud, yes that is quite terrible, excuse me. Mira, why don't you nip downstairs and find another book. I think there is a lovely story about a rabbit in my shopping basket. Yes, I know you like the Grandest Tigers in the Jungle but I think Little Grey Rabbit would make a nice change. Run along, dear, there's a good girl.'

'Who are you talking to, Elvira?'

'I have little Miracle staying with me for a few days and I don't want her to discover what has happened till I've had time to collect my thoughts. Good God, that is really terrible, both of them? Both dead?'

'Yes, Elvira, it's the most tragic thing I've ever known. But do you mean you have got Hugh Henrysson's child in your house?'

'Yes, Maud.'

'But you can't! You are a spinster. You don't know the first thing about children!'

'You seem to forget, Maud, you and I were both children once, too. Besides she's only here while her mother is away. Mira is good company. We play Old Maid together, most appropriate I am sure you will agree. Oh hello, Mira, that was quick. Now just let me finish talking to your Auntie Maud and we'll make some toast for tea. Goodbye, my dear, thanks for ringing.'

Maud hung up in disgust. 'Well! I've never heard tell of such a thing. That hard-hearted, dried-up old stick of a sister of mine has gone and got hold of Hughie's poor little girl. No good will come it. Mark my words.'

'Och, Maudie, quit fussing. You'll be getting to do the catering for the funeral. You'd best be applying yourself to yon instead of fretting about doings down South. You may have missed out on doing that fancy wedding caper, but I've no doubt they'll be calling on you the now, you did such a grand job when the old woman was gathered. Dinna' fret yourself with other folk's business.'

'Willie, you are impossible! It is my business. I'm talking about my adopted niece. At least Cecile will understand. Where is she by the way? She should be home by now.'

'She'll be coming by shortly. She's taken herself up the sands to have a look at the wreckage while the tide's away out.'

'What an odd thing to do. Why didn't she tell me?'

'Let the lass be, Maudie. She was awful distressed by what's happened.'

'But we all are, Willie! We don't all go and gape like sightseers.'

'Maudie, you and I both ken fine that it went deeper than that with our wee girl.'

Maud looked at Willie in amazement. Over thirty years of marriage and it was a rare day when he ever showed a vestige of sensitivity. 'You are a good man, Willie. I am lucky to have found you.'

'Now don't go getting carried away.' Willie stomped off to sort the lambs.

Summer 1975

*I*t was exceptionally dry, hot too, all most unusual, especially
on the soft, mild west coast. Typical of his calling, Willie Pollock
wasn't happy. The crops weren't sodden or flattened, but they
were short in the straw. Short straws are no good in any context.
The newish, rocket-shaped silos that stood beside the red-roofed
barn were redundant in a fine hay-making summer. The idle in-
vestment irked Willie almost as much as his wife and daughter's
preoccupation with the postscript to the fire and the custody of
the bastard which was, he stated firmly, none of their business,
even if the wee girl was the child of Maud's adopted niece and as
closely related to the Pollocks as she was to Maud's spinster sister
Elvira. Maud insisted that Elvira had no business meddling with
child-rearing having failed to find anybody to marry and give her
a baby of her own. 'You wouldn't expect a calf to be reared by a
barren heifer, now would you, Willie?'

'But your sister isna' suckling the bairn, Maudie.'

'Of course not! Don't be disgusting. At least Cecile understands.
She knows about nurture and nature.'

'Is that a fact?'

Behind the facade of worrying about brucellosis and lodged
corn, Willie worried about his daughter, who he did indeed love,
deeply. When Willie counted chickens he knew they'd die on
hatching; his geese laid only addled eggs.

Last year he had worried as he watched his only child bagging

129

up nicely, he'd worried that Hughie would have to make her an honest woman and though he'd been distressed when the brute had jilted her, he was also mightily relieved. Later he assumed that his Cecile's calf, if there had been one, had been lost or reabsorbed; these things happen in even the best regulated herds.

His worst moment was when Cecile had come under suspicion of murder when he'd realised that his wee girl not only had a motive, but also the opportunity. Whatever she had done, Willie was prepared to fight with his last breath to save her from being convicted of anything, even arson or murder.

Maud Pollock never had the slightest suspicion that her daughter was involved. She was furious at the merest hint or suggestion that she was guilty of anything, and refused to express relief when Matilda Gilmerton's testament that was read in court excluded Cecile from all suspicion.

But Willie wept like a lassie (secretly behind the byre) on learning she was exonerated. According to Tilda's sworn statement, the two old schoolfriends had spent the entire day in each other's company and were alone together, at Nether Dalmuirie, when they spotted the smoke rising from the summer house on the bank above. Who would doubt the sworn word of a bereaved sister? Certainly not the Procurator Fiscal, Tavish MacMaster.

The only surprise was the stated friendliness between Cess and Tilda, which was hardly evident before the fire and completely absent afterwards. Cess had worshiped Tilda in childhood and had not progressed. She blushed when they met and found it impossible to be natural, laughing too loud and too often, constantly over eager to please. She'd have walked into the winter sea and wrestled with pythons for Tilda; she fantasised about sacrificing herself heroically for her sake. Friends sometimes kiss on meeting, but Tilda had always ducked any physical contact with Cess, who she found sycophantic and cloying and her miasma of synthetic sweetness utterly repellent.

They'd clung to each other, paralysed by terror while the summer house burnt down, but that was the only time that Tilda had let Cess get closer than arm's length. She never gave her another chance.

Tilda should have felt sorry for Cess and maybe helped her to find someone or something else for her to love, a dog even? But Cess had red-rimmed itchy eyes and a perpetually running nose whenever she came near dogs or cats. Only smooth creatures, snakes or humans, were suitable companions for somebody with her affliction. Reptiles couldn't reciprocate affection and humans didn't want to.

If Cecile was truthful, she would have admitted that her first and only ever love wasn't Ben at all. She never acknowledged her inclination to anyone and especially not to herself.

At the double funeral, which was organised by Ian Parker, Tilda had stared ahead with dead eyes, as pallid and gaunt as a living corpse, speaking to no one. Irene Gilmerton stayed at home, numbed by sedatives and grief. Old Charles followed the remains of his only son and his bride to his family grave, supported on either side by Avis and Rodney Wishart. Tilda walked alone. The drops of water on her face were of icy rain, not hot tears. She refused Ian's offer of an umbrella.

Cess saw Tilda, standing silently with the rain soaking her long hair and her face completely blank, the embodiment of lost hope. She threw the first handful of earth over the coffin. Something hard fell on the brass plate, a wedding ring.

All through the spring and into the baking summer Tilda and her mother had remained invisible. They saw no visitors and never went out. The phone went unanswered unless Ian was there, in which case he would undertake to pass the message on having thanked the caller most politely, but not suggesting they should call back.

Ian did everything at Nether Dalmuirie, while Avis Wishart and Maud Pollock went on doing everything (unbidden and unpaid) for Charles, who was shrinking from life and retreating into the obscurity of senility, alone in his castle.

He no longer looked out across the sea or down to where his

heart was once gladdened by the sight of Irene's solo performances. She no longer danced in the big bay window; the curtains were always drawn shut, all blinds were down.

No longer did Cess walk along the beach to gaze up at the castle and the raw, charred scar where the summerhouse had stood. Instead she spent her ample free time inland, wandering amongst the coming heather and skylarks across Henrysson Hill, which her father leased for the broad grazing of his sheep and beef cattle in the summer months. Cess had no more interest in moorland birds or plants than she had in gulls and seashells, but she did like gazing down upon Nether Dalmuirie, her vision of the House Beautiful. From its full set of concrete teeth edging the roof to the over-sized reconstituted stone lions guarding the fake pillars flanking the front door, she loved every inch of rendered brick and pebbledash. She loved the sash windows that appeared afire in the morning sun and stared back like blank sockets in a skull at dusk. Cess adored the place. Literally.

It had been kind of her Uncle Rodney Wishart to give her his binoculars after she had dropped them in the sea. He said he didn't want them anymore, but the truth was that his eyesight was beginning to fade and he needed far stronger lenses if he was to see half the stuff that intrigued him, like the Dundoon fishing fleet and that damn Russian factory ship anchored off Arran. Rodney thought his niece was ornithologically inclined; Avis Wishart knew better.

Cess even trudged up to the closest obelisk. It commemorated fallen Covenanters about which she knew nothing despite having attended a dreary lecture on the subject, delivered in a monotone by Tavish MacMaster, without anecdote or visual aid to alleviate the tedium.

The view of all Dalmuirie from up there was magnificent. She felt a surge of excitement as she looked down and imagined how her life could be, if only.

From Dalmuirie Mains it appeared as if the obelisks were twins on opposing hills, but that was an optical illusion because the other one was further east, upon a higher hill that the Forestry Commission had decided to clothe with regimented conifers to supply the pit-props and telegraph poles that were no longer in demand. In fact it wasn't an obelisk at all but a tower from which neighbouring enemies could be spied and it marked the beginning of the great world beyond, commemorating a time when clans and tribes fought one another with just as much vigour as they fought Proud Edward and his English army. Like the Covenanters' memorial, this landmark was lonely and unvisited. It was also vanishing into the trees as they grew to prodigious heights, waiting for ever to be harvested.

Cess felt that she would never need to venture beyond that boundary provided she could have three wishes granted. She wanted Tilda's house, Tilda's wealth and Tilda's man. The fairy of the place, had there been one, saw to it that Cess got all three according to the letter, but typical of fairies, these wishes were to be granted spitefully and flawed.

★

Ben was not going to come to London till after the end of the academic year. He and his Aunt Elvira spoke often, always at Ben's expense. If he rang early, Mira would talk to him, too. He rang late if the business was confidential.

Elvira discovered that she was far more capable than she had ever thought possible, but it was exhausting.

After the fire, things began to change and Ben was in contact more frequently, but now he was primarily concerned with Mira's future, a future Elvira deduced, that did not include Dora's return nor did it seem to involve Ben's postponed marriage to Tilda Gilmerton. He never mentioned either Dora or Tilda and Elvira had sufficient insight not to probe. Relationships, she knew too well, could founder and end unexpectedly. Perhaps Ben or Tilda had found other lovers, their ardour may have dwindled, they may have changed. These things happen. Only Mira asked when she was going to see Tilda again.

'Some day.'

'When is that?'

'Go and find a nice storybook, there's a good girl.'

'Only if it is the grandest tiger one.'

'Not again, surely, Mira? I am fed up to the back teeth with those tigers.'

'When is Tilda coming then?'

'Very well, tigers it is.'

In June Ben asked Elvira to put his mother's house up for sale, though he didn't realise what a gigantic job it would be to make the little house in Wandsworth marketable. Nor did Ben realise how much work there was in looking after little Mira. She was lively, curious and generally happy, except at night when she was plagued by bad dreams. Elvira hadn't dealt with broken nights since the Blitz.

The dreams were all about Dora; Mira was petrified by the thought of her mother. Dora manifested herself as monsters, explosions, nameless terrors as well as appearing disguised as a witch or wicked fairy.

Elvira stopped reading fairy tales to Mira, notably those ones involving malicious females, which was virtually the entire canon. She dwelt instead on Beatrix Potter, Christopher Robin poems and Sam Pig, dismissing Mr Men as too trite and Noddy as plain silly and slightly sinister.

But Mira still needed to hear about the Grandest Tiger in the Jungle at least twice a week. She couldn't read, but she had the story by heart and knew when to turn the pages. Mo, the social worker who called, was impressed by this feat, though not by Mira's choice of book.

Elvira was the soul of politeness and Mira behaved immaculately. She showed Mo her bedroom and her toys and her wobbly tooth. 'Have you got wobbly teeth, too?' Mira asked, fascinated by Mo's protruding frill.

Over a cup of tea and some weird, home-concocted chocolate crispies, Elvira wanted to ask Mo who had sent her to call, but then thought better of it. She knew she wouldn't get a satisfactory answer. It was probably the Wandsworth neighbours, which was perfectly reasonable, after all. Elvira asked Mo to reassure Mr and Mrs Jenkins that all was well. Mo smiled benignly and said she could see that for herself and got up to leave. Elvira and Mira went with her to the door to wave goodbye.

'Thank you for seeing me, Miss Troubadour, and Mira, too. After all, this is only a temporary, emergency measure and that once Mum comes back I expect things will need to be monitored.' The door closed, Mo strode off down the street thankful that the commission was satisfactorily over.

'No! No!' Mira stamped her foot and started screaming. 'I don't want my mum to come back ever, I don't want things thermometered!'

Elvira promised Mira she would never leave her and that Mira's home, from now onwards, would be with her. She'd manage somehow. Nanny Westcroft was a great help, of course, but disapproved heartily of making any risky promises to children, or anybody.

'Supposing, Miss Troubadour dear, that the child's mother does come back, what then? If you break a promise to a child, you break all trust in their adulthood. Most of our criminals have been made such as a result of their early experience of untrustworthy adults.'

'I'll fight for her, if I have to.'

'Fine words butter no parsnips and blood is thicker than water. You are only her adopted great aunt and to be honest the authorities prefer children to be in a conventional family.'

'Are you saying that an old maid is incapable of looking after a child and making a good home?'

'I'm not, Miss Troubadour, but the world will.'

'Fiddlesticks to the world. What does the world know? Mira lives in terror of her mother. She's happy here. I can make it her permanent and stable home. You are about my age, Nanny, and nobody says you shouldn't look after children.'

'But I am a professional, I am paid, I can be dismissed. I have to forsake all my children, eventually.'

★

The news was not welcome at Dalmuirie Mains. Maud snorted with indignation dismissing the entire race of social workers. 'I've a mind to ask that wretched woman, who my stupid cousin's stupid son chose to marry, to return my lampshade. You'd expect a CA like Malcolm to be a better picker of brides. What an ungrateful hussy his Maureen, the so-called Mo, must be. After all my trouble, the only thanks I got was one sheet of Basildon Bond and now this! Clearly the woman knows nothing about what is good for children, any more than my spinster sister.

'Give over fretting, Maudie. It sounds as if the wean is just fine with your sister the now.'

'Willie! You may not understand about my sister, but your sister will, you can count on that. Sometimes you make me wonder whether you and Avis are even related. Cecile will understand, too. Where is she away to now?'

Cess was in Dalmuirie Post Office buying the *Advertiser* in the vague hope that a dream job could be found among the dross of Situations Vacant.

The septuagenarian postmistress dealt with pensions, stamps, the child allowance and gossip. She had a sharp eye and a sharper tongue and made no secret of her many suspicions. She spread rumours thickly and had a knowing way with defamatory embellishment and was unrepentant when proved wrong. She had been the first to condemn Cess as guilty of arson and then the first to announce that she had always said Willie Pollock's girl was innocent. Today she scarcely noticed Cess she was so busy relaying the latest sensation to the lengthy pension and postal-order queue.

'Gone!' she said. 'That flighty widow woman has flitted to Ireland on the Larne ferry. Just like that, without a word, and now we're told that's her off for good to live with relatives abroad. And do you know why? Will you listen while I tell you…her fancy man has taken up with someone else and that someone else is her own wee girl! No dearie, not the one that's deid, the other one. What's more they are living in sin in the big hoose. Did you ever hear of such a carry-on?'

Abandoning everything, Cess pelted home as fast as her fat legs could cope and was profoundly disappointed to find only her father there untangling baling twine caught in the tedder. 'Is that a fact?' said Willie, scanning the horizon for adverse weather. 'It just shows.'

'It just shows what, Dad?'

'That you never can tell.'

★

London baked in July. It was stuffy and enervating. The days were too long for Elvira, who found she was yearning for the dark winter evenings when Mira could be tucked up in bed at a reasonable hour and got up at a civilised one in the morning. Mira was not good at going to sleep in daylight, especially as the whole world, except her, was having a brilliant and noisy time outside.

Nanny Westcroft was firm about bedtimes. Small Tam was always in bed by seven-thirty when she was in charge. Elvira tried to be firm, too, but was becoming too weary to argue. 'Don't get me wrong, Nanny, I wouldn't be without Mira, I really love the little thing, it is just occasionally that I long for a bit of peace.'

'Of course you do, everybody does. Why else do you imagine people like me are employed? There is nothing wrong in feeling like that. You should take a break. Your health will suffer if you wear yourself to a shred and then where will we be? Up the creek without a paddle and that would never do, not in a month of Sundays!'

Mira, who was behind the sofa looking at a picture book, had heard every word.

'Why can't we go there?'

'Oh dear, I didn't see you there. Little pitchers do have big ears. Nobody wants to go up the creek, it's a horrid spot.'

'Why?'

'It just is. Now what are you looking at, not more tigers, I hope?'

'Look!' Mira held up a picture of children on a beach playing with buckets and spades.

'I wish I could make a castle like that. Tam says he always goes. Tam says there are donkeys, too. I wish I could go to the seaside.'

'If wishes were horses then beggars would ride. One day maybe. Now Mira, we'll all go for a nice walk in Kensington Gardens and see Peter Pan.'

'Peter Pan sticks in my craw and gets on my wick!'

'Mira , wherever did you learn such expressions?'

'Aunt El.'

'Surely not!'

'I am afraid she's right. I just couldn't face those infernal tigers again.'

'You, young lady, are so sharp one day you'll cut yourself. But maybe, if you wish very hard, eat up all your greens and go to bed without a fuss, just maybe, one day your dreams will come true.'

Mira continued to baulk at any vegetables, apart from baked beans, and tried every ruse to delay bedtime, but she did wish very hard. A month before Ben was due to return from the States, joy arrived in the shape of a letter for Elvira from Scotland.

Dear Elvira (if I may)

You will remember that I wrote to you before asking you if Matilda Gilmerton could lodge with you while studying in London. I am approaching you now with a totally different request prompted by your dear sister (my sister-in-law) Maud Pollock.

This whole area has been blighted by the terrible fire that killed both Hugh Henrysson and his new bride (Tilda's sister) this spring and the dreadful tragedy has also all but killed Hugh's father. Maud and I have been trying our hardest to help him, but I fear that any comfort we can offer does nothing

*to alleviate his deep misery. Old Charles Henrysson is the last
of his very long line except for your adopted great-niece, who
I believe is staying with you at present. I realise that this is a
strange request, but we were wondering whether the old man
could see his granddaughter once, before it is too late.*

*I understand that it is a lot to ask you to bring the little
girl all the way here. However, I have to come to London to
visit a sick friend in Penge in three week's time and would be
delighted to take Miracle back to Scotland with me, just for a
few days, so she could meet the rest of her family and hopefully
make her poor grandfather a little happier. I can assure you
little Miracle will be in safe hands. There are loads of lovely
things for her to do on the beach at this time of year and on
my brother's farm and even at Firthside Holiday Camp where
my husband is in charge.*

*Maud and my brother Willie will be thrilled to have Miracle
to stay and would be quite willing for Cecile, who has been
trained in child care after all, to travel back to London with
Miracle after this brief holiday.*

*I look forward to hearing from you and hope that you will
agree to this proposal,*

Yours Aye,
Avis (Wishart)

'Why does my sister get that nice Wishart woman to do her
dirty work? Answer me that, Nanny!'

'Because they knew you wouldn't even consider the proposal
if she did.'

'And should I? Should I take this proposal seriously?'

'Yes, of course you should, Miss Troubadour, provided of
course that Mira's uncle, as her closest relative, is consulted and
gives his consent.'

'Really?'

'Yes! A break from each other is exactly what you both need.'

Ben fell in with the plan provided he got to see Mira when she returned from Scotland. It was a pity that he couldn't reschedule his flight booking to Prestwick so that he could have travelled back with her. It was all remarkably simple until Mira realised that Elvira would not be coming to Scotland, too.

The nightmares multiplied and Elvira's wits frayed. 'You must tell me what is wrong, Mira. Tell me and I'll see if we can make it go away.' Elvira in floor-length flannelette, despite the heat, sat on Mira's bed, 'Don't you want to go to seaside after all?'

Mira shook her head, thought for a bit, then nodded it. 'Yes, but will Puff the Magic Dragon be there?'

'Certainly not. There be no dragons in Scotland,' said Elvira in her Pirate King meets Walter Gabriel voice that normally made Mira giggle.

'Will Dora be there?'

'Meaning your mum? No Mira, she's miles and miles away in another country.' Elvira hoped to God she was right about that; all this being truthful with children was tough. She had absolutely no idea where Dora was. All she did know was that she had not found a passport amongst the stacks of Dora's stuff abandoned in the Wandsworth house which at last she'd be able to clear properly with Mira out of the way in Scotland. She had not liked taking Mira there. The place stank and was full of dangerous memories.

To her surprise, she had found a passport for Mira which had been issued a couple of years before. Perhaps Valdite had been planning to show off her grandchild to the remnants of her Portuguese family, an expedition that had never taken place judging by its stamp-free pages.

Elvira's passport, which she renewed conscientiously, was almost as pristine, though she had been to Paris, once, in 1938, with her mother, which didn't really count as far as trips to Paris are concerned.

★

'It is the answer to everything!' Maud announced as she poured Willie a mug of strong tea.

'Is that a fact?' Willie replied from the depths of the *Scottish Farmer*.

'Of course it is! Aren't you listening?'

'I can hear you right enough,' said Willie, brushing bramble jelly off an article on slurry handling.

'Well. What do you think?'

'I doubt kelp is the answer to anything, or phosphates.'

'Who mentioned kelp? I was talking about Hughie's wee girl coming to stay.'

'Oh that.' He paused as if trying to find something helpful to say. 'Maudie, why is the house stinking of disinfectant? It's worse than the parlour when the ministry's down by.'

'Cecile is anxious about germs. She's getting the top back room ready for Miracle. She's taken to scrubbing.'

'Och well, right you are. I'm away down the byre. I'll take my tea along. I prefer muck to the stink of a public lavvy.'

'Oh Willie, please, just let me tell you why I think Miracle coming to stay is the answer to everything.'

Willie pushed his cap to the back of his head and sat down again. 'Fire away, Maudie, but don't linger. There's a heifer bagging up that wants watching and the milking to start.'

Maud explained. It was dead simple, a master plan doomed to success. Mira would thrive in the coastal countryside, be given a stable, structured and loving home life. Cecile would act as her keeper, guardian, mentor, substitute mother and then Mira's Uncle Ben, her own adopted great nephew, would feel compelled to ask Cecile to marry him and everyone would live happily ever afterwards. Elementary!

'But what about your sister Elvira? Might she not have a thing or two to say?'

'Irrelevant! It is the child that matters. She should be near her family. Don't forget, Willie, Charles Henrysson is her grandfather.'

'Aye, but that'll no do the wean much good. The man is skint, daft, too. And why should your scientific nephew want to marry our Cecile?'

'Adopted nephew, Willie. There's no danger of in-breeding if that is what concerns you. And who wouldn't want to marry Cecile given a chance?'

'There's no accounting for taste, Maud. Mind you a scientist would be that handy to have around the farm. Anyway, I thought Avis was telling you that the fellow was walking out with yon Matilda Gilmerton.'

'He was. Not any more. She's jilted him for Ian Parker, remember. And furthermore they were saying at the Post Office that not only are they living in sin but that they may have actually got married.'

'Parker is that canny. He knows what's what. He didna' come down the Clyde on a bike.'

'What do you mean, Willie?'

'I mean there's a man wi' his heid screwed on. He kens fine that yon widow would lose her fat settlement if she remarried and with the other lassie out the way yon Matilda is the sole heiress to all the Gilmerton foghorn, alarm and hooter empire. The man's a crafty one and no mistake.'

'I agree that this is all very surprising. Tilda always made out she loathed Ian Parker. Your sister thinks that perhaps she's of the kind that protests too much, the sort that says no and means yes.'

'You've lost me, Maudie. I'm off out now to start up the parlour.'

As Maud watched the cows ambling towards the dairy, their udders dribbling in response to the throb of milking machinery, she wondered if anybody anywhere could possibly want anything more. Then her jelly pan bubbled up and boiled over.

★

When Avis arrived at Elvira's house, Mira was so excited about staying up ridiculously late and going to bed on a train, that she quite forgot her forebodings. Avis was a person that a child could trust. Her own confidence gave everybody else confidence. She

142

was the sort you did not want to run from or disobey because she consulted you before suggesting what should be done. She praised without patronising. She had patience, time and the ability to be interested in everything without interfering or probing. She did not ask silly questions. She and Aunt El laughed at the same things and she did not mind one bit about Teddy being grubby. 'My boys loved the grandest tigers in the jungle too when they were your age. Now they are more taken by machines and superheroes and all that, though Tom is mighty fond of Nigel Molesworth. I'm afraid my days on the riverbank with Ratty and Mole are well over, especially now Christopher has got a scooter and a five o'clock shadow. I'd love to get some of those old stories out again. I think my favourite was Mrs Tittlemouse in her box bed. You can pretend to be her tonight in the sleeper. I'll let you in to a secret, Mira, I can't stand Chicken Lickin.'

'Nor can I,' Elvira, muttered. 'I could cheerfully wring that stupid hen's neck and those of the other rhyming ninnies, too.'

'I think Chicken Lickin is very silly,' said Mira, whose hearing was sharper than Elvira had thought. 'The sky can't fall down, can it?'

Elvira came with them in a taxi to the station. The ride through lit-up London was almost as exciting as the echoing station alive with incomprehensible announcements and people rushing all over with luggage.

Mira was delighted with her bunk, though she would have preferred the top one which Avis (now known as Auntie Bird) said was not a good place to be, especially if you needed to use the potty that lived in the cupboard beneath the basin in the night. She did not say clambering up ladders was too dangerous for little children. There was a hook to hang your watch, a net to store your things, a mat to stand on while you washed and lots of knobs for light and air and heat. The blankets were blackcurrant red and Auntie Bird told her all about how the improper use of the communication cord could cost you a whole £5.

The potential angst of parting was diluted by a gentlemanly

attendant asking at what time the ladies would be requiring tea in the morning. A whistle shrieked and the platform, with Aunt El waving upon it, slid back into the station.

As prompted by Avis, Mira blew Elvira a kiss. 'Come along, sweetie, let's see if we can get to bed before Watford so tomorrow we can wake up among the hills of my home.'

Elvira was used to loneliness, but had never experienced such a feeling of desolation before as she travelled home to solitude on the Victoria and Piccadilly lines. A whole week alone was no longer a luxury, but a sentence to be served.

Scotland 1975

The following afternoon Avis took Mira along to the Pollocks' farm where the first sight and whiff of her cousin distressed Mira so much that she grasped Avis's skirt and buried her head in its grey pleats. When Cess crouched to address her on the level, she screamed even more.

'There, there,' said Maud who was standing on the doorstep in a floral apron covered with flour. 'I'm sure I know a wee girl who'd like a bit of my sponge.'

'No Mum, please, don't interfere. Snacking cakes between meals is not good for children. I've been trained, remember. I have a certificate. Come along, Mira, you remember me. We used to feed the ducks. Why don't you come inside and see your lovely room? I've got lots of exciting games for us to play.'

Avis felt snot and tears penetrating through the Terylene skirt to her thighs. Mira was becoming hysterical.

Willie pushed his cap to the back of his head and remarked that those were fine lungs for a wean and suggested that maybe a jaunt to see the cows might be nice.

'Don't be ridiculous, Dad. The child should not be exposed to unhygienic environments.'

'There's nothing wrong with the cows. They've certificates, too, you ken, signed by the high heid yins of the Board itself.'

'But cattle trigger my allergy, remember?'

'I mind fine. A copper bottom excuse for not giving me a hand,

I reckon. See, the wee girl has quit greeting. You'd like the cows, wouldn't you, hen? Of course you would. Here, give us your hand and I'll take you down by. Your Auntie Bird will come with us. She and I were weans together. She's a great one for the cows, amn't I right there, Avis?'

'I think you were a bit keener than me, Willie.'

'I ken fine, you were the brains of the family, I was the brawn. I've some great wee calves wanting to meet you. Come along and I'll show you.'

While Cess objected like an incensed hen as Mira trotted off happily between her aunt and uncle. The hand Avis offered her to hold was considerably smaller than Willie's huge and hairy paw, when between them, they swung her over the muckier parts of the yard and helped her clamber upon a manger to lean on the rail surrounding the calf pen. Red and white calves with heavenly eyes and enviable lashes stared at the newcomer and then bounced towards her through the thick straw. Avis offered her hand to the boldest calf, a little Ayrshire heifer.

Mira shrieked. The calves took off vertically. 'Auntie Bird is being eaten up!'

'No, I'm not. She's just using me like a baby's dummy, she's got a lovely rough tongue. You try.'

Mira wasn't so sure about that, but then a couple of the other calves clamped their mouths on to her toes, and she began to laugh.

'There's a great girl now,' said Willie. 'You'll make a milkmaid yet. Mind, you'd better not blether to your cousin Cecile. I doubt she'd credit this caper as hygienic.'

Later Willie kept his promise to his daughter and did not let Mira down into the parlour pit with him, but made her stay on the level with Maud holding her hand and explaining what Willie was doing and why he squirted teats before putting on the clusters which hissed and sucked as the milk spurted down the pulsating tubes to the bulk tank. Mira laughed when Willie had to dodge the splatter from the cows' bottoms and learnt that the calves in the pen sucked milk through artificial teats on a bucket, but those with fluffy white faces in the field got milk from their mums because their dad was Bruce the bull with a ring in his nose.

'What is that called?'

'Ah well, that's what tells us he's not a lassie,' Willie replied.

'Is that his winkie?'

'Aye, I daresay.'

'And what are those things called under the cows, where the milk comes out?'

'Those are their udders. Times we call them bags.'

'Do people have udders?'

'Aye, in a way. Ask your Auntie Maud. She's the expert.'

Teddy was already frothing in the Electrolux by the time Mira could be persuaded to come into the farmhouse, where eventually, after quite a bit of bribery and bargaining, Avis had managed to leave, promising to return the next day with a pair of cast-off wellies for Mira and lots of exciting plans for outings, none of which seemed to fit in with Cess and her schemes, but were the only way to keep the peace.

Next to Auntie Bird, Mira liked Uncle Willie and Auntie Maud, who told her she was Aunt El's sister, though she looked nothing like her, being as round as a plump bun with curly hair, whereas Aunt El was a stick of celery with grey straight hair and pallid crinkles where Auntie Maud was smooth and florid. Cess didn't enter the competition. Mira's dislike of her was so obvious it even embarrassed Willie.

At night, when eventually Mira had been steered to bed, following an ugly scene about Teddy who was still damp and smelled wrong, then a bath which Mira told everyone she didn't want. 'Aunt El says I don't need baths, ever,' and pyjamas which were the wrong colour, 'Aunt El doesn't like pink,' she knelt down like a lamb and asked God to bless everyone, including Bruce the Bull, each calf, every cow and sheep plus Bubbly Jock the turkey and all the poultry, Aunt El, Auntie Bird, Auntie Maud and Uncle Willie and Granny and Grandpa (both with Jesus) and Uncle Ben in America – Aunt El had forbidden all mention of Tilda, even in prayer. Oh yes, and Tam and Nanny and the nice man on the train. No amount of prodding could persuade her to mention Cess, or for that matter, her own mother, Dora.

'She'll come round,' said Maud when she and Willie were alone.

'I hae me doubts,' Willie replied. 'Once a beast takes a scunner there's precious little to be done. We've a deal of trouble getting ewes to take on lambs when they've lost their ane. Times it helps dressing them in the deid yin's skin.'

Maud said that was not the same thing at all and surely Willie wasn't suggesting that Cecile could deceive Mira into liking her by wearing Elvira's cardigan.

'Aye well, maybe not.' He took off his boots and said that perhaps the wean would be happier if she spoke to his sister-in-law on the telephone, not for long mind, but he was prepared to foot the bill for three minutes after six o'clock.

Cess vetoed that, too. She vetoed everything. 'She's getting awful like yon Kruschev at the UN,' Willie remarked.

Cess depended for her opinions upon a generic creature called 'The Child' and Mira relied on prefacing most of her sentences with 'Aunt El says.'

The Child and Aunt El did not tally. They were at odds on principle; in fact, they refused to talk except through third parties. Things went well when Mira and Cess were apart, but together the situation was unworkable. Cess spoke much of roles and problems and concepts that were viable. Mira was delightfully chatty with Willie and Maud, but went stubbornly dumb whenever Cess attempted to intervene.

'We've heard all about Elvira and her Granny Valdite, she even mentioned poor dear Herbert, but never a word about her mother. Don't you think that odd, Avis?'

'Well, Maud, to tell you the truth, I think the little mite is terrified of her. Elvira told me that she'd been having nightmares and all sorts and seemed really frightened that Dora was going to return.'

'Aunt Elvira knows nothing about children,' said Cess, who was eavesdropping.

'I think your aunt has done a magnificent job,' Avis replied. 'Mira is devoted to her.'

'Of course she is, Aunt Elvira has spoilt her. Mira needs a stable, structured home with a suitable mother substitute, of similar age as her birth mother, not a chaotic life with an aged spinster.'

'You may be right, Cecile, but...'

'I am right. It's proved by childcare experts. It's in all the manuals. I can show you.'

'Yes dear, but children can't be reared by the book. Anyway, the chaos in Mira's life happened when she was with her so-called 'birth' mother, not after Elvira rescued her. What Mira needs is what she wants and what she wants is security with the person she loves best. In my opinion, that person is her Aunt Elvira.'

Maud Pollock tried to be loyal to her daughter, despite the facts.

Willie Pollock said nature was a weird one and no mistake.

★

The females that mustered outside Dalmuirie Castle the following morning were, for the most part, tired and tatty. Only Avis had slept comparatively well, notwithstanding the Commander's spasmodic snores. Maud had spent most of the night comforting either Mira or Cess, neither of whom could or would comfort each other. Mira had nightmares and then screamed if Cess went near her. In the end Maud slept in an armchair at the foot of Mira's bed and Cess shut herself in her room claiming that nobody understood, despite Maud's insistent protestations to the contrary. Dawn was very welcome and for once, Willie was not the only person to see it, even though the late summertime sun rose shortly after four.

Maud hoped that after such a ragged night, breakfast would set them up.

'That's my dad,' said Mira, pointing at the porridge packet. 'But he's gone to live with Jesus.'

'Well that's that sorted,' said Willie, his mouth crammed with mealie pudding.

'We're going to see your grandpa this morning,' said Cess, attempting to sparkle.

'No,' said Mira. 'We can't. He's with Jesus too, like Granny.'

'This is your other grandpa, hen. Your faither's faither.'

'Who?'

Uncle Willie means Mr Henrysson. Your grandpa is your daddy's daddy,' said Cess, attempting empathy.

'Then why isn't he living with Jesus, too?' Mira demanded.

'Good question,' said Willie. 'Poor soul. The man's got nothing to make him cheery. So maybe you'll be just the thing. Do you think you could try, Mira? Tell him about the wee calves.'

'Mr Henrysson isn't interested in calves,' said Cess. 'Cattle won't help him come to terms with his grief. He must work through the grieving process. He would benefit from counselling.'

★

Dalmuirie Castle's doorbell hung uselessly from its bracket, but as the door could no longer be locked, Avis leant against it till it opened enough for the four of them to squeeze into the vestibule. The trophy heads stared, glassy-eyed and dispassionately, down upon the dilapidation below as the party passed through and up stone steps to the hall, which no polish had sullied for decades and on down the passage to the library lined with unexplored bookshelves, containing all the most tedious literature of the previous century mixed with random, unwanted objects from the present, all of scant merit like the few, damp, chewed books which Lady Charity had given her husband, hoping to deceive others into thinking she had married a bibliophile.

Charles was sitting staring out of the window, gazing over the shaggy grass at Henrysson's Rock, no longer concealed by the sitooterie, now reduced to a blackened pile of charred timber which nobody had seen fit to disguise or remove. Given time, weeds would take over.

'Mr Henrysson, it's me, Avis Wishart. I've brought Maud Pollock and her daughter along, too.'

150

'How kind. I am, as you see, more dead than alive.'

'That's no way to talk now, is it? Especially since I've brought you a nice steak and kidney pie,' said Maud, 'and Cecile here helped me with nice seed cake and some nice shortbread.'

'How nice.'

'And we've brought someone else very special to see you, too. Come along, Mira, come and say hello.'

'What is that child? '

'This is Hugh's wee girl, Mr Henrysson.'

Charles took his rheumy eyes off the view and looked at Mira who was clinging to Avis while Cess tried to push her forward like the mother of a reluctant bouquet presenter.

'Good God! The bastard!'

'Mr Henrysson!' Maud tried to clap her hands over Mira's ears and suggested that they should all retreat, but Mira was having none of it.

'What's that?' she asked, pointing an elephant's foot in the empty grate.

'Don't point,' said Cess.

'What is it?'

'It's a leg,' Avis answered. 'For keeping pokers in. Now come and say hello to your grandpa, there's a good girl.'

'Is it yours?' she asked Charles.

'Every bloody thing is mine. Do you want it?'

'No.'

'No, what Mira?'

Instead of answering Cess, Mira abandoned all reticence and marched forward, to kick the old man on both his shins with the full force of her four-year-old, sandaled foot.

'Bloody hell! You are a proper little bastard! What was that for?'

'I always kicked my other grandpa before he went to live with Jesus.'

'No wonder he bolted, the battered old soul.'

'Say sorry to Grandpa for hurting him, Mira,' said Cess, as sweaty lakes spread beneath her armpits.

'Sorry, but you said…'

'No buts, come on, say sorry.'

'Mr Henrysson, please forgive her. My late brother had two tin legs. I expect Mira thought all grandfathers were like that,' said Maud.

Mira who hadn't thought much about grandfathers at all, did know she was thoroughly disappointed with this one's castle. Not a powdered flunkey or a chandelier in sight, no fairy-tale ballrooms, just musty murkiness and a familiar stench of decaying flesh.

'You've got rats,' she said, looking at the miserable old man in filthy tweeds, his face a mass of shaving scars with hair sprouting where his razor had missed. He smelled like Wandsworth bus shelters and the lift to Uncle Ben's St Pancras flat. 'The council won't like that. They get cross about rats.'

Never had she seen such long and fierce eyebrows, but as she stared, his miserable blank face began to change. It was like watching a windscreen shatter or china craze. A large teardrop meandered down his rutted cheek, his shoulders shook, then yellow tombstones appeared between his thin lips and his mothballed laughing mechanism came to life.

'You've got your father's eyes, your grandmother's, too.'

'No, they are mine! Both of them.'

'Of course they are. Don't take on so. I am just a silly old man whose family has gone to the dogs.'

'Where? I like dogs lots, only I think I like calves best. Uncle Willie said you might be cheered up by calves, too.

'You and I have got a deal of talking to do. Did you realise, young lady, that you are the last of the Henryssons?'

Mira looked a bit puzzled and then asked if the rug on which she stood was the grandest tiger in the jungle. The stripes were barely discernible beneath the filth, but the flayed tiger's stuffed head still bared alarming teeth.

'Once maybe. He's like the Henryssons now, pretty far through.'

'Through what?'

'His allotted span.'

'I hate spam. Poor tiger. Aunt El says spam is a bomination like marge and Mr Heath.'

'Quite right. Do I know the lady?'

'She's my sister, Mr Henrysson,' said Maud.

'Older spinster sister and thoroughly unsuitable as a child's responsible role model,' said Cess.

Charles looked at her and sighed. 'If only my son had had an iota of sense.'

Cess flushed pinker than the interior of the tiger's open mouth. Maud coughed.

'We are hoping that you will have plenty of opportunity to get to know Mira really well soon, when she comes to live here.'

'I'm bloody not! I want to live with Aunt El for ever and ever Amen.'

'Mira, who ever taught you to say things like that?'

'Aunt El .'

Cess longed to say she rested her case, but Charles Henrysson seemed perfectly happy to have his granddaughter swear; in fact he thought it funny. Of course one can never predict the reactions of the grief-stricken. It was all in *Introduction to Coping Mechanisms*, Chapter 4.

'Shh Mira, don't worry, of course you'll be with Aunt El again very soon.'

'Be careful , Aunt Avis. It is wrong not to be truthful with the young.'

'But I am being truthful, Cecile.'

'We'll see.'

'Mrs Wishart, why don't you take my granddaughter to see her forebears? I haven't the strength, and besides, you are the one who knows all about them.'

Mira brightened. 'I'd like that, lots.'

In the long gallery Avis noticed that yet more plaster had fallen from the ornate ceiling and that the copied portraits were now so dirty and damp that they might almost pass for the real thing.

Mira listened quietly, but was obviously underwhelmed by her array of boring ancestors.

'Where are they?'

'They're here, all round us. Look that lady there. She's your great great great granny and that blob behind her is the rock you could have seen out of this window if it hadn't been boarded up. Come outside with me and I'll show you.'

'Has that lady got a teddy on her head?'

'No Mira, I think it is a hat.'

'But where are they then?'

'Where are who?'

'Have they gone to the dogs, too?'

'In a manner of speaking, yes.'

'I want to see them.'

'Who?'

'The doggies. Dora said I could have a doggie, but she went away and I didn't.'

This was the first time that Mira had made direct reference to her mother and Avis was about to try and get her to say more, but Cecile chose that moment to come bumbling in, bouncing with artificial enthusiasm and suspect eagerness, rubbing her fat hands and suggesting a quick blow on the beach before going home for lunch.

*

Down south, in London, such emptiness had never afflicted Elvira before. All the sleep she had planned to reclaim eluded her. The nights she'd spent listening for Mira's nightmares were joys compared to these creeping hours of wakeful anxiety and remorse for indiscretions and gaffes, long forgotten by all concerned, except her. Demons of embarrassment prodded her with spears of guilty conscience for things both done and undone decades ago. And now? What was the point of her life? She was just a creaky spinster whose life meant nothing to anyone now, or maybe ever. She longed for Mira's mess and tiresomeness, she yearned for

Woodland Snap and even senseless Chicken Licken. Cooking for one was ridiculous, as was eating alone and shopping alone, or visiting friends alone, or changing a library book, or going to the cinema, all the things with which she used to fill up her pre-Mira days.

Once, at the hairdresser, while under the dryer, she'd read an article about how parents must learn to let go and how difficult it was to adjust to an empty nest. Elvira's nest had only been tenanted for a few months; parents were different, they'd had their fledglings from birth to maturity.

That was another thing, she hadn't been to Gino's Salon since Dora had disappeared. Perhaps she ought to do something about her shapeless greying hair now that she had the chance, but there again, why go to the trouble and expense? Nobody cared how she looked – they never had.

At first, Elvira had been convinced that Mira's holiday was only for a week and that she would be returned to her once it was over. Now things had changed. She should have known. She could have predicted what would happen.

She had been told, quite rationally and reasonably by Cecile Pollock, that Mira would not be coming back.

'You must appreciate, Aunt Elvira, a child of Mira's age requires the nurture of her kinship group and is happier in the surroundings of her extended family with a competent, and furthermore, qualified. maternal role model of the appropriate age.'

Had Elvira the strength, she would have told her niece (the appalling child appropriately known as Cess) exactly what she could do with her kinships and role models. but all she could do was grip the bakelite receiver in silent fury.

'So you see, we all think it would be preferable for Mira to remain here where she has security and space in which to develop her life skills, whilst retaining and strengthening the bond with her paternal grandfather. Consider the facilities on offer: a healthy environment, a supportive peer group, recreation and development opportunities, furthermore the headmistress of the excellent local primary school has agreed to admit Mira to the kindergarten class in September and waive the fees.' (This was quite untrue – Miss Stuart would never waive a fee, not even if Mary of Scotland herself had turned up at St Quivox requesting a place for wee Jamie.)

'Does Mira know about this?'

'She is very happy here, Aunt Elvira. You must believe me.'

'Must I?'

'What was that?'

'And what if her mother returns? What then?'

'That is a bridge we can cross if it happens, though it is abundantly obvious that the authorities would approve of the present arrangement and award custody where the most appropriate life plan is in place as opposed to the chaotic care offered by her blood mother or indeed the restrictions of life with you.'

'Please may I talk to Mira?'

'No, that will not be possible. It would be counter-productive and unsettling. Anyway she's gone for a walk on the farm with my parents. They are waiting for me to join them. Goodbye, Aunt Elvira.'

★

Mira could only evade Cess and her well-meaning, meaningful, play, by following Uncle Willie into the dairy and adjoining byres, where Cess could not go without sneezing till her weepy eyes were red as the cherries that embellished Maud Pollock's queen cakes. Mira liked cooking with Maud provided Cess was not there. She refused to eat anything cooked by Cess, but gobbled up everything, even fish pie, made by Auntie Maud.

Together they made pancakes and rock cakes and rock-hard melting moments. Once they made tablet which rendered Cess almost hysterical. 'Mother, have you considered the dangers of small children involved with boiling sugar quite apart from the risks of rotting teeth?'

'You used to make tablet with me when you were small. You must remember.'

'I do. But things are different now.'

Maud sighed. Things were not different now, but they were certainly not turning out as planned. Now she knew what she had always known but had not wanted to admit, Cess had no chance of usurping Elvira in Mira's affections, ever.

Mira always stood where she was told and never made any attempt to get in Willie's way. He maintained that she was no bother, grand company, as good as gold. This only served to make her disobedience and obstinacy with Cess even worse and did nothing to mend matters between father and daughter.

'What did you make of your grandpa then?' Willie asked while forking the straw for the dry cows

'He said I was a little bastard.'

'Och well, never mind.'

'I like being a little bastard. Why has your car got a wheel on its nose?'

'Yon's a spare, just in case.'

'In case of what?'

'A puncture or the like.'

'Grandpa's got a spare leg.'

'That's handy.'

'I didn't see the bears or any of his animals, only dead ones in bits.'

'Maybe another time, eh?'

Mira went silent. Willie saw that she was on the verge of tears; he was not going to be able to cope with that. 'Uncle Willie?'

'Yes, dearie. What is it?'

'I want Aunt El.'

'Soon, hen, very soon. Dinna' fash yoursel', yon calves canna' thole greeting.'

'Look, that cow has got a spare head! She's a push-me-pull-you!'

'Oh my, so she is! You are a sharp one. Why don't you run along back to your aunties while I get this sorted.' Willie could hear the rattle of his neighbour's tractor approaching the yard. Fraser from Dunholm was collecting hay bales and was a famously flamboyant driver. 'No, don't move, wee one, just bide where you are for the moment.'

Mira didn't stir from her perch on the trough but clung to the railings, wide-eyed with fascination as the cow in labour heaved to its feet, her coming calf's white head protruding from her rump, sticking a blue tongue out at life.

It took a full ten minutes for Willie to push the head back and reorganise the calf into a more suitable position for diving into the world, nose behind its cloven feet. There was a lot of muck and groaning, but eventually a long, wrapped-up body on a rope slithered out onto the straw where it lay, steaming in its mess till Willie removed the encasing membrane and tickled the newborn's nostrils with a straw. Then he dragged the breathing calf round by its legs to meet its mother, who set about licking her red and white baby clean, even before her own body heaved once more and delivered a slimy and deflated transparent balloon, full of what looked like a bucketload of liver, on to the floor of the byre.

Willie wiped his bloodied hands, and straightened up, having forgotten all about his audience. Mira had been transfixed throughout.

'Och my! There's no many bairns who get to see a calving in London I reckon. Look the wee one is trying to get to her feet already. She's a bonny heifer right enough. Shall we call her for you?'

Cess reacted as if Willie had taken the little girl to a public execution. Mira would be traumatised, psychologically unbalanced, emotionally blighted and everything else in the Freudian section of Introduction to Child Psychology, the part of her child care foundation course in which she told everybody she had excelled. Only Maud knew, or cared, that this excelling had resulted in a third, with a certificate that was less than worthless.

The next day Mira gave a complete account of the whole calving process while walking through Firthside Holiday Camp. Avis and her sons, Chris and Tom, were intrigued. Cess, thoroughly infuriated, tailed them, but Mira was far too excited to know or care about her, or the audience of campers. The Wishart boys were delighted with the show and egged her on appallingly.

'Let's hear that again, Mira!'

She screwed up her face and made the sucking, sloshing, spitting sound of a calf being hauled out of a pushing and groaning cow.

Cess glared. Nobody, except her, understood the first thing about children, not her parents, not her aunt, not her nephews, not these terrible trippers from Glasgow and emphatically not Aunt Elvira Troubadour.

Chris Wishart was on the lookout for goose-fleshed girls in bikinis to ogle, but Tom was too young for bathing beauties. He loved the funfair, especially the Ghost Train.

'No Mira, you are not going on that! Aunt Avis please, stop her, she's had enough trauma.'

'No I haven't!'

'Don't argue. Come with me. Let's go to the sandpit. You can build me a castle.'

'No! I want traumas.'

'Don't be silly, Mira, you don't know what a trauma is.'

Tom grabbed Mira's hand and together they joined the stream of jostling children mounting the steps to the Ghost Train.

'Stop flapping, Cecile,' said Avis. 'It's really very tame, awfully clunky and it leaks like a basket. Half the time you can see the sky. The rest is only a bit dark and creepy with flashing lights and skeletons. Why don't you go, too?'

Cess and fairgrounds didn't mix. Those devices that didn't make her sick gave her nightmares. For her there was no fun whatsoever to be had at the fair, but duty conquered terror as she pushed her way to the front of the queue. 'I'm with them!' she told the objecting campers. 'Let me through!'

'Hi Tom, back again?'

The youth in charge of the Ghost Train wasn't meant to let children under five on to the ride without an adult but he knew Tom well. 'Is it all right for you to take this wean wi' you?'

'Of course. Look, there's my mum down there.'

'Fair enough. Hey, miss, wait your turn. No you canna' get in this seat with Tom and his wee girlfriend. It wouldna' bear the likes of you. We'll get yous a seat on your ane just directly. We mustna' exceed the weight limit or the whole thing goes phut.'

'Stop the ride! I forbid you to let them go through!'

'Too late, miss! They're awa'!'

Tom and Mira's carriage jolted off through the rubber curtains into the jaws of hell where the louder you screamed the more you were enjoying yourself.

'In you get, miss, it's a snug fit but you'll be fine. Hold on tight now!'

Cess, alone in a carriage designed for two, was carried off in hopeless pursuit, panic mounting, eyes gripped shut.

Dangling hands brushed her face, a skeleton screeched as she was jerked through a pit of tortured souls howling in mechanical agonies. She opened her eyes and all was black, then a screen parted and revealed a rotting skull with worms in the empty eye sockets and fake blood dripping through its grinning teeth. More lights, more howls, more manufactured anguish, the ride was taking an eternity and all the time Cess could hear the children ahead of her screaming.

She could take no more. 'Stop! Stop!' she yelled while trying to stand up. Her head hit the roof; she was stuck in a tunnel suffocated by claustrophobia and terror. The carriage blundered on and she tumbled back into her seat as she was jerked through another curtain to the presence of the Devil himself. Old Nick was accompanied by his evil fiends with flashing red eyes, waving unconvincing pitchforks at a pit of hissing, plastic snakes. Nobody heard her, naturally they didn't, nobody does when you are damned to eternal torment. A blast of pretending smoke and flames, another creepy curtain then, with demonic laughter echoing behind, she was thrust out into sunlight and the delighted mockery of Tom and Mira who'd had a lovely time and were begging Avis to let them have another go.

Cess could barely stand, she was shaking so much. Her eyes

and nose streamed as she collapsed weeping on the Ghost Train steps, much to the mocking entertainment of all.

'Oh, you poor lamb!' said Avis.

If the Ghost Train was a vision of hell, Mira's heaven was Shamrock the donkey whose fluffy face and huge hairy ears was more lovely even than the calves with their knobbly knees. If only Aunt El could be there, too. Tom led by holding the bridle while Mira gripped the felt saddle's pommel. Avis walked alongside to catch her should Shamrock stumble in the soft sand.

Though Aunt El was lacking, at least Cess wasn't there either. She sat sulking on a bench far away from all things furry. Chris Wishart had sloped off to join three fat girls from Cowdenbeath on the waltzer.

'I wish I could stay with you Auntie Bird till I go home to Aunt El.'

'But Auntie Maud and Uncle Willie and Cousin Cess would miss you.'

'I hate Cousin Cess.'

'No you don't. You mustn't hate anybody.'

'But I do. I hate Cousin Cess.'

'But she's so kind to you. She goes to so much trouble for you. Why don't you like her?'

'She smells horrid and she doesn't like Aunt El. She says that she doesn't want me to see Aunt El again ever. I want Aunt El so badly.'

'Of course you do. Listen, I'll tell you what, if you are a really good girl and do what you are told I will get Aunt El to ring you up before you go to bed. Anyway, I'm sure you'll be seeing her soon.'

'When?'

'Look, do you see that big rock over there? That one like a bun.'

Mira nodded. 'But I still want Aunt El.'

'Of course you do, but maybe you'd like to come with me and the boys to sail round that rock tomorrow. We're going in a little boat and there will be plenty of room for you, too. Would you like that?'

'Will Aunt El be there?'

'Not tomorrow. Maybe another time.'

★

Again Elvira's call came at the wrong moment. Cess answered. No, emphatically no, she could not speak to Mira. And No, Elvira could not speak to Cecile's mother either, because she was out. Elvira was told that Mira was asleep, in bed. But it was only seven, Elvira protested. Not if you have risen early and been healthily active all day and are only four. But, Elvira persisted. She could hear Mira, even down the phone. It was impossible to muffle the heart-breaking, wretched sobs, the kind that sound far worse than those of a spoilt child's frustrated rage. What Elvira heard was despair and hopeless misery. Then there was a battering noise of someone desperate beating against a closed door and shouting. Elvira could have sworn that Mira was shouting for her. 'Aunt El! I want Aunt El!'

'What's that noise, Cecile? Is that Mira? Please let me speak to her.'

'No, Aunt Elvira, you can't. As I told you, she is in bed asleep.'

'But I can hear her.'

'No you can't. That is the television. Good-night!'

Leaving the telephone off the hook, Cess unlocked the door from the sitting room to the hall where Mira was standing and howling.

She didn't really hit Mira very hard. Cess told herself that it was more like a sort of shove which made the little girl lose her balance and clutch at a nearby table, which toppled, smashing a vase and scattering flowers and shards of Edinburgh crystal all over the tiled floor.

'You stupid clumsy idiotic child! No wonder your precious Aunt El never wants to see you again.'

Just then Maud returned from the garden with a giant cabbage.

'Never mind, wee one! Accidents happen. Oh dear, what a big bruise coming on your wee face. That was a nasty tumble you

162

took. I'll quickly put some Pond's Extract on it and you'll be right as rain. Never mind about the vase. It was a nasty old thing and we'll pick lots more flowers tomorrow. Clever Cecile will clear it up while I sort your face.'

'She fell, Mother, she just fell. One minute I was coming through the door and the next there Mira was, on the floor. And that's the truth, I swear.'

'Of course, dear, why on earth should I doubt you?'

The receiver wasn't replaced till the following morning when Willie discovered it after milking, still dangling.

The Rock 1975

Donald Begg's boat, the *Stupendous*, was moored down the coast at Dundrossan, a fishing village more picturesque than industrious and yet to become a haven for crafty folk selling pointless artefacts. Dundrossan had no tea shop with scones till the 1990s, just the Harbour Bar which sold McEwans according to the cavalier pasted to the window and no food to anybody and nothing whatsoever to tinkers. Women weren't very welcome either and strangers were received with frost. A chip van stopped by Dundrossan, once a week, and some rusty swings creaked in the ruined keep's shadow as if upon an expectant gibbet; that was all the village ceded to frivolity. A bus ran to and from Dundoon via Dalmuirie once a day. What more could one want? Donald maintained that as Dundrossan had been good enough for his faither and his faither's faither 'afore him, it was good enough for him. There had been Beggs in Dundrossan since the time when fisher folk relied upon the beacon atop the keep and a lonely bell tethered to Dundrossan Head to keep them off the rocks. There were no fancy lighthouses and foghorns then.

Provided his wife's washing was not being 'tossed aboot' Donald took passengers aboard the *Stupendous* to do a spot of mackerel fishing and maybe go round Ailsa Craig.

Donald Begg never moored at Ailsa Craig, not since the wife's sister had had words with the keeper's cousin in Dreghorn; the words were forgotten, but the grudge lingered. The *Stupendous* restricted her outings to circling the rock while Donald made disparaging comments about the state of the place and sometimes bellowed at the gannets through a megaphone. The Beggs ate lots of mackerel, but had not been blessed with bairns on whom to spend the extra wealth yielded by Donald's lobster pots.

Young Calum, Donald's aged nephew, was the crew. Unpaid Calum had expectations of his uncle, but as Donald looked the younger and fitter of the two, it seemed unlikely that Calum would be rich before he was a pensioner.

Leaving Dundrossan on a rising tide would enable the *Stupendous* to call at Henrysson's Rock for Donald's passengers to have a picnic on the way home. Avis had hatched this plan and negotiated terms the evening before. Donald hadn't the strength to deny her, but he did not approve, not one bit, No good came off that rock ever. It was a skanky hole either thick with rats or covered in poison; besides Mr Parker had banned all visitors.

'Mr Parker? What has Mr Parker to do with it? He's not the island's owner, as well you know. It belongs to poor Mr Henrysson and furthermore he has given us permission to visit it,' Avis lied with unassailable authority.

'Very well, Mistress Wishart, but we'll only be there an hour. The tide will catch us else. It's a driech spot for a picnic.'

'That's as maybe, Mr Begg,' said Avis, 'and I'd thank you not to go mentioning the Sawney Bean rubbish either, even if that is how you titillate trippers. We live here. We know that all that cannibal stuff is utter nonsense.'

The day of the excursion dawned fair and still, much to Donald's disappointment.

Avis parked her duotone Morris Traveller, known as the badger because of its colouring and not its smell, from which she unloaded a substantial picnic basket, several rugs, Mira, Tom and her friend Olive Smellie with her daughter, Isa. The *Stupendous* was moored at the quayside, where she was just able to float at low tide. Cess arrived in her mother's Austin alone; Mira had refused to travel with her.

'It'll no do, Mistress Wishart. I was counting on there just being the five of yous. I doubt we'll make it with six on board, plus me and young Calum, too.'

'Nonsense, Mr Begg. Mrs Smellie and her tiny daughter surely only count as one. After all they are replacing my strapping son, Christopher, a colossal rugby prop forward, not a wisp of a woman and her delicate child. Little Miracle is even smaller.'

'Aye, but yon Pollock woman is the size of two.'

'Mr Begg! Keep your voice down, please! My niece is very sensitive and anyway nothing like as large as she looks.'

Olive Smellie was no wisp either, but her Isa was a miserable specimen, shrunk in on herself and evidently unwell, too cowed however to voice her wish to be left behind. The ozone in sea air, her mother always maintained, was the best cure for everything, even having had one's tonsils out four days before. Isa was muffled up in a cocoon of furious misery. The anaesthetic had terrified her and now her gullet housed a serrated saw. She was the same age as Tom, but not his friend, or anybody's, that day.

Mira shook off Cess and went to inspect the picnic with Tom.

'We've got sick sandwiches and doggie doings sausages and lots of scab slabs.'

Avis shuddered. 'Tom don't be revolting, there's a dear. Now come along, all aboard.'

Cess held out her hand. Mira refused to take it and clung to Avis instead as they descended the stone steps, treacherous with slime. 'What happened to your face, Mira? That's quite a bruise. Did you have a tumble?'

'Yes she did,' Cess interrupted. 'It was all a clumsy accident. Wasn't it? Why don't you tell Auntie Bird how you were a silly girl and tripped over the nasty table, Mira?'

Donald started the engine and the sea air, of which Olive Smellie was such a fan, became a cloud of diesel fumes. Everybody was made to put on life jackets. Cess yearned for Brobat and a stiff brush; her yellow jacket was green for want of scrubbing. Tom and Mira were practically eclipsed by theirs and Isa tried to resist her mother's efforts to strap one on to her, probably because she felt that drowning was one of the better ways of getting through the day.

The sea was glass; Mrs Begg's washing hung to attention like soldiers on parade.

The *Stupendous* chugged away from the harbour pursued by hopeful gulls with an eye for Sandwich Spread and flapjacks, up the coast and out across the sound of Dalmuirie towards Ailsa Craig. Mrs Smellie, ever the teacher, was anxious to point out the wonders of nature, embracing geography, geology, archaeology, botany and history in a seamless stream of information.

'Listen, children, while Mrs Smellie tells you all about Ailsa Craig, look over there everyone, see how it is getting closer and closer.'

'Yes, and have you ever thought how amazing this place must have been when it was all blazing with volcanoes? Even this littler island we are passing now is just the middle bit of a great big volcano, the central plug. See there on our right, or rather as they say at sea, to starboard of us, we'll stop there later for our picnic.'

'But children, look, look over there on the left…how interesting!' said Avis, indicating an empty stretch of sea while desperately signalling her friend to explore the wonders to port because the *Stupendous*, having skirted Henrysson's Rock, was now in full view of Dalmuirie Castle.

'What's that, Mum?'

'A kittiwake, Tom.'

'And do you know why it's called a kittiwake?' Mrs Smellie paused to enquire before telling everybody the answer, to which nobody listened.

'No, up there on the shore, on top of the hill, those spiky black things and that mess dripping down below it like treacle.'

'That hill as you call it is Dalmuirie Brow. That mess marks where there was a fire,' said Mrs Smellie.

'*Pas devant les enfants!*' Avis hissed.

'What does that mean?' Tom asked.

'It's French, dear. *Pas* means not, *devant* means in front and *les* is the plural of the definitive article, in this case, because the object of the sentence is in the plural we do not need to bother as to its gender. *Enfants*, as you must know, means children and is masculine. So the whole means Not in front of...'

'What kind of fire?' Tom persisted, 'A big one? Did they get the fire engine?'

'Yes, Tom, I expect so. Now, I say, is that a seal?' Avis gesticulated in the general direction of Ireland.

'Did anybody die?' Tom persisted.

Olive Smellie looked to Avis for help.

'Yes,' Mira said. 'My dad got all burnt up and went to live with Jesus.'

'Wow! Who lit the fire?' Tom asked.

'Nobody, Tom darling. it was an accident. An accident with a paraffin stove.'

'Paraffin, children, is highly volatile,' said Mrs Smellie. 'Always remember that...and volatile means? Tom, you tell me, you are a bright lad.'

'Come on, Tom' Avis urged.

Tom shrugged. Isa remained inert.

Mira announced that Aunt El said only ninnies did volatile work for Mr Heath.

'What's that place up there with the towers?'

Avis rolled her eyes at Olive. 'You know full well, Tom. It's Dalmuirie Castle.'

'My other grandpa lives there, the one with the spare leg, not my grandpa with tin legs who has gone to live with Jesus like Granny and my dad. He's got bears.'

'Dear me,' said Olive Smellie. 'I think I know a little girl who is muddling the truth with fairy tales. Aren't you thinking of Goldilocks, Mira?'

'No, she had three. My grandpa has four, only I didn't see them because they'd gone out with the dogs.'

'One day, Mira, when you are older, maybe you'll write stories, too. Now who knows the difference between a gannet and a herring gull?'

Unmoved by gulls or views, Isa retreated further into her raw-throated resentment while Cess concentrated on squinting through her uncle's binoculars at the white building, resembling a set of disembodied dentures that formed the palace of her dreams. Every window of Nether Dalmuirie was blinded and there was no life in the garden, no smoke, no lights, no evidence of humans anywhere except for a flashy motorboat moored to a small jetty jutting into the sea below where the lawn ended and the coastal scrub began.

'Wow,' said Tom again. 'Being burnt must be horrible.'

'So much for tact,' said Avis.

Olive clapped her hands. 'Now, children, hands up those who have seen the Citadel in Dundoon.'

No response.

'Come along, Isa, I took you there last week and explained all about how they used to burn witches there. Only of course they weren't witches. Witches don't exist.'

Isa's glare contradicted her mother.

A sing-song was suggested. Something suitable, a shanty maybe, and did everyone know that sailors used to be ordered to dance hornpipes?

A groan came from the rug under which Isa was now hiding.

'I hate dancing class,' said Tom.

'I do dancing with Aunt El.'

'Do you, Mira?'

'I do everything with Aunt El. Aunt El lets me wind up her gramophone. We do Charleston and *Rock Around The Clock*.'

'Really?'

'And Dying Swan.'

The coast had now retreated beyond binocular range. Henrysson's Brow shut out Nether Dalmuirie and the castle's tower was silhouetted above the woods to its north, beyond which the shoreline running towards the Mouth of Dundoon was interrupted by the fungus of chalets and the garish fairground of Firthside Camp.

'I could dance with you, Mira. Would you like that? We could do the Gay Gordons,' Cess suggested.

'No!'

'No, thank you, Mira.'

Mira joined Isa under the rug while Olive rehearsed the entire history of Ailsa Craig from the dawn of creation, through its prehistoric eras, the indiscretions of abbots, the uneconomic cultivation of coneys and the bellicose intrusion of Spaniards foolishly claiming the rock for Rome. On she went, undaunted, through centuries of skirmishes till the building of the Stevenson lighthouse ('yes, children, the same family as Robert Louis Stevenson who wrote *Treasure Island* and *The Land of Counterpane*') concluding with the sad decline in demand for curling stones and the highly likely automation of lighthouses in the future.

The *Stupendous* drew level with the keepers' cottages. They all looked empty.

'Aye, they idle bodies will likely be away to their beds the now,' said Donald, gripping his pipe with his teeth and starting to circle the rock in an anti-clockwise direction following the old line of the railway that once led to the granite quarry, cradle of kerbs and curling stones. Straggly tree mallows had sprouted despite the inhospitable soil and some roughly hewn granite was scattered along the shoreline. Donald pointed sneeringly at the defunct gas works and said something most uncomplimentary about the foghorns.

Olive Smellie asked the children what fuel was needed to make town gas and Isa started to cry. 'I hate gas.'

'But this is different, Isa. Laughing gas like the kind doctor gave you is nitrous oxide. Town gas is made from coal, and where does coal come from? Coalmines, of course! Now who can tell me the name of the coalmine near Dundoon?'

Mira and Isa disappeared back under the rug while Cess gazed longingly at the remains of the mainland about to be hidden by the towering crags of Ailsa Craig's western face. Tom was transfixed by these sheer walls, all white with droppings and clothed in gannets. When Donald bellowed through his megaphone a few birds deigned to register modest alarm, but their hysteria was not the same now that the pleasure steamers had taken to blasting them with their foghorns. 'Aye, that's progress for ye,' sighed Donald, setting a course towards more bountiful fishing waters where he switched off the engine and let the *Stupendous* rise and fall upon the sickening swell. Calum fixed Tom up with a rod and offered one to Mira, too.

'No! She's too young,' said Cess.

'I'm bloody not!'

'Mira! We'll have to wash your mouth out with soap and water,' said Olive. 'Actually do you know what bloody really means? It is short for 'By our Lady' which of course means Mary, mother of Baby Jesus. Isn't that interesting?'

'Let the wee girl have a go. Calum here will give her a hand.'

'Only if I hold on to you.' The smile Cess forced through her rising nausea was terrifying.

'No!' Mira dived back under Isa's blanket.

Tom hooked nothing despite Calum's effortless success, Olive delivered a treatise on the different ways of round fish and their flat cousins, Donald gave a vivid account of landing a corpse on which mackerel had feasted and Cess heaved her breakfast into the water, which was pounced upon by thrilled gulls prompting Olive to switch from fish to why birds feed their chicks with regurgitated food. She also explained regurgitated. Tom asked whether chicks minded stuff that had been sicked up twice.

Avis sighed. 'Speaking personally, I think we've all had quite enough of rocking on the bosom of the deep.'

Henrysson's Rock looked paltry by comparison to its big sister Ailsa. Donald Begg thought so, too, and suggested that he took the party to another likely mackerel spot where they could picnic in the boat. All the women by this time were cross-legged. They were in sore need of concealing rocks. Calum had shown Tom how to cope over the leeward side. Mira said that Bruce had one of those, too, only his was enormous.

'Who is Bruce?' Avis asked, trying to appear calm.

'Uncle Willie's bull. He has the biggest winkie in the whole world.' Mira stretched her little arms as wide as they would go.

'Of course!' said Avis, somewhat relieved.

'My, you are a bright little button,' said Olive.

'Olive, please, please don't turn this into a biology lesson. Why don't you tell us about…oh I don't know, tell us something about Henrysson's Rock.'

'It's a wicked place,' said Donald, 'with a terrible reputation for terrible carryings-on.'

'Does anybody live there?' Tom asked. 'Look there's a hut behind those rocks.'

'Aye,' said Calum. 'It's just a wee shack. Maybe yon Parker uses it to store his poisons and the like. You couldna' bide there. Major Gilmerton used it for birdwatching.'

'He's the fellow that hanged hissel up at the big hoose,' added Donald. 'He was a rum one, for all his high and mighty ways.'

Avis signalled at him. 'Mr Begg, please. Remember what I said.'

'Och well, right you are, Mistress Wishart. You're the boss.'

Olive butted in brightly to ask whether anybody had heard of kelpies and water-horses? 'No, I thought not,' she answered herself, 'listen!'

These creatures, she said, went about luring children to ride them before galloping off back into the sea to eat them up. They spied on their potential prey from the water with one eye, looking rather like a jellyfish. 'You can spot a kelpie or a water-horse on land by its long dripping mane, though sometimes they disguise themselves as beautiful ladies and lure sailors into the deep, too.'

'Do the beautiful ladies eat the sailors?' Mira asked.

'I expect they change back into monsters first,' said Tom. 'It would be difficult for a lady to eat a sailor.'

'Not if she was a cannibal,' said Donald Begg.

★

Avis returned home clutching a soggy parcel of mackerel, a gift from Mrs Begg to repay her for the beans. The Wisharts had abundant beans because beans were Rodney's passion. He grew lots and applied himself to their cultivation with meticulous care, keeping an accurate log throughout their voyage from planting to plate.

Rodney was at the dining room table, calming himself after a highly frustrating day by stringing a mountain of runner beans and slicing them with mathematical precision.

Christopher Wishart was sulking in his room, gated. His escapade on the Lambretta had cost him and his pride dear. This week's Miss Firthside who'd been a willing participant in the venture had litigious parents determined to make something of her minor bruise and ruined stilettoes. The Windmill of Old Amsterdam lay in ruins, as did Christopher's plans for a school skiing trip at Christmas because he was now condemned to rebuild the windmill, albeit as a Crooked Little House, swap the scooter for a push-bike and appease the litigious family with his savings and new slingbacks for their daughter.

Avis sighed as she saw the bean mountain and gave her husband a kiss. Unable to forget Donald's story, she was off the idea of mackerel, particularly stout ones, but it looked as if fate dictated them for supper, especially as her sister-in-law, Maud Pollock, had called in a frenzy, at lunch time, with a punnet of surplus gooseberries. 'Just the thing with mackerel and beans,' said Rodney.

'But why the frenzy? Wasn't she having a restful day without Cecile and the child on her hands?'

'No, she wasn't. That chap Benjamin Troubadour had rung to say that he was on his way to visit his little niece.'

'The young man? The scientist? I thought he was in the States.'

'He's back and he wants to see Mira. Apparently Cecile had told Elvira to stay away and she was worried.'

'Poor woman.'

'Who?'

'Elvira, of course. She was absolutely all in when I collected Mira from her, but I could tell she was heartbroken to let her go and Mira is utterly devoted to her. I do hope that Benjamin sees that and insists on taking her back to London with him. After all, that was the original plan. She's a delightful child, but very complicated, precocious, and bright. I am afraid she and Cecile are utterly incompatible. I'm sorry for Cecile, too. She's been through a lot. I think she thought that having Mira live with her up here would compensate for something, or maybe lead on to something. She appears to have little else going for her except her dubious claim to a tragic past'

'Cecile tries too hard,' said Rodney.

'She tries too hard to be what she will never be. She's a donkey wanting to be a racehorse without the sense to see that she could be a delightful donkey.'

'Are you sure about that?'

'Not entirely.'

Later Rodney found Avis in their kitchen. 'Now, darling, you certainly do look all in. Let's get us a drink and then you can tell me about your excursion.'

For Avis there was no contest between missing the Archers and a chance to sit down with a welcome gin and orange. Their courting had been fuelled by gin and orange, when they could get hold of either, and it still induced a sort of contented melancholy of precious moments salvaged from amongst the bothersome bits of running their lives. They sat looking at the rose bed that Avis had succeeded in cultivating, isolated from the rest of their garden where ball games had worn bald patches in the lumpy lawn. Despite being less than half a mile from the shore, Ailsa Lodge had no sea view. Avis promised Rodney that one day they would grow old within sight of the sea.

'Now, tell me how things went on Henrysson's Rock. I'm all ears.' Rodney offered to light Avis's cigarette, she guided his hand, inhaled and watched the blue smoke rise and disperse.

'Well, Rodney, mooring was simple as it was almost high tide. the water was easily deep enough for at least an hour of picnicking and going behind rocks and Donald promised to return in plenty of time to take us all off. Then he and Calum chugged away to lift his lobster pots, but no sooner had the *Stupendous* left the jetty than the *Fair Irene* swept in with Ian Parker at the wheel, with a face like thunder and his ghastly, jaunty yachting cap. Once he realised that he could be seen the curtain rose on his habitual countenance of ebullient concern. "Ladies, ladies! Please take care. I implore you!" Why do you suppose the man talks like that, the worst of amateur theatrical courtiers? I said hello, calling him Mr Parker, to which he replied "Ian, please, dear Mrs Wishart." So I resolved to call him nothing, though nothing could stop Olive Smellie dashing forward, all flashing teeth and glittering specs and thrusting out her hand to introduce herself as a teacher at St Quivox and that she was just telling the children again about Henrysson's Rock being a fascinating volcanic plug.

'"Fascinating maybe, dear lady," the slug replied, "but exceptionally dangerous, positively toxic in fact. Please, I implore you go no further than this foreshore. The place is saturated with the most lethal rat poison on instruction from old Mr Henrysson himself, in a desperate attempt to rid the rock of these abominable and most dangerous of vermin."

'Personally, Rodney, I think that highly unlikely. The old boy hasn't taken an interest in anything, let alone rat-infested rocks, since poor Hughie died. Anyway, Ian was quite vehement. Then Olive became agitated and told the children that they must absolutely not to go exploring and began to list the horrors of bubonic plague and the dreadful consequences of mixing with rats. But only sulky Isa was there to listen. I expect she was hoping her mother would succumb to pestilential boils, because Tom and Mira had scampered off and were racing along the foreshore throwing seaweed at each other with Cecile lumbering in pursuit.

'Honestly, Rodney, I wouldn't have credited Ian Parker with being able to shout so loud. I reckon all Firthside could have been stopped in its tracks, though nothing, not even an explosion, could subdue those midges. They really are a curse and furthermore quite impervious to smoke, I smoked for Britain to no effect. Anyway, where was I? Oh yes, the shouting worked and Tom and Mira slunk back shepherded by Cecile, who looked scared out of her wits at doing anything to rile Ian, of whom she seems especially in awe. I wonder why. She's horribly eager to please. It's most off-putting. Anyway all was peace and harmony as I doled out the picnic, only I wish Tom would stop giving everything such repulsive names. Where does he get it from? I can't bear to tell you what he said about my home-made lemonade.'

'Boys will be boys, Avis.'

'Rodney! Did he learn that from you?'

'Possibly, or maybe from Christopher.'

'Sometimes I wish I'd had a daughter.'

'Like Cecile?'

'God forbid!'

'Go on, what happened when Parker discovered about Mira?'

'Well, I must give him credit for trying. He switched on his sickly charm and said he was delighted to meet the 'wee heiress,' and do you know what Mira replied?'

'I haven't a notion, tell me.'

'She said, very firmly, "No, I'm the bastard." Well of course that delighted me, stunned Ian Parker, outraged Cecile and got Olive all agog with facts about bars sinister and babies in warming pans which muddled everybody. I am devoted to Olive, but I wish she'd give the teacher in her a rest occasionally. Whiffy must get fed up with being crammed with information.'

'Whiffy has a head like a sieve, everything passes straight through. What happened then? How did you shake Parker off?'

'We didn't. We couldn't. He wouldn't budge until the *Stupendous* came back.'

'Did you ask after Irene and Tilda?'

'Well of course I wanted to, but somehow I didn't like to bring up the subject. I did ask how everybody was getting on, though.'

'And what did he say to that?'

'He said everything was as well as could be expected under

the circumstances and that time and travel are both great healers, oh yes, and there are consolations to be had on the Continent, whatever that was meant to imply. I rather got the impression that both Irene and Tilda had gone abroad, but whether together or apart I have no idea.'

'That is some weird marriage if marriage it is at all. We've had scant substantiation, only speculation. It can't last. Tilda will see sense and maybe Ian will go back to being Irene's poodle.'

'I hope you are right, Rod. He is not sporting a wedding ring, only the most ostentatious signet ring. So tasteless.'

'So what did you talk about? The weather?'

'We had a slightly awkward conversation about the difference between staying somewhere and living somewhere. I can't re-member how the argument went, but it ended with Mira asking if she could come and stay with us, and Cecile getting very red in the face and Ian Parker, much to everybody's surprise, saying how much he had enjoyed visiting Elvira in London. Most odd. Anyway I told little Mira that she could come and stay with us any time she liked, provided she asked Cecile first, and then I no-ticed that poor little Isa was dribbling blood and that we needed to get her to a doctor pretty sharpish. I rather hoped Ian would volunteer to take her and Olive to the shore in the *Fair Irene* but he was adamant and refused to move until Donald and Calum had come back with a boatload of lobster pots which left even less room for us passengers. Excuse me a moment, I must go and prod my pie. I think I can smell burning.'

Avis left Rodney watching Tom playing air cricket.

Avis returned, having saved the plum pie by scraping off the worst of the burnt bits. Rodney turned back from the window. 'So what happened?'

'When?'

'You were telling me about your journey home.'

'Oh yes of course, well it was the usual chaos .Whenever one wants children to hurry up, suddenly everybody disappears. I heard Cecile and Mira having quite a set-to about whether or not she could come here for the night. Naturally I had said we'd be delighted to have her any time. Goodness Mira has spirit, despite her size and angel face. She's quite devious, too, I think.'

'What makes you say that?'

'Well, I distinctly heard her ask Cecile not to hit her again, but I'm sure Cecile would never lift a finger to anyone, let alone a little girl, no matter how provoking.'

'You can't be sure, Avis. Not everybody is as self-possessed as you are.'

'I expect the child was exhausted. An early night will do her no harm. In fact we were all quite weary when the situation resolved itself with Ian volunteering to take the party from 'Dalmuirie Mains in his gin palace, which probably thrilled Cecile, leaving the rest of us and the picnic basket to cram into the cranky *Stupendous* along with those poor condemned lobsters which were quite distressing in a monstrous sort of way. Of course the *Fair Irene* outstripped us and Cecile's car had already gone by the time we docked at Dundrossan.

'We couldn't come home straight away because I had to drive Olive and Isa to Casualty in Dundoon. Olive was remarkably composed about the whole thing. Mild haemorrhaging is not uncommon following tonsillectomies, she said. I was very sorry for Isa, though. She was petrified, poor, over-informed, little scrap. She's OK, by the way. Olive has just rung to say that they are keeping her in overnight, but there is nothing to worry about. She also told me a lot of statistics about haemorrhages and cauterising. I'm afraid I was quite terse.'

'Quite right too, Avis! Now, tell me, do you honestly think that there is any chance that Mira will come to live up here?'

'I hope not, for everybody's sake, not least poor Willie and Maud. They like the child, don't get me wrong, but I don't think they reckoned on having their empty nest reoccupied by their daughter and a cuckoo who can't stand her. I really believe Mira hates Cecile. I can't see the situation changing either. You are bright, Rodney, what would you do? '

'I think we should wait and see. Who knows, maybe her feckless mother will reappear. She's the only one with a valid claim to the child. Blood ties really matter.'

'Charles Henrysson is her grandfather.'

'He doesn't count. This Benjamin fellow, Tilda's jilted boyfriend, may have a say in the matter, being her mother's brother.'

'I've heard he's a delightful young man, an academic scientist, just your type. But he's a bachelor; he doesn't need to be saddled with a child. So you see, apart from Cecile, albeit reluctantly aided by Maud and Willie, there is really only despised Elvira and of course, us.'

'No!'

'No?'

'Emphatically no, Avis.'

'But you don't mind her staying here the odd night.'

'Of course not, I'm delighted, but there is no question of her living here.'

'Rod, you are an angel. You always say the right things. What a relief. It still doesn't solve the problem of where the little girl is to go, nor would another drink, but I would love one anyway.'

'Of course. Sound scheme!'

'I'll take it with me while I get on with the cooking. Mackerel with beans and gooseberry sauce and plum pie in half an hour?'

★

Maud met Cess at the farmhouse door wearing her habitual floral pinny. Cess winced. 'I'm that glad to see you, Cecile! We've a visitor coming this evening. Did you have a nice boat trip? Where's the wee one?'

'She's staying with Auntie Avis tonight.'

'Why?'

'She just is. Don't worry about it.'

'I do worry, Cecile. You see, her Uncle Benjamin is coming here tonight especially to see her.'

'What? Why didn't you tell me? God! When is he coming?

Christ Almighty, why didn't you say? Here take this.' Cess thrust her seawater and sick-stained anorak at Maud and stamped up the stairs.

Willie was in the kitchen reading the *Scottish Farmer*. Maud went back to preparing supper. She wasn't going to pander to any transatlantic foibles: boiled fowl, parsley sauce and gooseberry pie would have to do any scientific young men arriving at short notice, even if his coming had caused her daughter to go berserk. She was delighted that at last there would be destiny for the bottle of Mateus Rose she'd won in a raffle and was longing to turn into a table lamp.

Ben had rung mid-morning. He sounded nice and explained that he'd been unable to get through on the telephone any earlier. He'd flown into London the day before and Elvira had suggested he come north to see his niece while the little girl was enjoying her seaside holiday. Maud wasn't surprised that her sister was behind this. So Elvira still thought Mira's stay was just a holiday. Poor soul. Maud found that for once she was quite sorry for Elvira. Maybe when Mira was settled and in school she could come and visit…then again, probably not.

Half an hour later Cess reappeared, with a bag of Mira's night things. Whatever she had attempted to do to her hair was not a success. 'I'll just nip these over to Aunt Avis.'

'Cecile dear, please fetch wee Mira back. Her uncle is coming all this way especially to see her.'

'He will have to wait till tomorrow. I'm not having her here being over-tired and silly.'

'She's only wee.'

'No, she's staying put and that's final. Ben will understand.'

'Will he?'

'Of course he will. Remember I am a professional.'

'So you tell us, but sometimes you know it's better not to do everything by the book.'

'No it's not! I'm right, I know what I am talking about. You don't! When is Ben arriving?'

'Soon I think. I don't even know how he is getting here.'

'You are hopeless!'

Cess slammed the door, rattling the trophy shelf. Willie looked up and asked what all the rumpus was about. Maud said it was love or maybe hormones, or both. Willie said he'd three cows waiting on the AI man.

★

When Cess appeared at Ailsa Lodge in a frantic rush, waving a carrier bag, Tom wasn't being a dancing class windmill or helicopter; he was the entire England team, bowling like a genius, batting prodigious sixes and standing in for his hero and fellow Scot, Mike Denness,

She shouted at him just as he threw himself to the ground and achieved an historic Ashes-winner of a catch. Reluctantly he came towards his cousin at the gate, while acknowledging the inaudible cheers and polishing the invisible ball on his corduroy shorts.

'Here Tom, give this to your mum!'

Not a please nor a thank you, just the abrupt command and she was gone. Her lank dampish hair still harboured a pink plastic roller clinging to the back of her head.

Tom chucked the bag beneath a laurel; the teddy bear inside could swell his ecstatic crowd of fans. He resumed his stylish approach to the invisible wicket, bowled a fiendish googly then, transforming himself into miracle batsman, hit yet another six.

Avis announcing supper stopped play. Virtual stumps were drawn. Autographs signed and the crowd dispersed. How they emptied the crammed stands was their affair.

Tom detested all fish that were not fingers, but a mackerel, almost caught by him, was different. He drew the line at gooseberries, especially those grown by fussy Auntie Maud, even though she didn't stink like Cousin Cess. Unlike her sister-in-law, Avis was not a good cook, but after so many years of marriage, a public school education and the war, Rodney was conditioned to leave a clean plate, though he was the only one to do so with gusto.

Baking the gooseberries into a pie did nothing for them or the pastry, which Avis had managed to convert to cardboard.

★

Cess realised, as she was driving home, that Ben would be expecting wine. Willie didn't go in for wine and Maud was very happy, and also got plenty happy, on the occasional cream sherry. Willie drank the odd dram to chase pints of heavy, but seldom at home. Jarring the brakes, Cess turned Maud's Austin back towards Dalmuirie.

Red or white, fizzy or flat, what would Ben expect? MacNab's Off Licence left her with little choice, Bull's Blood or Soave. 'I'll take both,' she said before discovering that she'd come out without any money. 'Please, let me have it, It's an emergency, I'll pay you tomorrow, I promise.'

Mr MacNab pointed at a notice. 'Please do not ask for credit. A refusal often offends,' and turning his back, asked if he could help the solitary next customer.

'Please, Mr MacNab. Here, take my watch. It's worth much more than the wine.'

'My dear young lady,' said a familiar voice, 'allow me please to spare you this embarrassment.'

'Mr Parker!'

'Call me Ian, my dear, please. We meet again. Here, let me. It will be scant repayment for the superlative picnic tea this afternoon.' He handed over a note and Mr MacNab put the bottles in a paper bag.

Mrs MacNab, the eyes and ears of Dalmuirie, came through from the stockroom. 'Why good evening, Mr Parker, we've not had the pleasure of seeing you for some time. I hope everything is in order at Nether Dalmuirie. You have been having a terrible time. We have all been thinking of the poor Gilmerton ladies. Was I not saying just that, last night after The News? Did I not say that no matter what terrible things are happening all over the world there is nothing to touch the tragedy right here?'

Mr MacNab grunted. 'Is it Johnnie Walker or Bells for you the day?'

'White Horse, Mr MacNab. I've only myself to please.'

'Are the ladies not at home then?' asked Mrs MacNab.

Without answering her question Ian told her that the house was all shut up, with a very sophisticated alarm system to detect intruders. 'I pass my time maintaining the grounds, for the moment.'

Cess was anxious to be off. 'Thank you very much. I'll pay you back, I promise. I'll bring the money tomorrow.'

'No! I forbid you to do any such thing. Remember that, if you wish us to remain friends.'

Ian followed Mr MacNab's quizzical gaze to where retreating Cess still had a plastic roller adhering to the back of her head. 'Ah', he said, 'we mere males are unable to question the whims of fashion to which the fairer sex are enslaved. Am I not right, Mr MacNab?'

★

Was it only a year since Ben had taken the same journey north, on the day after he'd buried his mother? Naturally he'd been sad then and anxious, too, but also hopeful. He had been going to see Tilda on his way to the States.

They had managed to meet briefly, as she was about to be discharged from hospital. but those minutes together had been enough to reassure them both that one day they would, should and must. be together. He had waved her goodbye as she was loaded into her homebound ambulance and then he'd imagined her waving to him as his plane rose from Prestwick and passed over Dalmuirie en route for the States. All had been well and all should have been well, as he crossed the Atlantic full of every kind of happy confidence.

As it turned out his fortunes, apart from his career, were in ruins by the time he boarded the eastward bound plane from the States a year later. Too much had happened in twelve months; events had stretched them into as many years.

Still recovering from the overnight flight, followed by a harrowing day and a second sleepless night. he felt like a man twice his age. His thick black hair had been invaded by white, his face was leaner, his nose more beaky and his irregular teeth looked yet larger, but his eyes, though red-rimmed with weariness, were as dark and bewitching as ever. The giggly girls on the train seat opposite certainly thought so.

He didn't notice. He stared unseeing at the passing of the Midlands, glassy Morecambe Bay, the layers of Lakeland hills, till the train climbed Shap and sped through Penrith to Carlisle and into Scotland. All the while, his mind was racing. He was too tired to think straight.

Since the last time he'd travelled north on the train, watching the Solway Firth disappear and be succeeded by wooded valleys and indifferent sheep grazing the Borders hills, he'd lost so much. Too much. He'd lost Tilda, his first and only ever love, and all his hope of that kind of happiness, unless there was to be a miracle.

He was a scientist, everything was miraculous, but he did not believe in miracles. He believed in something because he was yet to discover within himself, the ability to believe in nothing. His sister too was lost. Whatever way he looked at it, the Dora he'd known was gone. What remained? An adopted spinster aunt and a small child most unfortunately named Miracle whose own mother had called, accurately as it turned out, 'The Millstone'.

He'd only come back to make things tidy, sell the Wandsworth house and see that all was well with his aunt and niece. He'd had no reason to suspect otherwise despite the constant anxiety. Whatever happened, he knew Dora would never be able, or willing, to assume responsible parenthood. So, as long as Elvira was happy to have charge of Mira, and he saw no reason why not, that was the plan.

The sale of the house would provide enough funds, even though half the price achieved theoretically belonged to Dora. He'd set up a fund for Elvira to draw on for Mira's education and whatever children needed, about which he was extremely vague. Then, he thought, after maybe seeing a few of his old friends, he'd return to America and immerse himself in the work he loved, which from now onwards would replace all other forms of love in his life. It would be easy to get all this done, provided he didn't think too much and didn't go anywhere near Tilda, not even into the same country.

Yet here he was, not only in Scotland, but heading for Tilda's home, all because of Elvira.

Elvira had been utterly reasonable and sensible, completely credible, but miserable and anxious. She had also been impossible to disobey. Ben must go to Scotland, whatever it cost. She offered to pay. He refused of course, but he demanded to know why he had to go immediately. What was the urgency? Why didn't Elvira go herself? Then he offered to pay for her.

'Don't be ridiculous, Ben,' she replied, almost back to the vehement aunt who herded him and his sister round improving exhibitions and museums.

'All I want to know is that Mira is happy. All I want is for her to be happy and to have a happy upbringing. I thought she was happy with me. Maybe I was wrong. Or maybe I was wrong to consent to her going up to Scotland for a holiday. You see, originally the plan was for her to go north with my sister's very pleasant sister-in-law and then to be brought back to me by my niece Cecile. You know who I mean?'

'Yes, I remember. She was training as a nanny or something. I think she'd been at school with Tilda and her poor sister.'

'Yes, yes, wasn't that a dreadful tragedy? Let me continue before I forget what I am trying to tell you. I thought a week or so by the seaside would be fun for Mira. It would also give me time to get your place in Wandsworth ready for the market but then, Cecile rang me to say that Mira was not going to be coming back to me. She emphasised that, as she herself was a professional and more qualified to know about child-rearing, also that as Mira was just as closely related to her mother, my sister Maud, as she was to me, that her place from now onwards should be in Scotland. Oh she went on about the healthiness of country life, the joys of having an extended family, the excellence of Scottish education and so on. She didn't let me put a word in before she abruptly hung up. I've tried to contact her since, but I get nothing but rebuttals. My sister, at least, is civil; her daughter, however, is positively rude. Look, Ben dear, I don't mind, really I don't, as I said I only want little Mira to be happy and if, in your opinion, she is happy, really happy and doing well in Scotland so be it. I dare say the courts would endorse that, even if, or when, Dora returns, I suppose they would continue to find in favour of my sister's household. It looks better, healthier, too, I don't need to be told. But Ben, I do need to know if Mira is happy. You see it is quite possible to be unhappy in the very best of places.'

'Of course, I do understand, but what makes you think Mira is unhappy?'

'I've heard her.'

'I thought you said Cecile wouldn't let you speak to her.'

'She won't, but every time I do ring I hear Mira crying in the background. It is heart-breaking, Ben. I can't stand it. Perhaps I'm imagining things. Perhaps my old brain is playing tricks. I just want to know. Please Ben, please go and discover the truth, please find out what is going on and come back and tell me that I'm a fanciful, jealous, passed-over old stick and the sooner I subside into terminal senility the better.'

'I would never say that, Aunt Elvira, but I will go to Scotland, if only to put your mind at rest.'

'Ben, if you were silly enough to subscribe to such things, you'd be canonised. Now then I have a treat for you, a Dundee cake, your dear mother's favourite! Can I cut you a slice?'

★

At Carstairs, where the track divides beside the prison, Ben fell asleep and remained so till Central Station where he had to be roused by the ticket collector. He missed the first local train to Dundoon and caught the next, which stopped everywhere. Industrial legacy gave way to suburbia and coastal golf, till the train trundled into its last stop, where Ben was once more fast asleep. This time no ticket collector troubled him and it was only when a load of shrieking girls piled in for the return trip and an evening jaunt to Paisley that he realised where he was, that he got off and went in search of a taxi willing to take him the ten or so miles south to Mains of Dalmuirie.

The driver was a terse sort, dour even; he said nothing and drove regardless of his passenger, pedestrians, regulations or instructions. Aye, he knew the way. He also knew the longest and most profitable way of getting there, adding a further three miles by taking the coastal route and passing by the entrance to Firthside Camp, where a joker had removed the H and converted the 'I' of Firth into an 'A'.

The broken gates to Dalmuirie Castle hung open as they had done for a century, while those to Nether Dalmuirie House (which Ben recognised as Tilda's home address) were padlocked. Between the two gates stood the lodge, blinds down and showing little evidence of occupation. The taxi had to drive through Dalmuirie Village before doubling back upon the inland road to Mains of Dalmuirie. Two cars, a Jaguar and a battered Austin, were parked outside the MacNab's Off Sales. The rest of the place looked as dead as the bodies beneath the imposing memorials around the kirk.

Stopping at the farm gate, the driver refused to take his taxi through the farmyard to the house. Ben paid and approached the front door on foot, dodging chickens scratching for grubs in the dust. The door was open. A tantalising smell of cooking was emanating from somewhere: Campsie the collie, asleep beside her kennel, was drooling. The Ambridge cattle were lowing from an unseen radio while their Dalmuirie cousins answered from the byre across the yard.

Uncertain of what would be expected of him, Ben tried the knocker once or twice. Ambridge droned on; everyday country folk were far too busy to notice an unusual urban visitor.

He followed the lowing to a further range of buildings containing the milking parlour in which three cows were tethered contentedly chewing the cud. They gave him a languorous look with huge lash-fringed eyes, snorted, dribbled and went back to their ruminations. Ben followed a cluster of pipes into the next shed and found the refrigerated bulk tank and a man bending over a large metal flask. 'Ah there you are! You're awful late but never mind let's get on with it.'

'How do you do. I'm Ben.' He held out his hand.

'I'm Willlie Pollock. You're new, aren't you? Still you've got good hands for the job. I'd like to be able to do it myself, but with hands like mine, it's not fair on the cow. Come by now, where's your van?'

'I came in a taxi.'

'My, whatever next? Well, get your kit on.'

'Mr Pollock, I think there is some mistake. I'm Ben Troubadour, I've come to see my niece who is staying with you.'

'Och away with me. Here's me thinking you were the new in-seminator. So you are Ben, the scientist fella. I'm that pleased to see you, though right now I'd rather it was himself with the semen. Oh there's the AI van now, right enough. Excuse me. And there's the wife lifting tatties…Maudie! I've the wean's uncle here. Can you come and get him? I'll be in once we've got this lot sorted. She's a grand wee thing your niece, awful good with the beasts.'

Ben and Maud took to each other instantly. She was storybook farmer's wife, kind and capable, as warm and welcoming as her ample home baking. Apart from her race and gender, Maud bore no resemblance to her sister Elvira whatsoever. With increasing dread Ben was becoming convinced that this was the best place for a small child to be brought up. When Maud took him to the spare room, after showing him the room done up especially for Mira, he knew that he would have to break the bad news to Elvira, once he had witnessed Mira's happiness for himself. Maud said that Cecile would be back any minute. Ben hoped he'd be able to recognise her; more importantly would Mira remember him?

Cess drove into the yard just missing the departing AI van.

The driver waved and Cess told him to get out the bloody way. 'Give me cattle any day,' he told his faithful terrier.

'There you are, Cecile! Where's wee Mira?'

'I told you, Mum, didn't I, she's staying the night with Aunt Avis.'

'But her uncle has come all this way specially to see her.'

'He's here already?'

'Yes, I've just shown him to the spare room. He'll be down directly.'

'Oh Christ!'

'Hello, Cecile.'

She looked up and saw him. it all came back. How could she ever have thought that there was anybody else for her? A god made flesh with a hooky nose and squint teeth, sheer perfection in human form.

'Ben!'

She moved forward, hoping for a kiss. He held out his hand. Her face was on fire.

'Wait, darling!' It was Maud. 'Hang on a minute!'

Too late, as Cess lunged towards Ben the plastic roller sprang from the back of her head and bounced to the ground.

Ben dodged the kiss by stooping to pick it up and gave it back to Cess, who feigned total ignorance and tossed it to Campsie the collie. The kissing moment was passed.

'Away with you two while I get the supper sorted,' said Maud. 'You'll be wanting a bit of fresh air after your journey.'

★

They leant on a fence and gazed at distant cattle.

Beyond the cows there was a wood and beyond that? Tilda, of course. Ben knew the geography even though he was a stranger to the place and would make sure he was so again tomorrow, for ever. He turned from looking south to the west, where the sun appeared to be swelling as it started to sink. Cecile was talking. he must pay attention and try not think about the gulf between her and Tilda, so great that they could have been separate species.

'The reason Mira hasn't come home with me is that she is too frightened of you taking her back to London. Poor little thing, she hates living there. Oh, and Ben, there's a nasty bruise on her face. Now, I'm not saying Aunt Elvira is responsible for it, but everything points that way. Please don't question Mira about it. these things are best left alone. Unsupervised rehearsal of trauma is ill-advised with the vulnerable. It would be quite wrong to make too much of that sort of incident. One must avoid the subjective attribution of importance to life events, thereby initiating fixation.'

Ben didn't listen to the textbook gabble. he knew that what he was hearing meant it would be his duty to tell Elvira that Mira was not being returned to her care. Cess moved her hand along the fence towards his. 'I do know what I am saying. I am trained and experienced. I can empathise,' she said. 'Apart from needing a nuclear family, a dependable parent figure and role model, the child requires the interaction of kinship and peer groups within an extended family and secure environment in which to develop and thrive. None of which an aging spinster, like Aunt Elvira, can deliver. Whereas I, Ben, can deliver it all, and more too. ' She told him that she was prepared to dedicate herself entirely to Mira, adding, possibly too quietly for him to hear, 'for your sake, Ben'.

She then switched on a smile that didn't involve her pink and watery eyes fenced that evening by wandering lapis blue mascara. Teenage acne had left an oily legacy of open pores; a bit of carrot clung to her front teeth. Ben tried not to recoil from the sickly-sweet smell of her. Poor soul, she was a wreck. Still, he supposed she was talking sense; this place, with these people, would be preferable to London for a child like Mira.

Cess landed her hand on his in a gesture of empathy not in-cluded in the manual that counselled caution when invading personal space. Ben snatched his away, pretending to stifle a sneeze. 'I'd like to call Aunt El, please.'

'What for?'

'I promised I would.'

'There is no need.'
'I promised.'
'Mum has supper ready. Wait till after.'

Elvira had waited all day for Ben's promised call, even though she knew he couldn't possibly ring before seven at the very earliest. She'd paced the house attempting to concentrate upon long overdue tidying jobs. She cleaned everywhere, hating each moment, and wondered whether she should pass the time by going to the Academy Cinema on Oxford Street and seeing something intellectual, the sort of clever, ponderous hand-held camera stuff she couldn't do with Mira in tow. There were lots of things like that, but she didn't want any of them. No matinee, exhibition, concert had any appeal. She wanted to do childish things that adults didn't do without a child. Lonely people are advised to get dogs. Elvira wasn't the sort to give her heart to a dog to tear; her heart had already been torn by a child.

Seven came and went and so did eight: still nothing. She would be bold, she'd ring. Maybe that's what they'd arranged. She couldn't remember. Anyway, she could always say that she'd thought that was how they'd planned it to be. After all, it would have been difficult for Ben to ask if he could use the farmhouse phone, even if he did offer to pay or reverse the charges. But supposing she didn't get to speak to Ben, supposing she was fobbed off with chatting stiltedly to Maud or trying to understand what Willie was saying or, worse still, being insulted by Cecile. At eight thirty Elvira was just about to lift the receiver when the telephone rang. She answered, O joy! It was Ben.

Everything was fine, he said, his journey, the weather everything.

And Mira? How was she?

Ben said she was fine, too.

Did she look well? Elvira asked, unable to bring herself to say what she really wanted to know. Was Mira happy? Happy enough to stay in Scotland? For ever?

'I haven't seen Mira yet, Aunt E. She's staying the night with her cousins, the Wisharts. Apparently when Cecile went to fetch her she was having such a lovely time with the other children that it seemed unkind to take her away. Cecile told me herself. Would you like to hear it from her?'

'No Ben, I believe you. But when will you see Mira?'

'Tomorrow, early, before I catch the train back south.'

'You are coming back so soon?'

'Yes.'

'Why?'

'Things.'

'I see.' Elvira knew he meant Tilda, but she was too flustered to worry about that now.

'Ben, are you absolutely sure Mira is all right?'

'One hundred per cent. I promise you. Like I said, Mira pleaded to stay the night with her cousins, you know what children are. Cecile discussed it all with Mrs Wishart and she said it was perfectly fine. You said you liked Mrs Wishart yourself.'

'Yes, very much, but...oh, never mind.'

'Listen, Aunt El, I must go. These long distance calls cost a fortune. See you tomorrow. We'll discuss it all then, don't worry.'

But Ben did not tell Elvira everything. He couldn't say what Cecile had confided in the garden before supper about who she said was responsible for the bruise on Mira's face. It would be too cruel.

Everything shrivelled inside Elvira while her heart thumped a funereal beat and her stomach sank with all her hopes. Her body, like her life, was no more than an empty purposeless husk. There was no point to any of it, there never had been and never would be, ever again, apart from that brief episode when she had been indispensable. That had been an illusion; she had deceived herself with silly dreams. She longed for darkness, for oblivion and the death of remorse. She recalled those awful words – It might have been.

The summer evening was beautiful, still light but quiet enough to hear passing footsteps and small birds twittering. Other people were going to places, meeting friends, doing things. Elvira stood sightlessly staring at the street, abandoned and invisible.

She knew she wouldn't sleep. She couldn't do anything except exist, a good-for-nothing nuisance, a waste of space, a squanderer of air.

A young child in the house opposite, put to bed maybe for being naughty, was venting its misery into the warm evening. It was not Elvira's place to offer the child comfort in its anguish. The sound of weeping pierced her soul, she closed her window to stifle it. But it was still in her head; it was as if Mira was crying for help.

There was something she could do. She could risk everything and ring Avis Wishart. She had no more to lose. In the end, one only ever regrets things not done.

A man answered. He sounded English. Had she got the code wrong? 'I'm sorry to bother you so late, but could I possibly speak to Mrs Wishart?'

'Of course, who shall I say is calling?'

Elvira heard Commander Wishart call to his wife, 'Avis, can you have a word with Miss Troubadour?' Then he said, 'She's just coming. Aren't we having perfect weather?'

Elvira agreed and then heard the receiver being transferred. What was she going to say?

'Mrs Wishart?'

'Please, Elvira, call me Avis. How nice to hear you. I can't tell you what fun we had today with your little Mira. She really is a delightful child. We all went on a boating trip and had a picnic. Such a sporting little girl, gets on so well with everybody.'

Her little Mira? How kind to imply that little Mira was hers. Yes, Elvira did like Avis Wishart.

'I was wondering if I could possibly say hello to her. I know it is silly but I really would love to speak to her, just for a minute.'

'Of course, but I expect she's tucked up in bed by now and fast asleep.'

'Oh, I see. I'm sorry er…Avis. Could you possibly go and look, just in case she is still awake?'

'I would if I could Elvira, of course. But Mira is not here. Cecile took her back to my brother's farm after picnicking on Henrysson's Rock. They were transported in great style in a very smart boat while the rest of us returned to the harbour in a very fishy one full of lobster pots. Elvira? What is it? Are you all right?'

★

Earlier that afternoon while the party had been packing up on Henrysson's Rock, there had been an awful lot of shouting. Mr Parker shouted at every one to get down to the boats quickly. 'Time and tide, ladies and gents, please!' Donald Begg was blunter. 'Ye'll need tae get a move on, if you dinna want to walk hame once the tide's oot. I'm no waiting on you.' Avis was organising the packing up and Mrs Smellie was telling poor wee Isa, blood dribbling from her mouth, that there was nothing to worry about.

Cess was trying to motivate Mira into getting aboard the *Fair Irene*. 'For God's sake, child, do what you are told.'

'No! I am going with Auntie Bird.'

'No, you are coming with me.'

'No! I hate you.'

'What did you say?'

'I hate you and I am going with Auntie Bird.'

'How dare you say that.'

'It's true. I hate you. Please don't hit me again!'

Cess looked round. Nobody appeared to be listening. Ian Parker was getting yet more insistent. There was nothing she could do.

'You are a little liar. Have it your own way. Go on...get lost!'

For once Mira had done as she had been told.

★

Cushions of sea pinks grew amongst the rocks, some daisies, too, and yellow flowers that weren't buttercups. Aunt Maud said they were called bacon and eggs because the eggy-shaped flowers had tiny red bits on them. Granny had liked flowers, too, and grew lots of orange nasties in her garden. You could eat their leaves, but they weren't very nice. Aunt El liked red dailies best, but didn't have a garden, just the airy with a bay tree in a tub. Those leaves were nasty, too.

Once Mira thought she had been hidden long enough she shouted 'Cooee' because that meant people would start looking for her. That, and counting lots of numbers with your eyes shut, before shouting 'A hundred, I'm coming ready or not,' were all the rules of Hide and Seek. In Hunt the Thimble you had to say whether people were hot or cold, in Hide and Seek you said 'Cooee' again if it was taking a long time to find you. Jumping out and surprising your finders was, after all, the best bit.

Mira shouted, 'Cooee', many times. Only gulls replied.

Eventually she left her hiding place and wandered back to their picnic spot on the beach where the same gulls had demolished all the leftovers. There was nobody there. The water was just a little further away beyond a barrier of crackly seaweed. The ridges of damp, grey sand reminded her of Tam Westcroft's new corduroy shorts for school. Little waves lapped the shore without breaking, carrying multi-coloured jellyfish amongst the floating detritus. Sandy spaghetti strings of knotty worm casts had erupted where the tide retreated. The mainland was slowly, very slowly, coming closer as the island shore grew wider inch by inch.

Mira sat down and waited. She drew an M with a stick in the sand. It was lonely to have nobody to admire it. Aunt El had made her learn her address and telephone number in case she got lost. That didn't help if there was nobody about. When Dora had forgotten Christmas or gone away and left her alone, there had been kind neighbours ready to help.

The air was getting chilly; soon the sun would sink below the rock. Mira was frightened of the dark and her fear grew, along with her shadow.

Aunt El used to sing a song about whistling when you felt afraid. Mira couldn't whistle, but she tried to sing about humpy backed camels and chimpanzees and Noah filling his ark with them and green alligators and long necked geese, too. It was a sad song because the unicorns got left behind because they played silly games.

Mira shouted 'cooee' again and then…there it was.

A figure looking down from the top of the rock, dark and silent, blocking out the sun. An evil angel with a tangled halo of black hair.

Dora was standing there against the light.

At first Mira was paralysed, then she began to run towards the sea, losing both sandals in the weedy barrier. She careered on, impervious to a bleeding cut on her leg and the slicing pain of ridged sand on bare feet. She rushed into the sea, but a water-horse's eye was ready for her. Her screams joined the chorus of shrieking banshee gulls. On she ran, blind to rocks until she was tripped by a half-buried branch of drift wood. She was done for, lying face down on wet sand, incapable, spent and waiting.

A pair of bony arms encased her and held her tight.

They were not Dora's arms, nor was it Dora's voice that called her by her name. It was someone else, half familiar, yet unknown, skeleton thin with short cropped hair, androgynous. It was a kind voice, a beguiling voice, the deceiving voice of a hungry kelpie.

The voice murmured deceptive words of comfort, telling her that everything was going to be all right.

Exhausted, eventually Mira's sobbing stopped.

'Don't you know who I am?'

'A kelpie?'

'No, not a kelpie.'

'Are you going to eat me?'

'No, never, Mira. Why would I do that?'

'Kelpies do. They eat people.'

'Good Fairies don't. Do you know the story of Cinderella?'

Mira nodded her head.

'Well then, you should know what I am.'

The good fairies and fairy godmothers that Mira knew about were all sparkly in net dresses with wands and wings. But, whoever this was could read thoughts. Without being asked, this creature told Mira that it was in disguise and like all fairies, it was going to let her have three wishes, but only if Mira promised never, ever, to tell anybody anywhere anything at all about the things she'd seen and heard.

'Can you keep a secret, Mira?'

Mira nodded her head again.

'Promise?'

More nods.

'Good, because if you do break a promise or tell a secret all the worst things in the world will happen to you and none of your wishes will come true. Now then, what are your wishes?'

'I don't want to be with Dora ever again.'

'And the next wish?'

'I don't want to ever, ever live with Cess.'

'I see, and your third wish? Think carefully before you answer. I've heard of two things you don't want but what about something you do want, more than anything?'

Mira didn't need to think. She knew exactly what to say. 'I want to live with Aunt El for ever and ever Amen.'

It really was getting dark now. Had Mira dared to look up to the top of the rock she would have seen that both the figure of Dora and the sun had disappeared. As it was, she and the fairy stared ahead across the haunted ribbon of water towards the empty mainland shore.

'We'll wait together here, Mira. It will be all right, believe me.'

'When?'

'We'll just have to be patient. Tell me about your Aunt El. No? Well, perhaps you can sing me a song or tell me a story. What's your favourite?'

But the Grandest Tigers wouldn't come, nor would silly Chicken Licken and Mira could only remember the horrible Troll and not the cuddly Billy Goats Gruff, which made everything worse. Peter Rabbit and Mrs Tiggywinkle had gone into hiding, too.

They sat there for hours, or so it seemed. A full moon had risen and daylight had died when something could be seen splashing through the shallows.

'Oh look, Mira! Help is coming. Now stand here like a good girl. Be very, very good, won't you? Remember never ever tell anybody anything about what you have seen here today. Tell me you promise.'

'I promise. What is that? ' Mira pointed at the figure crossing the water as if rising out of the sea.

'Mira, let go! Please.'

'No. It's a water-horse!'

'Please, Mira, go and meet him. There is no water-horse here.'

'Yes there is. I've seen his eye.'

The water-horse reached the rock and transformed into a man walking, dripping wet, towards where the pair were hiding.

'Mira! Mira, where are you? Mira!' it said in a deceivingly man-like voice.

'Go to him, Mira.'

'No!'

It was coming closer. The features were quite plainly those of a dark-haired man. 'Look Mira! Can't you see who it is?'

'Who?'

'Come. Don't be afraid. It's your Uncle Ben. It really is. You'll be safe now with him, Mira. Don't forget your promise.'

When they got to where Ben was standing Mira was handed over without a word, or a touch, or a smile, or any acknowledgement of what had been seen.

Ben knelt down and wrapped his arms around the little, shivering child. She was freezing cold, scared and scarred. This was the child his sister had named Miracle, then abandoned.

Ben looked up and saw a void. There was nobody there, then or ever more, nothing for him to know, or understand…except that Miracle was his millstone now.

Part Two

Introduction

Ben's obituaries multiplied as the Washington cherry trees blossomed.

My uncle was at the height of his career and popularity when he was murdered there. The nutter who shot him then turned his gun on himself and saved the state a deal of expense.

Benjamin Troubadour, arguably the most recognisable celebrity scientist of our time – intellectual lightweight or genius? Our future must be his judge. Will his legacy be his works? Or will he be remembered for his engaging personality snuffed out as the random victim of a drug-crazed drop-out?

Troubadour's talent for communication was responsible for introducing many people to his subject. A popular presenter and an enigmatic lecturer; he could expound upon the obscure and esoteric in such a way that even those with no scientific education or background were transfixed. His murder at the age of 68 has horrified millions; his distinctive looks and voice were known world-wide, he had a following akin to that of a film star and yet he was modest and retiring, enjoying a quiet life of study within his close circle. Born Binjamin Warschauer, the posthumous son of Abram Warschauer a Polish surgeon, he and his sister arrived in England with their Portuguese mother in 1945 where the children were adopted by her second husband, Major Herbert Troubadour. Benjamin as he was then known, displayed a precocious aptitude for science and completed his education at Imperial College after which he pursued an academic career in the United States and South America devoting himself to the study of asteroids and inter galactic meteorites. For many years Benjamin Troubadour lived with his aunt by adoption, his niece and his housekeeper. This quartet travelled extensively but in recent years Troubadour divided his time between Mexico and New York City. He was unmarried.

'Whilst Troubadour's propositions were sometimes vilified as insubstantial his calculations were elegant, meticulously defined and exhaustively researched. A glib exterior belied the rigour of his irreproachable academic credentials.'

'Was rock doc gay?'

'His faith sustained him.'

'An enlightened agnostic'

'A beacon of humanism.'

'Prof was no poof.'

'Our world has been robbed.'

'Unassuming genius or genial showman? The debate continues.'

'What Harry Potter did for the arts Ben, Troubadour did for the sciences.'

'Counselling offered to grieving fans.'

'His loss is felt keenly by us all.'

'Benjamin Troubadour was unique.'

I made a collection of cuttings; they filled a file. It seemed that every journal and newspaper had something to say. Nothing written or declaimed was original, several tributes cited broken moulds. Many opined that we'd not be seeing his like again, not one of them was accurate; nobody really knew him. Neither did I.

★

I suppose we were a weird household, Professor Ben Troubadour, his maiden aunt Elvira, me (his little niece) and later, Sojourner, a large and joyful West Indian who arrived when I was about eight, while we were living in the suburbs of Boston.

Sojourner stayed. At first I think she had imposed herself as Ben's girlfriend, a role that later developed into his manager and agent, a job that she did extremely efficiently, albeit somewhat ferociously. She may have started out working in welfare as some sort of social worker, she certainly wasn't anything domestic. We all had separate bedrooms but I think Sojourner and Ben were occasional lovers. She certainly adored him, accompanied him everywhere and protected him from fans, loons and all sorts of predators, except the last. His followers ranged from besotted youths and autograph hunters to women wanting to have his babies. Sojourner taught me those bits about life and growing up which remained a closed book to my devoted and dedicated Aunt El.

I can recall no complications about setting up this arrangement though I imagine it entailed quite a deal of bureaucratic wrangling to get me and my adopted aunt to cross the Atlantic. Once there, Aunt El never returned to the UK which, apart from one brief trip to France before World War Two, she'd never left before.

She must have sold up everything, sacrificed the lot, to be with me and bring me up in the place of my disappeared and feckless mother. I hope she knew how much I owed and loved her. She died aged eighty-two having lived long enough to see me fulfil my ambition as a dancer and to know that I would never make it on the stage. She had encouraged me to follow my dream despite expressing a hope that I would not turn into 'another vulgar chorus girl'.

Aunt El did not talk much about her past but we all knew that her true love had been snatched from her by the younger member of a sister song and dance act, which almost topped the bill in seaside variety.

At first we three crammed into a service house in Arizona, a little ticky-tacky type box surrounded by scrubby grass. Our neighbours sprinkled, we did not, so our garden merged with the desert. Aunt El must have hated it. Then I think our next home was somewhere in Virginia, before Ben got an academic post in Boston and I learnt to sing The *Star Spangled Banner* as the flag was hoisted at school every morning. We first went to New York City when I was in 7th Grade and there I took more advanced ballet classes. I must have been promising because I recall the uproar when I was told we were moving on to Mexico and I had to relinquish the place I'd gained at ballet school.

Somehow, wherever we went, Mexico, Chile and Ecuador (where both Aunt El and Sojourner suffered horribly from the altitude at Quito) they managed to find me a dance class but the early promise did not endure. My height was not a factor in my failure to become a star; I stopped growing at five foot three. At college I majored in modern languages.

I travelled a lot and worked where I could. I did a bit of teaching and earned my living doing translation work, sharing apartments with friends. But home was always with Ben. I look a lot like him (apart from my eyes and straightened teeth) and many people assumed I was his child. I'm dark too but few would conclude that Sojourner, who towered impressively over us all, was my mother.

When Ben was killed in 2006, I was lost. Everything I'd relied upon had evaporated. I was immensely thankful that Aunt El hadn't survived to endure the insult of his inglorious end, shot at random by an inadequate on a spree. Elvira's appetite for heroism and valour would have been outraged to learn that her beloved nephew had been felled for no more than a fake designer watch.

Sojourner packed up and decided to rejoin her vast Jamaican

family, announcing henceforward her perpetual celibacy. 'My mission is accomplished. My life's love is over.' Before she went Sojourner, got things straight and, as ever, told me what to do.

'Quit this translation nonsense,' she commanded, 'write Ben's story. The world needs to hear your voice, not the voices of furry critters and cute reptiles.'

I had recently finished translating the improving adventures of a particularly didactic iguana called Dolores and her buddy, Juan (an earnest llama) for the Brazilian market and would have welcomed any change of job but having never written anything of my own, I was at a loss where to start.

Aunt El had been the writer in our household. Her stuff rhymed. She never published but did win a competition for a peon to a bar-becue relish and sold some soppy rhymes for greeting cards. She specialised in botanically inaccurate, pastoral verse and privately went in for random epithalamia into which she always contrived to insert a note of snide. Her true love had expressed himself in pom-pom dahlias in August 1944 and again that September to the cheap hussy who sang vulgar songs in variety shows.

She rarely spoke about the past except occasionally, when fuelled by sherry. Firstly, she was not my real aunt, or more accurately, not my real great aunt. My Uncle Ben and his sister Dorabella (my mother) had been adopted by Aunt El's brother when he married my widowed, Portuguese grandmother, Valdite Warschauer. I remember Granny but I'm hazy about Grandpa Troubadour; he had no legs. He died two years before Granny who I remembered dying, with yellow eyes, when I was four.

I knew Aunt El had a sister called Maud Pollock in Scotland who'd married a farmer and gone rustic, a most derogatory epithet in Aunt El's lexicon. I don't recall much grief when the Pollocks were killed in a car wreck; Aunt El disapproved of ostentatious emotion. But I do remember her saying that their only child, a daughter, was untrustworthy and that she was not leaving her a single penny of her non-existent fortune, even though she was the last of her line. However, Aunt El did approve of a woman called Avis who was Maud's surprisingly cultivated sister-in-law and married to a charming naval commander.

I knew that my father had lived in a castle in Scotland and was dead too and that he had not been married to my mother. I also knew that there had been a woman in Ben's life that nobody was allowed to mention and I knew, or rather didn't know, anything about my mother and did not wish to know anything about her. Only news of her death and reassurance that she was never coming back would have been welcome. The threat of her re-appearance had dogged my life since I last saw her, before I had turned five. Now, it is 2008. I am thirty-nine.

Ben was dead and so was Aunt El when I wed Pete Staple, how she would have revelled in the brevity of our union.

I was stupid to marry Pete who was not a fixed point in my featureless future. The staple that held us together was feeble, merely a mutual need for stability. All my previous relationships had been transitory but now I wanted a home. I didn't need to find a base until I realised that Aunt El, Ben and Sojourner were no longer there and that I belonged nowhere.

Pete was rumoured to have been engaged before to someone as suitable as I was not, but things had gone wrong between them. Later Pete accused me of stealing him from this golden girl called Barbara and blamed me for her descent into suicidal depression. I began to believe this to be the truth when the poor woman did succeed in taking enough pills. I felt terrible and Pete enjoyed making me guilty, he enjoyed taunting me for being an inferior imposter, inadequate in all ways. Pete's suspicious paranoia was matched by his aspiring infidelities; it was exhausting. Desire dwindled with the bride cake and the man with whom I'd briefly lived harmoniously in satisfying carnality, lost all interest in a loving, sexual relationship and frankly, I couldn't be bothered to attempt to re-ignite his desire.

It was my fault for imagining I could create a rock from a sand-hill and a lover out of suffocating vapour.

Had my body kept a grip on the baby, things could have been

different but that hope evaporated too, in a painful bloody mess, after two months of bloated nausea.

Had Pete lost his job I might have tried to stick with him for longer, but he didn't, unlike so many others. So I felt free to go, while he continued earning substantial sums. I would have worried about leaving him if he had failed, he was weak and I would have felt mean.

My flight must have thrilled his gold worshiping, status enhanced, snobbish family who put it about that I'd been a burlesque artiste wielding a feather fan, when the only feathers I'd worn were those of the shortest, boob-less cygnet in a low budget *Swan Lake* many miles from the Met.

The Staples had just forgiven me for being a bastard because my late father had fulfilled their aspiration by living in a Scottish castle, even though it was a tumbledown draught trap, inherited by bankrupts. Pete's folk worshiped at designer God who was white, spoke English and probably created everything in six days so He could play golf on the seventh. Their lives pivoted upon real estate prices, country club membership and the Right, which was always right.

Despite our split being inevitable Pete had insisted on taking me to the terminal, perhaps he wanted to make sure that I disappeared. After a perfunctory kiss, he turned and walked away clamping his ear to his mobile and waving his free, gold-ringed hand while eyeing a lanky, androgynous blonde. 'Missing you already!'

Dalmuirie Summer 2008

*T*he receptionist's plaid vest could not contain her exuberant flesh, she beamed at me with a cheerfulness that contrasted with my jet-lag. I knew my eyes were bloodshot and I suspected my breath was beyond the smothering reach of mints.

She looked up from her screen and smiled, her lapel badge said she was Yvonne, Manageress.

'Welcome to Dalmuirie House. May I have your name?'

'Staple, I booked online.'

I gave my married name. I've grown to hate the recognition and the assumptions that go with being Ben's niece and having to explain why I too am called Troubadour. Many people assumed I was his child anyway. So what? That didn't matter. I just hated the way they expected me to be his clone, someone whose math went further than the quadratic equation and who could converse about doings beyond my earthy universe.

'You'll be here for the funeral I guess?'

'I beg your pardon.'

'The funeral, Mr Parker's funeral, it'll be a big affair. It has all been shocking and awful unexpected. One minute, not more than a week ago, he was carrying on, larger than life and the next, there he was – dead. There's no telling when we'll be called to our reward, as my Mum used to say every time she forced us bairns into Sunday school.'

'But I made my booking three weeks ago.'

'Ah yes, Miss Staple, I have it here. A room with bath for a week.'

'It's Mrs.'

'Sorry, my mistake. Will Mr Staple not be joining you?'

'No.'

'That's grand then. Matilda is comfortable but not spacious.'

'Pardon me?'

'Your room, it is called Matilda.' Yvonne's name badge quivered as she sighed and asked me again whether I was to be included in the funeral arrangements.

'I do not know Mr Parker, I never met him.' Then, thinking I'd been harsh, I added that I was sorry he was dead. 'A sad loss for his family I'm sure.'

'Personally, I wouldn't go as far as that. I'll get Calum to show you to Matilda.'

'Why is the room named Matilda?'

'It belonged to a wee girl called Matilda before this place was a hotel.'

'What happened to her?'

Yvonne shrugged. 'Who knows? I'm not from hereabouts. She'll be getting on now, I reckon.'

A gnome was applying polish to the glass door and rubbing vigorously to display the hotel's engraved logo. Yvonne rang a bell, the gnome sighed, put down his duster and hobbled across to the desk. 'Was there something?'

'Calum, take Mrs Staple up to Matilda.'

Calum glared. I felt very sorry for him, he was exceptionally decrepit. 'No please don't bother, I'll find my way, I can manage my bag, just show me to the elevator.'

'There's nae lift at Dalmuirie Hoose – never has been, and I've known this place ever since it was turned into a hotel. It's a disgrace!'

'Well then, perhaps you know what happened to Matilda,' I said, picking up my case.

'Calum, please take Mrs Staple to the first floor.'

'Yin of yon's Matilda.'

Calum pointed at a large portrait of a stiff 1950s' family group. It was a really gross conversation piece, depicting a father, a mother and their two daughters. One was lanky and fair, the other dark. Both were dressed in striped, puff-sleeve dresses with stick-out skirts, white bobby socks and patent bar-strap shoes. An unbelievable dog sat on the mother's knee with bangs tied back in a ribbon similar to the ones worn by the little girls.

'Excuse me?'

'Matilda, she was the bigger yin o' they wee lassies. That's her mammy and yon sodger at the back is their da only he was deid.'

'I'm sorry?'

'Deid. No more. Passed over, gathered. He…'

'Calum! Sorry Mrs Staple, what Calum means is that the picture of the gentleman in uniform was painted posthumously.'

'He hanged hissel.'

'Calum there is no need to go into that, Mrs Staple must be exhausted after her journey. Here, let me show you to your room, give me your case. This way please.' Yvonne bustled me towards the stairs leaving Calum to mutter behind us 'Oot there in the garden.'

'You mustn't mind Calum. He only works here part-time. He is a touch fanciful. Dalmuirie House Hotel is an equal opportunity employer you understand. Interestingly enough that picture was painted by the late Mr Parker whose funeral is this week.'

'To which I am not going.'

'Quite.'

Sitting upon the double bed I felt horribly alone, a Hopper woman for the twenty-first century except I was not on my own in an indifferent city, amongst cheap rooming houses and diners, I was alone in South West Scotland, on a whim.

What had possessed me to come?

The business I had to transact required no face to face encounters and anyway, my business was exceptionally minor. Perhaps I should explain.

I don't think I ever met my father but I do remember being

taken by two women, neither of them my beloved Aunt Elvira, but known to me as Aunties, to visit an incredibly old man with watery eyes and a nose like a bruised orange and being told that he was my grandfather. This had puzzled me because I'd already had one of those who had died when I was a baby of three. I was now four, almost five and undoubtedly grown up. My dead grandfather used to laugh when I kicked his tin legs. This one didn't because his legs were his own. Despite this, I learnt later that he had designated me to be his residuary legatee which was a magnanimous gesture to his illegitimate but solitary descendant, though the residual legacy, into which I came on achieving years of discretion, was so discreet as to be negligible.

I wouldn't have come had Sojourner not insisted I investigate my roots. 'Get in there, girl! Find out where you belong. You might uncover something interesting, something you can call your own. You don't want to go through life just being your Uncle Ben's niece.

Sojourner had already made it plain that she had every intention of living out the rest of her days claiming to be Professor Troubadour's unwed widow. 'He was the love of my life, Mira, but I was not the love of his.' Whenever Sojourner said this I would reply that he was wed to his work but both of us knew that this was not entirely true, there had been someone, long ago, who had let him down and whoever this monstrous, treacherous harridan (according to Aunt Elvira) may have been, was never to be mentioned. Sojourner had been his bastion against the onslaught of others. 'I'm old, miracle child. I've had my day. I'm going home to dwell on my past, show off my scars, lick wounds and pray for his immortal soul.'

When I asked her whether she was going to investigate her own roots she said that she was fed to her teeth with folks going on about slavery and plantations and so forth and she had no desire to uncover any more wickedness committed by anyone in the eighteenth century, the twentieth having been sufficiently evil to be going on with. She disapproved then of the internet as much as she did of all things Bush, fundamentally Christian, or picky with food. Recently, I gather, she has plans to return to city life, conquer cyberspace and campaign for the Democrats, none of which surprises me as I am sure she'd be bored back home with the family she abandoned in her youth. We do keep in touch but only by mail or cell phone. Her conquest of cyberspace, like the apartment in the meat-packing district of Manhattan, is still conceptual.

The letter about my Scottish property, 'a small parcel without residential or agricultural potential and scant amenity value', had arrived after Ben's death and been forwarded to me by the attorney acting as his executor, a lazy man with whom I'd had no previous business. The letter had already taken over nine months to reach me. I didn't detect much urgency. Had it been a very small parcel of Manhattan, things would have been different. Apparently 'enquiries had been made by a party interested in acquiring the aforementioned property,' according to Mr Wallace-Falkirk, Writer to the Signet, of Wallace-Falkirk and Company. No sum had been mentioned nor did Mr Wallace-Falkirk suggest the purpose to which the amorphous party was going to put my useless parcel. It all seemed highly unlikely; I hadn't bothered to reply. I rather enjoy owning a bit of what is, after all, my fatherland.

It was still morning when I'd unpacked my bags, I was intending to stay for a week which I was beginning to think was going to be too long. I should have forced myself to stay awake, taken a walk, make some calls, anything to help me adjust to the time change.

I should have gone then to investigate my surroundings and see if anything triggered memories of my only previous visit. A four-year-old can remember quite a lot, but time distorts, facts get muddled by the accounts of others and the scale of things is unreliable. Great heights and distances become small and folk, thought to be impossibly ancient to a child, turn out not so very much older after all.

Why had nobody sent me any messages? I liked to think somebody was missing me, wondering where I had gone, even Pete. He had driven me to the airport, though perhaps that was to make sure of my departure. Our split, so far, had been a level-headed amicable affair, more of a disappointed drifting apart than a dramatic cleaving. A text from him would have been kind. He might think of me later, after all the sun would have barely peeked over the East River yet. Of course, he might not be alone. I didn't mind, really I did not, much.

I lay flat on the bed on top of the covers and stared at the ceiling on which I could just make out an azure paper, patterned with a regiment of stylised five-pointed stars, which had been painted over with a thin coat of white.

My eyelids closed and my eye sockets filled with tears.

★

Dawn was mighty early for kids to be out playing. They were having a great time chasing each other about in the undergrowth below my window, shrieking enough to wake the neighbourhood.

An obelisk like a granite fang threatened from the top of the bank beyond, picked out by the early morning rays. I was ashamed to have slept through the whole night fully clothed until I realised that the fang was being lit by the sinking, not the rising, sun. It was the start of evening and I had wasted most of what must have been a delightful day and woken to feel as rough as if I'd had an overindulgent night on the town. Now, thanks to my stupidity, I had to face an empty evening and a wakeful night alone. I reckoned that there was an hour or two left before absolute dark for me to fill with something more constructive than remorse.

No message on my mobile and no email either. Pete would be working now and too busy shuffling the losing cards in the global financial hand to contact me. Did he have to obey my request to be left alone quite so thoroughly?

'I'm going to take a walk.'

'Right you are, hen.' Yvonne was busy sorting papers when I passed her lobby desk. She looked up, 'Och, sorry Mrs Staple, here's me thinking you were one of they weans. You're that wee… sorry, I mean petite.'

'Wee is grand. Hen is good too. I like hens.' Petite reminded me of my ex mother-in-law, who was anything but; I wasn't sure what Yvonne meant by weans.

'It's a grand evening for a stroll, right enough. Will you be dining with us the night?' Yvonne's daytime gear had been replaced by a tartan skirt and sash, held in place by vast pin in the shape of a thistle. 'We've a big birthday party in the dining room but I'll find you a quiet corner, or maybe you'd like to take your supper in the room, there's a real scary film on one of one o' they channels. I love a good fright.'

I told her I'd prefer to eat downstairs, even if I was condemned to a quiet corner it would be better than being alone, besides I could use a drink and Aunt Elvira had conditioned me to always drink in company. 'Solitary drinking leads to alcoholism and certain ruin, believe me, Mira, I should know.' Aunt El worried that I'd turn into my mother and held unshakeable opinions about vices passed on in the blood. The Troubadours however were not afflicted with defective genes, Aunt El could drink alone with equanimity, whereas I, a merely adopted Troubadour, had to guard against all manner of inherited shortcomings, like my mother's addictions and indulgences, and my father's legendary feckless stupidity and lack of forethought that led inevitably to calamities and fatal accidents with paraffin stoves.

I was the first of us to own an automobile. Sojourner believed that anything mobile should belong to someone else and took cabs everywhere, Aunt El did go to driver school once, but it wasn't a success. Ben rode motorcycles or took the 'plane. He had quite a collection of bikes and lavished everything on these machines on which nobody was brave enough to ride pillion. He did his best thinking while roaring down the freeways, biking was his equivalent of pacing the cloisters for inspiration.

Aunt El sought inspiration by walking in town but hardly ever stirred when in the country, because of unreliable and virulent nature being all over rural parts and lying in wait to pounce. She thought during these urban walks and wrote her flower strewn verse indoors with her back to the view, while Sojourner devised yet more exotic dishes from mail order ingredients or stuff delivered.

Sojourner and Aunt El shared a serious dislike for anywhere without sidewalks and snarled up traffic. I often wondered how Sojourner could cope with abundant Caribbean vegetation and bumpy roadways. I'm not surprised by her threatened return to New York City. Our shots at country life in the States were futile, when we travelled, neither Sojourner nor Aunt El ever attempted to integrate but conformed to their stereotypes – Sojourner as the big hearted earthy provider and Aunt El as the wiry English spinster whose curiosity was sufficiently gratified by an intimate knowledge of the British Museum and the dear V & A, along with the Natural History and Science Museums where she had been material in inspiring Ben to become the man of renown, the super scientific guru, adored by millions.

When I was a really little kid I had to walk a lot because Granny never had a car either, though Grandfather Herbert received a strange device from a charity for the limbless that he propelled by means of turning a handle like the inverted pedals on a push bike. I don't think this machine ever exceeded my walking pace and I was scarcely three when Grandpa Herbert died.

He was the first of my family that I knew who went to live with Jesus. Later I came to figure that Jesus had too many house-guests altogether, something maybe to do with his father having many mansions. My father's father had a castle but I don't reckon he was long on mansions.

I believe Dora (my mother) decided to have a baby purely to give her mother a present. I arrived and was, presumably, an acceptable gift. Granny kept me, reared me and loved me while Dora disappeared on drifting adventures. When Jesus next held open house and admitted lovely Granny to his bosom, I became redundant, an unacceptable gift, that couldn't be returned to the store or exchanged for something more to my mother's taste, like dope.

There had been a woman who'd come to help Granny from time to time but I had hated her, she smelt of cheap, sweet face cream and tried too hard at everything, especially getting me to like her. Later she tried even harder which made me hate her all the more. I was terrified of these two women, the smelly trier and my mother; I was petrified that I'd have to live with either of them.

There was another too, a tall girl with lovely long hair who I adored, she was Ben's girlfriend and they were going to marry but then one day she was gone and nobody ever spoke of her again. When I asked Aunt El who she'd been I was told that she was a wicked woman and I was forbidden to mention her. So I didn't, but I did wonder about her a bit. I've forgotten her name but like Ben, she was extremely clever. I was going to be a flower girl at their wedding, I remember Granny buying pink silk fit for the Rose Fairy herself, at Arding and Hobbs, a shop whose name I knew as well as Buckingham Palace where Christopher Robin went with Alice or Banbury Cross to which a fine lady, with bells on her toes, rode upon a white horse.

In the end Dora abandoned me for good in Granny's wrecked house for Aunt E to discover amongst heaps of spent bottles and piles of garbage. Most of all I remember Aunt El's indignation at the sight of festering waste food. 'Anybody who lived through the war should regard wastage as crime.' That my mother had seemingly deserted me took second place to permitting maggots to get at the sausages in Aunt El's scale of misdemeanours.

★

'You'd best walk inland the now,' Yvonne told me, 'it'll be high tide soon and you don't want to be getting stranded on they rocks waiting on the turn, even with the kitchen shutting later at half ten the night, on account of the Commander's sons having to come through from Edinburgh to be at his party.'

'Can I get up to that monument?'

'Sure, you can walk up the avenue and turn left at the lodge or take the bridge across the burn and up the bank, though the path is kind of steep and a spot slippy.'

'What is it for?'

'What is what for?'

'The monument, does it commemorate anything?'

Calum came stumping through the lobby carrying a basket of small logs which he put down heavily upon a pale rug. 'Aye,' he said, 'aye, yon's got a history right enough.'

Yvonne bustled from behind her desk and picked up the basket and sighed loudly on discovering a grimy rectangular print where it had stood, 'Mind yourself with that basket you're making an awful stoor and the boss will not be wanting the place filthy for the Commander's party.'

'She's never going to get aff her bed o' grief for that.'

'She's not away to her bed Calum, she's practising for the funeral. She's minded to sing a suitable song during the service.'

'When I was a lad women didna' go to burials and the like, they stayed hame and saw to the tea.'

'When you were a lad Sawney Bean was still eating summer visitors. Now away and get the fire fixed, the Commander won't want his family to freeze on his big birthday.'

I decided not to stay to witness any more but set out up the sloping gravel to the spot where the roads divided at an unexpectedly large, ornate stone lodge, with every window blanked out by drapes.

A sign to Dalmuirie House Hotel stood at the top of the road up which I'd come and another indicating Dalmuirie Castle Residences marked the way along the other. There was nothing about either being closed to the public so I made a left and turned back towards the sea at a higher level, from which I could catch glimpses of the hotel and its gardens through the gaps between the rhododendrons, across where drifts of bluebells must have bloomed. I could hear the sea and the shrieks of gulls and something else.

A woman behind some bushes was singing Dido's lament rather well, except for a somewhat over-pronounced warble. She certainly was doing far better than Aunt El who worshipped Purcell but couldn't hit a note. 'Remember me – But Ah…forget my fate!'

The voice followed me as I walked up the metalled road between mown verges.

When I turned the final bend and saw what must once have been my father's home, the place meant nothing to me. All I'd anticipated was completely altered, gone entirely, along with fairy tales and childhood.

I remembered visiting a grey place, grey all over the outside and muddy brown within, huge and chilly. I had been told it was a castle and I was very disappointed. I had been expecting flunkies with candelabras and all the other trappings of proper Disney type castles; this place was more like the giant's evil lair or Hardup Hall where Cinderella toiled for her sisters. I was used to squalor by then but not on such a scale. It was as if my mother might have had possession of the place for considerably longer than the time it took her to wreck Granny's little Wandsworth house.

The stench of dead mice and stale smoke impregnated the threadbare rugs covering the draught-pierced floorboards. Dead stags stared from gloomy walls, dead fish and balding dead creatures swam or posed petrified, in murky glass cases. Domes imprisoned dead birds, dead butterflies and dead flowers, faded a century since. The only creature left alive was my grandfather and he didn't look that vivacious.

I had been counting now on finding the castle as it had been then, I almost thought I'd find the old man too, sitting at his desk, a taxidermist's triumph…but I was wrong. What remained of the old building was converted into several apartments, the stone was cleaned, the gardens neat. Much had been demolished and remodelled into landscaped ruins. It looked like a pleasant place to live, unpretentious and accessible, somewhat self-satisfied and over managed but certainly not the forbidding heap of superfluous masonry and malfunction that I'd carried with me these last thirty years.

'You are aware, I presume, that you are on private property?'

The querulous yet imperious voice came from a bundle of plaid rugs behind me. I turned and saw that the bundle was wedged into a wheel chair and contained an ancient lady with a hooky nose, tinged mauve. Her eyes were rheumy but her gaze steady and accusative. She wore a surprising hat, also in plaid, the sort that Scottish guys wear to be comic, or to trash the opposition's team on trips abroad, but her mouth was too serious to utter gags or drink till she was roaring.

'I beg your pardon ma'am, I was hoping to visit the monument.'

'Ah, an American visitor, foreigners are always the most inquisitive, especially those whose native lands are of scant historical interest. You may visit the Toorie at will but not the castle residences except by express invitation.'

'I'm sorry I didn't realise. I am actually re-visiting scenes from my childhood. I may sound American but I have an English passport, it was first issued when I was a really little kid.'

'What you mean is you hold a British passport. There are no such things as English or Scottish passports as yet, but one lives in hope.'

Rebuked I began to walk towards what I assumed the old lady had called the Toorie.

'Wait a moment please.'

I turned back, 'Can I get you something, another lap-robe maybe?'

'No thank you, but bide a while and tell me more about why you have come here. I would like to talk to someone rather than listen to that unsuitable lament.'

Dido was still at it somewhere behind the bushes. I sat down on the grass beside the wheel-chair. I could do with company too.

'She sings well.'

'Aye she always did, she was one of the few who were in tune but this pagan piece is highly unsuitable for a funeral. A wee bit pibroch at the graveside would be quite sufficient at the burial of the blameless but this carry-on for a man whose ways were suspect and lived in sin is both tasteless and wholly inappropriate.'

'Do you mean Mr Parker?'

'Indeed I do. Are you here for the funeral?'

'Everyone has asked me that. No I'm here on business, kind of, and to investigate my roots.'

'You look a little young for that. Genealogy is generally the reserve of the elderly, those whose span is perforce limited by age and infirmity. I, for instance, have discovered recently that I not only bear the royal name but that I am descended directly from the Queen of Scots herself.'

'Wow.'

'A predictably coarse reaction, but gratifying none the less.'

'I have quite interesting Scottish roots too.'

'Most people have.' She looked at me as if I had no conception whatsoever of what was interesting and then fell into a reverie, gazing out towards the sea where the sun was sinking towards a large rock that looked like a cup-cake. 'That's Ailsa Craig. It is a volcanic plug, extremely interesting to geologists, much frequented by gannets and formerly the habitat of slow worms and puffins which were eliminated by a plague of rats. Incidentally, you must not confuse the slow worm with a snake, it is a legless lizard, you can tell by its eyelids.'

'How?'

'The eyelid is absent in snakes. Furthermore the slow worm gives birth to live young, grows to considerable length and can shed its tail when attacked.'

I was about to ask at which point in a legless lizard's considerable length does the tail start when she informed me that the lighthouse had been automated and the keepers' jobs eliminated by technology.

'My uncle was a geologist.'

'I daresay. I am sure there are many rocks of note in the United States but none to equal those in Scotland for extreme age.'

'I'm sure you are right.'

'Of course, I check my facts.'

More silence broken eventually by Dido again – 'When I am laid in earth…'

'The sooner that happens to the late Ian Parker the better we'll all be pleased. By the way, let me introduce myself, I am Miss

Stuart, Miss Philomela Stuart, one-time headmistress of St Quivox School and now resident in the Scullery of Dalmuirie Castle thanks to the timely negotiations of Mrs Wishart, wife of Commander Wishart. They occupy the Gallery and Gun Rooms.'

'How do you do, I'm Mira Staple. Can you tell me about the Toorie please, I'm kind of interested to know why it stands there, I asked in the hotel but I couldn't get a straight answer.'

'You wouldn't, that place is manned by ignoramuses, not I must insist by ignorami as favoured by the ill-informed and pretentious who make the same mistake with the octopus whose plural is either octopuses or octopodes unlike the hippopotamus of course. However hippopotami, though correct, is archaic whereas stadium I consider is dignified by employment of the latin plural.'

'I have no latin.'

'I'd be astounded if you had. Now the Toorie, let me tell you what I know.'

'Has it stood there long? I came here once as a little kid and I don't remember it.'

Miss Stuart sighed, interruptions being uncalled for. 'The Toorie itself is as old as the re-building of Dalmuirie Castle in the late nineteenth century, which is of course quite recent to those who live this side of the Atlantic. It used to adorn the roof-top, off which unpredictable masonry and questionable battlements would tumble with alarming frequency, hence the necessity to demolish most of the castle following the death of the final Henrysson, the late Charles. The Henrysson family occupied a building on this site since the Middle Ages, without much distinction, except the ability to make good marriages and squander dowries. Incidentally there is no reason to believe that these Henryssons were connected to Robert Henryson, with the single "s", the renowned fifteenth-century writer of moral fables. I am afraid that these Henryssons were somewhat improvident, though the death of the heir was indeed a tragedy, even if the lad himself was a disgrace, even to a family riddled with disgrace. Hugh was the only child expelled from St Quivox School ever.'

Miss Stuart paused to give this bolt a chance to make an impact. 'The Toorie yonder is a memorial to Hugh Henrysson and his young bride who perished there together some thirty years ago.'

I was shaken, not by my father's errant ways but by the casual way this old woman was discussing him at all. I'd heard he was a wastrel, that he was also a school drop-out didn't surprise me, but discovering there were people who knew him, remembered and despised him, struck me to my soul and made my own myth real. Why had my clever, mad, beautiful mother fallen for him enough to conceive me? Was it really just because she wanted a tall child? Maybe. She was always on at me for being so small and dark but at least I had my father's eyes. I didn't want his eyes, I wanted my own. His are what I have and later on I became glad because I am told they look good; they are large and greenish blue. Aunt El said that my father had outgrown his strength and Ben, who never criticised anybody, said nothing. Perhaps Hughie Henrysson had been fun but dumb.

As I drew breath to say something, Miss Stuart raised her age-spotted hand for silence. 'You may ask questions later. Now the Toorie. It was erected upon the site of a rustic edifice placed upon the bank there as a sitooterie and to obscure the view of Henrysson's Rock, known colloquially as The Lumpie, from the castle on account of a most unfortunate incident there with a pet dog during Queen Victoria's diamond jubilee celebrations.'

I put up my hand, I felt I was back in 2nd Grade and needing the bathroom. 'Please Miss Stuart, what is a sitooterie?'

She glared and sighed. 'A sitooterie is a place in which one can sit outside. Something doubtless you would do on a porch or even a deck and is done in India upon a veranda and in Africa upon a stoep. Some might call it a gazebo or belvedere but that would be etymologically incorrect as this building was designed to face the castle and not the beautiful view of the bay for the reason already explained about the pet dog. Do you understand?'

'Yes, thank you.'

'Good. I will continue. In earlier times it served as a pavilion from where games of croquet, lawn tennis and putting could be observed but those days were long gone by the time Lady Charity gave birth to young Hughie and was never quite the same again. She spent a great deal of her time in the sitooterie, indeed she very often slept there during spells of clement weather. Her marriage was not of the happiest I surmise. Young Hughie was the result of enforced incarceration, I would deduce.'

'Incarceration in a penitentiary?' I asked.

'Gracious me no. In the bothy, during the war, while the military requisitioned the castle. Anyway Lady Charity was given to play-ing the violincello. Apparently her skill was much appreciated by the seals when she took her instrument down to the shore. Mind you, I was led to believe by my late brother that the moothie, or as you would call it, the harmonica, is more beguiling to a seal. He would play "Charlie Is My Darling" to great effect but that would have been unsuitable for Lady Charity to attempt, seeing as her husband's name was Charles. Now, as I was saying, one day she rashly perched herself and her instrument upon the De'il's Dyke.'

'What's that, Miss Stuart?'

'What's what, young woman? I wish you would refrain from interrupting me, I've now quite lost my train of thought.'

'I didn't understand what you said about a dyke.'

'The De'ils Dyke is a promontory of rocks leading out to the channel between the mainland and Henrysson's Rock. De'il is the Lallans for devil as in 'The De'il's awa' wi' the Excise Man' by Rabbie Burns. There are several similar promontories allotted to the De'il upon this coastline, however I digress. Now, it happened that Lady Charity was quite carried away with her own perfor-mance and failed to notice the incoming tide and as she scrambled towards the shore, she slipped upon some bladder-wrack and her 'cello tumbled into the sea and try as she might, she failed to re-capture it as it floated away to its doom. Lady Charity herself was quite distraught and was eventually discovered soaked to the skin and wailing at the edge of the sands. She took pneumonia and had it not been for the timely discovery of penicillin, by yet another brilliant son of Scotia, I warrant she would have died. As it was, she made but a partial recovery and for the last few years left to her, she remained in her room at the opposite end of the castle from her husband and only communicated with him through her son, when he was at home, and a series of expensive nurses. This, as you can imagine, drained the Henrysson resources still further and when eventually she died in the 1970s, there was not a morsel of her fortune left to leave. Ah there you are, have you done with lamentations for the day?'

A large woman with lank hair, wearing elastic waisted pants and a black stretchy top, dusty with undergrowth, appeared from behind a clump of rhododendrons. She was a hearty sort, probably too hefty to be either a cheerleader or an athlete but exuding the intimidating enthusiasm of a comedy girl scout.

'Shall I hurl you back home Miss Stuart?'

'This young lady, to whom I have been talking, is interested in the Toorie. She's from America you understand.'

'Oh?' The woman looked at me severely, through thick lenses.

'Cecile, she is staying at your hotel.'

'Oh forgive me please, I am delighted to welcome you, Miss…?'

'Mrs Staple.' I held out my hand: 'I'm pleased to meet you, you have a beautiful place.'

'Yes it is rather special, awfully spoiling.'

A spongy hand, a whiff of artificial scent and a clammy grip clutched at my guts. I knew that cloying smell of synthetic blossom and disinfectant, it belonged somewhere in my past, long ago, long before I'd left to live with Ben and Aunt Elvira but it wasn't a pleasant waft of nostalgia, not like Ponds Extract, Germolene or Vick Vapour Rub and Friar's Balsam all of which recall happy memories of being comforted after mishaps and cosseted during minor ailments. This woman's odour summoned my profound, enduring and inexplicable revulsion. It was sweet yet acrid, a mix of candy, pink soap and rotting greens, it clamped the top of my nose.

'You will find that everything at Dalmuirie House Hotel is designed to give the discriminating guest a memorable experience, our discreet and competent staff are there to ensure that all your requirements and needs are met. Our acclaimed chef will be happy to discuss your culinary preferences and the surrounding countryside offers a wealth of historic, cultural and sporting opportunities.'

'That's enough, Cecile, Mrs Staple may be from the States but she can surely read your brochure for herself. Furthermore, I doubt if she is an inspector, she lacks the zeal for that fashion of carry-on. Come away now or I will be missing the news with which I wish to be abreast, also I must change into more suitable clothes for the Commander's party as indeed must you, Cecile.'

'I consider it most insensitive that my uncle has not postponed this party in view of our great loss.'

'Not everybody sees the end of Mr Parker in the same light as yourself, Cecile. Furthermore, at ninety it is unwise to postpone celebrations. Good evening to you Mrs Staple, I enjoyed our conversation.'

'Goodbye Miss Stuart, it was a pleasure meeting you.' Miss Stuart waved a cotton gloved hand as she was pushed away at great speed by the woman called Cecile, who I did not know, but knew I loathed.

★

Why did I dislike this singing woman so much? Physically she was unattractive, yet not repulsive, or in any way alarming. I just disliked her, her personality repelled me, I was, I suppose, prejudiced against this middle-aged frump called Cecile. But prejudice is generally built on fear, fear of failing to keep a hold on power, a fear of one's own being overwhelmed by strangers. My dislike was animal, driven by the instinct to eradicate the weakling. A child can sense lack of confidence in a teacher and once the weak point is discovered, will return to it again and again like sharks sensing blood or hyenas following a wounded antelope, or wasps converging on damaged fruit. Whoever this woman was, or had been, to me I knew that she was weak,

vulnerable, convinced of her own inadequacies and utterly in-
competent with children.

I only went horseback riding once, I was utterly petrified, so
what did the beast do? This hitherto equine angel bucked me off at
its first opportunity, something its owners swore that their ador-
ably cute pony had never, ever, done before. It is a good thing we
humans can't smell each other's pheromones because if we could,
the world would not only stink but be in an even greater ferment
of sex and violence. Imagine the insults that we could deliver in
silence if we had wagging tails to lower with revulsion along with
ears to lay back and hackles to rise as mine certainly would have
done on encountering this woman called Cecile.

★

When I reached the headland edge, the sunset was half over, leaving a scarlet slice glimmering from behind the summit of Ailsa
Craig. When it disappeared completely the rock turned purple
and the breeze became instantly chilly. A shining path dwindled
over the crinkled silk sea towards the other, smaller, flatter and
meaner island, Henrysson's Rock.

I was standing on the spot where my father had died.

The Toorie, as Miss Stuart had called it, was like the tip of a
steeple and built of tapered blocks of grey stone, topped with a
weather-beaten blob that might once have been a pineapple or
possibly had started out as a smooth ball before the salt winds
eroded it. There was no plaque, nothing to say who or what it
commemorated; my father and his young wife had no memorial
there. I was all that was left of his family, and all that they had
left me was the scary rock in the sea below.

I knew then that I had been there before and that something
had happened to me there, something my memory refused to
retrieve, something horrible. Nobody had ever talked about it
to me and I had always known that it was something else I was
forbidden to mention. Now, over thirty years later, I no longer
knew what it was but I did not like that rock. I wanted rid of

it and its unreachable memory. Some places do have bad atmospheres. I could understand why the Victorian Henryssons had chosen to shield themselves from it with a summerhouse, notwithstanding the tragedy of the pet dog. Yet the place was compelling, my eyes were constantly drawn to it and the vision I conjured of poor Lady Charity serenading the seals with her ill-fated cello.

The sunny trail had vanished into the water and I set out back to the hotel down a woody path towards the bridge that Yvonne told me was kind of slippy. I was in a hurry to get inside and I crossed without mishap. The damp boards of the narrow bridge had been covered with chicken wire and some sturdy railings constructed to prevent accidents. Lady Charity must have taken her cello down to the beach this way. It was strange to discover now, that once, I'd had a musical grandmother. Most odd.

★

A family car had disgorged its load into the once tidy lobby, along with two girls aged probably, twelve and eight.

'I will not! I bloody won't and you can tell that sickly saddo that from me – with knobs on, tied up with gopping pink ribbon.'

The older and skinnier kid, wearing ripped jeans, was being mad at her defeated mother who was surrounded by heaps of bags. I edged my way past, mightily relieved not to be involved in this family vacation. The younger girl with a plumper face collided with me as she hurtled towards the door, dragged by a small yapping dog.

'What do you say, Phylida?'

'What?'

'Say sorry, Phylly, to the lady.' The kid glared and her mother reverted to appeasing her older sister, 'Patience, sweetie, please try and be reasonable, don't ruin Grandpa's party.'

'It's not about Grandpa's party, it's about my bloody uncle's bloody wedding and his bloody bride making me wear bloody pink. What part of Goth doesn't she get?'

'I like pink,' said the kid called Phylida who had now sat down in the middle of the lobby to concentrate on scratching the dog's bald belly.

'You would. You're so sad. You are pants.'

'I'm not, Patience!

'You are so!'

'Pardon me,' I ventured, 'can I just sneak by?'

The child didn't shift and the dog snarled. I like dogs but I wasn't too sure that this one liked me.

A tall man appeared and scowled, he had the kind of good looks that advertise middle-range limousines. 'For God's sake Caro, can't you keep them quiet? You aren't at home now.'

'You try! Take them down to the beach, take them anywhere and please let me have a break. My head is aching.'

'No change there then.'

'Please Chris, please.'

'Please what?'

'Take the girls to the shore or something and give me a chance to get straight.'

'Later maybe, I've got work to do, calls to make. I've got ends to tie up before close of business.'

'It's after six, Chris.'

'So?'

'Well aren't all offices already shut for the weekend?'

'And if they are? I've got things to do, people to talk to, things that do not concern you. OK?'

'Couldn't they wait?'

'Probably, if I choose.'

'Then please do me a favour, for once, Chris. Please take the children to the beach.'

'Yes of course I will but only when it suits me. Do you understand?'

'Say,' I heard myself, 'how about you two coming to explore the garden with me, I think I saw a tennis court. Do you kids like playing tennis?'

'Not much,' Patience replied. She had blackened nails and a dripping dagger stamped on her arm. I still figured she was no older than twelve.

'Ooh let's go down to the beach, I want to see the Lumpie, the cannibal island,' said Phylida.

'Patience! What have you been telling Phylly?'

'Nothing.'

'You did so! You told me that Sawney Bean and his huge family lived there and they ate up all the visitors because they were cannibals.'

'That's just a silly story. Really Patience, you know Phylly gets nightmares.'

'It's not nonsense, Mum. Daddy said it's true and that all the Bean family, even the tiny children were taken to Edinburgh and chopped to pieces in the Grass Market.'

'I give up.' She sank down upon a sofa, abandoning the pile of baggage and closed her eyes. Her mascara would have run in streaky black rivers, had she worn any.

'Are you kids here on vacation?' I asked as we strolled across the grass.

'Not really,' Patience replied and sat down upon a low stone wall staring out to sea. She was going no further. Anyway the tide was in and the path down to the shore between the gorse and brambles would be kind of steep and narrow to negotiate especially when it got darker. Phylida sat beside her and threw small rocks down towards the almost submerged promontory that I assumed to be the De'il's Dyke.

The Lumpie or Henrysson's Rock did indeed look even more sinister and gloomy, dwarfed by Ailsa Craig on which I could still distinguish some white buildings.

'My aunt used to say that sitting on cold stone could cause piles,' I said, for want of conversation.

'Bring them on!' said Patience.

'She also said you'd die if you wore damp socks.'

'I can't wait.'

'Oh come on, life can't be that bad, what is your little dog's name?' The dog was busy excavating. He had dug a sizeable hole beneath a heap of scrappy timber. I wasn't going to stop it; it didn't look that sociable, not the sort of animal to take a scolding from a stranger.

I didn't know what Aunt El meant by piles till I was grown; she didn't do insides apart from insisting on regular bowels. She and Ben delegated Sojourner to tell me the facts of life which she'd done with explicit enthusiasm.

Defying piles I sat myself between the bickering girls, with my back to the dog and asked what he was called. Receiving no answer I concentrated upon the darkening view. Now a light flashed from Ailsa Craig and another from further along the coast line, then another upon a distant outcrop on a mountainous island. 'Which island is that?' I asked.

'Vladarran.'

'Vladarran,' I repeated, 'I must remember that.'

'Vlad is the dog, silly, Arran is the island.'

'Oh.'

'Actually,' Patience said, 'his real name is Vlad the Impaler because of his teeth.'

'Don't you think it is wrong to give a dog a bad name? Perhaps if you'd called him Valentine or Valery he'd not be so aggressive.'

'But those are girls' names.'

'No they aren't.'

'Well they sound gay; Vlad isn't gay, He had puppies all over Edinburgh till Mum got the vet to chop off his balls. What is your name?'

'Mira.'

Moira?'

'No, Mira, short for…oh never mind.'

'Mira,' said Patience, 'I've read about Mira in a book Mum gave me last Christmas. Mira is an unpredictable double star of variable girth.'

'That's me,' I said.

'And if Mira replaced our sun in our solar system, it would reach out beyond Jupiter.'

'That's some star,' I said.

'Do you know any famous people?' Phylida suddenly asked.

'I don't think so,' I replied, 'but I expect you do.'

'Here we go,' said Patience, closing her eyes which I noticed had also been daubed black.

'I know the Queen.'

'You don't say!'

'She doesn't really,' Patience interrupted, 'she just saw her drive past.'

'But she waved at me.'

'She waves at everybody Phylly, that's what Queens are for, waving at silly little girls. It's what they do best.'

'Well I do know another famous person and you do too, Patience.'

'Who?'

'Claudia!'

'Oh her…she doesn't count.'

'Who is Claudia?' I asked.

'Claudia is the stupid woman our stupid uncle is going to marry. She's a total loser, she writes stupid books and has been on telly and everybody thinks she is wonderful, especially her. She wants Phylly and me to be her bloody bridesmaids in bloody pink like a couple of frigging marshmallow Barbie dolls.'

'I had a pink dress to be a bridesmaid once,' I said, 'only I wasn't as old as you are. I was just a little kid. I thought the dress was great.'

'What happened?'

'Nothing, nothing happened, the wedding was called off. My Granny had to cancel the taxicab, I remember that because I had never been in one before and I was almost as excited about the ride as going to a wedding.'

'What happened to the dress?'

'I trashed it. I wore it to the play-park and went on all the swings and slides till it was torn into shreds,' I replied, remembering that

was the first and only time I saw Granny cry. But she wasn't crying because of what I'd done to the dress. It was something else.
The whites of her bloodshot eyes were quite yellow.

'Who was getting married?' Patience asked.

'My uncle.'

'I wish our uncle would call off his wedding too. I'd love to
trash our dresses. Who was he going to marry?'

'A beautiful young lady.'

'Wasn't she awful like Claudia?'

'No, she was lovely. I liked her a lot. But something went wrong
and it never happened and my uncle never married anybody.
He's dead now.'

'Have you got a boyfriend?' Phylida asked.

'No, not at the moment.'

'Are you married?'

'Not any more.' I think that was the first time that my loneliness struck me. I really missed Pete then. That must have been
the jet-lag too.

'What was he called?'

'My husband? He was called Peter Staple.'

Patience giggled: 'He sounds like a paper-clip, like that silly
Office Assistant our mum has still got on her old computer. What
was your uncle called, the one that didn't get married?'

'Binjamin was the name he had as a baby but everybody called
him Benjamin or more often Ben.'

'So you called him Uncle Ben?'

'I guess so.'

'Did he grow rice?'

'Rice?' I said, somewhat baffled. 'No, he wasn't much good at
growing things but he knew a lot about space and rocks, he was
an astrophysicist.'

'Guess what,' said Phylida, 'I don't know anybody called Ben,
not properly like a friend. Only Bill and Ben the Flowerpot Men
that our granny likes and Mr Ben who I hate and Benjamin Bunny
of course.'

'And Benjamin bloody Britten who wrote that frigging Young Person's Guide to the bloody orchestra.'

'And Big Ben.'

'That's a clock, silly.'

'And Ben Nevis.'

'Idiot!'

'And Ben Troubadour, Patience. You like him.'

'Yeah, I suppose so.'

'Have you kids really heard of Ben Troubadour?'

'Of course, everybody knows him, he's really famous. He wrote that book about stars, the one about Mira being unpredictable and of variable girth. Mum loves him too, lots.'

'Loved you mean, Phylly. He's dead you know.'

'So? He's still on the telly, Mum still says he is her swoon.'

'Those are repeats silly.'

'So what's the difference? Can't you have a repeat swoon?'

'Gran said she nearly met him once, but that was years and years and years ago when Dad was our age I think. Cousin Cess said he was her boyfriend but I bet he wasn't.'

Patience turned to me: 'He lived in America, you sound like you come from there?'

'It's a big place,' I replied.

'Yeah, but did you know him?'

'A bit,' I answered.

'Now that's well cool.'

The children's father shouted for them to hurry up and come in and get changed for supper and for goodness sake get a grip on the dog too.

I stayed where I was as daylight faded thinking about the strangeness of this place coupled with a sense of familiarity, a knowledge of things forgotten. I almost heard the pathetic howl of a small dog marooned upon Henrysson's Rock and the twangs of a drifting cello, above the shoreline's whispers but I knew that was just the product of my mind, wearied by travel and overburdened by morsels of incomplete information. Lights carried on winking at me from over the water as I turned away to walk back across the mown grass.

★

My room contained proper furniture, not the stuff found in hotel bedrooms from Rio to Rome, stuff that fills climate-controlled, ergonomically correct, spaces for containing guests, all of whom are welcomed on a television screen by a clone of Big Brother. No CNN was going to bombard me here with big-haired females and strident males emphasising their earnestness and proclaiming their indignation. Here were no instructions on how to access adult entertainment or work the mini-bar. A tiny TV was the only concession to modernity in the room called Matilda, which had a real bookcase containing real books, the property of a child who signed them Matilda Irene Gilmerton, sometimes adding her address, Dalmuirie House, by Dundoon and continuing out through the solar system, galaxies and outer space but stopping short of that place Ben wrote about, 'The Surface of the Last Scattering'.

Ben's most popular book for kids was called *Nothing to Explain* but it was written long after Matilda had grown up and gone away. Her birthday, I discovered from another fly leaf was January 4th 1948, she'd be sixty now. There were leather-bound prizes that were probably untouched since the day they'd been presented at St Quivox School, for achievements as eclectic as mental arithmetic and deportment, composition and General Excellence, for which she'd received a weighty and much embossed tome called *Stories from Scottish History*, which I thought I might read, till my eye was caught by a shelf of scruffier books. These well-thumbed treasures must have been the books Matilda cherished and re-read. I was beginning to think I knew her.

Aunt El used to read to me when I was small, Granny did her best but I doubt if she was hot on reading aloud in English, especially as my favourite Beatrix Potter used such difficult words as 'implore', 'distracted' and 'soporific'. I think Granny took me to visit Aunt El in her tall narrow house across the river on the bus quite often, but I may be wrong. I don't remember so much about Aunt El's house except she owned a lot of weird and lurid pots which were rather special. One day they were no longer there, I think she sold them because she needed the money to fix her roof or something, Aunt El's house was always kind of creaky.

I used to sit on Granny's lap to look at picture books but Aunt El always made me sit on a footstool to listen to her. She read well and was good at voices but I don't think she liked the idea of anybody sitting on her. Her legs were like broomsticks, it would not have been comfortable. I loved Aunt El, really I did, I was so lucky to have her but even after I'd lived with her till I was grown, she never hugged me, the closest we ever got was an occasional whiskery peck upon the cheek to mark great occasions like birthdays and graduation and the first (and pretty nearly the last) time I performed in public. She had tears in her eyes and was ridiculously proud of the cygnet she'd championed. She was the one who had understood my driving enthusiasm and she was the one that made sure I took dance classes.

I was too old to need Aunt El to read to me when she gave me my most favourite book ever, for my eighth birthday. We were living temporarily in Manhattan, in a brownstone walk-up on the East side near the New York Medical Centre, within sight of Fifty-ninth Street Bridge where Aunt El told me there was an island asylum for addicts and there was no need to sing songs about feeling groovy, whatever that was. She was constantly watching me lest I sank into bad ways and even took me down the Bowery to look at the hobos as a warning. The poor soul was as ashamed of her niece, my mother, as she was proud of her nephew, my Uncle Ben. I believe she felt equally responsible for her downfall and his success.

The book, which was still alleged to be somewhat old for me, was *Ballet Shoes* by Noel Streatfield. I read it right through without stopping, resenting even the compulsory pause to enjoy my birthday tea and the pretty cake which had been ordered specially from Mr Carlo's Sweetie-Pie Deli.

Matilda must have loved the book too. Its green covers were faded to grey but there it was, the same in every way, the magic story of three children called Fossil, their strange upbringing and their theatrical aspirations. I wanted to be all of them, Pauline for her dramatic panache, Petrova for her dark independence and most of all Posy, the natural ballerina. I loved the line drawings of the extraordinary household and the bustling Nanna who reminded me of my dead granny but best of all I loved the pictures of Pauline and Petrova as flying fairies in *A Midsummer Night's Dream*. I never got to fly but I did stand on a stage to be blinded by footlights, I did smell the greasepaint and sit at a mirror surrounded by light-bulbs. I was lucky that way but I didn't have Posy's talent, one of the cygnets was as far as I got.

I wondered about Matilda. Did she ever fulfil her ambition? What became of the little girl who was generally excellent? I decided to re-read *Ballet Shoes* and take it with me to dinner. That way I could hide behind the pages and submerge myself in the story and not look so obviously alone.

★

If you are on your own, other people's conversations become the focus of your attention however much you try to appear deaf and detached. Even the tension of Pauline Fossil's first audition couldn't exclude what an elderly woman in, elegant but faded, black was saying to Yvonne when I came down to sit a while in the lobby before dinner.

'I see you have hung Mr Parker's portrait of the Gilmertons up again, I haven't seen it for many years, I'm surprised it's still here. Did Miss Pollock suggest it for the funeral?'

'Och no…I doubt she's seen it yet, she's been that busy dealing with the arrangements up at the lodge. She's not herself you understand, Mrs Wishart.'

'I do understand Yvonne, but what made you hang the picture there?'

Yvonne lowered her voice but I could still catch what she was saying: 'It was a Japanese gentleman Mrs Wishart, he had a wee accident with his bath overflowing and it made an awful mark on the wall. Calum found the picture in the attic yonder. To tell you the truth I didn't know then that Mr Parker painted it. Did you know the family yourself, Mrs Wishart?'

'Yes Yvonne, I did, so did the Commander, we all did, very well, including Miss Pollock, who may not be best pleased when she sees it there.'

'Oh my! Well I can't take it down the now, Calum is away to his home with the step ladder to sort his rones and I can't manage the picture on my own. It's that hefty. But I'll get it away tomorrow and find something else to put in its place.'

'Let's hope Miss Pollock doesn't see it tonight, we're expecting her to join the party, she is my niece, as well you know.'

'Did I not tell you? Och, I'll forget my own head shortly, I'm that busy with this funeral. They are not like weddings at all, funerals aren't. At least with weddings you know how many to expect, I just hope that enough people turn up for Miss Pollock's sake though I doubt there's many that will come for anything other than the spread. Now, where was I? Ah yes, Mrs Wishart, I've to tell you that Miss Pollock sends her apologies, she regrets that she can't join in the party, she says she needs the space to grieve…those were her very words on the telephone, not half an hour since.'

'Oh dear, well never mind, but hush my dear, don't tell the Commander, he's very superstitious.'

'Mrs Wishart, can you tell me why Miss Pollock would take against the picture? I don't even know really who the people are except that the two wee girls are called Matilda and Grizelda and that the soldier had already killed himself before it was painted.'

'It's complicated, Yvonne, oh look here comes the Commander with my son and Miss Stuart… . What kept you? I've been here ages, it was a lovely walk down through the wood. Oh look, I've not changed into my party shoes yet…take Dad through to the bar darling,' she told someone behind her, 'and get him and Miss Stuart a drink, while I sort myself out, everybody else should be here very shortly.'

She watched as the old man and a younger one, presumably their son, entered the bar followed by Miss Stuart walking with the aid of a cane and dressed in a long tartan skirt and knobbly cardigan, before continuing to explain the picture to Yvonne.

'The dark child was known as Grizel, she was the one who married the boy from up the old castle and they were the ones that died in that terrible fire on Henrysson's Brow.'

'Oh my! Mrs Wishart, is that a fact? Here's me thinking Calum was being fanciful, he's that keen on giving the guests the creeps. What became of the other wee girl, the one called Matilda?'

'Tilda? Ah yes that's a different story.' Mrs Wishart seemed to hesitate then she leant over the desk and whispered something into Yvonne's ear.

'Never! You don't say...who would credit that? I'd not have thought it possible!'

'Don't spread it around, please. That was most indiscreet of me, I apologise. Miss Pollock has enough on her plate just now.'

Tilda, that name rang distant bells in my long-ago memory. Could it be that Ben's beautiful girlfriend, the one he came within a whisker of marrying, the woman whose name I was forbidden ever to mention was Matilda Gilmerton, known to all as Tilda, the same Tilda whose childhood book had just dropped from my hand with a thud?

★

I counted fourteen places at table for the Commander's party. Balloons printed with 90 floated above each chair and glasses shimmered amongst the silver candlesticks. There were no drapes to obscure the view from the veranda dining-room even when, as now, the islands were only darker lumps in a darkened sea. I could see a string of street lights across the water and single lights winking back at the stars beyond the broken tracks of moonlight.

My table was in a corner; it would have been more tactful if I had chosen to face the wall I guess, but I love people-watching, especially people who are not my concern. If I end up muttering on a park bench gaping at the crowd, it'll be OK.

Most of the Commander's older guests were smoking on the terrace. Patience and Phylly were helping by handing round hors d'oeuvres and looked remarkably civilised; even the fake tattoos had been scrubbed. The kids seemed to relate far better to their grandmother than their mom, the woman called Caro. I could understand that.

Caro, meanwhile looked fragile and glamorous in eau de nil and was on a mission to down as many cocktails as was possible in the time allowed. Alcohol appeared to have done its work, either that or she'd been liberal with the blusher. Her husband didn't join the banished smokers but kept aloof and reminded me of a poem Aunt El used to recite about Godolphin Horne who held the human race in scorn.

It took Yvonne a while to persuade the party guests to come and take their seats for their first course. I was to get an identical meal of lox, followed by lamb (somehow Americans don't relish sheep meat as much as the Brits) with ice cream for dessert, though of course I would not be included in the birthday cake which Patience had been deputed by her grandmother to dress with ninety candles.

If there were any other hotel guests, they must have been seated in another section of the veranda.

The beaky nosed Commander was naturally distinguished, tall and stooping, dressed as if to go yachting, in a blazer gleaming with brass buttons, he entered on the arm of an old boy with hearing aids in both ears, wearing a gaudy dicky bow. This pair was followed by the old boy's loud wife whose shape had turned to jell-o. Was her strident voice the cause or effect of her husband's deafness? The Commander held on to the back of his chair and smiled all around and then asked if everybody was there. It was then that I realised he was blind.

'Yes all is in order, Rodney,' his wife replied briskly. 'Are you going to get Forbes to say grace?'

Forbes must have been the ancient guy, in a clerical collar, with an ebullient face who could have played Friar Tuck.

'All in good time. Where's Cecile?'

'She's not feeling festive, poor wee soul.'

'I am not sitting down thirteen on my birthday, not for anybody.'

'Run along Phylly dear and bring down Teddy, he can come to the party too.'

'No, stuffed animals don't count.'

'But surely all will be well if Forbes fixes it with the Lord.'

'Look what happened when the Lord sat down thirteen…an almighty calamity! No, someone will have to join us what about that woman on the desk, she sounds reasonable.'

Patience pointed at me: 'Why don't you ask her?'

'Don't be silly darling, Grandpa doesn't even know her.'

'So? We don't know Grandpa's friends and she's well cool. She's even met Ben Troubadour.'

I concentrated as much as possible on the doings of the Fossil children but I still felt like an exhibit at a freak show.

'Excuse me.'

I looked up and saw a youngish man, with a kindly face, faintly scarred beneath his right eye, standing between me and the party. 'Would you mind very much coming and joining our table? My father, for all his brilliant brain, is hopelessly superstitious and it would save us all a lot of hassle. I am very sorry to disturb your reading.'

I assumed this was the children's uncle destined to marry the detested Claudia, who wrote books and craved pink. She was obviously not at this party as the remaining female guests were ancient, one with a blue rinse, another with hair that matched the claret. The young man smiled and I decided that if I couldn't be Claudia I'd have to hate her. 'Thank you,' I said, 'I'd be honoured, but I'm not exactly dressed for a party.'

'Please don't worry about that. You are doing us a great favour. I'm called Tom Wishart by the way.'

'And I'm Mira Staple.'

'Come and meet everybody. Dad, I've found a perfect guest for you, her name is Mira.'

I picked up the old man's hand, it was forested with brown spots. He looked towards me with blue, sightless eyes then smiled, showing more teeth than a laughing horse.

'How do you do, sir, many congratulations on your birthday.'

'It's most awfully good of you to get us out of this scrape, when you are as old as me it is too late to tempt fate. Now let's make sure you know everybody here. Let me see…sorry my dear that's not a bad joke. Well why don't you introduce yourself to us all and we'll take it from there. Please don't be shy, nobody bites.'

'Hi,' I said, sounding like a game show hopeful, 'I'm Mira Staple and I've just come from the States.'

'We've already met,' said Miss Stuart. 'Mrs Staple is investigating her roots.'

'And guess what, she wrecked a bridesmaid's dress when she was little.'

'That's enough, Patience. Yes we met earlier, Mira was good enough to take the children down to look at the sea when we arrived and Chris was being most unhelpful.'

'You do talk rubbish, Caro.' The children's father stretched over the table and shook my hand rather too vehemently, 'I'm Christopher Wishart, Tom's older brother – come around here and take this seat between us and I'll give you the lowdown on who we all are. Our mother, Avis Wishart, is up there at the other end of the table between my daughters, Patience and Phylida, Miss Stuart who you have already met is between Phylida and Tom. The Reverend Forbes Farquerson, who used to be the minister at Dalmuirie Kirk is next to Patience and Winifred, his wife, is on Father's right with Mrs Whigham on his left and next to me. Her husband Dr Whigham is opposite me and next to my wife Caro, who is opposite you.'

I smiled at everybody including Blue Rinse who was between Caro and minister opposite Tom. 'Don't worry about introducing me, nobody ever remembers who I am,' she said.

'Of course we do,' said Tom. 'Chris is your godson.'

'I don't think he is, Tom dear. Nobody ever invited me to be anybody's godmother,' Blue Rinse replied.

'Well I think he should be.'

'Thank you, that's very civil of you. It is not easy being the widow of such a distinguished man and may I add, of such note-worthy local lineage, as my late Tavish. As a man's shadow, one disappears when the man himself is taken.'

I tried to commit all the guests to my memory. Winifred with the claret hair was the wife of Forbes the minister. Gregor Whigham was a retired doctor and profoundly deaf, as his booming wife Iona told me, while informing most of Scotland, that they had driven all the way from beyond Dreghorn, which sounded pretty intrepid. I didn't discover Blue Rinse's name.

'Are you one of the Galloway Staples?' the Commander asked from the table's head.

'Staple is my married name. I don't know anything about my husband's family except that they live in up-state New York.'

'Ex-husband's family, she means,' said Patience.

'How regrettable.' Miss Stuart sighed.

'Not always,' said Christopher Wishart, leaning against me.

'I heard that,' said Miss Stuart, 'you may be minded to aspire to the Lord Advocate's seat Christopher but divorce is not a call for flippancy.'

'Rebuked again!' He made a gesture of slapping his own hand.

'You always were one of my more precocious pupils. Intelligent certainly, but far too pleased with your own opinions. I advise you to watch out for snares and delusions.'

Forbes said a grace about thankfulness for meat and means to eat it; Caro crossed herself nudging Blue Rinse's side plate to the floor and was told by her husband to stop wearing her damn faith on her sleeve.

'Sorry, darling.' She glared at Christopher and Forbes intervened by asking me which were the roots I was investigating.

'The Henryssons.'

'How very interesting, how far back are you going?'

'My father was a Henrysson.'

'Ah yes, descended from another nineteenth-century emigrant I have no doubt. Well the person you should be talking to is Avis here. As I recollect she had the task of writing up the Henrysson family history, she will be a great help.' He turned towards Mrs Wishart who was obviously enjoying sitting between her grandchildren. 'Avis, my dear,' Forbes interrupted, 'Avis, this young lady claims descent from the Henryssons, I was telling her about you and the history written by poor Charles. Have you a copy still?'

'No, alas. The old boy lost all interest in his origins after the fire when he realised there was no future for his family. He asked me to burn it, but I put my copy in a biscuit tin in his grave. To tell you the truth, the stuff was an awful shambles and as speculative as those family trees in the Bible, lots of begetting and questionable statistics. I can maybe remember the important bits, such as they were. Which period are you interested in?'

'All of it, I guess, though I am really concerned with the recent past.'

'The most recent past of that family was a tragedy,' said Forbes. 'In fact, the funeral of the young Henryssons was the most harrowing interment I ever officiated at.'

'At which you ever officiated,' corrected Miss Stuart.

Forbes ignored the interruption. 'Burying old Charles Henrysson was a joy the year following, the man had lost everything, he needed out, but to have to bury the remains of two young people who'd died locked in a final embrace…that was terrible.'

'*The Mill on The Floss* springs to mind, does it not?'

'Indeed, Miss Stuart, you are ever at hand with the literary allusion.'

'Thank you, Commander.'

Mrs Whigham shouted at her husband, 'The tragedy…we're talking about the fire. Weren't you at the autopsy?'

'Indeed I was,' Dr Whigham replied. 'Not a duty I enjoyed, no not at all, not one bit. The remains were unrecognisable, such as they were. It was all highly unpleasant. The young man could only be identified by the Henrysson signet ring. I recall the young woman had perfect teeth, not one filling.' He lapsed into silence and Miss Stuart suggested that unpleasant was an understatement. Doctor Whigham then remarked that the blaze itself must not have been, by any stretch of the imagination, anything other than totally non-trivial.

'Wasn't Grizel wearing her wedding ring?' Iona asked.

'No, Tilda had told her to take it off as a precaution. There was a perfectly logical explanation,' said Avis, 'Grizel's hand had started swelling up after she'd scalded it that morning.'

'Women should never ever take off their wedding rings, it is terribly bad luck,' said the Commander.

'Nonsense, you silly old thing,' said Avis, 'I take mine on and off all the time and I haven't burst into flames once in all the years we've been married.'

'Not yet, maybe Avis, don't tempt fate.'

'You are impossible, Rod!' Avis blew her husband a kiss. 'Anyway, Tilda threw the ring into the grave at the funeral, that's what gave me the idea of burying the memoirs with old Charles Henrysson the following year, to give archaeologists of the future something to speculate about.'

'About which to speculate,' muttered Miss Stuart.

'I remember it well,' said the Commander. 'We could see the flames from Firthside Camp and the column of smoke from as far away as Dundoon. All the vegetation on the bank was burnt away, from the sea it looked like a permanent scar. I daresay it is all grown back by now.'

Caro clasped her hands like a martyred saint: 'Please, let's change the subject. I don't want the children getting nightmares.'

'Don't be ridiculous Caro, you dump them in front of far worse things on the television.' Christopher helped himself to claret, ignoring both my empty glass and that of his wife opposite.

Miss Stuart said that in her extensive experience, education is most effective when the macabre and brutal episodes of history are not skirted. 'The young,' she announced, 'have a phenomenal capacity for the morbid and tyrannical.'

'Tell me about Sawney Bean again, Miss Stuart, please,' Phylly begged.

'Lo! A perfect example! Can I trouble you for the wine, Christopher, please? Story-telling benefits from adequate lubrication and this end of the table is suffering from drought.'

'Was not your Tavish the Procurator Fiscal at the time?' Mrs Whigham shouted at Blue Rinse.

"Alas yes. A testing time professionally and socially. The verdict was that the initial cause of death was smoke asphyxiation as a result of misadventure, which I recall was quite a comfort to the bereaved.'

'And highly unlikely, in my opinion.'

'Miss Stuart! You are surely not casting doubt on my late husband's deliberations!'

'I am merely relaying received wisdom. There was one, recently taken from us, you will admit, who stood to gain from culling the beneficiaries to the late Gilbert Gilmerton's will. He was a man of great ingenuity, not beyond employing devious mechanisms.'

'Please Miss Stuart!' said Avis Wishart. 'That is a monstrous suggestion. Why should Ian Parker want to do that? He may not have been greatly liked but he was surely no murderer. That would be ridiculous.'

'As ridiculous as his marriage? I think not. Mr Parker was a sly creature, given to intrigue and clandestine dalliance. Furthermore, was not the reconstruction of the sitooterie a wedding present from himself, albeit paid for by the bride's own mother? Not that I attach any blame to that exceptionally shallow woman nor indeed to her highly commendable daughter, the star amongst the alumni of St Quivox.'

'I always thought that I was the star of the St Quivox alumni, Miss Stuart.'

'A galaxy is comprised of many heavenly bodies, Christopher, some more modest than others.'

Phylida relieved the subsequent awkward silence.

'I'm bored! Tell me again about Sawney Bean, Miss Stuart!'

'Very well Phylida, but not until I've heard the magic word.'

'Please,' Phylly whined.

'But before we embark upon cannibals I think you ought to be acquainted with the Abbot of Crossreguel.'

'Why? What happened to him?'

'He was roasted!'

'Yuck! Painful!'

Caro put her head in her hands. 'Oh please will someone pour me some wine. I can't stand this much longer.'

'You've had enough, Caro!'

'Wrong Chris! I will need a great deal more if I'm to sleep through Phylly's nightmares tonight.'

'Is roasting like being burnt alive, Miss Stuart?'

'Very likely. Now Phylida I don't wish to incur the wrath of your mother who looks most overwrought, so we'll revert to more sanguine subjects.'

'What does sanguine mean?'

'It means bloody, you tit,' Patience answered. 'I want to know who burnt down the summerhouse.'

'Nobody, darling,' said Avis.' It was a horrible accident. It's what comes of not being careful with matches.'

'Like Harriet, Granny? You know the girl that ends as a heap of ashes in that German book you showed us, the one that Mummy won't let us read. The book with the scissor man cutting off thumbs and Augustus who died because he didn't eat soup and Bold Agrippa who dipped rude boys in ink?'

'Yes, exactly,' Avis replied.

Caro bit her lip, the party was going off-track quite enough without any drunken tears.

'In my opinion,' said Miss Stuart, boldly gripping a bottle and pouring herself a substantial dose, 'despite your diverting tactics, I remain of the opinion that there were adequate grounds for suspicion of skulduggery.'

'Miss Stuart,' said Avis, 'I am sure that the evidence for foul play was exhaustively examined at the time. Who could possibly have wanted to murder either of those two sweet young people? I am convinced it was an accident.'

'I am sure that if my Tavish were here he would uphold your conviction, Avis, no doubt should be cast at the soundness of his judgement...ever.' Blue Rinse dabbed her eyes with lace trimmed hankie.

'Of course not, my dear,' boomed Mrs Whigham, 'But there are always rumours, some more credible than others. To hear the way some people talk you'd think nobody was above suspicion. Isn't that right, dear?' she shouted at her husband who roused himself from the reverie in which he'd taken refuge.

'What was that, Iona? I do wish you wouldn't mumble.'

'I was saying that nobody was above suspicion.'

'Suspicion of what?'

'Arson, Gregor, and murder. We are still talking about the fire.'

The table waited as the doctor composed his response. 'Well,' he said in a voice guaranteed to chill anxious patients, 'you are not incorrect, Iona. There were many theories as to blameworthiness of those connected to the young couple. For instance the jealous revenge of the jilted, the pecuniary aspirations of the ambitious, even sibling rivalry was cited as I recall, all far from unusual phenomena but in these circumstances probably quite without substance.'

'And totally preposterous!' Avis shouted.

'Preposterous but not without precedent, Avis.' Dr Whigham then retreated into his shell again while Miss Stuart listed murderous brothers and sisters of scripture, legend and literature, 'not forgetting the brutal disposal of my kinswoman, Mary of Scots by her cousin.'

'Cousins aren't siblings,' said Patience; 'Phylly and me are siblings.'

'Phylly and I,' replied Miss Stuart.

'Were those two wee girls in that picture siblings?'

'Yes Phylida,' said Miss Stuart.

'Well that's a matter of opinion,' said Mrs Whigham. 'Is it not a wise child that knows its father? Gregor dear,' she shouted across the table, 'did you not say that Irene Gilmerton's firstborn was a fine bouncing specimen for a premature baby?'

'She was indeed a sturdy child and a very comely young lady, as I recall.'

'Yes,' said Blue Rinse, 'Tavish compared her to the Maid of Norway.'

'Talking of Norway,' said the Commander, 'Gilbert Gilmerton received a medal from King Haakon in 1948, the framed citation used to hang in the cloakroom here, maybe it still does. Irene Gilmerton told me it was for being civil to that nice Norwegian stationed here after the war, you remember the tall blond chap, sound on heavy water as I recall.'

'One could deduce from what you are implying, Rodney, that Gilbert's civility went somewhat beyond the call of duty, into the realms of generosity,' muttered the minister's wife.

'That, Winifred, is a non sequitur,' said Avis very firmly.

'What's a non sexateur?' Phylly asked.

'A sexy nun of course, don't you know anything?'

'That's enough, Patience!' said Caro.

'Actually,' said Christopher, 'a sexy nun ought to be an oxymoron.'

Phylly looked puzzled. 'What's an oxymoron?'

'A stupid cow,' her father replied, staring at her mother, 'or maybe one should say a bull with special needs.'

'For goodness sake Chris, give poor Caro a break,' said Avis, 'Now where were we?'

'We were talking about the fire,' said Blue Rinse.

'I suggest that "cherchez la femme" might be a good idea,' said

Mrs Whigham, pursing her lips. 'Hell has no fury like the woman scorned and one needs to look no further than this very place to find one who had been roundly scorned. There is no possibility of Gregor ever revealing a medical confidence even if he was privy to such things, which I believe he was not, even though both Maud and Willie were registered as his patients but there were credible rumours that the jilted woman was enceinte.'

'Like an ancient Briton?'

'No, Phylida, certainly not!' Miss Stuart was probably the first to see the figure in the dining room doorway. 'Now remember children, both of you, gossip-mongers are mere sounding brass and tinkling cymbals.'

The table fell silent but the blind Commander blithely carried on, 'My niece may be somewhat short in the charm department perhaps, but the poor thing is no homicidal arsonist.'

All eyes, except his, turned towards the fat woman in black who had now entered.

'I am unable to conceive…' said Dr Whigham.

'Of course you can't, you silly old thing.' Mrs Whigham's false laugh reverberated through the dining room.

'Why Cecile!' said Avis. 'How lovely to see you, come along, draw up a chair, there is plenty of room.'

'I am not staying, Auntie. I just came to wish Uncle Rodney a Happy Birthday. I can see that I am not needed here.'

I made to jump up from my seat: 'No please, I was only invited to make up the numbers, I'll go to my room, I'm kind of bushed anyway. I would just like to say how much I've enjoyed meeting you all and thank you very much for inviting me and maybe I'll catch you some other time while I'm here.'

But the woman Cecile didn't attempt to take my place, instead she dumped a potted plant and a card on the table beside her uncle and turned back towards the door: 'Goodnight, everybody! I have no intention of bringing my misery to your happy party.'

Avis stood up.

'What's happening?' the Commander demanded.

'I must go after her, Rodney.'

'Sit down Avis, at once. I will not tolerate thirteen at a table.'

Avis grabbed both granddaughters, 'It's all right now, Rodney, I'll leave you with eleven…the eleven that went to heaven, remember? Come along, children let's get Grandpa's surprise.'

'Wait, Cecile please, we all want you to stay, don't we, girls?'

Tom caught hold of my hand, 'You can't go now Mira or we'll be thirteen again when Mother comes back. I'm afraid you are stuck.'

I didn't mind being stuck next to Tom but his brother Chris on my right, had hot breath and a hammy leg that kept overflowing his chair to nudge mine, especially when his Caro was watching.

Miss Stuart endeavoured to humour Blue Rinse by remarking that the late (and much lamented in several quarters) Procurator Fiscal had been a notable authority on the Covenanters.

'My Tavish was notable in many ways and an authority on many subjects. A man of integrity and respected for his competence.'

'Indeed!' said Forbes. 'He accomplished his role as Kirk Elder with exemplary zeal.'

A hand crept on to my right knee so I kicked Chris on his ankle. 'Bitch!' he hissed and turned his back on me to tell Winifred Farquarson of the claret hair about one of his many recent triumphs.

'Look,' said Tom, turning his head, 'They are talking about you.'

I looked up to the end of the table and saw the Commander bending towards Iona Whigham who was giving me sidelong glances.

I think the Commander must have asked what I looked like because I couldn't fail to overhear the thunderous whisper of her reply: 'Small and dark. Not entirely black, don't get me wrong but kind of Middle Eastern. She's very pretty.'

'Is she?' he asked, louder this time. 'I'd like to have seen her. What about her eyes?'

'Good, I think . Anyway she's not wearing glasses, unless of course she's got those contact lenses. They are marvellous you know. Have you tried them? Oh sorry, I didn't mean to be tactless.'

'You aren't, I like it when people forget this blasted condition. What colour are they?'

'Her eyes? I can't tell from this distance in the candle-light, even though they are very large.'

'What sort of age is she?'

'She's in her early twenties I imagine.'

'Oh, I was wrong, I was hoping she'd be a bit older.'

'Why Rodney?'

Just then Patience appeared carrying a cake ablaze with candles, followed by Phylly and Avis gripping the woman called Cecile firmly by the hand. We all sang Happy Birthday while Caro flapped about telling everybody to be careful. She was right in a way, the heat from that many diddy cake candles was amazing. The Commander needed no directions about where to blow. When he was told he had extinguished the lot, he rose to his feet.

'Before I make my speech…and don't groan, I will be brief, I just wish to propose a toast to those special friends who are unable to be here, specially the Smellies and of course my dear late brother and sister-in-law, Willie and Maud Pollock.'

We all rose and raised glasses.

'Are not the Smellies still with us?' asked Mrs Whigham.

'Alas, no, not entirely.'

'How not entirely, Miss Stewart?'

'What she means is that Olive is away with the fairies, quite out of it, in a home. Whiffy, I mean Wilfred, died a while back, mercifully before Olive went completely batty. Poor Isa has to cope with her mother alone.'

'Olive Smellie was the best teacher I ever employed at St Quivox, she was totally unqualified but she shared my great enthusiasm for imparting knowledge. She learnt and then taught, by osmosis.'

'What's osmosis?' Phylly asked.

'An absorbing antipodean law-giver. Now shut up and let Grandpa get on with his speech,' said Christopher who evidently felt that he was the better orator.

'Poor Isa Smellie,' sighed Miss Stewart, glaring at Christopher, 'another promising pupil who should have gone far had she not made an imprudent marriage. However she has her uncle to thank for taking her into his firm though I doubt she will scale many heights in her once blossoming career now. Opportunity knocks but once for most. Did you not court Isa yourself, Christopher?'

'Spare me, Miss Stuart. A momentary lapse in taste, give me credit for some sense, she's built like a wheelie bin.'

'I have never seen a wheelie bin,' said the Commander, 'so I am unable to comment but I do know that your lovely wife Caro is far prettier than poor Isa. As I recall, you were quite cut up Christopher, when she turned you down.'

'I can't remember that, but if you are right, she was the only one who ever did. Now why don't you get on with your speech?'

Deaf Dr Whigham, who hadn't been able to follow this conversation, said that he found it impossible to credit that an entire quarter century had passed since Maud and Willie Pollock had been killed. 'A fearful calamity, you will all agree, confirming the hazardous nature of continental travel. Had they stayed home as Willie wished, he would never have collided with a truck on the outskirts of Calais, not five minutes after disembarking from the ferry.'

'You must miss your parents a great deal, Cecile.'

'Yes, Aunt Avis.'

'Enough!' said the Commander. 'It's my birthday and I want it to be a celebration not a wake!'

He made a speech, thanking everybody by name and relating an anecdote about each. Iona Whigham was a doughty gardener, her husband Gregor, the doctor, played demon golf, Forbes the Minister could recite Tam O' Shanter (with gestures) and his wife Winifred painted charming water colours. Caro, the Commander's beloved daughter-in-law, was a perfect mother and her daughters, being his grandchildren, were naturally brilliant, albeit in their own way, Christopher's career in the law was the envy of all and Tom, whom he stressed was the most honourable of men, was managing to carve a great life for himself, despite his earlier difficulties.

I noticed the women, Winifred and Iona, exchanging glances with Caro, nothing was said but there was evidently something implied in the Commander's praise of his son.

Next, he laid on the flattery of his niece in spades. According to him she was a superlative hotelier, songstress and astoundingly wily business woman, as efficient as she was good-looking. Cecile simpered and then the Commander turned to Miss Stuart, who he addressed as the template for all dominies, adding, 'I can't recall the feminine for Scots school teachers.'

'Dominatrix!'

'Don't be ridiculous, Chris,' said Caro.

'What's a dominatrix?'

'Don't ask, Phylly,' Avis implored.

But Patience told her exactly what a dominatrix was and did.

'Really,' said Avis, 'the things they know! I had no idea where babies came from till I was fifteen.'

Having paused, the Commander then continued his speech by praising his wife of nearly sixty years for putting up with him.

'Please don't get uxorious, Rodney, there's still plenty of time for me to change my mind.'

'And finally…'

Blue Rinse coughed.

'What about Jonquil?' Avis hissed.

'Good heavens! How could I forget Jonquil?'

'With ease,' Blue Rinse replied. 'People do all the time.'

'Ah Jonquil, what can I say? The loyal widow of my old friend Tavish MacMaster and renowned for having had a mother who kept fancy fowl all through the war and came to our wedding in a hat trimmed with her prize-winning cockerel's tail feathers.'

Blue Rinse sighed and remarked under her breath, 'I never get credit for my embroidery.'

'Now for the welcome stranger in our midst who I hope has

a life as long as mine and lives to have four times more candles to blow out than she does at the moment.' After applause he sat down and the cake was taken away to be sliced.

It must have been the wine, or weariness, that compelled me to stand up and say, 'Thank you very much Commander, but actually you are wrong. I'm not fixing on surviving till the twenty second century. I am a child of the '60s, just.'

'In that case, my dear, I think I was wrong in another way. I don't believe you are a stranger.'

'What do you mean, Uncle Rodney? Mrs Staple only booked into the hotel today. I can show you the register, or rather I can show it to Auntie Avis.'

'No need, Cecile. I believe that this young lady is none other than your own mother's adopted niece and Hughie's daughter. I'm right, aren't I?'

'Yes,' I replied.

'No! Not little Miracle Troubadour! But this is sensational!' Avis jumped to her feet and came round the table and gave me a big kiss. 'Behold your Auntie Bird! And your Uncle Rod and your almost cousins Tom and Chris and of course, Cecile whose mother was your Aunt Elvira's sister, Auntie Maud. Oh what joy to see you again after all these years. How many is it? Twenty, twenty-five?'

'About thirty-three, I guess, maybe more.'

'As long as that? Well yes it must be. Oh I remember it all so well. You were such a bold little thing, you even loved the Ghost Train at the holiday camp and you trotted everywhere behind your cousins when we went off to Ailsa Craig for a picnic. It was a blissful afternoon, even the midges didn't trouble us. We all went – you were there too, Cecile – only of course you were considerably older than the other youngsters. You must remember boys…you made up rude names for the food and little Miracle found it all hilarious. Oh yes, and Ian Parker kept following us about in his fancy boat and intruding on our picnic.'

Doctor Whigham raised his hand: 'Might I enquire as to the cause of this consternation?'

'That young lady is Hughie's bye-blow!' Iona Whigham shouted.

'Well, I confess that I am not inconsiderably astounded by such an unexpected revelation at such a not inappropriate moment.' When he was included in the conversation Gregor Whigham had a delightful smile, but mostly he looked bemused, in the solitary confinement of deafness.

Avis was twittering on. 'That was the last time we saw you. The next day you were gone, vanished completely. Your uncle arrived and took you away, never to return until now. I don't know why you went so suddenly, though I believe there may have been a difference of opinion between your uncle and his Aunt Maud. Well, here you are, and you are more than welcome, isn't she?'

Everybody turned to look at me and I felt a flush creeping up my neck.

I remembered the woman who'd been singing 'Dido's Lament' and smiled at her. I used to call her Cess.

She stared at me. I have never been the object of such a venomous glare. 'Bastard!' she spat as she got up and left.

Now nobody followed her or begged her to stay. Miss Stuart broke the silence. 'In Australia, unless my information is wrong, that epithet is a term of endearment.'

Saturday

*T*ell me, Mira dear, what exactly do you remember of all this?'
I thought for a bit before answering Avis Wishart's question. She had invited me to drop by the day after the party which I was delighted to do. The hotel's atmosphere was tangibly fraught indoors, while outside the whole country was being lashed by torrential rain. I'd woken to find the window frames rattling a drum roll while the panes were bombarded with such force that the raindrops seemed like rocks flung by a furious mob. I no longer felt welcome, things were conspiring against my stay. Being Saturday, the attorney's office in Dundoon was closed, so there was nothing I could do but wait or take up the offer to visit my rediscovered Aunt Avis and her husband, who I knew I could never call Uncle Rod.

By mid-morning the rain had relented enough for me to walk up Henrysson's Brow through the soaked woods and over the wooden bridge with its planks wrapped in chicken wire and sturdy barriers either side. The swollen stream below was rushing to meet the sea that had risen to cover all the sand and was knocking on the cliff's edge.

The Wisharts' house was warm and well lit, logs burnt in the grate despite the season, brass gleamed and happy family pictures beamed from most polished surfaces that weren't covered with personal treasures amassed during their lengthy life together.

'I remember absolutely none of this,' I replied.

'Well I assure you this is not a new house but what is called "a sympathetic conversion incorporating original features" though in my opinion it has about as much of the ghastly old castle in it, as a set of capped and pearly root-fillings has of an original jaw-load of rotting and ill-assorted teeth. We are sitting now in what was once the central hall in which all the dreary old portraits hung until your grandfather sold them and replaced them with bad copies.'

'Painted by the late Ian Parker?' I suggested.

'Yes, that's right, he was a man of many parts.'

'And Cousin Cecile's lover?'

'I wouldn't like to go as far as that. I do not think that Ian Parker, even in his younger days, was much interested in being any woman's lover.'

'Not even his wife's?'

'There are things in this world, Mira, that neither I, nor my brilliant husband, can figure out and Ian Parker's marriage, which incidentally I believe is technically still extant, is one of them. Whether it was greed, spite, lust or just a deranged whim that motivated them to do it I doubt we'll ever know. I have heard of women being accused of protesting too much but in the case of Ian Parker's wife her declared loathing and distaste for the man were very convincing. The marriage rocked the district at a time when the district was enduring much rocking, not six months after the fire that killed Hughie and her little sister.'

'Whose little sister?'

'Matilda Gilmerton's sister Grizelda.'

'You mean Tilda became Mrs Parker?'

'And still is, as far as is known though nobody, except presumably the lawyer who handles her affairs, has had any evidence of her existence for decades. You look surprised.'

'I am. I am amazed. You see. I think I do remember Tilda, – just. She was lovely, really beautiful and I adored her. She was going to marry my Uncle Ben.'

'I know, my dear. After he went to the States I acted as their post box until…'

'Until when?'

'Until the fire, then everything changed.'

'In what way?'

'The grief of losing her daughter turned poor Irene Gilmerton's head. She would see nobody except Tilda. They became recluses, shut away in what is now the hotel with Ian Parker acting as their link with the outside world. Much the same thing happened to your grandfather after he lost Hughie, his only child. Charles Henrysson spent his final year in miserable isolation with me and my sister-in-law doing our best to keep him fed and reasonably comfortable. Not that he noticed, nor were we thanked. It was pitiful. You see, however badly Hughie and his father had got on, his father was devastated by his death and there were times when I thought that despair had destroyed his mind too. The only time after the fire that I saw him give even a glimmer of a smile was when you were brought to see him. Do you remember?'

'He called me the little bastard. I was rather thrilled, it sounded kind of exotic.'

'Tell me, Mira, dear, what do you remember of your mother?'

'That she was chaotic.'

'Nothing more?'

'There's plenty more.'

'Tell me please, I'd like to know everything. There is time.'

'Everything about her was confusion, not exactly cruel or wicked like a fairytale stepmother but wrong and very different, totally unconventional.'

At that point Avis went to answer the Commander's shout for help in finding his shoes. He was upstairs in his room. She told me he was nursing a hangover. 'Rodney insists it is indigestion but I know better,' she said, 'port does it every time. He'll live.'

Avis returned. 'Please go on, Mira, but wait till Rod arrives and can listen too.'

The Commander felt his way into the room, he didn't look that rough to me. He took my hand and told me that he was delighted to see me. 'I must apologise, Mira, for my somewhat dishevelled appearance, I am, as doubtless Avis has told you, a martyr to indigestion. Too much food last night, don't you know.'

Avis winked at me.

'Don't do that, Avis!'

'Do what?'

'Wink at Mira. I may be blind but I can hear your winks.'

'Well what about the hair of the dog then?'

'Damn good idea. What a gem you are. You'll join us won't you, Mira?'

I said it was a little early.

'Nonsense, it is never too early for Madeira and a bit of cake.'

Avis produced both, the Commander was right, it wasn't too early at all.

'Now then Mira, tell us, when exactly did you live with your mother?'

'It was 1974 I'm fairly certain.'

'Ah yes, Plant a Tree in '73 then Buy a Saw in '74,' said the Commander.

'It was also the year Lady Charity died and Hughie married Grizel Gilmerton,' said Avis The wedding was just before Christmas. She looked absolutely amazing in a velvet cloak trimmed with altogether excessive swansdown. Anyway Mira, go on tell us what you remember.'

'I remember that Christmas very well. I'd found Dora insensible on the floor sleeping off a bad trip or a binge, or both and then somehow got myself locked out in the freezing front garden, I think I was looking for Father Christmas who, despite all Dora's promises, had forgotten to come. The neighbours rescued me and contacted Aunt El who whisked me away in a taxicab and gave me the best Christmas ever. I don't know how she managed it, or indeed how she paid. She took me back to her place where she'd got a change of clothes for me and while I had a hot bath she told me that Father Christmas was a silly old man and gotten all muddled up and had left my presents at her address by mistake. True, there wasn't a monkey or a resurrected Granny (Dora had promised me both) but there were all sorts of little treasures, scent, soap, hankies, pencils, a little china box that I still have and best of all, a pack of Woodland Snap featuring Dr Bunfuzz, Hoppy Spadge and Millicent Littlemouse et al. After that she took me to church. Unlike Granny, who was probably the only Portuguese, Roman Catholic, Jewish member of the Church of England, Aunt El wasn't a church-goer at all but she held firm views on the benefits of Bible stories for the young and singing carols together. Anyway, I think she took me to Westminster Abbey; there were certainly great tombs with effigies of dead kings and queens. I fell in love with all the choir boys at once. After the service, she showed me a gigantic Christmas tree that had come all the way from Norway and then we walked to a place that looked like a palace where we had a proper Christmas lunch in the prettiest dining room ever, filled with sparkle and mirrors overlooking a park. Everybody made a huge fuss of me and Father Christmas himself kissed Aunt El who went all giggly. We walked back to Aunt El's house through the park and saw the stars come out.'

'It sounds as if she took you to the Ritz,' said the Commander. 'We haven't been there since the war.'

'How strange,' said Avis, 'how very strange.'

'Not really old girl, we've had neither the money nor the opportunity.'

'No it's not that. I wouldn't know what to do with myself there anyway. The tea costs something like £40…can you imagine? You and I used to get tea and a bath bun at Lyons for sixpence. No I was just thinking about Grizel and Hughie, I believe they started their honeymoon with Christmas at the Ritz. I know they spent it in London before going abroad. It said so in *The Times* I'll have a look in the album, I always liked to keep cuttings, people used to put all sorts of details in the matches column of *The Times* then, like "the bride wore a gown of duchesse satin and carried freesias". Paying for such banalities to be put in the paper is a wicked extravagance, almost as bad as listing the presents. We'll have none of that nonsense at the wedding next month, I trust.'

'We're getting more than our fair share of nonsense as it is. Claudia ought to think very carefully before she embarks on this marriage lark. Change the name and not the letter is a change for the worse and not the better,' announced the Commander.

'Oh Rodney, stop being such a superstitious ninny. Now let me have a rummage through these.' Avis opened a cupboard stacked with albums. 'Ah here we are, yes you are right, it was 1974 to 75. Things were pretty dreadful that winter but not I fancy quite as bad as the one before when we'd had a three-day week and everything shut down early and we had all those power cuts.'

'Can I see please?' I said.

'Yes of course Mira, we might even have a snap of you some-where.'

'I'd just like to have a look at… . Oh I remember those photo-graphs, they were in a very smart journal, Dora and I looked at them on a newsstand and she got me a copy of my own. I was fascinated by the beautiful people in beautiful clothes and excit-ing advertisements. I showed Dora that picture of Tilda in a big fur hood and she showed me the picture of my dad dressed to be the bridegroom. He didn't look right to me, too lanky, not like the brawny guy in the singlet and kilt on the oatmeal box at all.'

While I was looking through the album I chose not to tell my new-found aunt and uncle how Dora had gotten hold of the jour-nal for me, how she had leant over the display stand with her coat flapping and shoved it into an inside pocket after which she picked up a tiny pack of mints and gave me some more candy bars to hold. When she got to the check-out she paid for her mints and then turned to me and gave me a slap, calling me an evil little girl for stealing sweeties and made me put them back on the shelf and slapped me again. Naturally I bellowed and in the furore we left the shop. It wasn't just the journal, her pocket was full of other loot too.

I remember that Dora was very interested in Tilda; I suppose it must have been because she'd been Ben's girlfriend. She also read about the wedding with greater attention than she'd ever paid to me. We went to a library with snooty stone lions outside and she told me to sit quietly and look at a book. It had no pictures and I couldn't read so I watched her searching through newspaper cuttings and large works of reference, I'm not sure why, but I think she may have been looking up Tilda's family history. She must have liked what she saw because she took me to a tea shop and bought me a monkey made of cake which I didn't eat till he had cracked and crumbled to dust. A few weeks after that Dora made a bonfire out of all the junk in the garden and I threw my precious magazine on it too. After the Fire Brigade came and made even more of a mess by racing through the house with their hoses to douse the flames, the police did arrive. I hid under my bed till it was dark and everyone had left. Nobody bothered to look for me after all.

Later Dora told me that she was going to find a new place for us, far away where we could live by the sea like Puff the Magic Dragon. I asked her if I could have a dog and she said we would have the lots of animals, ponies to ride, cows and goats for milk, sheep for wool, chickens for eggs and pigs too, but she didn't tell me what they'd be for. We would live off the land and be happy ever after. That was probably the only time I had felt really close to her, the one time I felt she was a real mother.

The Commander interrupted my reverie. 'Penny for your thoughts, my dear.'

'Sorry, I'm being rude. I was just trying to think of the last time I remember seeing Dora, because quite suddenly, she was no longer there. She had gone, vanished, disappeared and Aunt El took me to live with her. I expect Dora had gone back out East, that's where she claimed to have her spiritual home. Aunt El told me later that she had left a note to say she'd gone to find herself. In order to get there, she'd taken her passport and all her documents and sold Granny's diamond ring which had once belonged to Aunt El's mother and was worth more than enough to get a ticket to Nepal.'

Avis took the album from me and turned a few more pages.

'Oh what a shame! Look, all the colour snaps I took that summer have practically disappeared. You can hardly make out a thing. I know we all went on a picnic to Ailsa Craig but quite honestly, we might as well have been in a Sahara sandstorm, do you see? I'm sure you came with us, along with Cecile and the boys.'

'I wasn't there,' said the Commander, 'nor was Christopher, it was the day he collided with the Windmill of Old Amsterdam with Miss Firthside riding pillion on his Lambretta. I spent the day appeasing her family, who seemed to be the entire population of East Killbride and most litigious. They demanded compensation, as well as a replacement for the stilettos which were the only casualty of the accident, apart of course, from the Windmill of Old Amsterdam, which was flattened. I think Olive Smellie and Isa went along with you, Avis. I know that you said Cecile was seasick and that Ian Parker was his usual intrusive self, oh yes and Isa started to haemorrhage from the mouth.'

'Good heavens Rod! Your memory is far more reliable than mine.'

'That's because I can't use the crutch of so-called visual aids. I have to keep my brain sharp.'

I peered at the photo; Avis was right, it could have been any group anywhere. One shape was squatter than the rest. That might have been me.

"What do you think happened to your mother eventually, Mira?' the Commander asked

'Rodney really! What a question! Have a bit of sensitivity.'

"No it's fine,' I replied, 'to tell you the truth I was more worried about her coming back than her staying away. In fact her returning to claim me was my worst nightmare, that and Ben or Aunt El going off to be with Granny and Jesus, because that would mean that I'd have to live with…'

'With who?'

'Other relatives I guess or maybe an orphanage, actually I quite liked the idea of that, it sounded sort of romantic like boarding school, which just shows how ignorant I was. Please don't get me wrong, I had a wonderful childhood, a touch unconventional and kind of unsettled but once I was with Ben and Aunt El I felt safe.'

'And you didn't feel safe with anybody else?'

'I did not feel safe with my mother, certainly.' I did not want to carry this further, had I expanded my answer I might have offended them. They were good people and anything disparaging about members of their family would have been unkind but the very thought of Cousin Cess being in charge of me still made me want to shudder, coupled with the memory of that terrible week which ended with something horrible that I can neither remember nor forget.

'And you never heard of your mother again?' the Commander asked

'No. I believe that Uncle Ben did get a message once saying she'd married an Irishman and was living near Cork.'

'Did your uncle look for her at all?'

I thought for a bit. 'Maybe he did, but like I said, I did not want him to find her and I wanted to shut out that possibility.'

'I see,' said the Commander, 'that is very sad. A lot of very sad things happened. You know, Avis and I grew very fond of Matilda Gilmerton. When she used to come and collect your Uncle Ben's letters here, on the pretext of learning chess. Actually, she was quite good at it.'

'And then?'

'The letters and so forth came to an end. Affairs do that, you know, especially when communications are so sporadic. It was before the days of emails and mobile phones able to reach all corners of the earth. We had to send Air Letters, which were at least an improvement on centuries before, when you had to rely on passing ships and obliging seafarers to keep contact with your best beloved.'

'Why did Ben and Tilda's affair end?'

'God knows. Maybe he met another woman who pleased him more. That happens too.'

'I don't think that happened to Ben,' I replied. I could not imagine my uncle in love. Sojourner was his shield against the hoards of females that flung themselves at him. He and she were devoted to each other, laughed at each other's jokes but love? Convenience yes, security yes, gratification perhaps, but passion? Passion, I think, did not enter the equation.

'It all happened around the same time as the fire and then, not many months later, we learned that Matilda had become Mrs Parker. Stupid girl! I suppose it was a perverted revenge for being jilted,' Avis interjected.

'I think there was more to it than revenge, old girl. I found the whole thing incredibly sad, such a waste. We lost touch with her and even though we knew she had separated from Parker we never heard where she was living or what she was doing or whether she ever completed her training. Somehow I doubt if she did. The spirit had gone out of her.

'But that had happened when she had that accident, she probably never did get shot of her limp. It was all, as I said, very sad.'

I'd have liked to say that it wasn't half as sad as the fact that he could not recover his sight but I kept quiet and looked out of the window to where Tom Wishart was walking from the Toorie towards the house across the grass, at the bank's edge. A dog was circling him excitedly as he flung a stick for it to retrieve.

'When did you find out that your father was dead?' the Commander asked

'I don't think anybody told me. I just got to know. I do remember asking Aunt El whether he'd gone to Jesus like Granny.'

'And what was her reply?' Avis asked.

'She said nobody could be sure.'

'A wise woman, your Aunt Elvira,' said the Commander. 'We should have kept in touch.'

A door opened. 'Is that you Tom, the one-eyed king in the land of the blind? Look we've got a visitor. Why don't you take young Mira here on a tour of the sights, I'm sure she'd relish an outing to somewhere other than this mausoleum peopled by us ancient relics?'

The dog was a kind of greyhound with a wagging tail that scattered a heap of papers as it greeted Avis rapturously.

'I'd be delighted,' said Tom after he'd kissed his mother, 'anything, even a trip round the sewage works, would be welcome after all this wedding palaver. Caro and those kids are driving me nutty. Why can't they wait and have it out with Claudia once she's done her book tour, she's the bride after all? No wonder Chris has sloped off.'

'Sloped off? Where?'

'Urgent business in Glasgow.'

'But it's Saturday.'

'Apparently his kind of law doesn't stop for weekends.'

The doorbell rang. 'Oh no, not the Jehovah's Witnesses again or those scrubbed young Mormons. Go on, Europa, you useless hound, tear them limb from limb.'

'No, Rodney, it is the Minister.'

'Same thing, Avis.'

'Come in my dear, pay no attention to Rodney, he hasn't got over his birthday. Now, what can we do for you, Katriona? You know Tom of course but let me introduce my adopted niece by marriage.'

Katriona didn't look like your regular kind of Presbyterian minister. She was wearing blue jeans and had her hair in a pony tail, which was a bit incongruous with a clerical collar. I suspect she was at least five years my junior. 'Hi Katriona,' I said, 'I'm Mira Staple.'

'I'm delighted to meet you, Mira, I've been hearing all about you. I understand we are actually standing in your ancestral home. News travels very fast in this wee neck of the woods.'

'Have some Madeira, m'dear!'

'That's very kind Commander, just a taste. Actually I haven't come round to scrounge a drink but to ask you a favour. You see, I'm in a bit of a quandary.'

'What sort of quandary?' Avis asked.

'A what on earth am I going to say at Mr Parker's funeral

kind of quandary, and seeing as how you knew him longer than anyone, I was wondering Commander, if you would do the honours.'

'Of course he will Katriona, the honour will be all his,' Avis replied while her husband looked aghast.

'That's grand. Thanks ever so much, Commander. That is one great load lifted, now I must be dashing away, Miss Pollock has asked me to source a piper. Thanks for the drink, it's much appreciated. See you tomorrow. Cheery-bye!'

'Christ! The funeral isn't tomorrow is it?'

'No Rodney, she means see you at church tomorrow. It's Sunday, remember?'

'Fat chance, Avis.'

'Katriona knows that. But the hearty faithful are given to hope.'

'They don't go in for wife murdering either but Avis I'd dearly love to strangle you. What, in the name of all that's sacred, is going on in your mind, out of which you undoubtedly are? Why would I be honoured to deliver anything pleasant about Ian Parker? It would be easier to explain String Theory to Europa here.'

Their dog wagged her tail and continued to savage a very tatty and faded teddy bear. I had a teddy bear like that once but I lost it.

'No need, Rodney, what Europa doesn't know about String Theory is irrelevant. Come on, you can do it, you used to do this sort of thing all the time.'

'I'm ninety Avis, I need a rest and furthermore I couldn't stand the man.'

'Nobody could, except your niece and old Irene Gilmerton of course. I wonder whether she is still alive. Oh well, never mind, you'll just have to apply yourself. Trot out the usual stuff.'

'What usual stuff have you in mind for a man who was a complete, ingratiating, oily, acquisitive, intrusive and insinuating sham?'

'Be positive. Think how good he was in a crisis.'

'He was like a pompous Chief Petty Officer with a whistle.'

'He was good at organising people. He could also copy paintings.'

'Very badly.'

'It wasn't his fault he had no talent. Think, Rodney, think of all those times he used to go to Milngavie Towers to visit that demented relative of his.'

'Alleged demented relative, Avis, I reckon he was haunting the Glasgow public conveniences for bum boys. Anyway, we heard nothing of his relatives, demented or otherwise, up until a few years ago. I am sure he had his eye on a likely legacy. Well he won't be getting one of those now.'

'No chance, Rodney, and even if both he and the mad old bat were still alive, she'd die penniless, like everyone else in Milngavie Towers, no matter how rich they were before.'

'Very well Avis, then if you are so resourceful, you write the wretched diatribe. Have you any idea where Parker came from?'

'You mean his origins, no he just seemed to have evolved. I did hear that the demented relative had a Polish surname, possibly Paderewski. Yes that would make sense, Paderewski to Parker, it's obvious.'

'Not to me, Avis. Not all Poles begin with P. Masses start with Ws for instance.'

'Like Wenceslas? I don't think Ian Parker's mad relative was called Wenceslas.'

'Wenceslas was a Czech.'

'Well no matter, you can skip the bit about where he was born and all that, just let him spring into life fully formed like that ridiculous goddess.'

'Athene was fully armed, Avis.'

'Stop quibbling Rodney, nobody can be fully armed unless they are fully formed first.'

Tom looked at me and smiled. 'Don't worry, Mira, they are like this all the time, that's why they're still married. Nobody else could put up with them. Oh God, I'd better go and see what's going on, I'll be back in a moment.'

Europa had abandoned the ragged rabbit and could be heard investigating the kitchen trash bucket.

'Firstly, build on what you know. Ian Parker, a well known local figure for over forty years.'

'Forty-five at least,' the Commander interrupted,' if not more, the fellow was built in with the scenery.'

'Fine, Rodney, forty-five. A man of many parts.'

'All defective!'

'Be quiet, or I won't help you at all. Now, what else? Yes, I have it. Assiduous and concerned with every aspect of the lives of others, a loquacious companion and one who enjoyed conviviality and indulged in life to the full.'

'And other people's booze, not to mention their money.'

'I thought I told you to keep quiet, Rodney.'

'Sorry Avis, please go on.'

'When desperate you can ask rhetorical questions. Where would we have been without Ian? How many of us have benefitted from his friendship? Who can count his many acts of kindness? Who can replace such a man in our hearts? You can keep this up for hours, Rodney, and don't forget that he really did apply himself to ridding the Lumpie of rats.'

'Should I mention his marriage?'

'Just say that Ian Parker was his own man, who made the best of every circumstance and enjoyed many companionable years living in our small community. Also,' Avis continued, 'he was as good as his word. That at least is true.'

Sunday

I had decided to spend my second evening in my hotel room. It was less embarrassing than having to encounter Cess again, somehow I felt I had intruded enough on the Wishart family, even if they were, in a distant way, my family too. Headaches are easily faked and British TV really is good, though on Saturday nights everybody seems obsessed with performing like someone else and voting zee list celebrities out of jungles and off game shows. One of the late-night movies was OK except that I fell asleep soon after the opening titles and never did get to learn how the good guys got to win. I like classic Westerns best, I can't hack car chases or American war movies, my real passion is for ancient musicals like *High Society* and the Ealing Comedies that Aunt El adored and Sojourner thought were trite junk. Sojourner could not understand why Ben loved *Lady Killers* and *Kind Hearts and Coronets,* which she considered to be both amoral and immoral. Her taste was more elevated, she professed a passion for Ingmar Bergman and Fellini though none of us believed her. The one movie we all agreed upon and loved was *Cinema Paradiso.*

I was the only person in the dining room for breakfast the following morning but I did overhear a very sharp exchange between Cousin Cess and Yvonne about how she should have been consulted before accepting my reservation.

'But Miss Pollock, I was not to know that you would object to Mrs Staple. She booked over the internet from the States and paid

270

double the usual deposit. You always say that the trans-Atlantic business should be encouraged and it is not as if we are snowed under with guests at the moment. We've only the three rooms let and all of those are to your family.'

'Mrs Staple is not part of my family, she is an imposter. She is base-born.'

'Miss Pollock! Surely you'd not be holding that against her!'

'All I am saying is that if Mrs Staple decides to leave early do not prevent her. I require her room.'

'Who for?'

'Me. From now onwards I will be living here. I want no questions or arguments about this. It is perfectly simple. The Lodge is part of Mr Parker's estate, his executors must decide what to do with it and have vacant possession.'

'Och Miss Pollock, that's awful sad. You've been staying up yonder for such a while, you'd think it was your home.'

'My home is here, Yvonne and it's Ms Pollock from now onwards, do you understand? I will start moving my things down today. Is Gilbert vacant?'

'You've the run of the place, Miss, sorry I mean Ms Pollock, bar the Irene Suite and Ailsa which your relatives are using and of course, Matilda.'

'I will take possession of Matilda as soon as you can shift Mrs Staple but meanwhile Gilbert will have to do. Please give me the keys, all of them. It is a fine morning with very little wind, I would like Calum to come up to the Lodge as soon as possible, I need him to mind the bonfire, I have rubbish that wants burning.'

'But Calum isn't in. It's Sunday mind, He's away to the Kirk. I doubt he'll be back till the morn's morn.'

'Oh typical! I suppose I will have to put up with being made to wait, yet again. Now please encourage Mrs Staple to leave, offer her a refund if necessary.'

Having heard all that, I felt more inclined than ever to stay. Why should this middle-aged woman resent me so much? I remember disliking her intensely when I was a child but I can't think I did anything bad to her, apart from saying that I didn't want to live with her. Maybe that was it. Perhaps nobody wanted to live with poor Cess, except the late Mr Parker, but I fancy that set-up was more a matter of convenience than an affair of passion though the up-coming funeral was set to be a showcase for my Cousin Cess's grief, as well as her voice.

There wasn't a soul about when I left the dining room and I noticed that there were no cars parked on the gravel either. Perhaps Chris Wishart and his fractious family had already left and I was now not just the only hotel guest but also the most unwelcome. Cousin Cess can't have grown prosperous on her brand of personal hospitality.

I went into a room, which was grandly labelled Library, to look for Sunday papers. Another room, also facing inland, was the Morning Room, both were empty. The books, I guess, had been purchased for their looks rather than their content and lined the library shelves like troops on parade. The journals on the tables promoted Scotland's vacation opportunities and the achievements of local enterprises and photographs of social gatherings, weddings awash with plaid and odd hats and awards ceremonies with people shaking hands while smiling at the camera lens. There were no newspapers in either room.

Cess was behind the reception desk when I went back through the lobby. It was impossible to pass her without being seen. Emboldened maybe by the hotel's Full Scottish Breakfast – a fried feast accompanied by oatcakes that looked and tasted of chipboard, I wished her good morning and commented in a British way on the weather (pleasant for the time of year but chilly in the breeze).

'Yes, Mrs Staple, was there something?'

'Please Cousin Cecile, call me Mira.'

'I'd prefer you to call me Ms Pollock.'

'OK. That's fine but I'm Mira and I am sorry that I have upset you.'

She looked up, our eyes met, I smiled and she turned away with a shudder. 'Upset is it? Does having my entire life blighted, my chances of happiness and good reputation destroyed, don't these qualify me to be upset? Obviously not!'

'Believe me, Ms Pollock, I have no recollection of doing any of all that. I haven't even seen you since I was a tiny kid. I think I remember staying with your parents on a farm, I recall a calf sucking my fingers and a bull with a ring in his nose. I also re-member going to an amusement park but I do not remember being mean to you.'

'What are you doing here now?'

'I have come to attend to some business.'

'Why?'

'I got a letter from an attorney to say someone was interested in buying my rock.'

'Well you are wrong. Nobody wants your rock and never will, so you can go away, now, as soon as possible.'

'I will leave, I promise you, just as soon as I've sorted the business.'

'I've told you, there is no business to sort, as you put it, not any more, not now that my dear friend Mr Parker is dead.'

She groped for something to mop the tears mingled with snot and dribble that coursed down her face, leaving pale tracks through her bilious orange make-up. I handed her the 'I love NYC' hand-kerchief from last year's Secret Santa. 'Keep it,' I said, not out of generosity but because I could not bear to touch it after she had snivelled on it. She revolted me as much now as she had revolted me then, when I was little.

A yapping dog was chasing a car down the hill towards the hotel. Cess fled through to the dining room and I retreated to the library while Chris Wishart parked his people-carrier outside on the gravel. Yvonne appeared from the kitchens to take over the abandoned front desk.

'Good morning again! Did yous all have a pleasant excursion to Dundoon?'

'Bloody awful, since you ask,' said Chris as he stomped past.

'Oh dear, I'm sorry to hear that.'

'Please forgive my husband, he has a lot on his mind and driving me and the children to Mass was not on his agenda.'

'Well I trust you and the wee girls had an enjoyable, or maybe I should say an uplifting, morning.'

Vlad the dog was scratching at the front door as I let myself out, he had a lump of compost in his mouth. Neither that, nor the reproachful tolling of Dalmuirie's church bell, troubled me as I walked towards its sound, hoping to find a store or gas station selling papers.

The Full Scottish Breakfast dwelt heavily despite my brisk walk to Dalmuirie Garage which sold me the only newspaper that it appeared to stock, *The Sunday Post*. I found a sheltered spot near the hotel with a good view, and sat on the almost dry grass to read.

Sunday papers in the US are fatter than old style mail-order catalogues. Pages of trash, cartoons and comic strips intermingled with information I never want or need. *The Sunday Post*, being easier to manipulate, contained much the same stuff, but was smaller and more parochial and much more engaging.

I read of outrage amongst councillors, epic domestic unpleasantness, stabbings in cities, rioting football fans, infuriated groups and corruption in public offices, inefficiencies in services and the quaint doings of cute pets and looked at pictures of under-dressed lassies and insinuatingly shaped vegetables. I learnt how to clean vases with rice, to use up odd ends of cheese in tasty scones and that it is never too early to plan next year's wallflowers. Dahlias were on special offer. Parking in Coupar was deemed even worse than in Hamilton, a survey revealed. World affairs, though given prominence, were dealt with briefly, football far exceeded everything. I marvelled at the comic strips, the Broons belonged to a time before my own childhood and Oor Wullie's antics were pure and joyful innocence.

Had I someone to be with, I might have liked to make my home there, but I had not. These reclaimed relatives would probably tire of me before I wearied of them. The root that connected me to that place was just a capillary.

From where I was sitting I could see the Lodge in which Cess had lived with Mr Parker whose body, I hoped, was in a funeral home somewhere and not in an open casket on a table in the front room. Scots possibly don't go in for wailing wakes like the Irish do in movies.

The Lodge was quite the nicest piece of architecture around, gothic, stone-built and compact, from what I could see it also had a spectacular garden, far more pleasant than either the hotel or any converted remains of the castle. Being at the top of the hill, dividing the two driveways, it also had the best views.

It would be a wrench for Cess to leave it now. She must be a lonely soul. I never thought I would feel sorry for her, I wish I could erase the thought that I had been responsible for blighting her life. How can a pre-school kid, however precocious, do that to an adult?

She walked down to the hotel carrying a couple of over-stuffed bags. I hadn't got the nerve to offer to help, I knew fine I'd be rejected, so I stayed put and started a questionnaire to see whether I was a Good Citizen.

When would I push my granny off a bus? a) Always. b) Sometimes. c) Never. d) If the bus was on fire.

When would I offer to help a crabbit neighbour with carrying heavy messages?

a) Always. b) Sometimes c) Never d) Only for money. Crabbit I guess means cranky but what is a heavy message? The Communist Manifesto? A shopping list hewn on tablets of stone?

I was about to grapple with the morality of vaulting the turnstiles into pay toilets when I saw Vlad the dog collide with Cess. One of the bags slipped from her grip, scattering papers all around. Heavy messages perhaps? I still didn't move to help her, I had already established that I was likely to prove to be a 'sometimes' type of good citizen.

Had she seen me I'm sure Cess would not have sworn so loudly or aimed a kick at Vlad who was now attempting flight in his pursuit of a seagull that was bugging him. Only the very worst citizens insulted dumb beasts. Cess crammed everything back in its bag and plodded on her way. Once she was out of sight I got up from my hiding place and strolled down towards the hotel too.

The photo, lying on the verge was still recognisable. I knew it at once as the official shot of Ben frequently used on the fly leaves of his earlier books. I turned it over and read the neat message on the back. 'To my own Cecile with all my love for ever, your own devoted, heart-broken Ben.'

Had this been Ben's hand I would have recognised it instantly. His illegible scrawl was unmistakable.

I'd always felt sorry for King John, who had his little ways and whose Christmas cards were never from his near and dear but only from himself. Now I felt really sorry for Cess.

I left the picture where she would see it, only half-hidden by some weeds and walked on to the desolate tennis court behind which I found a miniature headstone dedicated to Fifi, 1950 – 1966, Faithful and Devoted Friend. While I was looking at this monument to the embarrassed lapdog in the Gilmerton family portrait, Cess must have returned up the hill. I checked the roadside a few minutes later, Ben's picture had gone.

★

Tom Wishart and I had arranged to meet in the early afternoon, he was going to take me to see the district before he went to Edinburgh for what he called a ghastly family gathering.

'Your family?'

'No, mine isn't ghastly, Claudia's is. I've got to go to this do to give moral support. I've been given a three-line whip.'

'Are they into S and M?'

'I wouldn't be surprised, they are an alarming bunch but why do you ask?'

'The whip with three lines?'

'Oh that's just an expression, to do with Parliament. Haven't you heard it before?'

'Maybe but I guess not. I left this country a long time ago. Some things I remember well, others have passed away completely, but some forgotten stuff comes back, only looking a whole lot smaller.

The rest of Tom's family, apart from Chris who had taken himself to Doonbury to play prestigious golf, were recovering from too much of each other and lunch, as we scrambled down to the beach. Tom was touchingly pleased with himself and smiled broadly as he showed me what he'd manage to find – a frail dinghy that looked to me about as sea-worthy as a basket. It would have been churlish to have told him the very last thing I wanted to do in the whole world was to be taken across the sound to visit my rock, Henrysson's Rock, the Lumpie, the sole remaining vestige of my unsatisfactory breeding.

It was certainly smaller than I remembered, but not one bit less scary.

If it hadn't been Tom, I would not have minded inventing a phobia about water, a horror of boating, perhaps even a religion that forbad travelling on a Sunday, anything to get out of this trip. But he looked so thrilled by having pulled off this surprise, I couldn't deflate his delight. Fears, after all, are better confronted head on and he, of all people, was the one I'd be happiest to be with for such a confrontation, which would probably turn out to be no great production after all. It was truly just a rock, a rock of poisoned rats.

'You look worried, Mira.'

'Me? No I'm OK, I just didn't sleep too good, jet lag hangs on. Where's Europa?'

'With the parents, I'm not sure about her on a boat and I don't want her finding any old dead rats especially now that I'm moving away.'

'Are you re-locating?'

'To Spain, after the wedding, I've got a year's work lined up in the Pyrenees. Europa wouldn't take to living in the mountains, she doesn't do sturdy.'

I pictured that polymath Claudia and her peripatetic writing career thriving on crystal mountain air. I couldn't imagine anything more heavenly than a year in the Pyrenees. But then I was growing to think that anywhere, even a stinking slum, would be heaven with Tom.

'Doesn't Claudia like dogs?'

'I don't know. Not much, I suppose, she hasn't got one. Why do you ask?'

I pretended interest in a flight of gulls, I had to stop this nonsense. I was being absurd.

'Do you speak Spanish?' I asked.

'Only very basic. Do you?'

'Yes, fluently.'

'That is impressive, Claudia is the only other person I know who can speak it well.'

I wanted to go on and tell him about my French, Italian and Portuguese too, only I didn't want to hear that Claudia was also adept in all those plus, I would not be surprised to discover, of her competence in German, Russian and Serbo-Croat and her ability to decipher ancient runes while interpreting Chinese. The superstar Claudia's Spanish would undoubtedly be Castilian, mine was Mexican.

Tom took my arm and pointed: 'Look, there's a kittiwake.'

I saw just another seabird. They all looked the same to me, like the tops of choppy waves thrown into the sky. I really hadn't had a good night. My shallow sleep had been disturbed by nightmares and my sleepless hours by swirling worries. Worries that pester in the early hours often evaporate when it is time to get up. Sometimes they disappear into the bin which consumes dreams. Not so these ones. I was tormented with a hateful suspicion that something was being hidden from me. Someone, maybe several people, knew more about me than I did. They knew what I had sworn never to tell.

A dreadful truth was threatening me. The more I thought the more certain I became. Yet why? Surely it wasn't possible. Oh yes it was though, perfectly possible now that I had convinced myself that the fire which killed my father and his bride Grizelda, was no accident. It was deliberate, crazy of course but nevertheless a conscious act of deluded revenge.

My mad mother was the murderess. It fitted. Her interest in the Gilmerton fortune, her foolish promises of an idyllic life for me, her sudden disappearance and the fact that none of us heard from her again, ever. A woman as crazed as her would be capable of anything, including setting a summerhouse alight but would she really, deliberately do so with her ex-lover and his wife inside? Why not?

All those later sightings of Dora had been little more than speculative, her Irish marriage, her time in the East, everything had been so vague. Maybe she managed to disappear and survive, perhaps she was leading a respectable life in a smug suburb, or perhaps she had gone native in an unvisited jungle, joined a cult or died destitute on the streets.

What made it worse was that I was also convinced now that there must have been collusion in her disappearance. Surely Ben knew. Why else would he resolutely refuse to try and trace her? He had been a devoted and dutiful brother and then suddenly all blood ties were severed. Why else would he finish, suddenly, with Grizelda's sister Tilda? This fitted too. How could Ben and Tilda continue together if he was defending his sister for the murder of Tilda's sister?

I tried to dismiss all this from my mind as I joined Tom. Then I was struck with an inspired thought.

'Tom' I said,' I sure do appreciate you getting hold of this boat but the truth is I would really rather see what my rock looks like from a distance. Why don't we take a drive up there, I reckon the view must be stunning.'

'Where?' he said, straightening up.

'There, that obelisk in the trees,' I pointed towards a distant hill.

'No!' he replied so sharply that I was quite scared.

'Why not?'

'No!' he repeated. 'If you knew why you shouldn't have asked.'

'I'm sorry, I know nothing and I didn't mean to upset you.'

He grunted and continued to check out the boat while I prayed for him to discover an enormous hole but the tiny vessel appeared hearty and just sea-worthy. The water between the shore and the rock was as flat as ironed silk; the afternoon was warm and muffled. I tuned my petitions to praying for a tempest. I should have been more careful with my wishes.

After he'd rolled up his jeans and was pushing the boat off the sand into the sea, I noticed that it, I mean she, was called Happy.

'Tom', I said, hoping to defer his anger and delay matters with distractions, 'who do you think started the fire up at the castle?'

'I'm sure it was an accident, people love to speculate, it relieves the boredom, conspiracy theories add to the gaiety of nations. Jump aboard everything is ship-shape.

'And Bristol fashion? You know I haven't heard anyone saying that since I was a kid. An old nanny used to come to tea with my aunt and always said that when she was trying to get the little boy in her charge, ready to go home.'

Tom wasn't listening, he was taking a call on his mobile. I suspected it was Claudia who would doubtless have struck out for the rock, her svelte body slicing the ocean with an immaculate crawl and emerge the other side as enticing as Ursula Andress in the ancient Bond movie.

I looked with terrors multiplying at my beastly rock and remembered another of Nanny's nostrums, 'You must be big and brave, there are worse troubles at sea.'

The cavalry arrived just in time in the form of Patience and Phylida, I wanted to smother them in kisses like a delighted dog greeting a beloved owner.

'Where are you going? What are you doing?'

'I'm taking Mira to visit her rock.'

'Can me and Patience come too?'

'No!'

'Why not, Uncle Tom?'

'Because you'll go on and on and on about the wedding and I am fed up with hearing about it.'

'We won't mention it, we won't say another word about it… will we, Phylly?'

'We'll be wee mice,' said Phylida.

'Please, Uncle Tom,' Patience wheedled.

'No!'

'Why?'

'Because you haven't got life jackets.'

'We can swim. Really well, we've got certificates and I've even got a cup for most improved width, so there. And we told Mum you were going to look after us.'

'That, Patience, is an out and out lie, your mother would rather engage Beelzebub himself as your Universal Aunt before entrusting you both to me, as well you know.'

'Why?' said Phylly.

'I told you why,' said Patience, 'now shut up. But look, you can almost walk over to island if you stick close to the rocks, easy peasy.'

'Yes you can now,' Tom replied, 'but not in an hour or so at high tide. And anyway I can't fit you both into the boat with Mira there too.'

'Oh please,' I said rather too eagerly, 'please take the girls, I can watch you from the shore and I can always go another time. I guess the rock has been there since the pre-Cambrian era and doesn't plan on erupting again for another billion years.'

'No, no little girls. My foot is down. Hop in, Mira. Oh don't sulk, Patience, I can't stand Goths who sulk. Listen I'll see if we can get a boat from down the harbour to take us all to Ailsa Craig tomorrow if it's fine. How about that?'

'But we want to see the cave where Sawney Bean ate people.'

'Not without life jackets you don't, your mother would kill me.'

'She wouldn't, she only said we couldn't go in a car with you she never said about boats, did she, Patience?'

Patience gave her sister a kick.

Tom sighed. 'Run along, both of you. You could always go and take Vlad the Impaler for a walk, that's sure to wear him out.'

The girls walked dejectedly back towards the hotel.

'Poor little things!'

'Don't you believe it,' said Tom, 'they are both spoiled rotten. Here we go, all aboard the sky-lark. I'm bad at judging distances but I know it's not far. Sit tight.'

I am not a water baby. My swimming is rudimentary and I have no notion about boats and ropes and all that jargon about tacking and putting about.

Ben hadn't been a sailor either, his passion was burning up the open road on his bike which seemed strange for a man so gentle, learned and peaceable. He looked quite incongruous, encased in helmet and leathers. Aunt El considered the Staten Island Ferry rather rash and said the *Titanic* had it coming for her, which was somewhat obvious when you think about it. Travelling anywhere with Aunt El was a nightmare, she foresaw catastrophe with every alteration in an aircraft's engine noise and insisted on telling fellow passengers that there was nothing to worry about and we must all be brave and remember the Blitz and The Few, thus making everything much worse.

The short row across the sound was accomplished in four minutes which I thought stretched themselves to forty. By the time we reached the remains of a basic jetty I was shaking and my teeth chattered despite a sudden burst of sunshine through the muggy clouds, transforming the sea between us and the mainland into a glittering River of Life, back across which I would have to go in order to achieve salvation.

'Are you all right, Mira? Your hand is freezing.' I hadn't let go of Tom's hand since he helped me to the shore. I dropped it now; 'Sorry. I'm fine, really I am, I just feel as if someone has walked over my grave.'

'This isn't your grave, it's your kingdom! Come along, we had better start your royal progress, you must visit all quarters and be gracious to your subjects who are lining the route and cheering their hearts out.'

But the crowd had cheered as Louis the Sixteenth passed in

a tumbril, they cheered when Moussolini was strung up, upside down. For me there were only screaming birds and the drum beat of my thumping heart. I knew where I was. I knew that I should not have come back.

'I don't like this place.'

'At least have a look round while we're here.'

Tom was the last person I'd wanted to offend. His voice betrayed him, he was disappointed and resented my lack of enthusiasm.

'Of course we must, I'm just being chicken, you lead on, show me the sights.'

The land above the weedy, rock-strewn shore was strangely spongy, changing further up to scrubby grass at the low summit from where the ground fell away steeply on the seaward side of the island, invisible from the mainland. We picked our way down this western face until we reached a beach that was narrowing with the incoming tide. I looked for the legendary cave and was relieved to find nothing. Then Tom showed me a lofty slit in the rock just above what I assumed to be high water-mark.

As we climbed I smelt the stench of death.

I screamed. Tom turned. 'What the hell is the matter now?'

'Look there!' I pointed at a half-eaten corpse lying behind a heap of rocks.

He turned right round to his left and prodded the body with his toe.

I shut my eyes and shuddered, too horrified to move.

'Well that's one less seal for the eco-warriors to worry about. I wonder what's been eating it, gulls or rats, maybe both. At least they are doing something useful for a change. Take heart, Mira, nature in the raw is seldom pretty.'

'I'm sorry, I'm being ridiculous, I thought it was a child.'

'You've been hearing too much about Sawney Bean's gang. You know most of that story of cannibals is absolute junk, a lot of it put about by Daniel Defoe when he wasn't pretending to be a tart, or a highwayman, or a shipwrecked guy, or an eyewitness of the plague that happened when he was five. This version of the story with the Bean family living in this cave and pouncing on passing travellers was made up too, some sort of Jacobite mischief making. You'd starve to death before any dinner strolled past this rock. That aspect of the legend must have been entirely Ian Parker's own invention, while he conjured up his scheme to turn this place into the Sawney Bean Experience, a sort of Henrysson Rock of Horror. He couldn't of course because the rock wasn't his, even though he did spend a lot of time, and his wife's money, trying to exterminate the rats, obviously without lasting effect. The spongy stuff we walked over when we landed is undermined by labyrinthine rat holes. Rats get everywhere but only the real curse of Scotland will defeat us.'

'Curse! What curse? You said nothing about a curse.'

'The Midge.'

'What?'

'Bugs, Mira, don't look so alarmed. Just pesky, itchy, biting clouds of bugs.'

Some places are also cursed with a terrible atmosphere and my rock had that real bad. It was in no way desirable real estate, I recalled the attorney's words 'a small parcel without residential or agricultural potential and scant amenity value'.

'Look, down there, what's that?'

Tom looked towards where I was pointing at a heap of rotten timbers.

'It looks like a very ruined shack to me, perhaps it was a bird-watching hide or a store. It can't have been used for decades.'

We clambered up to the cave leaving the stink of putrid seal behind. The entrance was narrow and widened into a larger chamber from which smaller corridors appeared to lead back into the rock. I went no further than the entrance and Tom shone his torch to reveal nothing apart from trash blown in by storms.

He took my hand: 'Don't worry, there is nobody else here, there is nothing to be scared about.' His hand felt a bit too good and I know he didn't really need to squeeze mine like he did.

There was a scuffling behind us. 'Gotcha! Ker- ching!'

Patience was barring the exit in triumph: 'Wait till we tell everyone about this, Phylly!'

'For God's sake, what are you children doing here? I told you to stay on the shore.' Tom dropped my hand as if scalded.

'So? You only said you wouldn't take us in the boat, actually,' Patience replied, smirking.

'How did you get here then?'

'We paddled, it was easy peasy, I told you.'

'Well just go and paddle back then.'

Phylly started to wail. I could see the child was soaked through, everything dripped as her teeth chattered. 'What happened to you?'

'She fell over, the clumsy lump,' said Patience. 'Mum will go ape when she sees she's lost her trainers. We hung them round our necks but Phylly's fell off and just sort of floated away. They were new.'

Phylly's wails grew louder.

'Oh shut up for goodness sake,' said Tom, 'it's a mercy you didn't just float away too, the currents round here can be unpredictable. You certainly won't be able to go home the way you came, the rocks will be entirely covered by now. I've a good mind to leave you both here for the night.'

'No!' I was shouting now. 'No! You can't do that.'

'Of course I can't, Mira. What do you think I am? Come along, I'll row you two back now, in our life jackets, and then I'll come back for Mira.'

'Can't we all fit in to the boat together?' I asked, hearing my voice turn squeaky.

'I wouldn't want to risk it. You'll be fine on your own for maybe half an hour or so, probably less. Hurry up, you two.'

I watched as Tom rowed away. He couldn't wave of course but he smiled encouragingly. That was kind of him I daresay, though utterly ineffective. The kids had their backs to me and as the distance between us widened. I could see Phylly shaking despite the adult life jacket that enveloped her, but whether from cold or apprehension I couldn't say.

I was determined not to panic. Tom would be back just as soon as he'd docked and unloaded.

When they reached the shore I saw that he lifted Phylly out of the boat and put her on his back to carry her up to the house. He would make a wonderful father. Right now I needed a wonderful friend, quickly. The western sky had turned into a slate bruise, the gulls had stolen off and the sea surface was now crushed and wrung-out wrinkled silk.

I saw Patience tie up the boat before following Tom and Phylly up the path.

★

All nature sensed the coming storm, even the insect clouds dispersed in the sudden sharp breeze. In the distance, a hair of light cracked the sky followed by a grumbling roar.

My cellphone rang. Thank God for cellphones at least Tom could keep in touch and reassure me. Then, as I fumbled in my pocket I remembered that neither of us knew each other's number, so it could not possibly be Tom or anybody this side of the Atlantic.

'Hi honey, it's me! How are yo'all?'

'Sojourner!'

'I just wanted to say Hi. How are you doing?'

'I'm alone on a rock of dead rats.'

'That's quite some metaphor I take it. Is the UK that flaky?'

'No it's for real. I'm in the ocean, on a volcanic plug.'

'Like a bath plug? My, that sounds real bad. Is there anything I can do?'

'I wish you could. There is a storm getting up.'

'But you hate thunder storms.'

'Sojourner, for Christ's sake I didn't choose to be here.'

The signal died after a string of bleeps as giant drops plopped on the worried sea, creating spreading rings. I cursed silently, I knew that if I screamed, nobody would hear me and as I scanned the coastline for the boat, I realised that nobody could come for me until the storm had passed.

Behind me, a dog began to howl.

★

The howling was not the Baskerville, sharp fanged, blood- craving type but the terrified whimpering and crying brought on by hopeless despair. Had I been a dog I would have done the same. I was transfixed with fear, so petrified that I was barely capable of folding my body into a quaking ball and cowering behind the largest rock within range. I tried to convince myself that the howling was just my over-active imagination conjuring up a manifestation of the small dog that Miss Stuart had said caused the Victorian Henryssons such distress.

The thunder storm was very real. I blocked my eyes and ears and pleaded for it to stop, or at any rate for the lightning not to choose me. It was almost overhead now, I could barely count a second between the forked flash and the tumbling roar. Angels don't go bowling, the sky won't fall down. Everything passes, even terror.

Something nudged me, something with fur. My God! A rat! A bloody, plague-ridden, rat with wormy, whippy tail and a rabid bite. Better to be sizzled up by lightening than gnawed to a festering fragment like the seal I'd mistaken for a baby. I jumped up just as another flash briefly lit the blackened sky and I saw that the rat was actually Vlad the Impaler.

Neither of us could express how delighted we were to have found each other. I cuddled his soaked and shivering little body and told him that it was going to be all right. One always needs someone to say that to, even a snappy little dog.

Only our perishing is done absolutely alone. I understand we need faith in something. I certainly do, though I could never subscribe to organised religion or take part in the quaint, weird bits that are all in the pious package of impossible beliefs. I'd love to believe that the sign of the cross, a splash of holy water, consecrated bread and a laying on of hands will make things better, forgive sins and guarantee that all manner of thing shall be well.

But it does help a bit to tell, even a terrified little dog, that it will all be all right in the end.

Then I remembered, this is what had already happened to me right here, on this infernal rock, over thirty years ago.

As I gripped Vlad, so had another's skinny arms gripped me and whispered that it was going to be all right. The voice was gentle and persistent, things would be fine, the voice was sure but only if I kept everything a secret. One word about what I'd seen or heard and all the people I loved best would die and I would be given away to people I hated. Even then I knew enough of fairy tales to understand what happened to those who broke promises to fairies.

Those weren't fairy arms, they belonged to a skeleton with short and spiky hair.

The memory has lain dormant, vanished into the darkest recesses to re-enter my life now when all the people I loved best are dead and only one of the people I once hated is alive, unless my mother is living yet, but childhood monsters shrivel to irrelevance with age.

The storm did pass over. Five, ten, fifteen seconds elapsed between the flash and the roar till the thunder dwindled to a grumble over far- off hills. The rain stopped pelting and almost immediately the birds returned to wheel and shriek above the irritated, grey sea. I looked across the water to where the boat was moored – it was not there, only empty beach.

Surely Tom won't have set off back to find me while the storm was on the go. He couldn't have been that stupid, could he? It would have been far too risky, foolhardy even. Oh Christ! Supposing he had tried to get to me and the boat had capsized or been swept away and dashed to matchwood on other rocks. That would be entirely my fault, I would be a murderer. I clutched Vlad so tight again that he squealed.

I must contact someone. I tried my phone, there was a trace of power left, just. I decided to text Sojourner and get her to call the hotel and get help. She would have to use her initiative, of which she was in the habit of reminding me she had masses. It took a while to construct the message then I pressed 'send' to a 'frequent contact' before realising that it had not gone to Sojourner but to Pete Staple, my ex and the very last person I wanted to know I was in trouble, stranded and marooned on a hideous rock and possibly culpable of homicide.

The God in whom my belief was questionable was badly bothered by me that afternoon. I promised all sorts of things which would scarcely be of interest to Omnipotence, I'd quit all indulgence, I'd take up benevolence and give up men, especially those who belonged to other, better people. I'd devote my life to succouring the needy and doing good to them that hate me. I'd be complimentary to those I envy, I'd be pleasant to Cess, I'd leave her kingdom tomorrow, if only Tom were safe. Please God, please. I will leave Tom alone from now onwards, I won't even try to be friendly, I'll leave as soon as possible and never see him again, just please let him be safe.

I walked to the end of the island looking for wreckage, I scanned the horizon and shouted at the land. Nothing, no answer and no sign of the lost boat. Vlad stuck by me and barked a bit, quite useless. I felt hysteria bubbling up; I was going to lose it badly and disgracefully in front of the dog.

Tinkly music proved my phone not dead. It was Pete, touchingly agitated yet detectably irritated, ringing from up-state New York and wanting to know what was to be done. I heard his voice and I felt a surge of purest joy, not because it was him but because my heart had emphatically not leapt up. I did not want him back, there was to be no reconciliation. Even if I died, stuck alongside this small dog on this loathsome rock I would be happier than were I restored to Pete's bosom and that of the smug Staples. All I wanted was for Tom to be safe.

I told Pete to Google and call up Dalmuirie House Hotel and tell them I wanted a boat to get me and Vlad off Henrysson's Rock.

'Who the Hell is Vlad?' Pete asked.

'The Impaler and not your concern. Please Pete get on with calling the hotel.'

'Why should I? Get your lover to do your dirty work.'

'He's a dog, Pete.'

'So? That's not my fault, you should be more discriminating. You can't just walk out on me and expect me to help when you and your lover mess up.'

'I told you Pete, Vlad is not my lover, he's a dog.'

'And you're a bitch, a mongrel bitch. You and me are through, Mira. You should hear what Mom and Pop have to say about you. Comprennez?'

I told him to bugger off and felt a bit better for it.

There was still no sign of the boat nor evidence of wreckage but I did think that maybe the tide had started to recede. Perhaps it would not be long till the sea gave up its dead. No! Not that, oh please God not that, not Tom.

★

Two hours later, I waded ashore, thigh high in the coldest water I have ever experienced. I stuffed my cell phone down my bra and carried Vlad under my arm hoping like Hell I wasn't going to stumble over seaweed haunted by a cache of jellyfish. Almost at the shore, the sea-bed dipped, the water rose to my waist, I floundered and went under, I saw sky quivering through the water and Vlad wriggled free. I did not notice then that my cell phone had also wriggled free.

Both Vlad and I knew where we were going, it was too late to drown now and despite its efforts, the sea was not going to claim either of us, that project was now passed on to pneumonia. Once on the beach my legs became icy jelly and I collapsed upon wrinkled sand. Vlad did not approve of such lack of spine, he shook himself vigorously and scampered off up the bank, back to the hotel; I stumbled after, sneakers squelching and jeans clinging, sustained by anxiety and fury.

Shaking with cold and possibly shock, I staggered through the garden and made a dripping entrance into the hotel lobby.

Vlad's reception was sensational – mine, merely inconveniently messy.

'Oh my precious! My darling, where have you been? We've been looking for you everywhere. Thank God you are safe!' Caro Wishart scooped Vald up in her arms, impervious of the havoc he was causing her frilly shirt.

'Bloody dog,' said her husband Christopher, 'I've a good mind to have him put down.'

This triggered shrieks and wails from Caro and both daughters, Phylly with a gratifyingly bulky bandage wrapped around her ankle and Patience, thanks to anguish, more of a Goth than ever.

Christopher held up his hand as if quelling disorder in court. 'Shut up all of you. This time he shall live but if there ever is a next time, that's it, curtains, end of story. My word is paramount, do you understand?' Then he looked at me: 'I say,' he said, 'are you competing in a wet T shirt competition, my dear? If so, my money's on you.'

My teeth were chattering too much for me to make myself understood. All I could do was clamour for attention by shouting Tom's name.

'Now don't get your knickers in a twist sweetheart, what about Tom?'

'Where is he?' I spluttered.

Chris let go of my shoulders which he'd grabbed, and looked at his watch. 'He'll be almost through by now, I expect.'

'Through what?'

'Through to Edinburgh, about Mid Calder I imagine, why?'

'Are you sure?'

'Well, yes, barring accidents of course. Caro, what time did Tom leave you at the hospital?'

But Caro wasn't listening, she was wrapping Vlad in her cream pashmina.

Salt tears joined the salt water dripping from me. 'I thought he was drowned.'

'Tom? Never, he's much too canny for that. You aren't half making a mess of Cess's public parts my dear, would you like me

to come up and help you get out of your wet things? It would be
a rare pleasure to towel you down.' Chris made sure that Caro
had heard.

'No! I can manage on my own, like I've had to manage everything on my own today, even getting off that bloody rock on
my own.'

'Oh please don't swear in front of the children,' Caro pleaded as
I stomped up the stairs leaving sandy wet sneaker prints on each
step. Yvonne, who had gone to fetch Calum's vacuum cleaner,
followed me.

'Mrs Staple, there's been a wee alteration since you went out.
Your things are all now in Grizelda.'

'Why? I was fine in Matilda.'

'Miss Pollock said you were to be moved to Grizelda so I shifted
your stuff. I hope you don't mind. Grizelda has a sea view, it's
better by far.'

I was too tired, wet and angry to object but I did ask Yvonne
to tell me her version of what had happened.

'Well, when Tom Wishart brought the wee girls up to the hotel
before the storm their mum made such a fuss you'd think the one
they call Phylly had snapped her neck. Anyway she wanted to
call an ambulance, which was ridiculous, because she didn't want
Tom to drive her or her precious children.'

'Why ever not?'

'Oh you know, she can carry on , she even called him a half
blind convict which was well out of order, totally unacceptable.
Oh but she was in such a pother and, even if she could, which
she can't, she was in no fit state to drive.'

'But wasn't there anybody else available? Miss Pollock, old
Mrs Wishart?'

'No, Miss Pollock said she had to sort things here and I'm not
sure about Mrs Wishart, maybe she and the Commander were
sleeping off their lunch.'

'So what happened?'

'Well Tom told her she'd just have to take a grip on herself and let him drive her and the children to the hospital and then if the children's father could be raised at the golf he could fetch them from there. To be truthful I couldna' tell which it was, the missing dog, her injured child or the prospect of Tom's driving that troubled her the more. Anyway I said I would arrange a search party for the dog and Tom drove them off and said he'd have to go straight on from the hospital, through to Edinburgh I think, he's got some sort of business to attend to there. The turned ankle was dealt with that quickly at A and E that Mum and the kids came back in a taxi about the same time as their father arrived back from the golf club (I don't think he'd had much of a round) and then that wullie dog turned up, followed by you.'

'Didn't Tom tell anybody where I was? Didn't he ask somebody, anybody to come and fetch me?'

'Fetch you from where?'

'Henrysson's Rock, the Lumpie'

'You've never been stuck on yon all this time?'

'I have and I'm bloody freezing.'

'Oh my! And here's all us thinking you were just fine and gone up by to see the Wisharts.'

'Who ever told you that?'

' I canna' mind but there was such a rumpus going on what with all the shouting about the dog and the wee girl howling about her leg and young Mrs Wishart going mental and Phylly's missing shoes, I couldn't be certain about anything. It was a fearful scene. It was good that the lunch was over, you wouldn't want hotel guests to be embroiled in that kind of carry on.'

'Did anybody actually say I was with Tom's mother?'

'I'm not sure, but I think someone said you were OK. Now you'd better hurry up and into a bath. There's a good bathroom in Grizelda.'

'There's a good bathroom in Matilda too.'

'Aye, but I think you'll find the other room is better.'

I was way beyond caring but I was curious to find the door to

Matilda open and Cess herself sitting on my bed surrounded by her stuff, not mine.

She looked at me coldly. 'So you're back,' she announced with hostile composure. 'How may I ask did you find your rock?'

'How did you expect me to find it?'

'I have no idea, I have only been there once, as you may remember. I do not trespass. The late Mr Parker however was assiduous in keeping it free of rats for you. It is a tragedy that you were never able to repay or thank him. Now you will see that I've upgraded you to Grizelda at no extra cost. Please go and clean yourself up I don't want my guests offended or inconvenienced by unpleasantness.'

'What guests?'

I didn't wait for an answer. I couldn't be hacked to fight as I obviously qualified as the epitome of unpleasantness. I'd put up with a sea view, Anything so long as there was a hot, deep bath tub. My rock no longer worried me. Anyway I could block it out with the drapes.

I'd had enough of this place and the mad person who owned it. Just two more days and I should be through and then I could turn my back on the lot, start a new life somewhere else far away. In time I would forget all this, even Tom, especially him, the heartless brute for not bothering to tell anybody where I was and for giving me the worst, most anxious couple of hours of my life. For that I'd not forgive him. Not that he'd care.

Just as I was about to collapse, washed and warm into my clean white bed I heard a knock at my door. I opened it a crack half hoping it was Tom with an apology, which of course it was not, he was in Edinburgh with the human angel Claudia.

Yvonne stood in the passage and told me that she thought I might like to know that the boat had been found by the De'il's Dyke. It had broken loose from its moorings during the storm and drifted the short way along the beach. Nobody had taken the boat, everybody was safe. 'I didn't want you worrying, Mrs Staple.'

I thanked her for being so thoughtful but the truth was I had not been worried. I had only been concerned for Tom, the man who was so unconcerned about me that he'd neglected to tell anyone where I was. I felt ashamed of my lack of compassion.

Even if there had been another storm in the night or if Grizelda, the burnt bride, had returned to haunt her childhood bedroom, my deep and glorious, dreamless sleep would not have been disturbed.

Monday

onday morning dawned and my brain was clear, my cell phone was lost at sea but I was charged up and bristling with great intentions. Things that had bothered me had temporarily receded into the junk file with a good night's rest.

Perhaps the only thing left to be done was to discover a bit more about the late Mr Parker and what he had wanted to do with my rock. Whatever his plans, today was the day for getting rid of it, tomorrow the day for starting over, yet again.

Wallace-Falkirk and Company, Solicitors of Dundoon agreed for me to call though Mr Wallace-Falkirk, Writer to the Signet, who had contacted me a year ago was unavailable but Mrs Wong would be able to assist.

My vision of a Dickensian set-up of hunched gents and exploited clerks evaporated somewhat, when a chic receptionist greeted me and offered me coffee while I waited. I was further surprised to discover Mrs Wong to be a well built, streaked blonde of my age with a voice like Alastair Sim in the St Trinians' movies. She took me to her tiny office at the back overlooking a shaggy garden bisected by a washing line of grey garments that could have dangled there since hanging was abolished.

I liked Mrs Wong immediately; she was brisk and to the point. She explained that her specialism was marital disputes but that she was acquainted with the affairs of the late Mr Parker and was pleased to meet me but unable to offer much hope of a rapid and profitable disposal of my rock, now that Wallace-Falkirk and Company's client had passed away. He was the only person to express any interest in my rock whatsoever.

'Do you know why Mr Parker wanted Henrysson's Rock?'

'He had a scheme for turning it into a theme park, the Sawney Bean Experience or some such notion, but I think it was just folie de grandeur.'

'It's not a grand rock though,' I said.

'But people pay fortunes to call themselves lords of worse spots.' She spoke very rapidly and kept looking at the clock. 'The market for rocks is very flat. The sale of Ailsa Craig is a case in point, and Ailsa Craig has many advantages over Henrysson's Rock, not least some habitable housing, re-established puffins and of course, curling stones.'

I had visions of standing stones with perms but Mrs Wong was in too much of a hurry for irrelevancies.

Suddenly she stood up and shook my hand said it was nice to meet me, especially as she had been such an avid admirer of my uncle but that the initial interview was at an end. She walked with me to the door and came outside on to the step of the terrace in which all the professionals of Dundoon, from architects to accountants, appeared to have offices.

'Mrs Staple, forgive me, but I did not want to burden you with unnecessary expense. You see after the first twenty minutes, which are free, my uncle, who is the senior partner, insists that we charge exorbitantly for each subsequent six minutes. I would dearly like to talk to you further. Let's meet for lunch, entirely by chance you understand, How about the Shanter Cafe on the High Street at one today? I'm Isabella by the way.'

'And I'm Mira. That's great, the Shanter Cafe it is.'

'You can't miss it. It's between the Bombay Tandoori and Chinatown Carry Out beyond Oggs Fancy Goods. Occasionally the soup isn't bad, but I'd dodge the chicken if I were you, they're all spent battery hens boiled to rags. Now I'd better dash back to toiling at the coalface of crumbling marriages before my uncle's toadies report me for unpaid loitering.'

The Shanter Café's soup de jour was Scotch Broth, Isabella, who now told me to call her Isa, advised against that too. 'One sees enough of that on the pavements,' she said.

I wasn't hungry for anything in the Shanter Cafe but I settled for a Danish containing solid yellow custard, chased by a cup of exceptionally weak black coffee. Isa chose a flapjack and a vivid drink that I think she said was made from girdles. 'Nobody comes to the Shanter Cafe for the food, or anything else for that matter, it's the one place I can get a bit of peace. Now what would you like to know?'

'I guess I'd like to know about Mr Parker.'

'Well, let's see, one shouldn't speak ill of the dead, especially a dead client who paid, or rather, a dead client whose wife paid. And before you ask, yes, Mrs Parker was once rolling in it. She was the sole heir to Gilmertons, the dernier cri in foghorns, sirens, klaxons and hooters. I doubt there was a vessel afloat or a hazardous rock or a substantial works that didn't bellow at the world courtesy of Gilmertons. Not any more of course but Matilda Parker's father left his daughter more than enough to keep her oleaginous hus- band in idle splendour, free to seep into every cranny and keep the wheels of his little world at Dalmuirie well oiled.'

'You didn't like him?'

'Did anyone?'

'Cecile Pollock, is seriously distressed by his death.'

'Ah yes, poor old Cess Bollocks, as I'm afraid she is known, she'd be distressed by the death of anybody who flattered her even if they used her mercilessly.'

'Used her, in what way?'

'Oh nothing carnal, nothing venal, just to come and go and cook and sew and all that crap. Mind you, she used him too, they went everywhere together. Poor Cess, life is tough when you are alone, no matter how much you have.'

'Is Cecile rich too?'

'Not in the Gilmerton way but certainly not on the breadline. When her parents were killed, about twenty-five years ago, she inherited the farm and sold the place for a housing scheme and then bought the Gilmertons' house and turned it into a hotel.'

'You know a lot about Dalmuirie.'

'I've lived in this area most of my life I used to play with the Wisharts when I was a child, My mother taught at St Quivox School where my father was grandly called the Bursar. I got educated there for almost nothing till Mum realised I knew almost nothing and thrust me into the state system. She was bosom chums with Avis Wishart when I was little, they would gossip for hours. I drank it all in, specially the spicy bits. I was an only child.'

'Me too,' I said.

'And now I'm virtually an only adult.'

'Same here, I'm on my own now.'

'Have you and Mr Staple come apart? If you have I can put this down as a preliminary consultation. I'm not touting for trade, honest, but it would be convenient if questions are asked and any-way I derive great comfort from hearing about the matrimonial calamities of others.'

'Yes, it's one of the reasons why I've come here now, I'm kind of running away.'

'And the other reason is that you want to get shot of your rock?'

'Yes, that too.'

'And?'

'I'm meant to be writing Uncle Ben's biography. I felt I should look for his roots a bit. Only I haven't found out much yet, except that I'd had no idea how famous he was, here as well as across the pond. Everybody, especially the females, seems to have doted on him and either read his books or seen his stuff on their TVs, everybody that is, except Miss Stuart.'

'I wouldn't bank on that, the old Stewpot knows everything, she just pretends that nobody of any merit could ever come from anywhere except Scotland. So what happened to Mr Staple?'

'Pete and I just weren't right.'

'Take heart, you can't have been as wrong as me and Mr Wong, the bastard. We met at Law School, and I think now we got married to spite both sets of parents and to change my name, I was sick to death with being Miss Smellie. Anyway Mr Wong is now an astoundingly successful commercial barrister married to a tiny Taiwanese cellist with two children (one of each) both of whom play tidgy wee fiddles and they aren't yet four. It's sickening. Meanwhile, I've returned to my roots with my tail between my legs. My uncle has taken pity on me, given me this job and goes out of his way to show that nepotism has nothing to do with it. I can take no liberties and receive no favours. I should be grateful, after all there are loads of us law graduates waitressing and child-minding. Before he died my father forgave me for marrying Mr Wong but my mother's crowded brain went soft; she doesn't recognise me at all. Now I'm the one who has to work hard to keep her. Sorry Mira, it must be this place making me grumpy, let's throw caution to the winds and go to Corlioni's and get us a couple of cones, we can eat them on the esplanade and gaze out to sea like lovelorn maidens.'

'Can you see Ailsa Craig from here?'

'No, why do you ask?'

'No matter. What about your uncle? Will he not be expecting you back in the office?'

'I've told the office dragon that I am making a domiciliary visit to a potential client, it's almost true, everyone is a potential client and the fact that you are without a domicile means we are perfectly justified to conduct this interview from a shelter on the Low Green. Uncle Jock is away through to Edinburgh to where his blessed daughter is launching her latest work, and anyway he's far too preoccupied with how he is going to pay for her lavish wedding next month.'

''Is Mr Wallace-Falkirk's daughter by any chance called Claudia?'

'Yes, only she's dropped the Wallace when she's writing, too far down the alphabet apparently. Her public can't get that far. Do you know her?'

'No, not at all. I've just heard a lot about her from Tom Wishart.'

Isa sighed. 'Ah, poor Tom.'

'Poor? How? Everything seems to be going his way.'

'Well it may be now, but he's had a rough time. He's a great man though…a real Mr Right, unlike his pompous brother. Chucking Christopher was a rare pleasure, he couldn't believe that a great lump like me could turn him down. His face was a study in shocked consternation worthy of a Da Vinci. I think he only tried to get off with me because he thought he could. It was delightfully satisfying to throw him on the heap.'

'I daresay Claudia is a lucky woman,' I said.

'Isn't she just? Think of all that success and adulation, wouldn't I revel in that? Mind you I think her books are trash but I daren't say so because it sounds like jealousy, which of course it is. Now come on, Mira, tell me about you. Is Mira short for Miranda, worthy to be admired?'

'No, I'm afraid not.'

'Or are you named after the star? Mira according to one of your uncle's books is a massive capricious binary star, a red giant of variable girth; you don't look as if your girth ever varies, you lucky woman and only a stick insect could call you a massive giant, I don't know about the capricious or red bits. It's odd isn't it, the way something many times larger than our sun could be artful.'

'You study astronomy?'

'Incompletely. I was addicted to your uncle's programmes, he made it all so lucid. Then I went to evening classes and was totally baffled again by all those co-ordinates and technicalities. The tutor was useless and I only met a clutch of nerds, apart from poor Caro Wishart , the idiot woman who married Wanker Wishart. She's quite a bit younger than me and far brighter and capable of digesting all sorts of baffling data but her beastly husband complained about her going out in the evenings, can you beat it? Such control freakery is intolerable yet the poor bullied woman capitulated and stayed at home being a dutiful mother and downtrodden wife while he carried on groping anything and everything female he could grab. I admire Caro in a way, I envy her faith, she manages to believe in everything, however daft, and have a sound grasp of deep space and all those light years on the basis that once you've investigated the wonders of the universe and touched on quantum mechanics and transubstantiation, virgin births and risings from the dead are complete doddles. She's a convert, converts are always more ardent. She saw the light at her convent school and apparently was on the verge of taking the veil when Wanker Wishart pounced and she fell and shattered like a plaster saint off a pedestal. She's the most obsessed mother I know. Also I suspect she imagines being a martyr paves her way to heaven. After she left the class I gave up and went back to stargazing by myself. At my age it is very difficult for a woman alone to meet interesting people who don't bang on about the tedious doings of their dreary children, that's why I'm no longer matey with Caro. That and her inability to forgive or forget anything. But why complain? I've got a flat, a cat and a cat-flap, what could any old has-been want more? Now, come on, reveal all, if Mira isn't Miranda or a star with mood swings, what is it short for?'

'Miracle.'

'Miracle! Well I never. Wouldn't Caro like that? Loaves and fishes, water into wine and all that. Miracles are dead handy, embarrassing name though.'

'Nobody calls me Miracle any more, thank goodness, I'm always Mira.'

'OK, I understand.'

We walked down to the harbour and Isa told me how the streets were once cobbled and that Dundoon had been a busy port where fish were sold on the quayside. The Mission to Seamen stood alone beside the remnants of the town wall. The dry dock, shipyard and army barracks had all been demolished and replaced with an angular leisure centre. Desolate fairground rides covered the square on which, Isa said, troops used to be drilled.

'You could get a paddle steamer from here to Arran but I think we always had to go beyond Dalmuirie for a boat to Ailsa Craig.'

'Did Ian Parker come from here too?'

'No, his mother was in service somewhere near Stirling and his father appeared on his birth certificate as unknown, though Ian himself invented a gallant and eastern European past which was rather borne out when he became responsible for his demented relative in the same home as my poor batty mum. Only she died, Ian's relative I mean, not Mum who looks set to exist for ever, sans everything except the heart and stomach of an athlete.'

'In what way did you mean that Ian's past was borne out by this woman?'

'She had a Polish-sounding name, not that she ever spoke or anything, she just made a lot of noise for a while till one day she became totally inert and died not long after. It wouldn't have surprised me if Ian Parker had hastened her on her way. He was a resourceful sort, not that I would have blamed him. Anyway nobody ever suggested anything underhand and off she went to the crematorium with Ian as the only mourner. I hope that Cess has managed to persuade more people to come to his funeral tomorrow.'

I felt a lump of dread hit my stomach; there was the question I had to ask.

Isa paused: 'Are you OK, Mira? You look worried.'

'No, I'm fine, just a bit cold. I had a bad time yesterday. I got stuck on my rock during that thunder storm. It shook me up.'

'God! I bet that did. It's a beastly place, renowned for shady doings. I don't envy you owning it one bit. I went there once when I was a little kid, I was feeling rotten, I'd just been traumatised by having my tonsils out and all I remember is longing to get away home and have some ice cream for my poor throat. I think that's maybe why I love the stuff so much now. Here's Corlioni's. What flavour would you like? I always go for vanilla in a predictable way but Gianni has got plenty of other kinds.'

I told her I didn't really feel like ice-cream.

'Shame, I could have put it down to entertainment expenses.'

I felt my knees wobble, I clutched at Isa's arm. 'Sorry, I must sit down.'

After Isa shoved my head down between my legs I began to feel better. Thoroughly Scots, Gianni Corlioni, was most concerned and insisted on giving me a glass of his Italian grandmother's own very special, bitter sweet concoction which seared my throat, fumigated my sinuses and made my eyes steam. I was very grateful. Another slug and I would have been able to face anything, provided I could do it lying down.

Isa bought me a chocolate bar and made me eat it before we walked back from the shore to the town.

We parted at the street corner, out of sight from her office but before she left I managed to ask the question that had been torturing me. 'What was the name of Ian Parker's Polish relative?'

'I don't know, but I could find out for you. I'll let you know tomorrow, at the funeral.'

Did I really want to know the answer? What if it did confirm what I dreaded? Why would it matter? Why couldn't I dismiss it as something in the remote past? 'Besides,' I told myself, 'the wench is dead.' (Though it all happened right here and not in another country.)

I knew that I must get away as soon as possible. This strange sanctuary couldn't keep me, it was a temporary resting place not a refuge in which to get dug in. As I rattled back from Dundoon (I was pleased with myself for deciphering the bus timetable) I realised I had achieved nothing. The rock was still mine.

Isa was right, with the solitary, willing buyer dead there was little point in being a willing seller. I was not only willing but determined. I needed a rock but not a haunted lump of antediluvian granite, I needed a direction, a foundation, somewhere or someone with whom I could reconstruct my collapsed life. Now I was being jolted back to the one place on earth I could truthfully call my own and also the place from which I must get free and set out into the uncharted future. Ben had left me enough to subsist quite well for a while yet, though not enough for me to drift through life on the breeze of my fancy. Speculation must not turn to fantasy,

I was a stupid woman no better than a child crying for the moon that would never be mine.

★

It was almost as if Avis had been waiting for me. She was coming out of the Post Office cum general store as I de-bussed.

'Ah there you are! What luck, we can walk home together.'

Nobody argued with Avis but keeping pace with her was another thing, she strode as if she was embarking on some sort of competitive power walk in a cotton skirt and cardigan. As I panted along beside her, I told her I was leaving.

'Nonsense, Mira. When? You have only just arrived, you can't abandon us so soon. Poor Tom will be devastated.'

'I doubt it,' I said under my breath. (Why does everyone say Poor Tom? Are they hard wired into Lear?)

'What was that?'

'Nothing. I just said it was time I moved on.'

'Yes but on to where? You must leave a forwarding address, somewhere we can contact you and please at least wait till Tom comes back again. He came through from Edinburgh this morning and hung about hoping to see you before he was summoned back again by Empress Claudia to sort out some frightful wedding hoo-ha.'

'Wasn't he taking the kids to Ailsa Craig?'

'That's another story. Now, Mira dear, I do hope you can find it in your heart to forgive him.'

'What for?'

'For taking you to that rock on such a rotten afternoon and causing such mayhem with minor accidents and lost dogs.'

'I've gotten over all that. So, I hope, will Vlad.'

Avis paused and we looked down onto the flat calm sea beyond the roof-top of the hotel below us and beyond that to the great lump of Ailsa Craig.

'The expedition to Ailsa Craig was cancelled, you know. Caro got into a flap about the children nearly drowning yesterday, utter rubbish of course. She got a taxi to take them to a supervised adventure playground, where all fun is circumscribed by health and safety regulations, where dogs are kept on leads and their doings scooped into sterilised bins. Sharp objects are banned, there's no deep water, or anything more hazardous than tripping over one's own feet onto a padded surface. When I think of the risks at the old Firthside Camp it's a wonder Rod and I didn't end up in Barlinnie. Chris has gone to his Glasgow office and the whole boiling are loyally coming back tomorrow for the funeral, which is jolly decent considering none of them could bear Ian Parker but I told them they owed it to poor Cecile who is treating this event like the wedding she never had. Please stop a while longer Mira. Please, don't go, come and stay with us if my silly niece insists on evicting you.'

I asked her why she thought Cecile Pollock hated me so much. 'It's as if I am a compilation of all those possessed children in the horror movies. I swear she thinks me evil.'

'No, Mira, it can't be as bad as that. It is obvious she doesn't like you but poor soul, nobody likes her and you positively shuddered when she appeared the other night.'

'It's the odour, I mean the scent she uses, it brings back unpleasant memories. I don't like her, I never have, I don't really know why and I have no idea what I did to her. Maybe she was mean to me and I was mean back but like you say, I was only a little kid, whatever I did can't have amounted to much.'

'I don't know, Mira, and that's the honest truth but it must have been something that pierced her to the heart. But I know and you know that you wouldn't have done it on purpose. Your conscience is clear as far as Cecile is concerned.'

'I can't handle being hated.'

We walked on. Avis couldn't loiter for long. 'Yes but you have nothing to reproach yourself with, no lingering burden of guilt. You may even be doing her good if she gets some gratification from being vengeful. Now, I've been to all the houses in Dalmuirie imploring everyone to come to the funeral, and promising them all a fine tea. I hope no burglars were listening, they could have a field day tomorrow stripping all Dalmuirie of its knick-knacks if there's a market for china Scottie dogs and crinolined ladies that is. Are you tired, Mira?'

'No, I've just got short legs.'

'But I thought you were a dancer.'

'I was, but not a sprinter.'

I'm sure we banked like kids playing jet planes as we rounded the corner leading down to Ian Parker's lodge. The faster Avis went the louder she spoke. 'I hope Ian had the decency to leave his house to Cecile. It was his outright and it was the least he could do after all her devotion to him. He was just as unlovable as she is, there was nothing to choose between them. Whatever you are alleged to have done to her, Mira, it would not have made any difference to her life. The poor child was un-endearing from the cradle. Her parents died you know, slap bang the coach they were travelling in went straight into an oncoming lorry outside Ostend on their way to Westfalia with a group of dairy farmers to look at milking machines. It was their first trip abroad and virtually their first excursion beyond Dalmuirie. My brother always said no good would come of it, which it didn't, except arguably for Cecile.'

'Didn't she like her parents?'

'Yes of course she did, Mira. Children do.'

'I hated my mother.'

'Yes well, that was different. What I meant was if dear Maud and darling Willie hadn't been killed, Cecile would never have been able to sell the farm for a housing scheme and get enough to buy this place, not that I imagine she's got much left now.'

'Do you think that now Ian is dead she'd be in the market for Henrysson's Rock?' I asked while in urgent pursuit.

'No chance, Mira. I fear her business haemorrhages money as it is. Unless she has been left the Lodge and can put it on the market she'll be in trouble keeping the place going.'

We were nearing where I thought our paths would part but Avis said she was coming to the hotel to make sure there was enough ham. Ham, she explained, meant a lot at funeral teas and she'd promised all Dalmuirie plenty. We continued past the hedge surrounding the Lodge garden.

'The trouble with Cecile is that she always throws herself at every man she meets and they throw her immediately back. She is most off-putting. She's her own worst enemy, developing crushes that are figments of her imagination. She chases after love but needs companionship. She overwhelms anybody even slightly pleasant with her desperate generosity. It scares them. She can't cope with settling to be herself. She can't cope with a face that will never be her fortune and looks for beauty in a jar when she'd be better off scrubbing up and learning to smile. She wants to be perceived as a woman she could never possibly be. If she wasn't set on being an object of desire she wouldn't be an object of repulsion. If she settled for normal, everyday friendliness, she'd bumble on through contentedly. Life doesn't need to go to extremes. There's oodles of space for ordinary personalities between Helen of Troy and the Witch of Endor. We can all pity Cecile but she doesn't make it easy for us to be fond of her. Her father was probably the only man who ever cared for her, so apart from that, her relationship with Ian Parker was the best thing that happened to the poor woman and that was no more than a matter of mutual convenience.'

We both saw a head appear briefly at an open window; there was only one person to whom it could belong.

'I'll tell you one thing Mira, Cecile has a truly beautiful voice. She sings like an angel.' Avis shouted loud enough to acquaint the entire district with this fact; only I saw her wink. 'You'll hear her tomorrow, it will be a real treat,' Avis bellowed.

As we neared the hotel's Palladian-type porch, Avis took my hand. 'Please, Mira, wait and see Tom before you go. He really deserves a little kindness, he's been through so much.'

'What do you mean?'

'Oh well, if he hasn't told you, never mind, but his life has been quite a tragedy.'

Why was Avis telling me all this? Was she trying to extract my sympathy?

'He's doing OK for himself now,' I said. 'He seems fine to me.'

'He puts a good face on it, Mira and at least he's landed a splendid job managing Caro's brother's projects in Spain. He's his best friend, he's stood by him for years. He's his Best Man, you know, and though I say it myself, my younger son is that, a gem. My husband was right in his speech, Tom really is honourable. He is about the most considerate and selfless person I know. He deserves to be happy.'

'And I hope he is,' I said somewhat coolly. 'Thanks Aunt Avis it has been great talking to you. I must go and get started on the packing.'

'No, Mira, wait. Please tell me, in strictest confidence. What has Tom done that makes you dislike him so?'

'Nothing, he's done nothing.'

'There must have been something. Please Mira.'

'He did nothing. That's what. He did nothing about getting me off Henrysson's Rock. He did nothing, he just went away and left me there alone till the tide had turned and I struggled back to the shore with the dog. I tell you, Aunt Avis, Vlad the Impaler had more concern for my situation than your son. When I could see the boat was missing I went half-mad with anxiety, I thought that he'd had an accident while trying to fetch me. I thought I was responsible for him drowning. Honestly, I went to Hell and back during those hours stuck on my horrible, creepy rock.'

'Surely he told somebody where you were, even if he couldn't come for you himself because Caro was making such a palaver about Phylly's foot.'

'He can't have. Everybody was very surprised to see me when I eventually fronted up, all dripping wet and frozen. They were more concerned with the mess I was making. Though Yvonne was good enough to tell me later that the boat had been found and that it had merely slipped its moorings.'

'Well Mira, I'm astonished. No wonder you are furious. I understand that part entirely, but the rest baffles me. I expect you think I am just being a typical doting mother.'

'I wouldn't know. I didn't have one of those.'

She kissed me on the forehead and told me to be sure and leave a forwarding address. I didn't tell her that I hadn't got one of those either.

Tuesday

I could see that the morning promised good weather for Mr Parker's funeral when I went downstairs to use the hotel computer to access my email. There was little of any interest, except one message from Isa Wong to say we needed to talk and she'd left something on voicemail, but my cell phone was drowned, the message would enthral the creatures of the deep, not me.

I needed a strong drink first; at nine in the morning strong coffee would have to do. I asked Yvonne to prepare my bill, I'd be checking out before noon as stipulated, though she told me I was welcome to keep the room all day. Calum deposited the hat stand he was shifting and told me that a body had been asking for me.

'Where?' I asked.

'On the telephone.'

'Who was it? When did they call?'

'I couldna' say. '

'Did you ask?'

'I canna' mind.'

'He means he can't remember,' said Yvonne.

'Yon lass kens fine whit I mean,' Calum replied, stomping off with the hat stand, sending the brochure display flying as he went.

'I'm sorry. We've had words. Calum knows he isn't meant to answer the phone.'

I helped pick up the scattered leaflets, all advertising attractions

311

that I'd never see. What a lot of enthralling stuff I'd miss now that I'd resolved never to return to Dalmuirie.

'Don't worry, Yvonne,' I said, assuming that it had been Isa trying the landline too, 'I expect whoever it was will call again.'

Yvonne sighed and shrugged. A feather-enhanced pin heaved upon her tartan bosom. Smoke signals were possibly more effective than Calum's telephone technique.

With this terrible fuss about Mr Parker's funeral and the great tea to fix, Yvonne said it was all hands to the pump and any port in a storm.

With some storms all pumps and ports are useless. I didn't want to speak to anyone. I needed to pack up and go.

I had decided to travel south overnight and had booked myself on to the sleeper train that left Glasgow near to midnight. I'd be in London for breakfast but beyond that I had no idea where to go or what to do. The prospect was more depressing than frightening. I was going into a lonesome future quite unknown and unconnected except for continuing to be the unwanted owner of a rotten, unwanted rock.

It is better to arrive in the morning before everybody is established in their niches if, like me, you have no niche. I remember the chaos of evening starlings looking for ledges on which to spend the night. Every one of them found somewhere, they all got places and I would too. It was not as if I was an asylum seeker, an illegal immigrant, I had a British passport and I seem to remember that Aunt El held that to be of paramount importance and a splendid protection against tyranny and exploitation. Provided you could say 'Civis Britannicus Sum', all would be well. I don't believe she ever tested this thesis or if she had, it would have carried any weight. Still, Roman citizens allegedly found it handy when in sticky confrontations with barbarians and gladiators.

I'd fix myself somewhere, then send to New York for my things. Or maybe not. I didn't want to open boxes full of the stuff from which that life had been constructed. I wanted to start afresh completely, without trailing roots. I still had not tried to receive Isa

Wong's message. If I didn't face it now, I would be forced to do so later. Confront your fears, they say, and impossible obstacles melt into insignificance.

This one did not do that. My dread was confirmed.

Isa had official evidence, in writing. The woman who the late Ian Parker had visited so assiduously and for whose care he'd paid, until she finally succumbed to her chronic condition, completely incoherent and demented, had been called Dorabella Warschauer. That was all I needed to know, I didn't hear the rest. Like the convicted once sentence is pronounced, what follows is mere detail

Both my mother and Ben had retained their birth name on official documents though they had assumed the surname Troubadour when their mother had remarried the kindly Herbert with the two tin legs.

So much for being rootless. Here was a bloody great shackle of a root. I felt the weight of it crippling me. I should be thrilled, excited and intrigued that the woman who had abandoned me had resurfaced, albeit as a handful of scattered ash. At least she was now truly dead; that alone was comfort. The fact that she had been alive throughout most of my life was horrifying, but my ignorance then and my knowledge now, were both good. Dora was over and I must get over her, she had given me nothing except birth and left me nothing except the blighted legacy of having died quite young, of a chronic degenerative disease that was almost certainly genetic. Her known death was a blessing marred by this curse. How could I know whether I was to be spared? Perhaps the malign symptoms were waiting for their cue to manifest themselves in me or through me to any children I might miraculously conceive. There was still time for that, just. But I must forget all prospects of motherhood now that I knew my tainted genes could condemn my babies too.

I stared at the rock in the sea through the window of the room called Grizelda and knew then that I was right. I had seen Dora all those years ago, standing there, on the summit of Henrysson's Rock with the sun behind her, like an infernal angel.

It had been neither a nightmare nor the imagination of a terrified child, who believed in fairy-tale junk. That had been, and was, reality. Ian Parker, for whose funeral the kirk bell would soon be tolling, must have been much more than an ingratiating fixer.

Lacking all concrete evidence, I was now utterly certain then that my mad mother, the woman known as Dora Troubadour, had been guilty of arson and double murder. For some reason, she had been protected by Ian Parker, reputedly a Pole himself and quite possibly connected to the vaporised family Warschauer. I may not have inherited my mother's sins, but I did have the double burden of her genes and guilt to bear.

Dora had not been on that rock alone, there was another, the one who had sworn me to silence that evening as the sun sank. I assumed this person who had called themselves a fairy had been a woman, though it was hard to tell. Like Ariel, it was androgynous. The low voice had been kind but very firm and the arms that had held me were as hard and thin as sticks. I could still see a face, gaunt like The Scream, with hair cut convict-short.

I sat in silence as if waiting for someone to tell me what to do. What could I do but disappear into my future and try to start over with what was left?

I would write Ben's life, I'd research his works meticulously and re-create him from solid evidence. It would be a dry objective work, without emotion. No infatuated contributions from the women who thought they knew him. By science alone he would be known. The rest would live on in all our imaginations. He was, till the last, entirely his own, unimpeachable, property.

My Ben belonged to nobody else. My Ben was mine alone and certainly not his. Nor was he the man that Cess and all the rest had constructed for their own idolatry.

The clatter of catering preparation filtered upstairs, the hotel was busy making this funeral tea into a big production.

Voice exercises were coming from the Matilda room. I was overwhelmed with a terrible pity for Cess, the pathetic woman responsible for this warbling, who'd wasted her life as an infatuated, exploited, unattractive and despised object, not only of ridicule but also of suspicion, the victim of whispered accusations and false condemnation for a crime of which she was utterly innocent.

I wrote a note to put under her door wishing her well, then adding that I hoped she'd find it in her heart to forgive me.

For what? For being my mother's daughter?

I would put *Ballet Shoes*, in the Matilda pigeon hole as I left. There was no need to see Cess face to face, ever again. The bus would take me back to Dundoon and from there I'd get a train to Glasgow. I had masses of time to waste. If I checked out soon I would not need to explain anything to anybody.

The floorboards betrayed me. The scales emanating from Matilda stopped just as I stooped down to slide the note under the door, it was opened and I fell into the room my nose almost touching a pair of feet with horny nails, hammer toes and bunions. Looking up I saw a clown. Cess in face pack and rollers was glaring at me with red-rimmed eyes. She must have been weeping as rivulets had bored through the lavender-tinted clay on her cheeks.

'I am very sorry.'

'What the hell are you doing, Mira?'

'I was delivering this note.'

'Why?'

'To say I'm sorry.'

'Why?'

'Because I am. I don't know what about. But I am sorry. And now I'm going. Goodbye Cecile. I won't be bothering you again, ever.'

'Good. Get lost!'

I'd heard her say that before, somewhere. I scrambled to my feet but as I was closing the door behind me she called me back.

'Wait!'

Amongst the chaos of half-used cosmetics on the dressing table there was a photo frame which she turned around before towelling her face vigorously and ripping the rollers out of her hair. The mirror snidely reflected the framed publicity shot of Ben, its faked message inverted.

'Don't do that, Cecile, you'll wreck all your hard work.'

'I'm a wreck anyway, as well you know. Why should it worry you? You've got what you wanted. Not that it matters any more.'

'Listen, Cecile, please. I've never wanted anything from you, ever. Nothing at all.'

'You rejected me, you made it your business to sabotage my life. You separated me and my true love for ever. You denied me the chance of happiness. You condemned me to a life sentence of solitude.'

'Steady on, Cecile. That's quite some accusation.'

'Don't be so trans-Atlantic and flippant. I mean every word. You are responsible for my unfulfilled potential, for my lonely existence.'

'I was a little kid, I don't know how I could have all those things. Four-year-olds are pretty powerless.'

'You weren't. You managed to ruin me, completely.'

'How?'

'You rejected me. You refused to do anything I suggested. You wouldn't even try. You didn't like me. You are responsible for wrecking my reputation, for having me known as an unsuitable woman.'

'Unsuitable for what?'

'Unsuitable as a mother.'

'But you aren't a mother, Cecile, are you?'

'No I am not, thanks to you. You destroyed all my prospects, Nobody ever trusted me to even look after a child again after what you did. Everybody knows that you got left on the Lumpie and everybody says that it was my fault. But you were to blame, though I have been blamed for what happened ever since.'

I suppose a decent, kinder person would have admitted it. But I couldn't. Besides it wasn't even half true. I had done what I'd been told and got lost. That I hated her was however the whole truth but I was also very sorry for her too.

'If only you had made an effort, if only you had co-operated, my whole life would have been different. I was prepared to devote myself entirely to you. But you just kicked me in the teeth and forced me and Ben apart. I suppose you realise that you are also responsible for your poor uncle remaining single. You were like a parasitic leech, sucking out all our hopes of happiness together.'

I guess thirty years is time enough to manufacture bitter fictions. There would be little point in trying to put her right. She liked holding on to her version of history, it would be folly to attempt to disillusion her.

The phone was ringing downstairs again, nobody answered. The ringing stopped. Cess could see me in the mirror as I retreated towards the door.

'Stop, Mira! I haven't finished.'

'There's more? Isn't ruining somebody's entire life enough? I've said I'm sorry for whatever you think I've done, I am also very sorry that you've been under suspicion for causing the fire that killed my father. That's really mean.'

'That fire was an accident!' She pounded the dressing table top with her fist and made the bottles and jars jump, Ben's picture toppled back leaving him staring at the ceiling of faded painted stars. I said nothing.

'Not that I didn't have good reason. Oh yes I had plenty of reason for vengeance.'

She paused, waiting for me to ask for more. I obliged and she did; this was her story.

She'd been pursued, raped and impregnated by my father, Hugh, then abandoned by him for Grizelda Gilmerton and her fortune. Grizelda had always had it in for her, Cess said, right since they'd been at school, something to do with Cess having the better voice. I couldn't rightly follow what all that was about but it was obvious this story was as fictitious as her passionate love affair with Ben. She didn't say what had happened to her baby, I did not ask. It would complicate matters to have to account for my lost half-brother or -sister.

I figured I must have taken on the part of scapegoat from Grizelda in the blighted life of Cess. Grizelda was responsible for her wretched childhood and I was to blame for the rest.

By now Cess was sobbing, head down upon the dressing table amongst the ineffective cosmetics and the picture of her make-believe lover

The telephone was ringing again. Still nobody answered, the clattering and rushing about was rising to a crescendo of shouted instructions and exclamations of distress. Eventually there was a knock at the door.

'You stay where you are, I'll answer it.' I opened the door a crack, it was Yvonne, tight-lipped and furious. Calum had gone and lost the ashets.

'Assets? What assets?' I asked.

'Ashets…big oval dish things for putting things on. He says they are in the press in the attic but he canna' mind where he put the key.'

'I suggest you just use some other plates for the moment, Miss Pollock is kind of overwrought and while you are at it perhaps you'd bring her a little brandy? Thanks Yvonne.' I shut the door firmly and shot the bolt.

'Come along, Cecile. You have got to brace up. You owe it to yourself and the memory of Mr Parker and all the people who love you who are coming to support you today.'

'Nobody loves me. Nobody ever has.'

'That's rubbish and you know it. What about your parents, what about your aunt and uncle, I know they love you. What about Mr Parker?'

'Especially not him. He didn't love me, I was just his unpaid housekeeper, his slave.'

'Why did you live with him then?'

'He took me places.'

'Well then he was a good friend. He was your walker.'

'If you say so.'

'And you were his arm candy.'

'What?'

'Oh never mind. Yvonne is fetching some brandy which will do wonders for your voice.'

'Really?'

'Sure. All my singer friends swear by it.' (I have no singer friends, at least none that rely on just the one brandy.)

'Also I could help you fix your hair and make-up if you like. I know a lot about that sort of thing.' (Another lie, my make-up technique is tragic) 'What are you planning on wearing?'

She pointed at a coat hanger on the picture rail from which a black sack was dangling, a close relative of a rural Mediterranean widow's garment of choice, except for a weird attachment of black lace around the neckline and wrists.

'Very chic,' I lied and the telephone started up again. This time it was answered at the third ring. I went downstairs to fetch the brandy myself as Yvonne was deep in conversation with the caller who apparently wanted to know the time of the funeral.

'Why folk can't read the notice in the paper beats me. Mrs Wishart herself put it in the *Advertiser*. Oh well on we go. Is that you away now, Mrs Staple?'

'I'll take this brandy up to Miss Pollock, then I'll go.'

'Are you wanting a taxi?'

'No thanks, Yvonne, I'm fine.'

'Is Tom Wishart giving you a lift then? He's been asking for you.'

'No, Yvonne. I've made my own arrangements.'

'What shall I tell him when he comes back?'

'Tell who?'

'Tom Wishart. He said he'd drop by in the late forenoon.'

'Tell him I've gone.'

Cess was in a right state again when I got back with the brandy. Her hair was damp and limp. When she cried, she did it messily, with a dripping nose and dribbling mouth. Her eyes were scarlet now and buried in the puffiness of her blotchy cheeks. Something had to be done.

'Look Cess, I mean Cecile, I've said I'm very sorry about all those things you blame me for but right now you must smarten up. Now, as I said before, you owe it to yourself, if not to Mr Parker. Now drink this and stop crying and if you will let me I'll help you.'

The torrent eventually spluttered to a stop; she downed the brandy in one and turned towards me. 'I owe you an apology too.'

'Well don't let's worry about that now, the main thing is to get you sorted. Supposing I pin your hair up, that would look very smart and you wouldn't need to worry about it.'

'I've got a hat.'

'Even better, You'll look wonderful.'

'You must listen to what I have to say.'

The hat looked like something worn by Granny Giles. Every Christmas Ben would give Aunt El the Giles Annual. I loved that cartoon family far more than Peanuts. Aunt El sometimes looked a bit like Vera, only taller. Nobody looked like Ben, or Sojourner, I rather fancied myself as the mop-haired kid given to catapults.

'Perfect,' I said. 'With your hair up you will look most elegant. Have you got any drops for tired eyes? If not I may have some in my purse. I'll go look for them while you put on the dress, then I'll fix up your hair while you put some foundation on your face, I can see you've got masses of it, foundation I mean, not face.'

It took a while but we did it and half an hour later not only had she confessed everything that had troubled her, she looked great. Well almost.

I could see that she felt better too. The Catholics may have got it right about confession. Her admission that she had lied about me all those years ago and repeated the lie recently was penance enough. Knowing that I had suffered no ill-effects from either incident was her absolution. It was easy to forgive her for the first lie because her failure to care for me had ensured my return to my beloved Aunt El, the second lie, that being so recent, was very different.

It turned out that Tom had begged Cess to get somebody to rescue me from the rock. The reason he had not come himself was because Caro was in hysterics about her kid being in shock and had realised that the only way of getting her to hospital was to get Tom to drive all of them, meanwhile everybody else was sent to hunt for Vlad the dog.

'You mean that Tom had asked for someone to rescue me?'

'I told him that was not necessary,' Cess replied.

'Why? Of course it was necessary, I was marooned.'

'I told him you were fine and that I had seen you and that you were perfectly OK just a bit cold and that you were in good hands and there was nothing for him to worry about as you were now warm and safe.'

'But I wasn't, was I?'

'You weren't in any danger and I had seen you, that wasn't a lie.'

'But it was. Why did you say that, when you knew it was untrue?'

Cess shrugged and replied, 'It wasn't untrue. I had seen you and you did look all right.'

'How?'

'With these, from Grizelda when I was moving your stuff.' She pointed to an ancient pair of binoculars. 'I knew that if you waited you could wade ashore at low tide, I didn't expect you to try while the water was still deep, except along the De'il's Dyke but that is quite tricky when the rocks are under water. Possible though, if you know the way.'

'Which I don't and Tom knew that.'

Cess shrugged. 'Maybe he did, maybe he didn't. Anyway I managed to convince him you were OK so he set out for the hospital with a car-load of hysterical Wisharts. It was a joy to see them go. I promised I'd look for their dog.'

'And did you?'

'No. I knew where he was, where both of you were, I thought you could keep each other company.'

'I see,' I said. 'So it didn't matter to you that I was terrified, frozen and furious. So it didn't matter to you that I thought Tom had come back for me and drowned in the attempt when I saw the boat was missing. So it didn't matter to you that I blamed him for abandoning me when I discovered he was safe. I went through Hell on that rock.'

'I didn't realise you thought that. I'm sorry but if you'd waited just a little longer than you did, you'd have found it easy.'

'Well, there it is. It's over now, I won't be seeing any of you again I expect, so let's deal with the job in hand.'

So, Tom wasn't to blame. But what did that matter? There was to be no more Tom for me, whatever I felt. I had no business feeling anything for him, he belonged to a woman and a place quite removed from my increasingly un-rooted world.

Cess turned away from the mirror, quite collected now and not looking too awful. 'Tell me Mira, was there anybody else there with you?'

'Only Tom and the kids, that is until the accident, then he had to row them to the shore.'

'Not then, I mean when you were small, when Ben rescued you. Was there anybody else there with you then?'

'No, Cecile, not a soul.'

After so many lies, what difference would another make? But perhaps it wasn't a lie, maybe I didn't see anybody else, memories can be false and imagination, especially that of a terrified child, can be vivid and compelling. If you believe in Santa Claus you must be able to believe in anything, good fairies as well as demons.

No, I was sure. I had seen my mother, Dora Warschauer, on that rock. Furthermore, her name had been confirmed as that of the woman who had died in the care home visited so zealously by the late, fellow Pole, Mr Ian Parker.

Then I realised that I could not remember what Ian Parker looked like, there were no pictures of him anywhere, nor could I recall his voice, if indeed I had met him at all that summer of 1975. It had never occurred to me before that my androgynous good fairy, short cropped and skeletal, could have been him and not a woman after all. That almost made sense but not quite.

If that was the case, why had Tilda Gilmerton married him? Furthermore, why had she married him if that was not the case?

★

Cess was ready and waiting for the undertaker's limo when I left her. I made the excuse of not wanting to muss up her face and shook her hand instead of kissing her goodbye. I expect I only imagined the sickly, sweet stink of her but I made for the restroom to wash my own hands again before I finally checked out of the hotel.

Yvonne was fussing about fixing towels and soap. She was trying to poke some red dahlias into an already crammed vase. 'I've just found these flowers and I've not the heart to chuck them in the bin but really I've not the time to arrange them. Would you like them, Mrs Staple, with the compliments of the hotel?'

'No thank you, Yvonne. I couldn't manage them on the bus or the train.'

'It's a shame you won't let Tom drive you, he could get you to Glasgow after the funeral.'

'I prefer to be independent.'

'You're that right enough,' she said, bundling the remaining flowers up in newspaper.

'No wait, Yvonne. Don't throw them out, I will take them, I've got time before the bus to take them up to the church.'

'To the funeral?'

'To a grave.'

I slipped out of the hotel by the back way and took the woodland path up to Dalmuirie, wheeling my bag behind me and carrying the red pompom dahlias.

Speckled leaves danced in the breeze above calm seas of fern, wild garlic and dead bluebells. Standing still, I could hear the trickling burn at the bank's foot concealed by dense rhododendron. A squirrel, maybe red like Nutkin, scampered up a gnarled beech and disappeared. My bag bumped over the rough, uphill ground, the wheels catching on straying roots.

The paths forked, one led back towards the beach the other up into the rest of the world. I'd missed the noon bus, I could have lingered but I didn't. Whichever way I chose would make no difference. I arrived at Dalmuirie as the single bell started tolling and decided to find myself a vantage point from which to observe the mourners arriving, without being seen myself. I'd have time during the service to find where the Henryssons were buried. The bus shelter was too far away so I found a neglected spot on the south side of the cemetery and sat upon a horizontal gravestone behind a substantial broken column commemorating Euphemia MacMaster who'd died much mourned, thought evidently not much missed by subsequent MacMasters, who'd let ivy and willow-herb vie with each other for domination over the abundant stinging nettles on their plot.

How lucky that no ardent plant hunter had thought to introduce poison-ivy to the United Kingdom to cover careless picnickers with itchy pimples. I used to love scratching the rash to make water spurt from the spots, driving Aunt El mad. Poor Aunt El, she hated anything about bodies or their quirks.

A few people began to arrive; they were the prudently prompt. It was still a lovely day, unlike the usual rainy scenarios for movie funerals when neat, bleak widows meet alluring mistresses in seductive mourning, beneath large umbrellas, at the open grave of the dear, unfaithful departed.

Black came in touches rather than total immersion, here a skirt, there a tie but nothing to up-stage Cess and her ensemble of gloom until I saw Caro in a black lace mantilla shepherding her daughters towards the church. Phylly was going in for ostentatious limping while Patience stomped ahead, an apprentice vampire hoping for an open grave. She'd be out of luck there, unless she fancied following the cortege to the crematorium.

The only other headgear was on Miss Stuart, a rather startling dark plaid turban, which she gripped firmly, as Avis Wishart in dog-tooth checks, pushed her wheelchair to the church door.

I wasn't going to see Tom here now, or ever again. He was already inside the church where I knew Cess had recruited him to be an usher in charge of service sheets.

I'd apologise on a postcard from London; that would do. It would be for the best.

Had I not hidden behind Euphemia's monument I might have met him, but not now. It was all too late. Anyway I'd express myself better in writing without betraying my confusion and misery. I'd wish him well in his marriage too, something I couldn't trust myself to do calmly, face to face.

Why wait to get to London, why not now? I had both postcard and an envelope in my purse. I'd scribble my contrition on the back of a picture the Citadel in Dundoon. I'd planned to send it to Sojourner but she'd far prefer Buckingham Palace to the site of the last witch burning in Scotland I'm sure.

Dear Tom,

Please forgive me for being mad at you for leaving me on the rock. I know now that it was not your fault. Sorry. I hope the wedding goes really well. Good Luck in your new life!
Give my love to your family, it was nice knowing you all.

Mira

Should I put a kiss? No, better not. I could not bring myself to mention Claudia, the luckiest bride in the world, I hoped the wretched creature appreciated her immense good fortune.

While I was writing a southbound bus drew up and a single passenger got out.

I chose a moment when the flow of people into the church had abated and, leaving my bag and the flowers beside Euphemia, I gave the card to a guy, in a long black robe at the churchyard gate. He looked kind of official, maybe a verger. I explained about not being able to stay for the service on account of the bus and asked him to direct me to the Henrysson graves. 'The Henrysson Lair' he corrected, and indicated a part of the churchyard beyond the MacMaster plot.

He also promised to deliver my note to Avis Wishart who'd pass it on to her son. He knew Mrs Wishart well, he said. Everybody did in these parts, a fine woman and no mistake.

I needed to get out the way quickly as I saw a stately black limousine, with Cess in the back, drawing up at the churchyard gate. This parody scenario was too creepily bridal to bear.

I waited beside Euphemia's grave till all the congregation was inside, then dragged my bag silently over the grass to a seat beneath one of the church windows and went to look for where my forebears lay.

The last resting place of the Henryssons was neither layer as in cake, nor lair as in a wolf's or a robber's hideout but a sort of avenue of flat tomb stones leading to an obelisk. The departed Henryssons were somewhat better tended than poor Euphemia, probably because they'd been alive more recently. The obelisk had been erected by a Victorian Henrysson called Horace for his subsequent descendents. Previous bearers of his name, who didn't concern me, must have been languishing, quite forgotten, beneath illegible stones and bumps elsewhere in the graveyard.

Names of the dead were carved upon the obelisk in descending order, my father and Grizelda were second from bottom above his father, my grandfather, who was the last. There was no room for any more, or me, which was just as well. Peaceful as it was, I had no intention of rotting in the company of ancestors.

There was something quite weird about standing on the remains of my father. Should I bow my head, kneel in prayer? Feeling somewhat foolish, I placed the dahlias where I thought my father and his wife might be buried, and walked back towards the church.

At first I thought a ghost was standing on the path. Though skeletal and supernaturally pallid, the figure was not translucent. Nor I reasoned, did ghosts go around in baggy tracksuits and sneakers. Hard to tell but I assumed it was a woman, virtually bald, worn out, not quite old but well past youth and without doubt, very sick. She turned away from me and went to sit on the seat where I'd left my bag.

The organist's ponderous Nimrod had been succeeded by a hymn about thanking our God who had, from our mother's arms, brought us on our way.

When I sat down beside her I saw she had been trying to read my bag's label. 'Hello,' I said, hearing myself sound awkward, 'May I join you?'

She made room for me and indicated that we should keep quiet. Cess had begun to sing.

We two, I and this strange woman, listened and were amazed. The querulous warble was gone, replaced by strength and clarity as Cess sent her voice soaring. 'Remember Me!' The final lines came and faded away, 'But Ah…Forget my fate.' I longed to burst into applause, I suspect the congregation did too but we sat in seemly silence on that memorial bench and listened through the window as the congregation, with shuffling acquiescence, obeyed the exhortation 'Let us Pray.'

I noticed that the woman was crying. 'Cecile sings well,' I whispered.

'Yes, she always did.'

'You know her?'

'Yes.'

'And the late Mr Parker?'

'I know most people at the service.'

'You ought to go in, there's bound to be a space for you. Everybody is invited. I'm just a visitor, I have to catch a bus in a few minutes. Why don't you let me help you to the church door.'

'No. I don't belong here any more.'

'You lived here once?'

'Long ago.'

Next came the eulogy, spoken with vehemence and expertise by the Commander. We couldn't hear a word of it but the way in which it was delivered was convincing. A man of his word was being fittingly commemorated.

We continued sitting in silence till the congregation sang about the sun that bids us rest is waking brethren 'neath a Western sky.

'Do you miss Dalmuirie?' I asked, just for something to say.

'Only the sea. Where did you put those flowers?'

'On my father's grave. Look, I must go, the bus is due in a couple of minutes. Bye, it was nice meeting you.'

While the organ was still playing loud enough to muffle the sound of wheels on gravel, I dragged my bag through the church gate as the northbound bus was coming down the hill towards me.

Somehow the woman had managed to follow me and, just as I was about to mount the step she clutched my elbow with a brittle grasp It felt as if a skeleton was holding me. 'Goodbye, Miracle. Thank you.'

'What for? How did you know my name?'

Either she didn't hear, or wouldn't reply. I watched her turn away and take the path towards the shore.

The driver pulled out but he had to stop again to let the hearse drive away from the church gate, with Cess alone following in the oversized limousine. The congregation was assembled like the cheerful crowd that throws rice at the departing newlyweds, only they didn't. Nor did they wave and cheer, though not one of the faces that I could see from the top deck, where I'd chosen to sit concealed, showed symptoms of grief. They were having a jolly time, and looking forward to a jolly tea before Cess returned from the crematorium to dampen the merriment with mournfulness.

I shrank back in my seat, watching. Most of the cast of my brief stay in this circumscribed district was there. I saw the verger give my note to Avis. If only I hadn't written it – too late for regrets now. I saw Isa Wong in conversation with Tom Wishart and longed to know what they were talking about. Was it me? Of course not, why should it be?

The policeman at the cross-roads saluted the coffin as the hearse went by and the bus moved on. Tom did look up but I doubt he saw me. The little crowd dwindled to pin men and women as I passed out of their lives and on to find mine, drifting and pointless as it was now bound to be.

Tuesday Evening

I don't know when it came to me, but somewhere on the road between Dalmuirie and Dundoon I had one of those moments (without the thunderbolt and voice from heaven of course) but Damascene in its own small way. I must rid myself of my only piece of real estate and bequeath it to the only person who could possibly want it, Cess.

It was so easy, so simple and obvious and best of all, something constructive I could do right away, this very afternoon. If she took it as an apology or peace offering it would be no matter, let her continue to manufacture her life story.

I bought a pad of paper and wrote a note addressed to Isa Wong asking her to make the necessary arrangements and took it to her office. Wallace-Falkirk was on my way from the bus to the train station in Dundoon and as I mounted the porch steps, the reception clerk came out.

She recognised me at once. 'Now here's a stroke of luck, Mrs Staple. I was just leaving but I expect you have come to collect your letter, you'll have doubtless got the message I left at your hotel. I'll away and fetch it for you and ask you to sign, please come in.'

I explained that I was wishing to deliver a letter not pick one up.

'No problem, Mrs Staple. This arrived here late forenoon after Mrs Wong had left for the funeral. I texted her about it but it seems she was unable to contact you so it is just a wee stroke of luck that you happened to be passing. I know fine that it's for yourself, there's no mistaking you Mrs Staple. Everybody knows who you are. Professor Troubadour was as well known as Nelson Mandela I'd say and you look that much like him, your uncle I mean, except for your eyes and your teeth of course. You Americans are just great at dealing with crooked teeth.'

Thankful at least not to be recognised as the child of a mad murderess, I zipped the envelope into my bag and went on my way against the rush of homeward-bound Glasgow commuters.

The train for Glasgow was short and empty, but just as it was about to leave, a squawking gang of fat girls, wearing very little, bar angel wings, invaded and arranged themselves on the seats around me. Their glittery tops above and skimpy skirts or over-stretched leggings below, framed expanses of bare, pneumatic belly. Those with the vaster thighs, wore ballet shoes, others had encased their feet in sturdy boots.

The bride-to-be had a bit of net on her head, and a tutu fit for an elephant at the spot where women used to have waistlines. 'Jade' was written on an L plate round her neck. She, poor soul, was the most sober and drab of the bunch.

They were returning home for further celebrations after a binge-ing day at the seaside, making noisy nuisances of themselves and goading anything male.

I felt very old being, quite possibly in some instances, older than their mothers. As the train made its halting journey along the coast, which mainly consisted of bungalows punctuated by golf courses, the girls boasted about how much they'd drunk, intended to drink and how incredibly sick they expected to be, before their hen party was done.

I began to feel older than their grandmothers. Reading was virtually impossible but I was prepared to try.

Singing began, a girl with Bev written across her boobs started it and urged the others to join in the chorus which involved a lot of butt-shaking and pelvic thrusts.

I opened the envelope. It contained at least six handwritten pages written in a shaky hand. In no way was it going to be an easy read.

Bev, along with her fellow ring-leaders, Caitlin, Isla and Kimberley (they'd all had their names printed on T shirts) rounded on Jade who was looking more dispirited with every passing minute.

'Come on hen! Lighten up. You're getting married, not getting your heid chopped off!'

Jade shrugged: 'I don't know,' she said, 'I'm no' so sure.'

'What's not to be sure of?' Bev asked. 'It's not as if you are that Shakira who has been made to wed that Paki boy who canna' speak a word of English. Your folks won't strangle you – they like your Hammy. What's not to like about Hammy?'

'Don't go there!' Kimberley muttered.

'Shut it,' said Caitlin.

'I'm no ready to settle down.'

'Come on hen, let's face it, Jade, at your age you've got to grab what you can and it's not as if you are the sexiest lass in the box, you're bloody lucky to have caught Hammy, I can tell you. Any man is better than none and at least your Hammy has a steady job down the abattoir, amn't I right, girls? Don't we all fancy a stunner?' Bev shrieked with delight at her own joke. 'Get it, girls? Hammy's a stunner!'

'In your dreams,' said Kimberley and those who were still upright fell about. Jade looked dangerously close to tears.

Isla put an arm round Jade's fat shoulders on which a recently tattooed seagull perched. 'Cheer up, hen, think of your mum. She'd go well mental if you backed out of the wedding now, she's spent a small fortune on her outfit and had her highlights done and got the venue sorted. And what about your dress? You'd never sell it now, not after your Auntie Min's been fixing it to fit you.'

'Aye, true enough. It's just…'

'Just what, Jade?'

'I'm not so sure I want to spend the rest of my life with Hammy.'

'Och dinna worry. That's just wedding nerves,' said Kimberley, offering Jade a swig of her vodka mix.

All this was going on while I was trying to at least decipher the letter's signature which was no better that a spindly scrawl.

'Come along girls let's ask this lady here. 'What would you tell Jade to do?'

'Are you meaning me?' I asked.

'Sure,' Bev replied. 'You tell her, she's bloody lucky to catch any man, isn't she? After all isn't any man better than no man once you are over the hill like Jade?'

'I think no man is better than just any man,' I replied.

'Och, this woman's rubbish girls, she's a Yank anyway, they understand nothing.'

Caitlin lurched down the carriage, probably to have the first vomit of the night.

'Are you gay or something?' Bev asked; her breath smelt volatile. I pretended to be absorbed in my reading as the entire carriage of drunk girls began taunting me. I was aware that sweaty Jade had taken refuge beside me.

'Don't sit there, Jade. Yon yank's a dyke. You don't want Hammy getting notions about that fashion of carry on.'

Kimberley looked at the envelope on the table in front of me. 'Is that you?' she said pointing at my name. 'What kind of name is that?'

'It's mine.'

'What? You are Miracle Troubadour?'

'Yes.'

'Whoever gave you a name like that?'

'My mother, I suppose.'

'My mother, I suppose!' Kimberley made an attempt to ape my accent.

Caitlin had now returned looking chastened, wiping her mouth and chewing gum. 'What's wrong wi' being called Miracle? It's no worse than being called after a hole in the ground like you Kimberley, or were you named for the folks that make the paper for wiping your arse? And Troubadour's nice too, like that salon where my nan gets her perms.'

'That's Pompadour you daftie. Troubadour's the carry-oot down by the Leisure Centre, the one the council shut.'

Isla's glazed eyes stared at me. 'I know you!' she said, prodding me in the chest with an azure nail. 'You're famous. You're off the telly!'

'No I'm not. I'm sorry to disappoint.'

'Rubbish. You were in Big Brother. You were crap! What's yon?'

'A letter,' I said, trying to stuff the pages back into the envelope.

'Let's see,' Kimberley said.

'No, I'm sorry, it's private.'

'Then you've no business reading it in a public place! Come on, girls!' Kimberley made a lunge towards me, seized the envelope and held it aloft, upside down. Everything cascaded to the floor, then picking up some pages, she tore them into scraps before throwing them over the bride: 'Confetti!'

Finally she christened the mess with the remains of vodka mix.

Just then the train arrived at Paisley and mercifully the whole posse made to tumble on to the platform. Jade turned to me as they dragged her out, her fake veil all askew. 'Sorry Miss,' she said.

The next stop was Glasgow Central, I had five minutes to salvage the pages and get them back into some semblance of order. Though crushed, the first and last two pages were just about intact; the stuff in between was ripped in to soggy fragments. If there was anyone else on the train, they certainly didn't offer to help.

I'm not sure that anybody's spirits lift at the prospect of a three-hour wait on Central Station. One minute beneath the glass and iron-work canopy at the station's entrance convinced me that I'd seen all I wanted of Glasgow, with its streets and people sodden. I had no Atkinson Grimshaw vision watching the dripping scene, while the world's worst piper alternated between 'Scotland The Brave' and 'Baa Baa Black Sheep'.

Anyway I had a case to drag and I felt no urge to explore this former City of Culture in the pouring rain. I needed somewhere quiet to sit where I could piece the letter's remains together.

A morose vendor, standing under a memorial to the dead of the Caledonian Railway who had perished in the wars, sold me an *Evening News*.

Nearby, six small shell cases surrounded a large central one, like infant missiles suckling their mother bomb. It was a collecting box for the Ladies Auxiliary Board to buy gifts for hospital patients. The world is full of wonders. Did perhaps an Auxiliary Lady present a gift to Dorabella Warshchauer, bought with this pensioned lethal weapon's stomach contents? Nobody around looked likely to know, or care, yet the cross-shaped brass plate on the centre shell was worn down with much polishing and the slot for donations still gaped.

When I collected my tickets from the machine, a young girl, still in her teens but with a careworn face, approached me and asked if I'd buy her a ticket to London. She needed to see her mum, quickly. She didn't want money, just a ticket. I told her to go away, which she did with meek resignation.

The Central Hotel had the air of decayed disapproval, a supercilious butler standing by watching the excesses of his vulgar employers, while lamenting the decorum of earlier days, when places were known and boundaries weren't only there to be breached. I went in past a doorman in a peaked cap and found myself in a dark lobby smelling of ancient spirits and the contents of vacuum cleaners that had patrolled lengthy corridors of murky carpets for far too long. I was a woman alone, among several unattached others whose purpose I guessed, was not the same as mine. I was after solitude not the company of strangers. I might be less conspicuous on the station concourse.

I wasn't hungry but I could use a drink, a quiet one, alone in a silent corner. Drink I could get but not the silent corner. I found a bar upstairs in one of the chocolate-coloured wooden bulges that form Central Station's shopping parade and sat with a large scotch at the smallest table I could find beneath a wide-screen TV showing a football match that nobody was watching. The excitable commentator was drowned by thumping music and the bleeps of flashing amusement machines. The noise was so indefinable as to be the next best thing to silence.

Glancing at the *Evening News*, I saw it contained mostly sport and outrage about local injustices, plus quite a bit about the cost of the Scottish Assembly and Tram Scandal in Edinburgh. A Celebrity had Called It Off, a Priest had Denied Gay Slur, a Dog had Savaged Tots and questions were being asked about Corruption in County Buildings. I'd leave What's Hot in Scots Fashion for later, along with the crosswords. My stars, I noticed, advised following my heart and going for it.

I'd try to get the trashed letter in order. Whether the light was at a better angle or I had merely gotten used to the spindly handwriting, the signature now appeared clear. The letter, written in blue ink, was from Matilda Parker.

I used to quite enjoy jigsaw puzzles, Aunt El always insisted on wooden ones, we did them at Christmas time each year. Sojourner and Aunt El would bicker quietly about whether it should be edge first or middle first and accuse each other of hiding vital pieces. Uncle Ben worked as diligently upon reassembling The Bar at the Follies Bergeres as he would upon an astronomical formula. He'd have had this heap of scraps sorted and interpreted in a trice.

> *Dear Miracle,*
> (The letter started without date or address,)
>> *This will reach you after it's all ended. Originally I planned to meet you and confess face to face but my dread of imposing the burden of knowledge on you, or anybody else, prevents me. So you can judge whether I am being cowardly or considerate. Neither conclusion will trouble me.*
>>
>> *The time for secrets is over. There is no one left. Thank you for keeping your promise.*

I read this unspoilt section of Matilda's letter through three times. What was the secret that I'd kept for this woman? What was the promise I made? I only remember her as Ben's girlfriend, the one he was to marry and then later as the one Aunt El forbad me to mention. Now I know her as the little girl in a kitsch group portrait whose room I'd first slept in at the hotel, who'd had stars on her ceiling and later married Ian Parker, a man nobody much liked.

I know that my marriage was seen as a sham. My entire life since the fire has been a sham too. I made a promise that I should have broken. I am guilty of deciding one life was worthless and another worth an unforgivable lie.

Here the writing had become almost entirely illegible, certainly not something I could make out by the light of the bar, I decided then to read any of the unharmed bits and leave the rest for a moment of well-lit calm and sobriety, I was enjoying the whisky very much. I needed to eat.

The congenital disease that killed her, after decades of decline into total dementia, had already taken hold, enhanced of course by her persistent use and dependency on drugs, of which I am ashamed to admit, I was totally unaware. I was not only naïve but wrong, there is no excuse.

I read this paragraph with a sickening conviction that all I had feared was being confirmed. My mother had not only wrecked herself, but had been wrecked by her inheritance from a gene bank now obliterated. I alone could be a carrier as the sole survivor of a vaporised line.

Up until ten years ago we managed to survive, moving through Eire to Argentina before settling in Morocco. Mother could adapt herself to anything and reinvented herself as a chanteuse of German descent called Renee Susskind and sang torch songs in dusky night spots accompanied by a Maltese gambler with a shady past. When she died, I decided the disease had reached the stage when it was safe to return to Scotland. My husband, to give him credit, supported us both and arranged

*for terminal care in Milngavie Towers, albeit paid for by me
with my almost entirely extinguished fortune.*

I wanted another Scotch but I didn't want to give up my seat. I thought about what I had read so far and what I had discovered about Matilda, this tortured old woman I'd known as a young beauty called Tilda.

It was a message from a lonely exile, a puppet with severed strings. Was she saying that she had devoted her life to being in charge of my mother? Why would she do that except out of misplaced devotion to Ben, Dora's brother? That too was ridiculous. My mother had murdered this woman's sister. Blood counts surely, I wouldn't know of course, not having any siblings. All sorts of ideas flashed through my head including the notion that Matilda and Dora had been lovers.

A man, stinking of drink, lurched towards my table. Rocking on his feet, he gripped the back of the chair on which I'd placed my things. 'You looking for company hen?'

'No thanks.'

'Aw go on, have a wee dram wi' me. You canna' sit in a bar on yer ane, not a fine lassie like you.'

'I'm OK thanks.'

'Have you no got a boyfriend? I could be your boyfriend, I could show ye a thing or two and no mistake.'

Why do all drunk Scots want to know about my boyfriends? Appealing to the bartender seemed a bit harsh and probably ineffective, after all I did look lonely but hardly on the pull.

'Och get away hen, shift your gear, let a fella take the weight off of is feet.' He swayed towards me, his breath stank. 'Gie'us a wee kiss!'

'No! Go away! Please.'

'Not unless I get ma kiss. Just a wee kiss, that's all I ask.'

A man's voice interrupted. 'Listen here, you! Go on, shove off!'

The voice belonged to Tom. This time he had really come to my rescue.

'Who the Hell are you to tell me to shove off?' The drunk drawled.

'Never mind. But if you don't cut it now I'll…' The rest of what was said was inaudible but effective, the man staggered back towards the bar, jeered by mates.

Tom Wishart sat down opposite me and smiled. 'Hello,' he said.

At first I couldn't believe it, Tom, of all people, here in this tacky bar, how? Why? Dumbfounded I lamely answered, 'Hi.'

He grinned. 'God, am I glad I found you.'

'I'm glad you came but why? Did you get my card? I really am very sorry for judging you so harshly without checking my facts. I really did think you'd forgotten me on that vile rock.'

'Forget that too. It was a misunderstanding.'

'I expect I will, eventually. Right now I'm ashamed. I think I've been very silly.'

'Only in that you snuck off without saying goodbye.'

He really did have a wonderful smile.

I smiled back, praying that he couldn't see the betraying surge of embarrassment flushing my face. 'What was it you said to that drunk guy?' I asked trying to appear calm.

'Oh just that I'd fix his face so his teeth stuck out his ears, or words to that effect.'

'Is that usual round here?'

'It was where I learnt to fight.'

'You a fighter? A boxer?'

'I was never good at hitting people for fun.'

'Oh I see I guess I didn't know you were a vet.'

'God no, I like animals but not enough to deal with their re-pulsive diseases.'

'I didn't mean a veterinarian, I meant were you in the military?'

'No, my record blighted that ambition as surely as a well aimed punch buggered my left eye and my dream of batting for Britain.'

'Who punched you? Why?'

'My face didn't fit. Toffs are considered fair game where I spent my early twenties.' He shrugged and smiled, 'So there you are. Now, how about you? What are you doing hanging out in this awful hole?'

'I might be asking the same of you.'

'That's easy, I was looking for you. I knew you were taking the sleeper south so I was hoping to catch you before you left. Now you've got to tell me, what are you doing with all these scraps of paper?'

'I've had a shock.'

'I can see that, but why in this bar? Come with me to somewhere quieter and you can tell me all about it. There's plenty of time.'

'Aren't you on your way to somewhere?'

'Aren't we all?'

'My train goes in a couple of hours.'

'Oh bugger! That's my phone I had better answer it. Oh God!' he said as he pressed the button. 'Hi. OK, wait a second it's too noisy in here I'll go outside.' He motioned to me to stay where I was, raised his eyes in stagey anguish and mouthed that he'd be back, then pointed at the TV screen behind me before leaving the bar with his phone clamped to his ear.

I twisted round in my seat and saw a reporter standing upon the black sands of Dalmuirie beach with Ailsa Craig silhouetted against the evening light, behind her. She was talking to camera but inaudible, the wind tangling her hair in the mike. She then started interviewing a policeman who was having grave difficulties with his cap.

Tom returned and asked me what had happened.

'I don't know, something to do with Ailsa Craig.'

'Probably golf, they like using Ailsa Craig as a backdrop.'

'With cops?'

'Corrupt golf, then. Let's get out of here. No, look there at the text.'

I read the words rolling along the bottom of the screen. A body had been washed up on the beach.

'Poor soul,' said Tom.

A further shot of the empty sea and then the weather forecast.

There would be rain. Naturally there would, one didn't need a girl in an ill-fitting dress to tell you that in Scotland.

'Give me your case, we'll go and seek a bit of peace in the tawdry grandeur of Central Hotel.'

'I've been there, it's full of hookers.'

'My father calls them Ladies of Negotiable Affection and nobody will bother you if you're with me, they'll merely think you are a canny negotiator. It's due to be completely done up, Caro's brother wanted to have a go at it but it needed even bigger boys to get it right, that's why he's sticking to the Spanish plans instead, thank God. I don't think I could stand all that retro palm court stuff.'

We found a bar and sat at a round, glass-topped table with brown, cane legs. Tom ordered the drinks and he then asked what was distressing me.

He listened while I told him about the stuff Tilda had written.

'This is as far as I have read,' I said giving him the less damaged pages. 'Please read it, I don't understand any of it except that she seems to be saying that she spent most of life protecting my mother. I don't know why, I don't know what to do or to think.' To my acute shame I began to cry. He covered my hand with his.

'Don't distress yourself, Mira, we'll get to the bottom of this somehow. Firstly, wouldn't it be better to read the letter all through first?'

'It's kind of trashed. Look!'

'Christ Mira! Did it spend Saturday night in Sauchihall Street?'

'A hen party was having fun.'

'Some fun, it looks more like a massacre. What's all this sticky stuff?

'Vodka mix I think.'

'Oh well, at least the hens didn't set it alight. Do you want it kept a secret or would you let me try to decipher it? I may be Cyclops but my one eye is very good, I think it compensates for being rubbish at distances. The sticky lumps won't trouble me as everything looks flat. I'll take it to a stronger light, these lamps are designed to conceal rather than reveal.'

I read the first part of the letter again but I couldn't concentrate, so I took Tom's glass over to him.

'Tom, sorry to interrupt, but do you think that this letter is a suicide note?'

'Quite possibly.'

His phone was ringing again and I took it to where he was standing beneath a bronze bracket lamp. 'You answer it, Mira, tell whoever it is I'll call them back.'

'Hi,' I said, 'Tom Wishart's phone. Who is calling please?' I'd done temping, I knew the drill. I could see Claudia's name on the screen.

'Tell that bloody gaolbird that I want to speak to him now. He is there, isn't he?'

'Do you mean Tom?'

'Of course I mean Tom, how many other gaolbirds are there? Put him on the line immediately, whoever you are.'

'Hold on, please.'

'Hurry up!'

I gave the phone to Tom and said, 'You should take this. It sounds very urgent.'

He put the papers down on a side table and marking his place with one hand, took the phone from me with the other.

'Oh it's you again, Claudia. I'm sorry, I can't help…I told you I don't know… . Yes, I had to go to a funeral… . No, not tonight… . No believe me, not since Friday, no I've not had a call nor an email…I'm in the Central Hotel now, in Glasgow…I promise you. No I don't know where…what was that?…No…no…I'm here alone with a friend… . Don't be ridiculous, of course not… . Look I've told you the truth… . Good night. Try to get some sleep.'

He turned the phone off and gave it back to me. 'Oh dear, what a mess.'

'Wedding nerves?'

'Histrionics. Now listen, Mira, this letter is far more important than that and far more interesting than you thought. Give me a few more minutes'.

'Tom?'

'Yes?'

'Why did she call you a gaolbird?'

'Because Mira, that's what I am. Didn't you know?'

'No Tom I didn't. Why?'

'Why didn't you know?'

'No, why did you go to prison?'

'Do you mean what did I go to prison for?'

'Yes, isn't that the same thing?'

'Not entirely. I was sentenced to three years when I was twenty-two for causing death by dangerous driving, driving whilst drunk and taking a vehicle without consent and leaving the scene. My girlfriend's father's car went off the track on Dundoon Hill. She wanted to go up to see the moon at midnight from the Covenanters' Memorial obelisk on her family's estate. It was her twenty-first birthday party. She was an only child.'

'Oh Tom, that's terrible. I am so sorry.'

'She didn't seem that badly injured when it happened, we were both thrown clear, it was an open car and we didn't wear seatbelts. I left her by the trackside and ran for help, no mobile phones then, but when I returned she'd passed out, she was in a coma for months and died without ever recovering consciousness.'

I couldn't think of anything to say, Tom appeared so calm and accepting, almost complacent. 'Her parents sold up and moved south; they've set up a charity, Clara's Fund, in her memory to help other people who've lost children. I get a card from them every year on her birthday to remind me of what might have been. I think it helps them, a little bit.'

'That's terrible, Tom.'

He shrugged. 'This on the other hand is much more interesting, give me a few more minutes, get another drink, I think we'll need it.'

I wondered why I was still feeling quite sober. What was going on?

I gave Tom his drink and he clasped my arm. 'Mira , tell me, what do you think you know about your mother?'

I felt the dreadful grip of foreboding in anticipation of admitting the hideous truth.

'Come on, Mira, tell me.'

Tom's hand in mine gave me courage. 'She's dead, Tom.'

'Yes. Go on.'

'There is more, much more but that's all I really know for certain.' I couldn't stop the tears coming.

Tom crouched down before me and took both my hands in his. 'All right, Mira. Please stop crying and try to stay calm. Suicide note or not, this is certainly a confession. Here you read the last page, it is comparatively unspoilt while I complete this sodding puzzle.'

I took the page and sat in an armchair lit by a tarnished bronze standard lamp.

At first, amid the turmoil, I didn't think about the consequences of my impetuous decision but as I threw Grizel's wedding ring on to the coffin, I knew I had thrown away everything – all prospects of love and freedom and condemned myself to a life of guilt and fear. I deserved to be caught, we all did and to be punished for the terrible crime of deception we had committed. I wish now I had been caught.

It is extraordinary that we did get away with it for all these years. The nearest we came to being discovered was the time that I found you near where she was concealed, drugged and sedated, on Henrysson's Rock. Amongst his other roles, Ian Parker was the local supplier, he'd been providing Grizel and possibly even Hughie, with what they needed for ages, – I didn't know that either.

So that was why the voice of my good fairy was somewhat familiar but the short haired skeletal creature who comforted me on the shore was nothing like the lovely Tilda I'd known before.

So she'd been the one who made me promise not to say what I had seen. That was the promise I'd kept all this time out of fear that my mother might return or that Cess would become my guardian. I was right, I had seen my mother there standing in front of the setting sun. But why? Why should Tilda sacrifice herself to protect a demented, drug crazed, murdering arsonist?

I read the final paragraph.

Ben and I never met again after that brief moment when I handed you over. I will never forget the look on his face, I think he understood, I hope he forgave me. I've never stopped loving him.

I hope Ben found happiness. I hope, Miracle, you do too.
I have found no way in my life to be forgiven, my hope for redemption is oblivion.

With sincere remorse,
Matilda Parker

I waited for my agitation to subside before going to see how Tom was getting on with piecing together the scraps. I could see by the lay-out on the table that the job was done. He looked up and I noticed his injured eye for the first time. It did not detract from what I found beautiful. I must not lust for forbidden fruit that was the deal I had made with whatever made sure I survived, the second time I was abandoned on Henrysson's Rock.

'It's OK Tom, I do know.'

'What do you know Mira?'

'I know my mother lit the fire that killed my father and his wife Grizelda. I know that Grizelda's sister, Matilda Gilmerton, Ian Parker and her mother managed to protect my mother till she died of some kind of congenital dementia. Surely that's enough. Tom, I ought to go to my train.'

'You've got over half an hour. Now sit down, you've got it wrong.'

'How?'

'Yes, the fire was lit by someone known as Dorabella War-schauer.'

'My mother.'

'No, not your mother, Matilda's sister. Grizelda lit the fire and fled to hide on Henrysson's rock, Parker found a bag in the bushes containing a passport in the name of Dorabella Warschauer. Parker was prepared to take the risk and convince Matilda and her mother that they could protect Grizelda from detection because the woman in the summerhouse had been a nameless tart, the sort who is never missed and Matilda agreed in order to keep her promise that she'd stand by Grizelda whatever happened. Then he told Tilda that the woman was Ben's sister and she realised that was the end of everything for her, she gave up and allowed Parker to blackmail her into marrying him.'

'You mean?' I couldn't go on.

'I mean your mother died with your father, they are buried together at Dalmuirie.'

'So my mother wasn't a murderer? She wasn't genetically insane?'

'That's right.'

I was dumbfounded. It was too much to take in at once. Everything had changed. Deferred guilt disappeared the dread of inherited insanity evaporated. A burden tumbled from my back and had a life to live and perhaps, a future. I was suddenly overwhelmed by pity for the one who had lost her love and hope while being crushed by persistent guilt throughout her entire life. However, I was free to start over without secrets and utterly alone.

'Poor Tilda.'

'Yes,' said Tom. 'We should never make promises that can't be wiped out by time, money or crafty lawyers. We should not make promises that damn us if we keep them and damn us if we break them.'

'But Tom, what do you mean exactly?'

He didn't answer.

'Tom?'

'Yes Mira?'

I think the whisky had made me very bold: 'Were you driving that car?'

He looked at me and smiled. 'I promised Clara I'd say I was, she was terrified of her father and I told her I'd take the blame.'

'So you let yourself be convicted for a crime you didn't commit?'

'Stupid, wasn't it? Stupid and proud and bloody ridiculous, except that as her passenger, I was complicit, though the bit about leaving the scene of the accident was most unjust. I was going for help but by the time we got back, Clara was in a terminal coma. I was too idiotically proud to change my plea after she'd died. I was naïve and idealistic I suppose and I couldn't face the idea of being condemned as a liar and cheat. I thought it was better to be condemned for something I had not done than to risk the ignominy of my innocence not being believed. My promise certainly put my life off course but it didn't blight it completely like Tilda's promise did. I had the luxury of a clear conscience not perpetual haunting guilt.'

'Tom, your father was right, you really are an honourable man. Do your parents know what you did?'

'They may have guessed but I never told them.'

'Do they, or anybody else in Dalmuirie, know the truth about the fire?'

'Who knows? Maybe they all do, maybe none of them. But I swear I did not. Are you going to tell them the truth now?'

'I don't know. Would you?'

'Not unless you say so. I can keep secrets.'

I saw the station clock jerk on another minute, we had to hurry. I had a train to catch and a man to leave.

'Thank you for everything Tom, Claudia is an exceptionally lucky woman. I hope you both will be very happy in your future life together. Now I must go. Here, can you hold my ticket while I cram these papers into my bag? Maybe someday I'd transcribe them but right now I've got to go.'

'Mira, wait! What did you say?'

'That you are an honourable man.'

'No, about Claudia.'

'I hoped you'd be happy together.'

We were running towards the platform entrance where the car attendants were checking tickets.

'Stop Mira!' He grasped my arm and turned me round, my case hitting a fellow passenger scurrying by.

'I'm sorry,' I said to the indignant businessman's back.

The girl who'd begged me for a ticket, was still imploring the embarking passengers to help her. The businessman pushed her aside.

'Here you,' said Tom offering her my ticket 'take this. Quick they are about to shut the gate. Don't thank me, it's a present from Mrs Staple…run!'

'Tom! Why did you do that?'

'Because you are not going anywhere till we've got this cleared up. I am not, never have been, nor ever will be involved in any way with that queen of all bitches, Claudia. As for marrying her, God the thought alone appals me. I'd sooner marry Cousin Cess or Miss Stuart, even.'

'But the children told me that their uncle was marrying Claudia. You are their uncle, aren't you?'

'Yes, so is their mother's brother, my good friend Tamburlaine Westcroft, who I hope to God has finally seen what a manipulative woman Claudia is. During last week's debacle she decided to call the wedding off, before changing her mind back again tonight. That was what those calls were about.'

'Oh, I see.' What else could I think of to say on that emptying concourse? I watched my train gliding out of the station. 'Tom, what happens next?'

'You tell me, Mira, it's your story.'